DISCIPLINED BY

HARDSHIP

BOOK THREE OF NATONUS REFUGE

MATT LEVIN

For anyone who's been made to feel like they don't belong

CHAPTER I

From the viewscreen aboard the *Caretaker*, holding high orbit over Enther, Tanner Keltin couldn't see them, but he knew that Junta vessels were just now arriving at the planet Ikkren. The war he'd engineered—that he'd manipulated Michael Azkon and the rest of the Junta leadership into starting—was proceeding well. That meant it was time to start the next stage of his plans.

Plans that would lead, ultimately, to the destruction of the *Preserver*.

For months, Tanner had spent nearly every day coordinating a counterinsurgency campaign against the Ashkagi rebels down on Enther's surface. That was part of the deal he'd struck with the Junta: while they blockaded the outer rim and invaded Ikkren, Tanner dispatched his Offspring to defend the home front from the rebels.

The Junta had invited Tanner and some of his senior followers to one of the remaining warships in orbit to coordinate with the rest of the command staff. He'd chosen some of the men who'd been in the Offspring the longest. Those who were steadfastly loyal to him beyond a shadow of a doubt. Those who would do whatever it took to complete their crusade.

It was only the second time Tanner had ever been on a starship in his life, and the first time was aboard some boring commercial spaceliner. But the *Caretaker* was a warship. Tanner could feel the sheer *power* of the vessel in the way the metal alloys of the floor panels vibrated underneath his boots. The vessel might be decrepit compared to the Union navy's latest warships, but it still possessed firepower that could shatter continents. Or other starships.

From today forward, Tanner was going to rid himself of the minutiae of counterinsurgency planning. It was time to move on to his real objectives.

The door to his left slid open, and a uniformed Junta officer walked in. He was absorbed in a datapad, only briefly glancing up to give him a slight nod. Tanner withdrew a shiv hidden in the folds of his suit, walked over to the officer, and stabbed him in the chest.

Tanner had killed two people: the newar Russ Kama, and the old Ashkagi radical leader Brandon Zahem. Killing others wasn't a new experience, exactly, but doing it with a knife felt different. He was close enough to see the sudden register of shock on the officer's face, close enough to get splattered with blood, close enough to feel the heat of the man's breath from a sharp exhale.

And then there were the *sounds*. The thud-ping of a plasma weapon insulated you from the grim reality of it. The stabbing was a symphony of clean slices as his blade slipped through skin, blood, and organs, interrupted by the crunch of bone as the shiv wedged, temporarily, through the officer's clavicle and ribs.

Soon enough, the man couldn't do much else besides gurgle. Tanner withdrew the shiv and let the man's corpse crash to the ground. He straightened his back, whispered, "Thank you for your sacrifice," and crouched down to wipe his blade on the hem of the man's pants.

Then he slid the blade back into a hidden receptacle on the cuff of his suit and pulled up his wrist terminal. He dispatched a simple message to all other twelve Offspring aboard the ship: *It is time.*

He walked to the edge of the corridor, took one last look at the blanket of space and stars outside, and exited via an adjacent corridor. One that brought him to an intersection where he took the leftmost path, leading him to a security room. There was only a single soldier on guard, and he only managed to get a "Hey, you're not supposed to—" out before Tanner cut a deep knife wound across his torso. He caught the lifeless body before it slammed into the ground, laid it down softly, and closed the dead man's eyes gently.

Naval warships didn't need a huge crew, since automation and computing technology made the need for a high volume of staff redundant, even on an older model like the *Caretaker*. But forty-eight Junta officers still crewed the ship—*forty-six*, Tanner thought with a smirk—meaning his people were outnumbered.

Good thing he could access the ship's security network from a nearby terminal.

Tanner had already cracked the ship's encryption codes days earlier. They weren't easy to bypass, by any means, but it wasn't as hard as the high-level encryption used by most megacorps in Union space.

He pulled up a grid view of camera feeds from around the ship. By now, the other twelve Offspring onboard had split into two teams:

one was slicing its way toward engineering, the other was dicing its way toward the ship's CIC. The engineering crew could still overload the ship's engines if they got spooked and felt they couldn't defend themselves from the Offspring, meaning securing engineering took priority. Only problem was, the CIC could override all commands coming from any security office elsewhere on the ship, so the Offspring needed to storm both targets simultaneously.

Tanner turned his attention to the camera feeds. Both teams had encountered minimal resistance, but that was to be expected. The Junta crew didn't keep weapons on their persons, but there were emergency weapons lockers at various points throughout the ship. The problem was, firing a plasma weapon aboard a starship was basically suicide without an enviro-suit equipped, since a misplaced shot would tear through the hull and vent all the oxygen into space. *Never bring a knife to a gunfight* only applied when firing your gun wouldn't kill you.

The hallways leading to the CIC and engineering began to resemble sacrificial pits as the corpses of the Junta crew piled up. Trails of blood and carnage led to both target destinations. Tanner furrowed his brow as he saw one of the hallways with a gaping hole in the side. Sure enough, one of the Junta crew had actually gone for an emergency locker and fired a plasma weapon. Stupid but understandable, given their desperation. They didn't live to appreciate their fuck-up, however, with the officer's corpse slumped over next to the breach. Three Offspring were caught in the hallway, trapped by emergency doors automatically thrown up by the ship's computer to contain the breach.

Tanner tightened his jaw as he watched the three helpless Offspring. The hypoxia setting in, they too collapsed to the floor. They'd died as heroes.

And they wouldn't die in vain.

Three other Offspring had arrived at the entrance to the engineering room, while the other six were almost at the CIC. Tanner immediately lifted the security locks on all doors across the vessel from his terminal. His people swarmed into both the CIC and engineering almost simultaneously. Sure enough, the camera feeds cut out seconds later, once some tech in the CIC must've figured out that the network had been compromised. Hopefully, it'd be one of the last actions they'd ever take.

Tanner stepped back from the now-useless console and again turned to his wrist terminal. *Meet me at the hangar bay once your work is done,* he dispatched to the two Offspring teams. *And bring the bodies of the fallen Junta.*

He received a message reading *Engineering is secure* only moments later, easing any apprehension that the plan wouldn't work. Another minute later, he received a second message: *CIC secured, one casualty. We're working on returning authorization to your security station. Then loading the casualties onto a cart and heading to the hangar.*

Tanner figured they weren't *quite* out of the woods yet, but victory was practically assured at this point. There was no chance of the Junta crew blowing the warship up anymore, and he now had sole access to the ship's security network. It was all too easy to lock out the remaining Junta forces' access to the computer system. He then returned to the camera feeds.

Once their work was done, the surviving five members of the team sent to seize the CIC left and headed for the hangar. Tanner figured he'd meet them there. He shut off the security console, picked up the body of the guard he'd killed earlier, placed it delicately on a nearby trolley, and left the room. After a brief detour to collect the original officer he'd knifed, he broke for the hangar.

The bay itself was small, barely big enough to fit a handful of shuttles. The *Caretaker* was far from the carrier-class warships the Union used. Tanner wasn't even sure a squadron of fighters or drones would fit inside the hangar. As old as the ship was, however, he had to give credit to its crew for their upkeep. The metal still looked almost pristine, with only a few blemishes and scratches visible. Too bad he'd never get the opportunity to pay his compliments to the crew's maintenance habits.

Soon enough, the surviving eight Offspring filed in, wheeling in carts full of bodies. "These people were not our enemy," Tanner said solemnly once the others had gathered. "They were native Natonese, just like us. But it was only through their deaths that we now possess a warship of our own. It is only fitting that we honor their sacrifice by giving them each a hero's funeral."

"Warships like this ought to carry plenty of coffins for exactly that purpose," one of Tanner's followers said: Claude, one of his earliest recruits. Claude had been one of the first Offspring to back Tanner's claims to leadership after the Offspring's founder, Owen Yorteb, had been imprisoned by the Union. He couldn't quite recall if Claude had been dishonorably discharged from the Union military, or just given an entry level suspension during basic. "We'll scrounge some up for you."

"Good. Thank you," Tanner said. A handful of the others headed toward the hangar bay exit.

Tanner walked over to the pile of bodies, trying to count them all and failing. "Computer," Tanner said, "how many life forms are still aboard the ship?"

"My scanners are reading ten life forms aboard the *Caretaker*," the vessel's computer replied.

By the time Tanner realized that meant there was still one Junta crew member left alive, he heard rustling behind a crate on the far side of the room. A woman in an officer's uniform darted for one of the exits. Tanner commanded the two closest Offspring to stop her. As they ran after the sole survivor, Tanner tapped into the ship's security system from his wrist terminal and locked the exit door.

The Junta officer reached the door before the pursuing Offspring could reach her, but her attempts to force the door open failed. She sunk to the floor as the two Offspring cornered her, shivs drawn. "Please," she called out to Tanner, "I have a husband and two kids back on Enth—"

A hand signal and an "I'm sorry, no" from Tanner was all it took. Once his two followers had silenced her protests, they picked up her body and brought her over.

"Lay her down next to her fallen comrades," Tanner said. "And go get those coffins."

. . .

It was a solemn sendoff, jettisoning all fifty-two coffins into the vacuum of space. At least it was a more peaceful enterprise than the sudden, violent tempest that'd resulted in the Offspring seizing the *Caretaker*.

Tanner didn't enjoy killing native Natonese, and he mourned the deaths of the four Offspring who'd lost their lives, but he knew that all fifty-two sacrifices were necessary.

For the first time, the Offspring possessed nuclear weapons.

But there was still plenty to do. As soon as the last casket disappeared from view, swallowed by the black void, Tanner turned to Claude. "The Junta military will be expecting routine status reports from the dead captain," he said.

"We can go through his private logs, analyze his speech patterns, and piece together a voiceprint simulator," Claude said. "We can even use his logs to simulate a fake holographic projection of the old captain. So if Junta command ever wants a holographic report instead of a written one, we should be able to make a highly convincing fake."

Tanner wasn't expecting them to have much communication from the Junta military. If the brass cared about the *Caretaker*, they wouldn't have let it sit in Enther's orbit. It was a dead-end assignment for officers whose careers were going nowhere. He figured the Junta wouldn't suspect for even a second that something had gone wrong. Especially while their attention was drawn to the war on Ikkren or setting up the blockade along the asteroid belt.

That gave him all the time he needed.

Tanner said his goodbyes and headed for the captain's quarters, cordoned off from the regular dormitories. As he strode triumphantly through the ship's narrow, bloodstained corridors, he gained an appreciation for the name *Caretaker*. His crusade, after all, was to take care of all his native Natonese brethren.

Specifically, by *taking care* of the newars.

Tanner arrived at the dead captain's quarters and settled in at the desk. He pulled up the desk terminal, bypassed the old security, and inputted a new password. Then he activated a holographic projection of the outer rim.

Junta ships were closing in on Ikkren, with another handful

heading to various checkpoints along the asteroid belt, and two deployed to Calimor. But right now, Tanner was more focused on a single holographic blip. He used his thumb and index finger to zoom in on the projection of the planet Bitanu, where a single speck hovered in orbit: the *Preserver*.

The newars had moved their cryo vessel out of the way of the Junta navy, and apparently they were even constructing a planetary defense matrix to protect the *Preserver* from any incoming missiles. Originally, Tanner had hoped seizing the *Caretaker* was all he'd need to do—other than fire off a missile salvo that would annihilate the *Preserver*.

But the newars' defense matrix meant a missile attack would be more likely to fail than succeed, and firing the *Caretaker*'s nukes too early would give away his ruse. He had to be patient, had to find the right time to strike.

Which worked just fine for Tanner. After all, he'd made it this far. With the *Caretaker*, he now possessed the means to destroy the *Preserver*.

All he needed was the opportunity.

CHAPTER 2

The embassy room where Isadora Satoro used to conduct cabinet meetings had been converted into a war room. An old mahogany table had been whisked off, replaced by a holo-projection of the Natonese outer rim: the planets Calimor, Bitanu, and Ikkren, all of them on the far side of the system's asteroid belt. Blips showed the Junta navy closing in on Ikkren like hungry beasts, circling their prey.

A late summer Obrigan storm rumbled outside. The projection flickered in response.

Riley Tago's security staff were everywhere, moving around with sleep-deprived, caffeine-addled looks in their eyes, always late for some strategy meeting or planning session. Isadora looked around the war room as a half-dozen security personnel practically ignored her, absorbed by the holo-projector as they tracked Junta fleet movements.

For almost three months, all manner of weapons had been flying across the Natonese outer rim. Whatever fleet the Horde possessed had been decimated after a series of naval engagements. So far, most of the fighting hadn't taken place on any planets. But that was about to change. A Junta blockade along the asteroid belt was cutting off shipping from one end of the system to the other, and the *Preserver*—not to mention all the refugees' colonies—was caught on the other side.

The door opened behind Isadora, and two individuals filed in. The first was Riley, who seemed to wear a grim expression everywhere she went these days. Isadora had learned only recently that Riley had been soliciting advice from her predecessor, Russ Kama, who was now floating across Natonese space in a makeshift coffin. Heading on his final, everlasting journey. Riley was all alone now.

The second was Nadia Jibor.

She'd been Isadora's settlement adviser once, but it was hard to say what she was now. Especially when it would be a while before it was safe to transport anyone off the *Preserver*. She was the only refugee who'd stared down the Offspring leader Tanner Keltin—and lived. Riley made the rounds with the other defense personnel in the room, while Nadia hung back, leaning against the wall and surveying the room.

"Thank you for coming," Isadora said. "Based on current projections, Junta ships are about to reach orbit over Ikkren. They've already announced plans to place the Horde settlements under military occupation. It's time we get off the back foot."

"I've been trying to get in touch with my counterpart in the Junta military hierarchy," Riley said. She crossed over to the central holo-projector and leaned against the side. "But they've been ignoring my message requests. Still, they haven't made any explicit mention about our Ikkren settlements. And if they were planning on destroying them, they could've launched missiles from space."

For the previous few months, Isadora and her staff had been desperately contacting all their outer rim colonies, coordinating with local leaders, coming up with lockdown plans, shutting off trade depots, and creating standardized neutrality protocols that wouldn't put them in anyone's crosshairs.

And despite all that, it still wasn't enough. Even if they were reasonably confident that their actions over the last few months would keep their colonies safe, there were no guarantees when it came to the *Preserver*.

Today was the day they were going to stop just doing crisis management. Today was the day they were going to seize the initiative. To do anything they could—whatever they could—to either end the war, or somehow bring 30 million individuals out of cryo, and fast.

"There is little we can do for our Ikkren colonists at the moment," Isadora said tiredly, "other than not provoke the Junta." She turned her head so she could search Nadia's face for a reaction.

The lines of her face were all drawn down, accentuating her taut jawline. "We can't trust any assurances from the Junta," Nadia said, defiance in her eyes. "They've betrayed us at every turn."

True enough. Isadora knew that too well, remembering how the Junta had shot at her, at Nadia, at a team of special forces led by Russ Kama before his death. Isadora the woman would never forgive them, but Isadora the politician knew she had to suppress such feelings. The Junta weren't their allies, but they held the capability to destroy the rest of her people. Better not to stir up the hornets' nest.

"We simply cannot afford to antagonize the Junta at this juncture," Isadora said. "Right now, the lives of our colonists across the outer rim are contingent on not provoking the Junta into attacking them. That's to say nothing of the *Preserver*."

"The Junta isn't even our biggest problem," Nadia said. "They're just a cover for the Offspring. *Tanner Keltin* was the one who pushed for this war. That means, as long as the fighting continues, none of us is safe."

Another rumble from outside.

Isadora's thoughts went to the one spy they'd successfully put in the field: Carson Erlinza, a man she'd never met, but whom she'd still ordered out of cryo and trained as part of their espionage program. As part of the operation that'd killed Russ, Carson had infiltrated the Offspring's ranks. But with his handler dead, they had no way of contacting their one source of information on the Offspring. If he was even still alive.

"For the moment, we know all we need to know," Nadia continued. "The Offspring have partnered with the Junta. No matter what he's planning, Tanner will find some way to use the war for his advantage. And if the Junta are helping him, they're our enemies too."

It was an impossible problem, really. Provoke the Junta, and they might attack their people's colonies, or even the *Preserver*. Do nothing, and the war would give the Offspring the space they needed to operate. For months, all while desperately coming up with emergency plans to keep their colonies safe, Isadora had been trying to figure out how she could possibly come out on top in a no-win scenario. Indecision would be the worst choice, but making the wrong one would be little better.

But perhaps there were ways to do both. The best politicians were those who refused to be cowed by their apparent choices, who instead found ways around their limitations. Not that Isadora considered herself that highly—far from—but she knew her people deserved the best. So she'd try to act the part.

"This is why I've called you here, Nadia," she said. "It may be possible for you to fight back the Junta invasion of Ikkren. But it would require the rest of us disavowing your actions, at least in public."

"My crew and I are ready," Nadia said without a moment of hesitation. "I don't care what kind of blockade the Junta set up. The *Exemplar* is faster than any of their naval vessels, and they won't be able to take us out as long as our missile scrambler is working." The fire in her voice was all too familiar, but Isadora wasn't used to it coming from her. It was almost like Russ was still alive, still standing in the room with all of them.

Isadora walked over to the projector and zoomed in on Ikkren. "If there's any hope of fighting the Junta, it begins with the Horde. They've fought to defend their planet from invaders before, and they can do it again. But according to our intelligence, their leader has disappeared. The first step is finding Tori Hyrak, then providing whatever assistance you can to help her unite her people and push the Junta off the planet. Of all the people to send, we think you're the best, given your prior dealings with the Horde."

"We would have to issue a declaration of neutrality, of course." Isadora continued. "Deny that we had any knowledge of your mission to aid our allies. And you'd be going in alone, without backup or access to our resources. In fact, it would probably be best if the two of us refrained from as little direct communication as possible."

Isadora's heart fell as she finished the last sentence. She felt like she so rarely got to see Nadia. The last three months of having her in

Obrigan City had been a welcome reprieve from their usual distance.

Especially while Meredith is barely talking to me, she thought unwittingly.

No. She couldn't let herself think about her problems with her daughter right now. If she did, she knew she'd always prioritize repairing her relationship with Meredith. Keeping her work and her personal life separate was the only way forward.

"I think the plan could work," Riley interjected. "I'm sure the Junta would have their suspicions that you were acting under orders from us, but we'd have enough plausible deniability to counteract them."

"When do I leave?" Nadia said almost immediately.

"We could arrange something tonight," Riley said. "That'd give us enough time to issue a statement of neutrality on the war. And then we'd have to pretend to try to stop you. Which we'll make sure doesn't actually work, of course." Isadora thought she could see a faint wink from her.

"Good," Nadia said brusquely. "I'll go brief my crew and prep the *Exemplar* for departure." She spun toward the war room exit in a violent arc.

"Nadia..." Isadora said.

She paused at the door. "This isn't goodbye," she said, one hand resting on the doorway. "But I have to go. I have to do whatever it takes to stop Tanner."

Isadora's blood chilled, but she couldn't tell whether it was because of the way Nadia had said *whatever it takes* or the way she'd nearly spat out *Tanner*. "I understand," she said quietly. "Just...be safe out there."

Nadia turned her head and attempted a grin, but it looked too obviously artificial with the anger still burning in her eyes. She departed the room.

Isadora returned her attention to a terminal next to the projector unit. She uploaded all the intelligence and satellite surveillance data the Union had passed along to the *Exemplar*.

She wished it was possible to convince the Union to intervene and stop the conflict. But as much as Prime Minister Tricia Favan wanted to help, the Union Parliament was plagued by political gridlock in the lead up to the elections at the end of the year. They weren't about to stick their necks out and approve a deployment of the Union war machine.

Isadora had been crestfallen when Tricia had given her the news. The Union prime minister had tried to smooth things over by passing over a mountain of classified intel—including the data she'd just forwarded to Nadia's vessel—but even then, there was only so much she could do to help. Then again, Tricia had been willing to skirt the law to help Isadora's people so many times that it made sense the rest of Parliament was dragging their feet on a military intervention.

She looked up and saw Riley studying her. "Your plan for Nadia makes sense. What next?"

"While Nadia is working on finding Tori, we should approach the problem from all angles," Isadora said. "As I see it, we have three objectives: (1) prevent the Junta from winning, (2) stop the war as soon as possible, and (3) figure out what the Offspring are up to. Nadia's handling the first, and Carson Erlinza is handling the third. With our colonies as secure as they can be, I'm planning on switching my full attention to the second.

"We've already failed to convince Parliament to intervene," Isadora continued, pacing around the projector. "But if trying to convince the Union government to do something about the war is a non-starter, then it stands to reason that I should instead focus on the Union *people*."

It wasn't as far-fetched of an idea as it sounded. Isadora knew the Natonese public had grown sympathetic toward her. For the longest time, she'd found her popularity with the Natonese people darkly ironic—it was too late for that to actually matter, and it was difficult to care what the Natonese thought about her when she'd been fighting for her political life.

But now, popularity with the Union citizenry was just what she needed. "I'm going to try to start an anti-war movement," Isadora said. "Something that could put pressure on the rest of the government."

Riley looked thoughtful. "Ambitious, but if you can pull it off, I think that could really help keep our people on the *Preserver* alive. Especially alongside what Nadia and Carson are doing."

"My first stop is the planet Sarsi. Polling data suggests the populace there is more sympathetic to our people than those here on Obrigan," Isadora said. "I'm going to head back to my office. Let me know immediately if we hear anything from Ikkren."

"I will, ma'am. I'll work on getting in contact with our militia forces." Riley stiffened her back and saluted. On cue, the rest of the defense staff who'd been hurrying around the room stood erect and saluted as well. Isadora returned the salute. *Guess I'm a wartime leader now.* She left the war room and headed back to her office.

The closer she got, the louder the storm got. The sky had turned dark grey, with boiling clouds crisscrossing over each other and savage strikes of lightning interrupting the darkness settling over the system's capital. It was only late afternoon, but it looked like dusk.

Isadora's eyes flickered toward the holographic projection on her wall: 30,210,617. She'd gotten a lucky break with the deal her chief diplomat and her attorney general had hashed out with the Sarsi planetary government. They'd signed a joint treaty overriding the Union settlement charter ban. And then they'd pulled a full 6 million out of cryo to set up colonies across Sarsi. Which felt like an enormous victory, but one that now paled in comparison to the danger that the remaining 30 million were in.

Isadora returned to her desk and placed her head in her hands. On top of the crisis and her fractured relationship with her daughter, she'd been having nightmares as well. She already slept so little that she desperately needed the few hours she got. Instead, horrific memories of the Hegemony invasion of Earth—the event that'd forced her people across the galaxy to the Natonus System—had been keeping her awake.

She remembered the confusion of how the invading fleets had escaped Earth's long-range scanners. Remembered the terror that followed when they announced they were placing the entire Sol System under their control, just like the rest of humanity's scattered colonized systems. Remembered the anguish that former colonists who'd left Earth generations ago were now returning in conquest.

Maybe those memories seemed more vivid now because Isadora was in the middle of another solar war. Maybe it was her mind's way of telling her she was trapped once again. She supposed it didn't really matter why.

She rubbed her eyes and went through her wrister messages to wake her up. Nothing new, other than an update from Vincent Gureh. Once it'd become clear that the Junta fleets were heading toward Ikkren, she'd ordered her chief engineer to reposition the *Preserver* over Bitanu. For the past few months, he and the rest of the engineering staff had been working around the clock to construct a defense matrix on Bitanu, where surface-to-air laser turrets could protect the *Preserver* by intercepting any incoming missiles.

It was only a temporary solution. The *Preserver* would never be safe so long as the war was going on.

Construction on the laser defense matrix is going well, the message from Vincent said. *We're estimating that about 60% of batteries are now operational. Which means we'd be able to protect the* Preserver *from a decent-sized salvo, but nothing beyond that. And if the fighting spills over to Bitanu, this might all be for nothing.*

Which brings me to my next point. I've been having some...concerns about the long-term sustainability of our settlement efforts. Nothing terribly time sensitive, but also something I'd rather talk about in person, as opposed to sending via wrister. Which might be difficult, considering the Junta blockade. Just let me know if you ever make any plans to visit the outer rim.

Isadora furrowed her brow, wondering briefly if she should route Nadia to talk to Vincent before heading to Ikkren. But if he wasn't willing to discuss his concerns even over their encrypted channel, would he be willing to talk to Nadia? And he'd said they weren't time sensitive. Better to just sit on the message for the time being.

Isadora closed her wrister and turned to stare out the window. Somewhere out there, Union security forces were arriving at the house of a teenage girl named Rebecca Keltin, and informing her that her period of house arrest would now be lifted. The investigation into Rebecca's possible ties with her brother—which had morphed into an investigation of Tanner's past, once it became clear Rebecca had no contact with her estranged sibling—had concluded. Which meant

Meredith could go back to spending time with her.

Since she'd informed the Union about Rebecca's connection to the Offspring, Isadora and Meredith's relationship had been badly strained. The investigation had lasted longer than Isadora would've liked, but Rebecca had been treated very well, she'd been assured. Meredith didn't see it that way.

Maybe seeing Rebecca again would change things. Another lightning bolt crashed outside, just a few blocks away from the embassy.

Isadora sighed. If she couldn't repair her relationship with her daughter, then she'd just have to end the war and defeat the Offspring with a broken heart.

CHAPTER 3

The storm had parted at last, so Nadia Jibor didn't mind sitting on the rooftop of her people's embassy. Her legs swung over the sides as she looked out to the east, away from all the other government buildings, toward the rest of the city.

A smell—that *post-storm* stench that was hard to put into words— hung in the air. It was nothing like the pristine smell she'd gotten a whiff of back on Enther, or on her old farmstead back in Kansas after a vicious American Midwest rainstorm. It was an industrial smell, the kind produced as rainwater had slicked through metropolitan grime and refuse and left it washed over the side of every skyscraper or pedestrian platform. Of every tenement housing unit filled with countless individuals just trying to scrape by.

She'd been on Obrigan for almost three months, and she couldn't wait to leave. There was a time, back when she'd been shuffling from planet to planet on the Natonese outer rim, when she'd dreamed about seeing the sprawling, massive city at the heart of the system's core worlds. To see the city lights kissing the night sky, to hear the music blaring through the air from dance halls and drinking dens in a place where sleep was always negotiable.

And now she'd seen it, and found it hard to care. She just wanted to get back to the outer rim. She was a creature of the frontier now. There was a war going on, and lounging around on some planet too insulated for anyone to care felt like a betrayal of all the millions still in danger.

And it felt like a betrayal of Russ.

Every time Nadia slept—hell, every time she closed her eyes—she saw him collapse from Tanner's plasma blast. The man who'd almost killed her died to save her. How the fuck do you get over that?

She stood up, toes to the edge of the embassy roof, and looked out. Sure enough, the dance halls were all lit up with neon lights. She spotted ecstatic crowds through the windows with every flash of light. None of them would ever get it, she thought with a sneer. They were innocent, childlike. Oblivious to the threat posed by the Offspring. They needed someone like her to go out and bring the fight to Tanner so they could enjoy their empty lives in peace.

But without knowing where Tanner was or what he was planning, the only thing she could do was to push back against the Junta offensive, apparently. Which meant finding Tori Hyrak, providing whatever logistical help she could to the Horde resistance, and seeing where that got her.

Her war against the Offspring would be fought via proxies. At least until Carson figured out what Tanner was really up to.

Hopefully.

Nadia checked her wrister. Isadora's declaration of neutrality should've come out about an hour ago. Boyd and Derek had already prepped the *Exemplar*. They were bringing the vessel to the landing pad outside the embassy courtyard right now. It was time for them to leave.

She headed for the stairwell that took her down into the embassy proper. Paused at the office suite on the topmost floor. Isadora's suite. Part of her yearned to say goodbye one more time, the other part wondered what there was to say. She knew she'd see Isadora again. She refused to consider an alternative possibility.

Shaking her head and steeling her nerves, Nadia pressed onward.

The next story down, she ran into a tired Riley Tago. The woman had dark circles under her eyes and looked thinner than Nadia remembered. Flanked on either side by a defense personnel with a beret cap on, Riley excused her two followers and beckoned Nadia into a side room.

"I figure you're about to be on your way, but I just wanted to say a quick good luck," Riley said. Nadia had a few minutes to spare before her crew arrived with the *Exemplar*. She entered Riley's office.

The room was far more barren than Nadia would've figured. There were no decorations on any of the walls, no pictures, no holo-emitted profiles of friends or family. Just blank walls and an empty desk, minus a personal terminal. The only sign of life in the entire room was an elegant prayer mat splayed out on the ground: an Ashkagi rug, almost identical to the ones she'd seen back on Enther.

"I know we've never really gotten the chance to talk much," Riley said, sitting at her desk. Nadia leaned against the wall. *When is the last time we've talked one-on-one?* Nadia wondered. *Ever?*

"I just wanted to say, I really appreciate what you're doing," Riley continued. "What you're about to do is both extremely brave, and extremely dangerous. But someone has to take the Junta threat seriously, and the political limitations are hamstringing us here." She struggled to maintain eye contact as she spoke.

"All I can hope for is that the fight against the Junta leads to the Offspring. And, by extension, Tanner Keltin. He deserves everything that's coming at him for what he did to Russ."

That was when Riley burst into tears.

Nadia looked at her feet and tried to figure out what to say. She knew Riley had been close to Russ. "I'm...sorry," was all she could manage. She shuffled over to Riley's desk and laid a hand on her shoulder.

The cry was as fast as it was vicious. Less than a minute later, Riley was composing herself, wiping at her nostrils with one of her index fingers. Nadia retracted her hand.

"Thank you, but I'm sorry too. I didn't mean to have an outburst like that," Riley said.

Nadia had been so busy thinking about the war, about Tanner and the Offspring, that she hadn't realized how hard her heart had grown in recent months. She'd always thought of herself as having a comforting persona, but now, all she could think about was making Tanner pay when Riley had been crying.

"It's okay. I've been thinking about Russ every day since we got back from Enther."

Riley stared at her hands. "He was my best friend in the system."

Just like Boyd for me. There was a time when Nadia had contemplated what losing him might feel like, back when he'd been taken prisoner by the Offspring. Instead, it was thanks to Russ' sacrifice, as well as the sacrifices of almost a dozen trained soldiers in their colonial militia force, that Nadia never had to actually experience what Riley was going through.

"I was in contact with him the entire time," Riley continued. "I was constantly asking him for advice back when he was working for the Syndicate. Not that he was any help, of course. He usually just told me I knew what I was doing, and to trust my instincts."

Riley snorted, though her jaw wavered for a moment. Nadia returned her hand to her shoulder. "I can imagine him saying that."

"He could be a real ass." Riley chuckled, but the grin faded instantly afterward. She adopted a solemn look and finally turned her head to face Nadia. "Did I ever tell you about my husband?"

"I...don't think so? I didn't realize you were married." Nadia's logical side caught up too late. If Riley had a spouse, he'd have been brought out of cryo too. Which could only mean—

"He died during the Hegemony invasion. We shipped to Mars when the Hegemony fleets reached the asteroid belt. I still remember the dark specks of their warships hanging in the air. Or the way the entire Martian landscape lit up when the nukes fell." Riley's face lowered. "I was the only one of my squad to make it out. My husband included."

"I'm so sorry," Nadia whispered. "I didn't know." For every refugee aboard the *Preserver*, there were dozens of family members they'd left behind on Earth. Everyone had lost someone. But seeing your spouse die next to you in combat was something different from what the rest of their people had been through.

Comforting the grieving was always agonizing. What else could you say, other than stringing along a countless number of *I'm sorry's* or *I'm here if you need me's* or *It will get better's*? It was the twenty-fifth century, dammit, and humanity still hadn't come up with anything better than platitudes.

"No one did," Riley continued. "No one except Russ. And now he's dead too. Right now, that feels like all my life is going to be. A long string of ghosts. Everyone I've ever been close to is dead. Maybe I'm just not the kind of person who ever gets to settle down with close friends or family."

Nadia squeezed her shoulder, retracted her hand and brought her knees down to the floor, finally figuring out something to say. "You've been defense adviser to Isadora for almost two years. That means you've been keeping millions of people safe this whole time. Back after the Offspring attacked New Arcena, how many lives did you save with your new security measures? Hundreds? Thousands?"

Riley didn't acknowledge what she was saying, but she blinked quickly.

"*We're* your family, Riley," Nadia pressed. "It's hard to remember, because now we're spread out all over the system. But we are a common people, and we all owe something to you. I know it isn't what you wanted, but it's something."

Maybe she was imagining it, but Riley's eyes seemed less stricken. "That's probably kinder than I deserve, but I appreciate it." She straightened her shirt—an old, well-pressed EDF uniform—and sat up in her chair, back straight.

"I should get going, but if you ever need anything while I'm out on the front lines, then please...reach out." *Think I got through the entire list of platitudes.*

"Thank you. And I'll expect regular reports on your progress via an encrypted channel. Even with security measures, it would be better to keep the chief coordinator out of the loop. Plausible deniability and all."

Nadia nodded. "What about the last third of our operation? Isadora and I know what we need to do, but what about Carson?"

Riley's mouth twitched. "I actually have a plan for him. You understand that I can't go into specifics, but I have...a contact on Enther. Something of a spiritual adviser. For now, that's all I can say."

"Of course." Nadia pushed herself back to her feet. "I'm glad we could talk before I departed for Ikkren."

"Me too. And really...thanks. I know I'll be okay. It's just the path I'm on right now—but it feels like I've been wandering in the wilderness for so long. I just want a destination."

Nadia nodded, said her goodbyes, and left Riley's office. It was getting late, and the embassy was mostly deserted. Except for Riley's uniformed security personnel. Ever since the war on the outer rim had begun, it felt like there were always defense staff wandering around with those dark circles under their eyes.

After taking a stairwell to the ground level, she walked out into the courtyard, where the gentle trickle of the stream was mostly drowned out by the noise pollution of the nearby entertainment district. Nadia walked along the crushed gravel path toward the landing pad.

That was when the *Exemplar* cut through the night sky, water still dripping down its sides from the storm earlier, while neon lights danced on the aft hull plating. The vessel circled the landing pad and came to a rest.

A minute later, Boyd and Derek exited the vessel. Derek leaned against the cockpit while Boyd inspected the hull. Both of them turned to wave at her as she approached.

She thought back to her conversation with Riley, to what she'd said about family. It wasn't just the refugees, because she practically considered both Boyd and Derek family, and both men were native Natonese. Maybe *family* was something even more expansive, something totally different from blood or point of origin.

Maybe everyone in the entire system was becoming part of some bigger family. Maybe the Offspring were the real outsiders. The barbarians at the gates. Not because of who they were by birth, but because that was their choice.

Once, Nadia had envisioned her role as bringing people together, both old and new, from every corner of the system. But now, she was a guardian of all those who'd made the choice to come together. And she was leaving to make war against those still on the outside.

Nadia surprised herself with all these thoughts. It was like she was still her old self, the kind that had entertained starry-eyed delusions about what she could hope to accomplish. The kind that had faded after the Offspring attacked New Arcena. Maybe it was important to hold onto that kernel in her heart, and to make sure that all the simmering rage that had lodged around it didn't fully crush it.

But she could entertain such thoughts later. After they'd stopped the Junta war machine, after they'd foiled whatever the Offspring were planning.

After she'd killed Tanner Keltin.

She walked up the steps to the landing pad and embraced both Boyd and Derek. "We're all ready for departure," Boyd said, his voice steadier and less frantic than she remembered it being before his captivity.

"By the time we'll get to Ikkren, the Junta will already be entrenched, meaning it will be even harder to find Tori," Derek said. He was talking about *his* planet, Nadia thought, but whatever dread or anxiety going on inside the man's mind hardly appeared in his tone of voice. "But I know I can get by the blockade. Especially with a ship like the *Exemplar*."

"I know you can," Nadia said. "Let's get going. I'm already sick of this planet, and I'm not inclined to waste any more time." She followed her two crewmates to the landing ramp at the rear.

The whole time, she was thinking back to what Riley had been saying about paths and destinations. She'd been talking about Ashkagiism—Nadia didn't even need the hint about a *spiritual adviser*—but religious implications aside, it felt just as relevant for her as it had for Riley.

And though Nadia didn't know if Ikkren would be her final destination, she had an inkling that she was heading toward a resolution of her years-spanning mission.

That soon, everything would be different. One way or another.

CHAPTER 4

The smell of fire and ash was starting to feel all too common for Carson Erlinza. Another village of Ashkagi rebel sympathizers, abandoned just before the Offspring's attack. Another village put to the torch.

Thanks to a brief partnership with a splinter faction within the rebels, the Offspring knew exactly which of the many remote villages dotting Enther's jungles sympathized with the Ashkagi. Now that they were partnered with the Junta instead, their primary task had been destroying the villages that were secretly funneling supplies and man-power to the rebel cause.

Each time they arrived at a village, however, it'd been abandoned first. Which was thanks to Carson. Or at least, he liked to think so.

He'd been with the Offspring for only three months, meaning he wasn't the guy in the room when decisions were being made. But the organization wasn't a military force, and operational security seemed more like a suggestion than a rule. There were always overeager members willing to talk about what they'd heard, or what their friends higher in the Offspring's haphazard hierarchy had told them. So Carson had contacts of his own who *were* in the room when decisions were being made.

It wasn't hard for him to piece together a list of all the villages the Offspring were planning on striking. And then, he transcribed those names of villages onto a simple piece of paper, which he hid in the ruins of each village they passed through.

Carson and his patrol partner, a jumpy young man with a lazy eye named Bradley, walked slowly through empty village streets. Past empty log houses with thatch roofs and nylon tarp coverings. The row of dwellings gave way to an Ashkagi temple. As they passed by the temple door, Carson cocked his head, hoping it wasn't obvious he was faking it. "Do you hear that?" he muttered. Carson liked keeping his excuses to wander off fresh. He hadn't used a fabricated, mysterious sound in a while.

"It's your imagination," Bradley said.

"There it is again," Carson said, ignoring his comrade. "It's coming from the temple. I'm gonna go check it out."

Bradley shrugged. "Whatever you say. Shout if you run into anyone, brother."

"Will do."

Carson pushed open the door to the temple, drawing his handgun from a hip holster and aiming it through the slit in the door. Inside, there was an empty stone floor where he suspected attendees would lay out their prayer mats. A wicker bin on the far side of the room contained a single mat, probably overlooked in the retreat from the village.

Rows of elevated plant berths lined the walls, where some of Enther's famous breathing flowers were still buried in dirt. The kind that bloomed and contracted in slow cycles that you could sync your breath to during prayer, if that was your kind of thing.

Carson looked over his shoulder to make sure Bradley wasn't following him. He paused for a moment, keeping his body perfectly still so he could focus entirely on his sense of hearing. There was the low murmur of voices as the other Offspring moved throughout the village, or the sound of splashing as his comrades doused the entire village in oil.

He pulled his piece of paper with an updated list of targeted villages out of a fold of his suit. Then he walked over to the stone wall on one side of the temple and carefully removed one of the loose blocks. He then withdrew a bottle of liquid siliconized ammonium phosphate from another suit fold and coated the paper with a built-in brush. He slid the intel into the gap behind the loose block of stone and pressed it back in. Finally, he drew a large X on the stone's face.

If anyone else happened to walk into the temple, it wouldn't look different at all. But a fire—one that wouldn't destroy the temple, but would probably char the surfaces of each exposed stone—would leave an extremely obvious X-mark left from the fire-insulating coat he'd just applied. And that would lead an observer to the intel hidden behind.

The state of the civil war on Enther had grown dramatically simpler in recent months. Various rebel factions had united under Noah Tasano, a respectable and devout Ashkagi. With most of the Junta military redeployed elsewhere, the Offspring were holding down the home front against Noah's rebel forces. Carson could only hope that various members of the rebellion, or perhaps simply a rebel sympathizer, were getting his drops.

He allowed himself a grin as he put away the bottle of chemicals. *Not bad for a therapist.* "This one's for you, Juliet," he whispered. To be fair, he said that every time. It was a practiced ritual, but one he enjoyed. What would Juliet say if she could see him now? Juliet, who'd once chastised him for his utter inability to pull off even a basic intel dead-drop?

Probably *Don't get cocky, motherfucker.* Carson imagined his deceased, would-be handler rolling her eyes while trying to suppress a small grin. And it was good advice. A single error, and Carson might give himself away.

Back when the refugee leadership had first pulled him out of cryo to infiltrate the Offspring, he'd figured he was doomed to give himself away with some little oversight. If he even managed to infiltrate the Offspring's ranks at all. But here he was, behind enemy lines, and no one had caught on to his deception. Yet.

Carson headed outside, where Bradley was leaning against one of the nearby houses. "It was just a loose stone," he said, suppressing a grin at his white lie.

"Figured. This one's just like all the rest. A ghost town."

Carson fell into step alongside Bradley, and they continued to move through the village. Other teams crossed paths with them every so often, spreading more oil in the village. The rain had almost stopped. Perfect time to burn.

The mission wasn't to indiscriminately kill rebel sympathizers in the Enther countryside. They just wanted to deny them a resource base. Carson figured no one particularly cared that the villagers had already abandoned the settlement. Burning the crop fields was most of what mattered.

But at least the villagers wouldn't die along with their livelihoods. Carson liked crediting himself with that, even though he knew it was just as likely that they had scouts deep in the jungle that could track the Offspring's movements.

It helped with the anxiety, the constant crushing weight of responsibility to find out something, *anything*, that could give his people an edge over their adversaries. That could provide insight into what Tanner Keltin was up to. If he could get out information, hopefully, to the pro-rebel villagers, that meant he could do so for his own people.

Plus, it helped with the fact that he still hadn't found out anything significant. He'd mostly just been going on these village raids for the past few months, and he hadn't so much as seen Tanner since his first day with the Offspring. The same day they'd killed Russ.

Carson and Bradley arrived at a central square, an asterisk-shaped intersection of muddy pathways interspersed with the occasional stone. Other Offspring had started to gather, each team of two describing how they, too, had found nothing of value. And how they'd prepped the village for a burn.

Three Offspring walked up from one of the adjacent paths, two of them flanking the third. The one in the middle was Emil Gurtrin, who'd served as Carson's orientation adviser during his first month in the organization. Emil was a bit higher in the don't-call-it-a-chain-of-command chain-of-command than anyone else Carson knew, and he liked to talk. Which made him just about the perfect person for Carson's uses.

"I'm guessing no one found anything worth reporting?" Emil

asked.

"No rebels yet. Can't wait to actually find some," an eager man named Marcus said. In any group of scared, insecure young men, there was always bound to be someone who cloaked his feelings in overaggression and machismo. For their unit, that was Marcus.

Emil, meanwhile, hadn't quite made the rounds of eye contact with the other patrol teams before he continued, "All right, let's burn the whole fucking place down."

The two Offspring flanking him each took lighter devices out of their suit belts, walked over to one of the oil-coated houses, and activated them. The village burst into a plume of fire in seconds.

The others formed up behind Emil as they strode through the empty streets, like conquerors surveying the destruction left in their wake. *Not a few of them are just kids acting out for attention*, Carson had to remind himself. Even when they spat out racist vitriol at the Earthborn while he was in earshot. At the *fucking newars*, they always called them. At some point, kids acting out turned dangerous. Murderous, even.

But Carson knew from his old life that they weren't hopeless. Especially Emil. The way he'd said *let's burn the whole fucking place down* would've convinced almost anyone else, but not Carson. The people who put a lot of effort into telling you how badass they were, how willing they were to commit violent acts, were usually the ones who were trying to paper over the fears and insecurities imploding them.

It was the people whose tone never changed when they were talking about violence that were the hardest to help. Carson had only met him once, but he'd marked Tanner as that kind of person. Someone who could tell you to murder hundreds, or thousands, or millions in the same tone of voice he used to describe his favorite flavor of ice cream.

The flames crackled and licked their way down doomed building walls, across thatch roofs, along wooden fences that marked individual plots. Carson looked around at the others marching in formation beside him, and discovered that most of them were grinning. Which was, again, probably a good sign. *Kids acting out for attention*, he reminded himself. If they ever actually ended up in a fight, ever ran across a village that wasn't already abandoned, he figured most of them wouldn't be smiling afterward.

They exited the village and took position on a hill overlooking the burning settlement. "Let's take five, then we'll head back to the transport," Emil said. "And then it's back to base."

Most of the Offspring sat down and pulled nutra bars or water bottles out of gear packs to watch the village burn. Carson withdrew a bottle of water he'd filled back at the base, checked to make sure the purifier tablet he'd stuck in had dissolved, and took a long drink. *Still too used to Vancouver*, he thought with a grimace. Enther was humid enough already to make him perspire on the regular, and that was before walking through a blazing village.

He put his bottle away and joined Emil at the base of the hill. Most everyone else was still transfixed by the fire they'd started, watching as the settlement slowly crumbled to ash. Not Emil. He was leaning against one of the giant trees, frowning.

"Another empty one," he said once Carson was in earshot.

"Isn't the goal to cut off the rebels' supply lines?" Carson asked. The same things that made a good therapist made a good spy, too: ask questions, redirect the focus to the speaker. Just like telling a patient what to do made them mistrust you, it'd invite suspicion from the other Offspring.

Emil shrugged. "True enough. I guess it's a win either way. But I figure the fighting's going to start at some point, and I just want to get it over with."

Scared, Carson thought. He knew from his frequent talks with Emil that the man had never been in a fight, never watched anyone die, much less even held a gun before signing up with the Offspring.

"Sometimes, I get the feeling that the trees are watching us," Emil said, sending dark looks to the surrounding foliage. "That must be how they're always able to figure out where we're gonna attack next."

Do you think we could have a spy in our midst? Carson might've asked. On one hand, him bringing it up might be a way to put himself above suspicion, if he was the one suggesting it. On the other, it was just a little too on-the-nose for comfort. He said nothing.

He didn't even know how the Offspring went about screening its members, although he knew that their recruiting drives had reached their zenith right before he joined. He'd never asked Emil whether they were doing background screenings on all the new recruits, and again, he wasn't sure he was comfortable with the idea of planting the thought in the other man's head. But he did know that recruiting had since dried to a trickle, which either meant that no one else was interested in joining—unlikely—or that they already had the numbers Tanner needed.

"I bet they're watching us, even now," Emil continued, his head darting back and forth between the trees. "But like you said, I guess it doesn't really matter." He stretched his hands up into the air and yawned. "Somewhere out there, our fearless leader is off fighting to save our solar system, and we're here pouring oil and lighting fires in abandoned villages."

His voice was biting, snappy. The same way he was whenever he talked about his family: a subject he'd alluded to often, although one where Carson wasn't yet ready to press him for the full details.

But hearing him use the same tone of voice to describe Tanner made it difficult not to react. Any one of *Are you having doubts?* or *Do you think Tanner might be wrong?* or *What would you do differently if you were in charge?* was almost too tempting to ask. An innocuous "What do you mean?" was what Carson went with instead.

"It's just...it's just hard when you come here expecting to do one thing, and instead, you get grunt work assignments like this. I thought I was gonna *be* somebody, but the others higher up and closer to Tanner aren't telling me everything. It's easy to be mad with them, to question whether I should've even—woah," Emil said, rubbing his forehead with his hand. "I'm sorry. I shouldn't let myself get carried away like that. Everything's fine, and we should trust in Tanner's leadership. He's a strategic genius, he knows what he's doing." The words spilled out of him fast.

But it was all Carson needed. If he was having doubts, that meant he might be willing to share even more intel in the future, assuming he could properly prod him. Emil had been his primary source of information so far, which was especially valuable considering his semi-leadership role. Maybe he even had some intel on what Tanner was up to.

Carson stretched out an arm and placed his hand on Emil's shoulder. "Don't worry," he said softly. "I'm glad you shared that with me, brother."

Every time he said the word *brother*, an image of Stacy flashed through his head. Somewhere on the other side of the asteroid belt, Stacy was about to get caught in the middle of a war as Junta ships tightened their noose around the outer rim. He'd heard most of the fleet was headed to Ikkren, not Calimor, but he still feared for his brother. He was a filmmaker, not a soldier.

"You can tell me anything you want," Carson blurted out. It was risky, and made him seem almost desperate for more information. But while Stacy was in danger and Carson was one of the only people who could do anything to help him, taking a risk and pushing his relationship further with Emil felt like the only right thing to do.

But as he turned to look at Emil's eyes, his breath caught in his throat. Would the other man see through his desperation, his sudden urgency? After a second, however, Emil's eyes softened instead. "I'd like that, brother. Maybe we can talk more back at the base. You've been a good...friend, Carson." The edge of his mouth curled for a moment.

The two nodded at each other and stared out over the burning remnants of the village. After a few quiet moments, Emil got up to round up the rest of their people and head back to the transport.

CHAPTER 5

Isadora's first meeting with Rebecca since her house arrest had been lifted—and the last meeting on her schedule before departing for Sarsi—was to take place in Eltanos Park. Isadora had never been, although she'd always wanted to. It was one of those places she kept wanting to visit, until work got in the way. And *work getting in the way* was probably one of the best ways to sum up Isadora's life ever since the *Preserver* computer had put her in charge.

She glanced around at her surroundings, at the endless rows of low-hanging oak trees and the large lake right in the park center. She'd seen the Obrigan hinterland before, with its translucent-capped fungal growths and weirdly depressing monotone flowers, but the park didn't feature any of the native flora. It was like the entire city was curated to resemble an old-Earth megalopolis.

At least the sonic dampeners along the perimeter kept it peaceful. Isadora turned her eyes skyward, where there was a line of air traffic sailing by. Not a single engine whine could be heard from below. Enjoying the gentle rippling of the lake, she let herself enjoy a deep breath.

When the refugees had fled Earth aboard the *Preserver*, they'd been told that Natonus was supposed to be the most resource-rich system that humanity had discovered. The crown jewel in colonized space. Even so, the scale of development in only a century—at least in Obrigan City—still took Isadora aback sometimes.

If only it wasn't so hot. Growing up in Seattle, Isadora had rarely experienced a truly sweltering summer. She missed walking along Elliott Bay in the cool, misty summer mornings. Obrigan City had Seattle summers too, but here, they called it *spring* instead.

She considered taking off her blazer, but she could already feel the sweat seeping into her sleeveless blouse. She'd stopped feeling self-conscious around her staff a long time ago, but meeting Rebecca was different. After months of unsuccessful attempts at repairing her relationship with Meredith, Isadora was increasingly convinced that the only way to truly begin to mend things over with her ran through Rebecca.

Isadora looked up and saw her approaching. She wore a long black cardigan that almost reached her knees, seemingly unperturbed by the heat. She walked up, sat across the park table from Isadora, and crossed her legs.

"I got you coffee," Isadora said, hoping reaching into her satchel would help her avoid awkward eye contact. "Meredith said you like...mochas, right?" She passed a coffee cup to Rebecca.

"Yeah. You?" Rebecca asked, immediately taking a drink.

"Oh, just black," Isadora said.

Rebecca snorted.

"Is that...funny?"

"Yes. I mean, no. Inside joke."

"I see," Isadora said, and looked down at her fingers. She pursed her lips, trying to figure out what the hell to say. *So sorry you've been incarcerated for the last few months* sounded more like something Tricia Favan might say, but she couldn't figure out how to phrase the same sentiment in her own voice.

"I imagine you must understand how sorry I am," she finally said, hating it immediately. "I'm—"

"—look," Rebecca interrupted, "I'll tell you the same thing I told Meredith yesterday. I'm not mad at you. Honestly, I don't really go out a lot, so house arrest wasn't that much of a downer. Except for not getting to see my awesome girlfriend in person for the past few months." Rebecca had the kind of dry, acerbic voice where it was damnably hard to tell how much of her emotions were genuine, and how much she was joking.

Still, Isadora closed her eyes and felt a hesitant wave of relief. Part of her had wondered if Rebecca would just scream at her, or dismiss her with a sneer, and then declare that she wanted nothing to do with Isadora or Meredith ever again. She wouldn't have blamed her.

"I'm guessing you asked me here to talk about my brother," Rebecca continued.

"Yes," Isadora said, her voice growing quieter and graver. "Yes I did."

"You know, I think the people interrogating me all summer wrote up a big report on everything I told them about Tanner."

"I am aware of that," Isadora said. She was also aware that the report had been hundreds of pages, and included lengthy chapters such as *Preferred Chess Strategies* or *An Analysis of Tanner's IT Problem-Solving Patterns* that made her mind numb. Reports were just words. She wanted the real truth at the heart of the matter.

A smirk spread across Rebecca's face. "You didn't read the report."

"I read it," Isadora protested. And then: "I suppose I may have skimmed a few sections. But really, I've always felt that even a short conversation with you could help me get a better sense of Tanner than memorizing some report."

"You're acting exactly how I do when the teachers call on me and I haven't done any of the reading." Rebecca's voice was still dry, but her eyes twinkled in amusement.

Isadora grinned. It didn't sound like Rebecca had any hard feelings, and if she didn't, then Meredith would come around too. Hopefully.

But behind the young girl's snarky facade, Isadora could tell there was something else. Tanner had departed her life almost two years ago. The intelligence report indicated the siblings hadn't had any contact since. Which meant Rebecca hadn't known about Tanner's involvement with the Offspring.

It must've been jarring to suddenly learn that someone you thought was out of your life forever was back, that they were at the helm of a dangerous terrorist organization. Even if they'd mistreated you.

Isadora thought back to Meredith's father, back to how frustratingly long it'd taken her to accept that he was little else but a toxic influence on their lives. If she'd suddenly learned he was a terrorist leader a couple of years after cutting him out of their lives, how would she have reacted?

She discovered a swelling sense of respect for Rebecca.

Plus, Tanner Keltin was now a household name. Isadora looked over her right shoulder at a holo-billboard that loomed over the park. It was actually promoting Calimor spices cultivated by her people—at an insane markup, naturally, with the Junta blockade cutting off shipping and limiting supply. But she wouldn't have been surprised if the billboard instead featured Tanner's face under a MOST WANTED caption.

Rebecca took another long drink of her coffee. "Tanner was...well, he was always distant. He never had that many friends growing up. Not that I can remember, or anything. But he always spent a lot of time helping me. He helped me study for tests, saved up as much money as he could to help me go to university, that sort of thing."

"It sounds like he really cared about you," Isadora said cautiously. Her natural inclination was disdain, to say something like *Tanner seems like the kind of person who thinks he deserves a medal for taking care of his sister*, but she stopped herself. Perhaps there really had been a time when Tanner Keltin was a good, self-sacrificing person.

"He really did," Rebecca blurted out. "I don't know when he started getting involved with the Offspring, but I have some guesses. It was almost like a light switch. He stopped spending time with me, he never told me what he was doing, he always hid things from me on his wrister."

Isadora nodded sympathetically. She was not well-versed on radicalization, but it was a believable story. Everyone had dark impulses, and when people became exposed to certain kinds of information or other stimuli at just the wrong time, it could bring those impulses to the fore.

"I understand he became distant. But did you ever get a sense he was getting involved in something like the Offspring?"

Rebecca shook her head. "I remember a couple of arguments where it was clear he didn't like your people. No offense. Don't worry, I argued back. And then, he...left." She lowered her head and rubbed her neck.

Isadora didn't press further. She remembered all too well what the report had said, how Tanner had struck Rebecca before abandoning her. Meredith's father had never laid a hand on her in that way, but she was no stranger to cognitive dissonance about someone you used to know. Rebecca would need to come to terms with the man her brother had become on her own.

"So where does all this leave me and Meredith?" she blurted out. "Are you going to tell me I can't see her anymore, or you'll tell the Union to lock me up in my house again?" Isadora was mostly sure she was trying to sound sarcastic, but there was an edge of anger in her voice.

In truth, though, it was a question she'd been mulling over for a long time. What was Isadora to do about her daughter dating the sister of her greatest adversary?

"Rebecca," she said, using the voice she reserved for only the most solemn occasions in her job, "Meredith cares worlds about you. I see no reason to put an end to you two spending time together."

She couldn't, not when their relationship was everything she'd been fighting for. Her goal was always to make a home for her people in the Natonus System. One day, that meant they'd become Natonese in their own right. Settling down and falling in love with those who already inhabited the system had always been part of the endgame.

Even if their last name was Keltin.

Meredith had pointed out the hypocrisy of the situation during one of their many fights over the summer. "We're fighting against people who want us dead because of where we're from and who we're related to. And you're telling me it's okay we hold Rebecca prisoner because of who *she's* related to?" she'd said.

Isadora knew how far it was from being that simple, but the elegance of her daughter's point still stuck in her head.

And there were political considerations as well. She was about to set out for Sarsi to drum up anti-war sentiment. What could be a better symbol of that than her own daughter dating the sister of Tanner Keltin? She'd never wanted the media to focus on Meredith, but acknowledging the reality of her relationship with Rebecca could be a powerful card to play at some point.

Isadora cast a grin at Rebecca. "If you break her heart, however...all bets are off the table."

Rebecca snorted. "Noted."

Isadora stood up to leave. "I have to be off. My transport leaves for Sarsi in a few hours, and I need to stop by the residence and say goodbye to Meredith first. And...thank you for meeting me. I promise I'll make this right."

Rebecca finished her coffee and made eye contact with her. "Thank *you*," she said. "When you found out who I was, the first thing you did was to think about Meredith's safety."

Isadora struggled to understand her meaning, but as soon as she realized the full implications, her heart dropped.

By the time Tanner was fully lost to the Offspring cause, he'd stopped protecting Rebecca like that. And although Isadora's protective instincts had been directed against her, she was mature enough to appreciate the intentions behind them. A flood of sympathy for the young woman swelled in Isadora's abdomen. And a growing appreciation for the choice Meredith had made in a partner.

"I'll always make sure Meredith is safe. Her and everyone close to her," Isadora said with a sad smile.

Even if that means eliminating your brother, she couldn't bring herself to add.

·   ·   ·

When Isadora entered the residence, Meredith was curled on the couch with a holo-reader in her lap. "Hey mom," Meredith said. Her voice had lost the brightness it used to have when Isadora got back from work, but for once it wasn't tinged with hostility, as it'd been the whole summer.

Isadora hung her blazer on a coat hanger next to the door and fanned herself. "I just got back from meeting with your girlfriend."

"Yes, mom. We *do* talk, you know."

Isadora rolled her eyes and grinned. "I don't see any reason why you two shouldn't continue spending time together. The Union ISB's investigation has shown that she has no contact with her brother."

Meredith frowned. "I know. I could've told you that."

"I understand. But I had to be sure." Isadora kept her voice devoid of anger—no *you'll see when you're my age* or *you don't understand because you're not a mother* admonishments. Just a calm, honest acknowledgment of the position she'd found herself in.

Meredith had turned seventeen at the start of the summer, a birthday that'd been a quiet affair. As hard as it was to reckon with, Isadora had come to appreciate that she was growing up. She was past the age where Isadora could rely on the old condescending platitudes.

Meredith was almost an adult. She deserved to be treated as such.

But it also made Isadora's heart ache. Back when Meredith had still been in cryo, one of the things that'd sustained her during the hardest days of separation was the promise of returning to normal. But after she'd awakened Meredith, there was hardly any normal left to return to. And within a year, her daughter would be a full-fledged adult. *Normal* was just a specter of the past by this point.

"Summer reading?" Isadora asked, craning her neck to look at the holo-reader.

Meredith shook her head. "I finished that a month ago." Then she cocked a grin. "Rebecca told me she still hasn't started."

It was hard remembering that this was going to be Meredith's final year in secondary school. In the Natonus System, Isadora had learned, going to university was relatively uncommon. Higher education hadn't seemed necessary during the first few decades of colonization. And after that, basic income had removed the need for a sizable class of educated professionals.

Even if going to university was just *what was done* back on Earth, Isadora wasn't about to force Meredith to follow their old traditions. And even for Natonese who went to university, taking a gap year or more to get some work experience was fairly popular. "Have you thought any more about what comes next?" she asked.

Meredith looked thoughtful. "I dunno. I've been talking to Rebecca about it, actually. She's not sure she wants to go to university, even if she's got the funding."

It took Isadora only a second to process that. For someone who'd been raised to follow Tanner Keltin's expectations, rejecting the opportunity he'd given her was one way of Rebecca reasserting her agency. It made Isadora like her all the more.

There was a part of her that wanted to question the wisdom of basing one's plans on a teenage relationship. Hardly any of them lasted, and that was before factoring in being related to two heads of warring factions. And as someone who'd once allowed herself to be swept off her feet by someone who was no good for her, Isadora almost wanted to throw cold water on Meredith's insistence that she and Rebecca make joint plans.

But telling Meredith all that would just ruin what was promising to be their most civil conversation in months. And sometimes, you had to let your children make the mistakes they were going to make. Meredith certainly wouldn't be the first person to go chasing some doomed teenage love affair.

"I'll support you no matter what," Isadora said finally. "And I'll always be proud of you, whatever you decide."

It was fleeting, but she caught a grin flash across Meredith's face.

"I'm sorry, but I can't stay," she continued. "The first wave of war refugees is arriving on Sarsi, and I'm going to make sure they know they have a place to stay at our settlements."

Meredith nodded. "Don't worry, I can take care of myself."

Isadora walked closer to the couch. "I'm sorry about all this. It seems like I've been having to leave the planet all the time for the past year." First, it had been to travel to Calimor after the Offspring had attacked New Arcena, then it was to travel to Enther for her failed attempt at a dialogue with the Junta. Hopefully, this trip wouldn't be as depressing.

"It's what you do," Meredith said. Isadora struggled to figure out the sentiment behind her daughter's words, whether it was supportive or resigned. Maybe it was both.

"This will all be over someday. This job isn't meant to last for-ever."

Isadora always been too busy to consider a life after her job was done, but she felt a sudden urge to settle down and, if not get back to normal with Meredith, then build a *new* normal on top of the old ones' ashes. But there were a lot of ifs to get through first.

If she could keep the *Preserver* safe during the war, *if* she could overcome the Offspring threat, *if* she could accelerate the pace of awakenings after the threats of war and terrorism were gone. Anxiety crept into the base of her skull like an old friend.

But for the first time, she could almost see past it all. To a future where she and Meredith were a mother and a daughter, nothing more.

Meredith shot to her feet, laid down her holo-reader, and crossed over to Isadora. The two wrapped their arms around each other. "I know, mom. I love you. And I know you'll make it happen."

Isadora's heart caught in her throat, not daring to question whether this sudden outburst of affection was real. It was the most she'd gotten in months. She'd take it.

But there was bittersweet nostalgia too. Isadora remembered what it'd been like when Meredith was short enough that her forehead came up to Isadora's shoulder. Now, she was a fraction taller than her.

"Go save everyone," Meredith finally said, pulling back from their embrace.

"I love you, and I'll try," Isadora said. She turned around, grabbed her blazer, and headed back outside. To the nearest spaceport, where she was going to start on her journey to hopefully do just that.

CHAPTER 6

Nadia had missed the simplicity of sitting around the *Exemplar*'s canteen table with Boyd and Derek. The old rituals were easy enough to resume: the coffee, the textured egg protein, the pre-buttered toast that still ended up soggy no matter how hard they tried. The casual conversation, usually about nothing at all.

"The trade was stupid," Boyd insisted. "The Obrigan Developers objectively got a better deal with Porgins."

"A great netball team is more than the sum of its parts," Derek countered, his voice more drawn and thoughtful than Boyd's. "Porgins is the better player, but Bennil fits better in the Sarsi Explorers' system."

Boyd waved his hand in dismissal. "That's just the Explorers' PR team covering up the fact that they haven't won shit in years, and can't afford Porgins."

Nadia hid a grin behind her coffee tumbler as the two men's debate continued. When they'd first boarded the *Exemplar*, their backgrounds and beliefs were so conflicting that something as simple as a sports disagreement was a welcome change of pace.

But not everything was the same. Boyd talked slower and more deliberately than he used to. He didn't obsess over every single imperfection or inefficiency in the *Exemplar*'s systems. Derek, meanwhile, had an edge to his voice and his movements she hadn't seen before. His manner of speaking had always seemed ponderous to her, but now, his drawl sounded more forced than natural. Like he was trying to disguise emotional tectonics.

Derek must've caught Nadia looking at him. He cleared his throat and announced his intention to return to the cockpit and begin the vessel's descent through Ikkren's atmosphere. Which left Nadia and Boyd finishing up their breakfast together, in what would've been an eminently comfortable silence if it hadn't been for the missile scrambler in the back.

They'd activated it when they got close to Ikkren, just in case any of the Junta warships in orbit got any ideas. And they'd coated the ship with radar-resistant stealth materials before leaving Obrigan, so they could hopefully fly around Ikkren undetected after entering the atmosphere.

Their destination, recommended by Derek himself, were the ice caves underneath one of Ikkren's largest mountain ranges, located in the planet's dry northern latitudes. The caves were directly below the destroyed husk of the original Modrin settlement. The one that'd been nuked by the Union over a decade ago. Derek had explained that the original Modrin settlers—who founded the Horde defense alliance—would retreat underground in the face of an overwhelming adversary. The Junta occupation probably qualified.

"How are you feeling?" Boyd asked.

Nadia released a tense sigh. "Just thinking about where to even begin. The hidden site Derek gave us is a start, but there hasn't been a clear sign of a unified Horde response to the occupation. And with Tori Hyrak disappearing, I'm worried the organization might've splintered."

"The Horde allchief will want our help," Boyd said calmly, a thin smile on his face. "I'm getting the feeling she won't be too hard to find. And the people of Ikkren don't want to live under enemy occupation. When we show them we can get results, they'll unify."

Hearing Boyd made Nadia realize that her biggest source of anxiety wasn't Ikkren, but the broader situation. She understood the necessity of coordinating a resistance to the Junta occupation—if they didn't know what Tanner Keltin was planning, then fighting his allies made the most sense—but a large part of her wanted to hunt the Offspring leader down. The Ikkren occupation be damned.

Nadia cocked her head. "I'm having a hard time understanding your optimism. You were the Offspring's prisoner for almost a month. You know what our enemies are capable of."

"I also know what *we're* capable of," Boyd countered. "One time, we won an entire planet from the Junta. Then we actually brought the Horde to the negotiating table. And did I forget to mention that we prevented your people from getting into a shooting war with the Union?"

Nadia's mouth contorted until it was somewhere between a grin and a grimace. "And then utterly failed to stop the Enther civil war and got you kidnapped. In fact, we just pissed off the Junta more and drove them into a partnership with the Offspring."

And I couldn't save Russ, she didn't add. She'd replayed her confrontation with Tanner countless times, always dwelling on the what ifs. Namely, what if she'd just drawn her own weapon and shot Tanner first? Her hesitation had cost Russ his life.

Boyd wore a sloppy grin. "And that negates all the earlier stuff how, exactly?"

"How are you this calm?" Nadia asked.

Boyd leaned back and placed his hands behind his neck. "I dunno. Maybe my time in an Offspring cell taught me something."

"I'm glad you could get all reflective while Derek and I were worried sick."

"Look: before I got captured, I practically spent all day thinking about the next thing. The next settlement project, the next land-use evaluation report I had to write up, the next maintenance check I had to do to keep the ship running. Sometimes, I even thought about what comes after. One way or another, this job is gonna end someday."

Nadia's fist tightened around her tumbler. The *Preserver* being destroyed by a stray missile felt like an increasingly plausible way it could all end.

"But being the Offspring's prisoner? I dunno...everything was just so uncertain, all the time. I spent the first few days hyperventilating from all the unknowns, but then it just...got better. All I wanted was to get back to the *Exemplar*. So now that I'm finally here again, I've been able to relax more. Live in the moment. Not all the time, but it feels different from before."

I'm glad someone can relax was the first thought that swam into Nadia's brain, but she kept that to herself. Because the second actually slowed her down. The entire time she'd known Boyd, he'd been exploding with energy. She tried remembering a time where he'd been able to stay still, but she just drew up blanks.

This was a big moment for him. She looked around, trying to

remember all the little details—the bowl of unfinished egg protein that Derek never remembered to take to their washing unit, the sudden hiss as the air recyclers kicked in, the loose strap Boyd had forgotten to buckle on his suit's chestpiece—so she'd give this moment the place it deserved in her memory.

"That makes me happy, Boyd," she said with a faint smile. "Happier than maybe you realize."

"Good. I can tell you've been on edge ever since you rescued me. Which makes sense, but the thing is, you haven't come back down to normal yet. And I get it—I know you've been through the ringer, believe me—but some days, I'm wondering if you've forgotten what it means to be you."

Nadia froze, her eyes locked on her tumbler.

"You haven't been able to stop talking about the war, or more specifically, Tanner," Boyd pressed. "And you've been spending practically your entire free time on drills."

Nadia couldn't argue with that. She'd been diligently practicing all the tactics on the datapads Russ had left behind. She was a decent shot, but spatial awareness had never been her strong suit. Luckily, she was starting to turn that around.

"It was your optimism that drew me and Derek to your crew in the first place," Boyd continued. "It was your optimism that got us over our differences. And it will be your optimism that gets us through this as well."

"It's not that simple," Nadia protested. "I can't fly us between our people and the Offspring and convince everyone to get along. That only worked last time because Tricia Favan is a good person. Tanner isn't."

"I understand that. But Old Nadia would've insisted that hopeless optimism might still open some doors for us. Even if we don't know how everything is gonna shake out."

Nadia opened her mouth to respond, but Derek's voice over the intercom interrupted them. Boyd gave her a long stare as he moved everyone's dishes to the washer unit. The two of them headed for the cockpit.

Turbulence gave the *Exemplar* a light shake as they took their seats. "We're breaking through the atmosphere now," Derek said. "The mountain should be coming into view soon."

The Junta occupation, according to Union satellite data, had proceeded rapidly. Most of the major Horde settlements were under direct occupational authority. Some of the smaller ones had stayed out of the enemy's crosshairs, but it was only a matter of time.

The planet's landscape was an interweaving pattern of brown and white, of mud and ice. Derek brought the *Exemplar* to ground just above one of the entrances to the caves at the edge of the mountain ridge, and the trio headed for the airlock. Once they'd made sure their gear was on right, with Nadia finally pointing out the unbuckled strap to Boyd, they ventured out into a cold that was both familiar and yet still shocking, somehow.

A gust of wind raked across Nadia's body. She cursed. "I'm never getting used to this ice cube of a planet," she said, although she was fairly sure the sound of her teeth chattering drowned her out.

"Me neither," Boyd concurred.

"Just give it another few decades," Derek said with a wince.

Nadia's body had become accustomed to shivering intermittently by the time they rappelled into the caves. They walked up a steep incline before entering a deserted cargo area. The walls were solid ice, a deep cerulean blue emanating from within. There were a series of heat lamps located around the cargo area, but each one was tragically depowered

"Where is everyone?" Derek asked. The echo was his only answer.

"Could they be deeper inside?" Boyd asked gently. "I say we press on."

"The Junta might've found out about this place," Nadia said, drawing her handgun. "Let's take our corners carefully just in case."

All three of them took their weapons out and cautiously worked their way through the cargo bay. Then exited into a series of tubular ice tunnels. Nadia had to concentrate to keep her boots from slipping, even with the traction provided by their lugs. The echo of their boots' thuds made her anxious—what if there was a Junta fireteam lying in wait, and she couldn't hear them? She gripped her handgun tighter and pressed forward.

The trio arrived at an intersection where there was a patch of metal fixed to the ground, but there were still no signs of life. "There should be some kind of command center this way," Derek said, indicating the path in front of them.

"Assuming the Junta hasn't already gone through it," Nadia said, gritting her teeth.

"Do you think it's possible the Horde resistance didn't even bother coming here?" Boyd asked. "We haven't seen any signs of battle, much less a hasty retreat."

"Maybe, but it wouldn't make sense," Derek said. "I'm not aware of any other rallying points. And it wouldn't be like them to give up."

"We should keep moving," Nadia said, looking back over her shoulder.

They entered a small antechamber, where they took cover on either side of the far door. They spun out of cover in unison, weapons brought to the ready, but no one was waiting for them in the command center. They fanned out and covered each part of the room.

"I...I don't understand," Derek said.

"It's easy enough to understand," Nadia said, in a voice that was almost a hiss. "Nothing ever works out right."

"It's okay, both of you," Boyd said sternly. "Let's search this room for clues."

While Boyd stayed by the door, Nadia moved toward a central holographic unit, where she pulled up a projection of the planet. Derek, meanwhile, crossed to the far side of the room.

There were only a handful of datapad receptacle cabinets along the far wall. *Makes sense*, Nadia thought. The Horde had never been big on bureaucracy. Derek started going through the datapads.

Fairly certain they weren't about to fall under attack, Nadia turned her full attention to the projector. She searched for a recent activity log, hoping that anything in there might give her a clue as to the Horde resistance's whereabouts. Sure enough, someone had accessed the device only a week earlier.

Nadia brought up the commands the previous user had inputted. The holographic map of Ikkren zoomed in to the southeastern hemisphere, which elicited a furrowed brow out of Nadia.

When she'd first signed a trade treaty with the Horde, paving the way for refugee settlement, the southeastern hemisphere had been the least developed part of the planet. Which meant that most of the colonies there were inhabited by Earthborn refugees.

The projection continued to zoom in. Thankfully, the colony Cleevan—the one where Nadia's parents lived—moved outside of the range. The projection stopped once it had centered on Lethock.

When Nadia and her team had initially surveyed the site that turned into the Lethock settlement, it hadn't seemed particularly promising. But when they'd discovered a series of hot springs in a deep underground cave, the colony grew rapidly thanks to an influx of tourism. It'd quickly become the largest refugee population center on Ikkren.

This all but confirmed that the Junta had raided the ice caves. They must've decided to attack Nadia's people directly. Hell, maybe Tanner himself had spurred them on. She'd need to get to Lethock immediately and do whatever she could to keep her people safe.

Nadia closed the projection and was about to storm toward the exit when Derek interrupted her.

"Nadia?" he said softly. "I don't think the Junta was here at all." He held out a datapad. "This was the only one I could find that hadn't been wiped. But it's revealing. This suggests that the Horde splintered after the occupation began, and that some in the leadership are actively blaming Tori for allying with your people."

Nadia should've seen this coming. Tori had told her plenty of times just how fragile the coalition she'd built really was. Under the stress of the Junta invasion, it would only make sense that the Horde would devolve into squabbling factions.

But if one of those factions were coming for refugees, she didn't care. She needed to get to Lethock and stop whatever the renegade Horde members were planning on doing.

Boyd, meanwhile, walked toward them. "You know who might've done this?" he asked.

Derek nodded sadly. "A man named Gus Pallek rallied support by denouncing Tori, according to the datapad. He was a classmate of mine when we were young. We signed up for the Horde's expedition force at the same time."

"If he's targeting my people, then we're going to have to stop him," Nadia said firmly. "We should get to Lethock as soon as possible." She spun on her heels and began striding for the exit. Derek pocketed the datapad and followed her, Boyd alongside him.

As they reentered the antechamber, Nadia frowned. They weren't any closer to finding Tori. If anything, the information they'd gleaned from the ice caves suggested the Horde was in disarray. It was hard to maintain hopes of setting up a planetary resistance to the Junta.

All she could do was follow the path that'd been laid out in front of her. Right now, that meant ensuring that Gus Pallek and his renegades didn't sell her people out to the Junta. Or worse.

CHAPTER 7

Life at an Offspring depot on Enther was all too familiar to Carson. He'd never been inside a terrorist camp before, but he'd read plenty of reports. The Offspring schedule consisted of time blocks highly similar to those back with the eco-terrorist cell he'd worked with back home: meager rations distributed for breakfast and dinner, drills and shooting practice throughout the day, ideology sessions in the afternoon, unstructured time in the evening.

Carson was almost at the end of the ideology meeting for the day, and he was trying really hard not to yawn. Which was a better reaction than he'd had a few months ago, when every violent denunciation of his own people had produced an ocean of nausea in his stomach.

"And that's why we must do whatever it takes in defense of the Natonese people," a recruit two chairs down from him said. He wasn't in Carson's unit, so he didn't know his name. "We have to stop the newars."

He'd forgotten to pay attention to what, exactly, was the justification for the recruit's conclusion. He was more focused on how unsure the recruit had sounded. How they all sounded in their mandatory denunciations of Carson's people.

It made sense. People weren't born wanting to inflict violence on each other, meaning it had to come from *somewhere*. But it was harder for Carson to maintain that humans naturally tended toward cooperation when his days were filled with burning villages and these meetings designed to manufacture outrage. Maybe *people are naturally cooperative* was the lie he robotically repeated to himself, just like how the Offspring repeated *the newars are dangerous and must be defeated*.

Carson looked around and saw a handful of faces that were smug, cocky, or angry, like Marcus from his unit. But most looked scared. Scared of the judgment that'd rain down on them if they ever questioned the Offspring's official line.

Fear was useful to people like Tanner Keltin, because fear made it more likely that these Offspring would follow orders no matter what. It was a testament to how easily decent people could commit evil acts, if manipulated in the right ways. Thinking that only sociopaths were capable of evil was a comforting lie, one that people told to protect themselves. *There's no way I could do something like that*, they might think. *There's no way I would ever do something like that*.

Carson had always wished people could more easily admit their dark impulses, their flaws. If the public could admit its own collective dark side, it would've made his old job a lot easier.

Just like me, Carson thought as the ideology session came to a close. *I'm a killer now, I've done terrible things in service of a greater good.* He frowned, remembering what Juliet had told him long ago. He felt like he'd fully embraced his dark side now. Few weeks went by where he didn't have at least one dream about the recruit he'd had to kill during his infiltration. Today, the images passed through his mind like a brief, waking nightmare.

Carson walked over to a table of refreshments, only to find it had already been picked clean by the other meeting attendees. His stomach growled in displeasure. The Offspring's strict food rationing had worn everyone thin. Every few weeks, one of the superiors would do a shopping trip to one of Enther's cities, taking orders from each individual. The order lists always ended up short, since most of the recruits had already wiped out their discretionary funds just getting to Enther in the first place. And most of what people wanted was more food.

Carson was luckier than the others, since he still had access to a decent chunk of funds supplied by the refugee government. But it wasn't a bottomless well, since they couldn't wire more natons to him without breaking the contact barrier, and he didn't want to draw too much attention to himself by requisitioning lots of items.

But he still made orders every once in a while. It was how he'd gotten the liquid siliconized ammonium phosphate he used to relay information to the villagers. He'd explained it was because the edge of his wrister had gotten melted off when he was standing too close to the flames in a village.

For today, he'd requisitioned something else.

He walked outside, where the rain had mostly subsided. Walked along a perimeter wall. The Offspring mostly hopped around from abandoned Junta weapons depot to depot, making camp with the inflatable tents and mattresses they all kept in their backpacks. The depots all looked the same: rusted metal bunkers that were half-subterranean. Carson gazed down the perimeter wall, where it looked like the steel was sinking into the mud.

At the other end was Emil Gurtrin. He always liked taking walks outside in the unstructured time before dinner. He looked over his shoulder at Carson and grinned. "Finally get out of the meetings?" he asked, a lopsided grin across his face.

Carson shrugged. "I don't hate them. It's good to remember why we're here."

"You're a better Offspring than I am, then," Emil said. "Those things bored me to tears. Now, hey, don't get me wrong, I hate the newars as much as the next guy, but I don't think repeating how much I hate them every day is gonna change anything. I'd rather be out there," he said, gesturing aimlessly at the sky, "finding some way to stop the invasion."

Carson had always suspected that ideology sessions were not as effective as radical leaders thought they were, but he'd rarely had someone straight up admit their inefficacy.

He crossed his arms over his chest and stared off into the trees. "I hear you," he said. "It's weird...I've never even seen one. I thought I'd be out here fighting them face-to-face."

Emil sighed. "That's what I thought too. I can't say I've met the enemy face-to-face either."

"You think you'd recognize them if you saw one?" A little on the nose, but it was hard to resist.

"Of course. I'd know instantly," Emil said. Carson hid a grin. "I've looked at all the depictions on the Offspring netsites. I know what one of those animals would look like." By this point, Carson didn't even cringe at the word *animal.*

The two men stood in silence, until Carson reached into the folds of his suit and pulled out a pouch. "Hey, brother. I know it's gonna be your birthday tomorrow. It's a little early, but I got you this." He handed Emil the pouch, filled with liquid nitrogen-frozen balls of ice cream. "Hard to get a cake in the supply runs, so I went with this instead."

Emil's eyes widened momentarily. That, Carson was prepared for. But he wasn't prepared when Emil's eyes watered, too. He brought his arm across his eyes in a violent arc, quickly drying them. "Thanks, brother," he whispered.

Emil tore into the pack immediately and crammed a whole handful of the frozen ice cream balls into his mouth. *Not one for delayed gratification.*

"You want one?" he asked, handing a few to Carson. By the time he'd put them in his mouth, they were half-melted.

"No one's remembered my birthday in fucking *years,*" Emil continued, his voice growing quieter.

Carson laughed unwittingly. "That can't be true. Right?"

Emil nodded his head bitterly. "Lost touch with all the people I graduated secondary school with, so the birthday wishes dried up after a few years of *oh-why-don't-we-ever-talk-anymore?*'s and *let's-make-sure-to-stay-in-contact*'s. Never really made friends with anyone in my government job. And even my parents stopped wishing me a happy birthday three years ago."

"Your parents?" Carson repeated. There had to be a story there.

"It was because of my brother. He was always my parents' favorite. He got amazing grades all through school, I got *pretty good* ones. He was the star of every sports team he played on, I was *decent.*"

Emil snorted. "Honestly, being an utter failure feels better than crushing mediocrity."

It wasn't a surprising sentiment. An unfulfilled desire for attention had been highly common among Carson's old patients.

"Anyway, after graduation, my brother set up this big adventure guide company to the mountains around Obrigan City. After a few years, he was one of the biggest names on the scene, because of fucking course he was. And then, three years ago, just two days before my birthday, my parents get a call in the middle of the night.

"It was a mountaineering accident. He died getting every single one of his clients off the mountain, safe. Became a media hero overnight. All his clients put together a big fund to pay for his funeral expenses, plus a lot more. Sent over a commemorative plaque thanking my parents for my brother's sacrifice.

"Ever since, my parents would invite me over on my brother's death day, along with our extended family. We'd all gather around and share our memories of him. And then, three days after that, my parents would always forget to call and tell me *happy birthday*. After the first two years, I decided to stop going to their little remembrances. Then I came out here."

Carson opened his mouth, but found himself unable to find the right words. If he'd still been back home, or really anywhere other than undercover with the Offspring, he'd urge Emil to seek professional help. From the tone of his voice, it sounded like he didn't even *like* his own brother anymore. If he ever had. There were so many layers to his trauma that Carson wasn't sure where to begin.

But *being an utter failure feels better than crushing mediocrity* was the heart of it. Carson could see past the hard exterior Emil was trying to project, and peered into the real man: a scared kid, who talked a big game about wanting combat experience or hating the refugees, but just wanted someone to care about him.

Or at least wish him a happy birthday.

The stories were always different, and few had made him feel as emotionally hollow, but Carson had worked with plenty of young men like Emil. The need for solidarity and recognition was so fundamental to the human experience that desperate people would join up with someone like Tanner just to attain it.

"Wow," Carson finally said, forcing himself not to talk like a therapist. "I had no idea."

Emil shrugged. "I haven't really told anyone all of that before. But you've been a good friend, brother." Carson felt a sudden chill at his usage of the word *brother*.

"Way better than any of the assholes I used to work with," Emil added with a smirk. "It was hard to care when they fired me."

"What happened, exactly?"

Emil shrugged. "Caught me looking at the Offspring's netsite on my work terminal. I wasn't even seriously thinking about joining, I was just curious. But after I got fired, I reconsidered."

Carson wanted to slam his forehead with his palm. If you had a population of individuals who desired solidarity and recognition, social ostracization was practically doing the radicals' work for them. Emil had been looking for a way to stand out, and the Union government had practically slapped a sign on the entire Offspring organization that read HEY, JOIN US AND YOU'LL BE A FEARSOME BADASS.

Carson thought back to his mission. Pictured a missile, cutting through the overcast Enther sky until it exploded Emil's body into fractions. It felt like a grim capstone on a grim life.

Emil wants to kill me, Carson reminded himself. *Wants to kill Stacy.*

Did he? If he really had the choice, was he the kind of person who could pull the trigger? How many of the Offspring recruits really could, if the choice was in front of them? From his experience, Carson knew that plenty would—but not all of them.

"I thought this was gonna help turn my life around," Emil continued. "At first, it did. I like the camaraderie, the brotherhood. And I believed—*believe*—in what we're doing. But you're still the only person who's reached out to me, and we're stuck on this jungle backwater, fighting someone else's civil war."

Carson thought back to their conversation outside the village they'd most recently attacked. He knew Emil had been having doubts. And he'd always been his biggest source of information. If he could press that advantage further...

"Are you having second thoughts?" Carson asked, then tried not to wince. It was too far. Too suggestive. Emil would see through him right then and there. He'd tell everyone who Carson was and then they'd—

"Yes," Emil said.

Carson was so taken aback at his honesty—and still reeling from his dumb question that'd somehow worked—that he couldn't figure out how to respond.

Emil placed his head in one of his palms. "Look, not like that. Don't report me to the loyalty officer or anything like that." He chuckled, a little too nervous for Carson to tell if he was fully joking.

"But I came out here to *be* somebody," Emil continued. "Somebody that would stand up and defend the people of this system. Even if no one cares about me or who I am." He still had a smear of ice cream at the edge of his mouth, which Carson found it damnably hard to ignore

"And you can't do that while we're stuck on this jungle backwater, fighting someone else's civil war," Carson said. He was pushing Emil, but in a way that felt empathetic. Hopefully to the extent that Emil didn't even realize it was a push.

Emil looked at him and grinned. "You get me."

"You've been a good friend to me too, brother," Carson said: a sentiment that wasn't utterly untrue. He and Emil were close, and a part of him didn't want him to come to harm. As therapists had to empathize with their patients, so too would a therapist-turned spy empathize with those he was leaning on for information.

"Thanks," Emil said. "I'm glad to hear it."

The two of them stood in silence for a few seconds before he continued. "Maybe things will turn around soon. I hear we have a lead on a way to cripple the rebels' supply lines. Maybe with a victory there, we can finally be done with this civil war and return our attention to the newars."

Carson tensed up. So they weren't just going to some other village next. He wished he'd known about the new plans so he could've included that in his last intel drop.

"According to Junta surveillance, the rebels are using some ruined old city named Kal Jova as a supply depot. It looks abandoned, but the footage picked up rebels moving arms, food, and medical supplies through the area. That's why we haven't seen many results from burning their village plots. So we're gonna deploy to Kal Jova."

Carson considered, briefly, how to respond. The information Emil had been giving him had been a trickle so far, but he was starting to wonder if it could turn into more than that. Still, it'd be smart to be cautious. For now. He went with, "And you think that will finally end the war on behalf of the Junta?"

Emil shrugged. "The civil war's been going on for longer than I've been an adult. I'm just hoping it'll be enough of a win that the Junta will consider our end of the bargain fulfilled. And then the rest of us can join Tanner on...whatever he's planning." Carson couldn't tell if Emil also didn't know Tanner Keltin's plans, or if he was still hiding that information from him.

But either way, he felt a sinking feeling in his gut. He didn't have any way to let the Ashkagi rebels know their supply operations were compromised. He just hoped he'd be able to figure out some way to render assistance to the rebels once he got there.

Emil stretched, yawned, and headed back into the complex. "I think it's almost time for dinner. You coming?"

Carson flashed a grin. "Of course, brother." He followed Emil back inside, wondering the whole way just how far he could push him to open up.

CHAPTER 8

After getting used to life in Obrigan City, where you'd usually see people wearing muted whites, greys, or blacks—*maybe* a deep navy, if you were lucky—colors abounded in Hovina, the second largest city in the system and capital of the planet Sarsi. Isadora caught coral greens and bright oranges and flashy pinks all around.

The most professional garb she'd seen was a banded-collar dress shirt, shorts, and semi-casual synthetic sandals, even though it was still the end of the workday. Tattoos and all kinds of piercings were common. Especially gauged earlobes. They seemed to *love* their gauged ears here.

Isadora was here to add fuel to the fire of a growing anti-war movement, deploying her political popularity with the Natonese to carry out a calibrated political stunt. But it was hard to focus on her goals when the city looked so vibrant. A little under 9 million people lived here, and Isadora could understand why it was such an attractive destination.

"How have I not come here earlier?" she mused. While a scorching late summer had settled over Obrigan City, most of the neighboring Sarsi enjoyed a temperate, if humid, year-round climate.

The planet also diverged sharply from Obrigan's politics. The Sarsi electorate had overruled the Union's charter ban, allowing for Isadora's people to settle there. Almost 6 million refugees had been relocated to the planet, a full million of those settling in the newly constructed suburban districts outside Hovina.

Isadora hadn't been to her people's most recent outposts, but the war had given her a reason to. And it was the perfect site for her planned stunt.

To her left, Valencia Peizan shrugged. "Because you're a workaholic who shuts herself in her office most days?"

Isadora shrugged. "I suppose you might be right about that."

Valencia had spearheaded her reelection campaign. She liked the other woman enough to reassign her as her chief of staff, a decision that had been paying off immensely over the past few months. She could devote more of her days to actual planning, decision-making, and meetings when she didn't have to schedule everything personally. Or keep track of it all.

Plus, she had a soft spot for Valencia's attitude. When Isadora had been starting out, she'd been so worried that her staff wouldn't respect her that she'd come off a little too cold and professional. Katrina, Gabby, and Alexander rarely joked with her, and Riley only sometimes did.

Now that Isadora felt more comfortable in her role, she didn't mind a little well-intentioned sass from Valencia. She didn't have to project her authority anymore, it was just assumed.

She and her staff continued down the promenade toward the train station, where the city's mayor was waiting for her. The municipal government had ensured that the blocks between the spaceport and the nearest train hub were properly secured in advance of Isadora's arrival. But plenty of pedestrians were still around, and she saw sporadic flashes from media crews on the edge of the promenade. She spotted a few people who looked like police—they wore matching shirts, at least, although they didn't tuck them in—who waved at her. None of them carried so much as a baton.

Isadora, Valencia, and their security detail met the reception outside an elevated train station. At the front was Jim Dexargo, the Hovina mayor. "It's a pleasure to meet you, finally," he said with a big grin, striding forward with his hand outstretched.

Isadora shook his hand and regarded the man. He was barrel-chested, with large feet that made his sandals look small. A bushy beard obscured most of his lower face, but she could still make out a tattoo running along the entire left side of his neck. It wasn't an image she recognized, but it looked like twisting vines in shades of crimson and indigo.

"The pleasure is all mine," she responded, giving him a reserved, diplomatic smile. "Hovina seems like a vibrant city, Mayor Dexargo."

The man chortled. "That, it is. And it's just Jim. Wanna see it from a couple dozen feet off the ground?"

Jim and his staff led Isadora and her entourage up an escalator to a train station, where an empty electric car pulled up. "We never had the growth boundaries the capital did, so Hovina's got a bit of a sprawl going," he explained as the train came to a halt. "So we built a grid of electric, elevated trains over the city."

Isadora followed Jim inside, both of them followed by their respective staff. The train gathered speed as it shot out of the station.

She walked to one of the windows and looked out over the sprawl. Even the structures were flat. She was pretty sure she hadn't seen a building over five stories. There were no skyscrapers, just sprawling office complexes with what looked like tram lines between sections.

From what she could tell, the most common material used for the buildings were red bricks and beige sandstone blocks. Roofs were constructed with mint-green tiling. The larger promenades had the same sandstone blocks, the smaller alleyways were cobblestone.

"When I read that Sarsi was a swamp planet, this isn't exactly what I'd imagined," Isadora said. "Your city is beautiful."

"We get that a lot," Jim chuckled. Isadora frowned for only an instant—was the man just *too friendly* that standard political backslapping and flattery just weren't effective?

"The original settlers had a lot of reclamation work to do," he explained. "They say it's one of the reasons the city got so big. And then we filled 'er up with all kinds of coffee shops, juice bars, or just plain 'ole bars. We drown out the swampy smell with coffee, fruit, and hops." He wore a triumphant grin on his face.

"I don't think I've gotten a bad smell yet," Isadora said. The primer on Sarsi she'd read said that in the districts closest to the swampy wilderness, you could still get whiffs of hydrogen sulfide or methane.

A strange musical medley came out of the train's speakers. "We have our trains advertise local bands on the loudspeakers," the mayor said. "This is an electronic ukulele/synth-chord duo that got big a couple of years back. Hometown heroes, or something like that."

The train passed by a large public square, where Isadora was surprised to see a large gathering. Many were holding signs. A few were old-fashioned text on paper—which somehow didn't surprise Isadora in a city like Hovina—although most were laser dot projections.

Isadora thought back to her first year in the system, when she'd encountered an Offspring protest during a staff retreat to the Obrigan wilderness. She felt her chest constrict and her breathing falter as she looked out over a sea of what had to be protesters. Sarsi had seemed too perfect. There had to be a dark underbelly.

But when the train pulled closer, she could actually make out some of the signs. WE <3 YOU ISADORA one of them read. She looked out and found another legible one, reading OUR LONG-LOST COUSINS FROM EARTH ARE ALWAYS WELCOME HERE. And, toward the rear, ANYONE CAN SETTLE MY PLANET.

The signs made her eyes water for a moment. She wiped them before Jim or any of the others could see. Valencia had been telling her for months that she was turning into a popular political figure, that the Sarsi citizenry had always been the most receptive to their people. But actually seeing it, just months after Isadora had only narrowly won reelection, was totally divorced from reading an opinion poll.

It was enough to make her forget, but only for an instant.

On the other end of the Natonus System, there was still a war raging. Still a band of murderous xenophobes who could now operate unchecked in the dark. 30 million lives were in as much danger as before she'd landed on Sarsi.

But after years of toil and never-ending anxiety in what increasingly felt like a thankless job, it felt *damn good* to be appreciated for once. Isadora let the feeling linger in her system, relishing it. She found her lips pursing as she waved out at the crowds.

The train careened around a bend in the track, heading for the new districts where Isadora's people had congregated. "You know," Jim continued, more quietly and more seriously, "I let your people know that they're welcome to settle wherever they want. Most wanted to stay in the new suburbs, I imagine because they'd feel more comfortable surrounded by others like them. But I don't want it to seem like I'm cordoning your people off."

"I understand and appreciate your thoughtfulness," Isadora said. "I'm sure our settlers here understand where you're coming from."

She felt the train below her slow down as it approached the terminus station in one of the new districts. She straightened her blouse and cleared her throat. "And you're sure that the details we discussed are all right with you?"

Jim nodded. "Of course. I really appreciate what you're doing here."

The door slid open, and Isadora stepped out onto the platform. Jim and his staff took the lead, riding an escalator down to the ground level. The workday should've let out by now, meaning they'd hopefully have a good crowd waiting for them, both resettled refugees and native Natonese. Isadora used the time to check her wrister.

There were the usual status updates from Riley on every Junta military movement on the outer rim: the asteroid belt had been effectively blockaded, but none of their settlements had been attacked yet. There were updates from their settlements' security forces as they tried to track the Offspring, but they'd seemingly gone dark.

And then there was a new message from Vincent, reiterating his request that Isadora go visit him on Bitanu to talk about the *Preserver*.

"Valencia," Isadora muttered. Her chief of staff walked a step further down on the escalator. "The Junta have blockaded the outer rim, and they've already shot at a vessel carrying both of us once. If I asked you to get me safely to Bitanu, do you think you could do it?"

"So...the impossible?" Valencia asked with an obviously forced smile.

"Yes. Exactly that."

Valencia sighed. "I'll have a chat with Riley when we get back to the capital."

They arrived at the bottom of the escalator, rounded a support pillar, and saw a massive crowd waiting for them. Isadora had expected maybe a couple hundred at best. From what it looked like, there were almost a thousand. She widened her eyes in surprise. The crowd erupted when they saw her.

She recovered quickly, smiling and waving at the gathering. Most of those among the crowds who were refugees had come out of cryo either at the end of or after her reelection campaign. Without having experienced the bitterness of the election cycle, it stood to reason that they were more amenable to her than some of Sean Nollam's diehard supporters.

Her grin widened as she took the stage. An adoring crowd was every politician's dream.

She scanned the closest individuals as she settled in at a central podium at the edge of the station. They could've come from all over Earth. They were different from the first 4 million she'd brought out, which'd been dominated by hydroponics workers, technicians, engineers, and construction crew. This crowd mainly included restaurant workers, chefs, home service workers, and bankers to work in Sarsi's dominant financial sector.

"My fellow Earthborn," Isadora said, casting her voice out to the edge of the plaza, barely aided by the voice projection box at the edge of the podium, "welcome back to life." She grinned, and the crowd erupted. "And on behalf of all of us, I want to extend a warm thank-you to our gracious hosts." She gestured at Jim and his staff. The crowd echoed her gratitude.

"I will not mince words," she continued. "We are facing the gravest threat we've seen since we arrived in the Natonus System. Our people are in mortal danger. And until the guns fall silent across the outer rim, they will remain in danger.

"I stand here before you to call for an immediate and unequivocal ceasefire," she said, forcing each word out as though it were a declaration. Cheers met her, as did waving signs calling for peace. WAR IS NOT THE ANSWER, one read. Isadora wondered briefly how many times in human history the same sign had been flashed at some protest or gathering. "Nothing can be gained from fighting. *Everything* can be gained from peace, from working together." More cheers.

She paused and looked at Jim Dexargo, who nodded at her. "But in the meantime, we realize that the war has created mass numbers of people in the same situation as us: war refugees, fleeing devastation and the collapse of solar supply chains. We know the pain of being driven from your home. So, in consultation with the local authorities, I hereby announce that our settlements here on Sarsi are open to *all* war refugees."

Although the majority of the 6 million who'd emigrated to Sarsi had resettled in Hovina, others had constructed new settlements in the untapped planetary wilderness. It was a rough slog—it would include plenty of desludging or artificial island construction—but there was still plenty of available, resource-rich land for grabs. When Isadora had discussed the possibility of allowing war refugees into any new settlements her people constructed, the planetary government had quickly agreed.

"We cast our voices to every corner of this system," she continued, eyeing the media drones at the edge of the plaza, "to tell you that, no matter who you are, no matter where you are from, no matter what you are fleeing from, we hear you. We see you. And you are *welcome* here." Her voice rose in a crescendo until it thundered out toward the crowds like a shock wave. And even still, the crowds drowned her out.

"We are all the same. We all share a common destiny. Let us go forward and end this needless, destructive conflict in the name of our shared humanity. Let Earthborn and native Natonese forge ahead and join hands—hands that will always be outstretched in peace. Thank you."

The crowd erupted again. Isadora straightened her back and waved her hand lightly. She hoped the grin could disguise the disingenuity of her closing statement.

It was hard to say that she was only interested in peace when she'd ordered Nadia to take covert actions against the Junta. Or if Carson gave her the intel that would put Tanner Keltin in her sights. She'd order him dead without hesitation, because that was what someone in her position had to do, and she had to play the part.

But right now, her task was rallying as many people as possible against the war. So she'd play that part too. Whatever it took.

She invited the Hovina mayor to take the stage, then retreated to the edge of the platform to confer with Valencia. They stepped back behind one of the pillars to hear each other over Jim's booming voice.

"That was beautiful. I honestly might've choked up a little bit," Valencia said.

Isadora arched an eyebrow. "Really?"

"No."

"I figured. So, what do you think?"

"That it was good politics. We've managed to one-up the Union Parliament, doing what they weren't willing to do for us when we showed up in their system. I'll bet Union media is gonna treat you like a hero for that speech. That gives you political capital that can be leveraged."

"So, you think the plan *worked*, in other words."

Valencia smiled thinly. "I do."

As the two of them continued to look out over the gathered hundreds, she continued: "You know...look, I realize it feels like we're powerless while the *Preserver* is in the middle of a war zone. But this level of popularity? That's *power*, right there. More than I thought we'd have."

"I agree," Isadora said. "Bottom-up power. Which may be one of the best kinds to have, in politics." Except that people power was most potent in the long run, and Isadora didn't know how much time she had.

But it was the hand she'd been dealt. She'd keep playing the game, keep making moves until disaster struck. Or, more hopefully, until the war was over. Or the Offspring had been utterly destroyed. Hopefully both.

CHAPTER 9

Lethock had been founded as a tourist town in the middle of a tundra, back when Nadia and her crew had first surveyed it. Now, it looked the part.

As the *Exemplar* flew in toward the colony, Nadia had to blink to make sure her eyes weren't deceiving her. Bright neon signs interrupted the white and blue landscape, and what used to be a mass of basic prefab shelters had instead turned into a sprawling colony with hotels, pricey restaurants, upscale bars, and a circle of large landing pads outside of the settlement. Clouds of steam from the underground hot springs wafted through colony streets.

And now it was a target.

Nadia had come to Ikkren to find Tori and rally the Horde against the Junta, but the allchief had apparently disappeared after infighting within the Horde's ranks had cast her from power.

Once Nadia had learned that some of the renegades had developed a plan to occupy Lethock instead of fighting back against the Junta, and without any good sense of where to search for Tori, she'd set out to stop them. Unfortunately, she wasn't certain what their plan was, much less what kind of force the renegades had deployed to the settlement.

She supposed it didn't really matter what they were planning. If it involved putting refugees in harm's way, then Nadia needed to stop them, not understand them. After that, maybe she'd be able to coerce the renegades into giving her information on Tori's whereabouts. But she wasn't holding her breath.

A shrill beep from the *Exemplar*'s control console cut into her thoughts.

Derek cursed. "Sorry. I forgot to radio in our approach." He began frantically typing away at the pilot's station, while Boyd gave Nadia a concerned look. They'd never seen Derek forget an important step like that.

But he could be forgiven. One of his childhood friends, Gus Pallek, was the mastermind behind the renegade Horde faction seeking to depose Tori. And Derek had already been on edge ever since the war began.

Once they landed on one of the raised platforms outside Lethock, a detachment of local militia forces headed out to meet them. That, at least, was a good sign. Whatever Gus was planning, it seemed like he hadn't started shooting anyone yet. But Nadia was well aware that bloodshed was a probable outcome. She paused at the airlock to make sure her handgun was easily accessible.

The door opened, and a squad of colonial militia personnel were there at the ready. "When we saw the *Exemplar* coming in, we almost couldn't believe it," the militia captain said, striding forward to shake Nadia's hand. "Kate Hossi, ma'am."

"Please, it's just Nadia," she told the captain, shaking her hand brusquely. "We're here because we have intelligence that suggests a renegade Horde cell may be targeting Lethock."

"They're already here," Kate said. "A group of Horde gunships arrived and took control of the militia headquarters. We weren't sure whether we should defend ourselves, especially after the chief coordinator's neutrality proclamation, so we stood down. Then we ordered the tourists away—not that there are many, with the war going on— and issued lockdown orders for all colonists."

"Sounds reasonable. Any idea what their intention is with occupying the colony?"

"None, ma'am."

"Fair enough. We're here to talk to the renegade Horde members." Nadia walked briskly to the elevator at the edge of the landing pad.

"They said they'd fire on anyone who came into the headquarters," Kate said.

Nadia looked back and exchanged glances with Derek, who shrugged. "I'm betting they won't fire on *me*. And if they do, then we'll figure out how to beat them." Kate's face registered skepticism, but she seemed to accept that.

Nadia, her crew, and the militia forces took the turbolift down to the ground level. The colony was eerily deserted, with flashing holo-billboards giving a false sense of life. Nadia thought she could see eyes peering out at her from the shelters, but she mostly kept her own eyes straight ahead. She didn't think the renegades would be so brazen as to fire on her unprovoked, but she figured she should be ready for anything.

The rest of the trek to the militia headquarters was uneventful. Once they reached the plaza outside, Nadia quickly assessed the setting. Multiple alleyways converged on the plaza, which would make for useful cover if the renegades fired at them.

Then again, Nadia wanted to do her best to avoid getting colonists shot at. It might be better to lay down smoke grenades and escape if they fell under fire. She asked both Boyd and Derek to ready a pair of grenades, then strode into the center of the plaza, her long hair whipping her face as a gust of wind rolled through.

One of the headquarters' windows opened. "We told you to stay away!" a voice bellowed at her.

"I'm not militia!" Nadia called up.

"Then who are you?"

"You know who I am."

More windows opened. At least a half-dozen gun barrels were pointed at her. She recognized one of the renegades as Gus Pallek. "You're the reason we're in this mess!" he shouted.

"And I'm here to help get you out of it. But I can't do anything if you're here, threatening my people."

A pause. "When we came here, I honestly wasn't sure what we'd find. But locked away in the headquarters' computer system is a *very interesting* message from your leadership. One that described your crew's mission in great detail. One that contradicts everything Isadora Satoro said about your people staying neutral."

Nadia tensed up. Riley must've sent classified information to all militia forces on Ikkren explaining what she was up to. It implicated Isadora in a lie: one where she'd secretly dispatched Nadia to help the

Horde fight the Junta despite her official proclamations. If the Junta found out about that...

"Honestly, the message went far beyond what I was *hoping* to find," Gus continued. "I bet the Junta would be very interested in its contents. Maybe they'd even reconsider putting our planet under siege."

"You can't be serious!" Derek's voice.

Nadia turned to her right to see her crewmate joining her. "Gus, I know you. I know you're smarter than this. Nadia's here to *help* us. The Junta can't be trusted. And Nadia's people have only ever helped us." Nadia was just grateful that Derek was speaking up.

"You want to talk to me about *intelligence*, old friend?" Gus barked back. "How about this: the only reason we're in this predicament is because of Tori's alliance with the refugees. They've lost us our planet!"

Nadia's hand twitched, instinctively wanting to dart to the handgun at her hip. But with who-knows-how-many rifles pointed at her, she figured that'd be a bad idea. She turned around to look at Boyd instead, planning on giving him a signal to ready a grenade.

She saw him mouth, "Negotiate!" at her. And then: "You're *Nadia Jibor*, dammit!"

She paused, her hand inches away from the grip of her gun. *Stop*, she had to remind yourself, *why are you so eager to fight?*

She recalled what Derek had told her about Gus earlier. About how he'd always been brash, insecure, reckless. He'd respond to forceful negotiation, but he'd back down if challenged.

"Derek's right," Nadia said. "You can't really think the Junta will negotiate with you, no matter what you bring to the table. The thing is, right now, I'm the only outsider in the whole system who's trying to *help* you. You can either cower away from your real enemies here, or you can help me win back your planet."

"Think about it," Derek pressed. "When has an off-worlder ever done anything for us? If you want to beat the Junta, do it honorably, alongside our allies. Not through betrayal and subterfuge."

Nadia flashed Derek a grateful grin before returning her attention to the militia headquarters. The Horde renegades' silence had grown tense, making her reconsider reaching for her weapon.

Finally, Gus gave her a response. "Fine!" he growled. "Let me think about it!"

.   .   .

They'd been thinking for the rest of the day, which Nadia took as a bad sign.

At the very least, they were still holed up in the militia office, and they hadn't turned over Riley's message to the Junta. Otherwise, Nadia figured, Junta ships would've shown up to capture her already. Or they might've just started bombing refugee colonies across the planet.

Meanwhile, she and her crew had stayed in one of the vacated tourist hotels. She kept trying to schedule another round of negotiations with Gus, but the renegades had maintained radio silence.

At least the bed's nice, Nadia thought, looking down at the luxuriously soft and squishy mattress in her hotel room. She'd always found the *Exemplar* plenty comfortable, but it couldn't compare to the rooms here.

She got herself out of bed the following morning, took a shower, and found Boyd in the deserted hotel lobby for breakfast. They'd been feasting on all the food stores that hadn't gone bad, considering the hotel was overstocked. "Morning," Nadia said groggily after grabbing a cup of coffee. "How's it goi—"

"—you should talk to Derek," Boyd blurted out.

Nadia blinked several times, still trying to wake herself up.

"He skipped breakfast this morning," Boyd continued. "Said he was gonna go check out the hot springs. Tell me: we've known Derek for years now—when has he *ever* skipped breakfast?"

"A fair point," Nadia conceded. "But he's your friend too. Why don't we go talk to him together?"

"Because it's different. I'm the guy he jokes around with, talks to casually. He *respects* you."

"You know as well as I do that Derek respects you *plenty*, Boyd."

"Well...yeah. But it's different. He'll actually listen to you. And besides," Boyd added, giving her a look that was uncomfortably perceptive, "I think a conversation would do both of you some good."

Nadia sighed, but agreed. She ate a breakfast sandwich, refilled her tumbler, and headed out for the underground hot springs.

The colony was still deserted, with the militia trying to keep everyone indoors. She hopped over several rows of snow-covered railings, where tourists would normally queue up to enter the caverns.

The air felt instantly warmer inside. Translucent steam rose from spring-fed pools lining the rocky path. She found it a welcome relief from Ikkren's chill at first, but she was sweating by the time she got deeper in the cave system. She adjusted the temperature controls on her suit and stepped into the next cavern.

Derek was inside, sitting on an outcropping that stretched out over a large basin, draping his feet over the edge. His book of Ikkren poetry sat in his lap. He turned around when she approached.

Nadia cleared her throat. "Reading?"

He closed the book. A plume of dust escaped from its pages. "Trying to," he said. The rich velvet of his voice filled the ice cavern with a satisfying echo.

"Look—"

"—you're here because I haven't spoken to Gus since yesterday."

Nadia nodded. "We really need you on this one. You're our best hope of getting him back on board and pointing us in Tori's direction."

"That's all true," Derek said, followed by a deep sigh. "But I've been worried about what I might say if I talked to him at length. The truth is...I'm angry."

"Angry?"

"Yeah. Like there's this miasma of rage constantly going on in my gut."

"Miasma of rage"? Sounds like someone's been reading too much poetry, Nadia thought.

"When I was younger, all I could think about was getting off this planet. Leaving the outer rim. But then I went to the sunward planets for the first time as part of our mission, and all I got were dirty looks and hostile glares."

Nadia thought back to their time wandering around the rainy cities of Enther or the claustrophobic subterranean tunnels of Rhavego. Plenty of people seemed to have known who Nadia was, and by extension, who Derek was. And although most people had been nice, Nadia still remembered hearing the occasional *newar scum* hurled at her, usually followed by a wad of saliva.

For every encounter like that, Derek got at least five such comments. And then, when he finally came home, to a place where he shouldn't feel like an outsider, it was under military occupation from a hostile outside force.

"Maybe it's good to be angry," she said. "We're in the middle of a war. Anger can help us get through this."

"That's a strange thing to hear, coming from *you*."

Only a few days ago, Nadia had gotten a *look-how-much-you've-changed* earful from Boyd. She wasn't particularly keen on another lecture. "The problems we're facing are different now," she said. "I'm just being the person I need to be. And what about you? Are you becoming the person *you* need to be?"

Derek furrowed his brow. "What do you mean?"

"You want to save your planet. I get that. But right now, there's this massive leadership vacuum, with Tori losing her people's backing and rival factions competing for power. The way I see it, your people need someone to step up. I'm not saying you need to take charge or anything, but there *are* things you could be doing."

Derek stayed silent, so she continued. "The whole time I've known you, you've been content to live in the shadows. You read your poems, you fly the ship. But you retreat from others. You've always let me and Boyd take the lead. Every time someone treats you like an outsider, you use that as an excuse to turn inward even more."

She worried her voice was coming out harsh, so she took a deep breath and spoke more gently. "You are someone your people should look up to. You've faced down Offspring, the Junta—multiple times—Ashkagi terrorists, hell, even the Union military. You've traveled from one end of the system to the other. You were the first person who saw the potential of an alliance between our two peoples, and through that, you've helped bring your planet out of isolation. If there's someone who can convince Gus to back down and help us find Tori, it's *you*."

Nadia was used to Derek looking quiet and contemplative, but she'd never seen him look genuinely taken aback before. For almost a minute, neither of them said anything, and the only sound in the cavern was the gentle hiss of the steam and the babbling of the water.

Derek snorted, finally. "Fine. I see your point. I'll go talk to Gus."

.   .   .

Nadia had thought it'd be better to allow Derek time to negotiate with Gus on his own. It seemed like that was the right choice.

The renegades had announced their intention to pull out of Lethock without sending Riley's message to the Junta. They were preparing to ship out to the various occupied settlements around the planet to begin resistance activities against the Junta. It didn't really feel anything like a victory, with a mountain directly in her path still left to climb, but it was the first step nonetheless.

Nadia stood at the edge of the landing pad where the last Horde gunship was about to take off. Gus was helping load ordnance and supplies into the vessel. She cast a look over her shoulder, where life had returned to something resembling normalcy in Lethock.

People had left their dwellings, and Kate's colonial defense forces were taking control of the militia headquarters again. After Nadia's urging, she'd wiped all traces of Riley's secret message from the headquarters' computer system.

After he'd finished loading supplies onto the transport, Gus walked forward to join her. "Surely you have to see the injustice of it all." He indicated the refugees going about their daily lives. "The only reason the Junta attacked us was because of our alliance with your people. But now, with your leader's neutrality statement, your people get to live as though nothing's changed, while mine have to fight for our home."

Nadia nodded. "I *do* see the injustice of it. And that's why I'm here, fighting for your home alongside you."

That shut Gus up. "That's what Derek told me," he said finally. "And that's why I'm telling you this: Heykan."

"Heykan?"

"It's the largest settlement on Ikkren. Right after my people broke away, the rumor was that Tori was heading there. Supposedly, she was planning something big."

"Well then. My crew and I will set out for Heykan immediately. Do you want me to pass along a message?"

Gus wrinkled his nose. "Tell her I still blame her for getting us into this mess. But...maybe I was wrong. Maybe there's a new generation that can get us out of it. Tell her I said all that." He walked toward the gunship without saying goodbye. The engines fired, and it sped off.

After the Horde ship disappeared from view, Nadia looked over at the *Exemplar* resting on an adjacent landing pad. *First step down,* she thought. And she knew where the next one was.

CHAPTER 10

Carson couldn't see the ruins of the once-great Kal Jova from the windowless interior of the Offspring transport, but he figured they were close. His ears popped as the transport lost altitude. After another few minutes, he felt the lurch of the landing gear, and the transport came to a rest. The side door slid open. Must've been facing away from the ruins, since the only thing Carson could see was more jungle.

"Okay people," came Emil's voice from the cockpit. "We're here. I want to remind you all that we believe the Ashkagi rebels are using the ruins as a supply depot. Junta satellite surveillance suggests no one's home, but it's possible we could encounter hostiles."

Carson looked at the others. Considering the strategic importance of investigating the Kal Jova ruins, the Offspring had dispatched multiple units. The majority of the others looked familiar, though he'd only met them briefly, back during his orientation period.

And then there was Marcus, who wore a grin that was equal parts smug and angry. "Here's hoping we *do* encounter hostiles," he said eagerly. Two others echoed the sentiment.

Emil ignored Marcus' outburst. "We've been training for this. Just be careful, and watch each other's backs. And remember that this is just an initial recon mission. If you find anything, report back immediately. We don't need heroics. Meanwhile, I'll be monitoring your progress from the transport. Natonus for the Natonese."

"Natonus for the Natonese!" the others repeated. If anyone questioned the irony of the chant, as they were heading out to potentially engage other native Natonese in combat, no one commented on it.

Carson unstrapped from his seat, followed his patrol partner Bradley out, and nodded to Emil along the way.

Both he and his partner drew their sidearms once they left the shuttle. "I'm betting this is gonna be another dead end," Bradley said.

"What makes you say that?" Carson asked as the two of them trudged up a muddy path.

"Every village we've been to has been deserted. That means the Ashkagi are watching us. No reason to think that the ruins will somehow be different."

Except there was, of course. Since Carson had only just found out about the Kal Jova raid, he had no way of alerting the rebels that the Offspring were coming.

The two of them arrived at the top of the short hill, and the ruined city came into view. All other thoughts ceased. After spending all of his time on Calimor, Enther, and Rhavego—the underdeveloped parts, more specifically—Carson had forgotten what a truly massive city looked like. The ruins of Kal Jova represented the most expansive urban landscape he'd seen since he left Earth.

The dead city sprawled out as far as he could see, even though most of the buildings looked like they'd been reduced to fractions of their previous height. Most of them were rubblized husks now. Piles of building blocks and debris covered the streets.

Maybe a decade ago, that's all it would've looked like. But now, the jungle had reclaimed the ruins. Through every refuse pile were the twisting corkscrew-shaped Enther vines. Ivy and moss had crept up the destroyed buildings' sides. The city was a tapestry of decay and natural rebirth.

Carson let out a long breath. "I'm forgetting my history," he said. "What happened here, exactly?"

"City got attacked," Bradley said.

No shit. Biting his tongue around the Offspring was painful sometimes.

"It's what set off the civil war. The one that destroyed the old Theocracy, let the Junta come to power."

"I'm surprised no one ever rebuilt it."

Bradley snorted. "With what money? The Junta's broke. It's why they need us to fight the rebels for them."

Carson shrugged and gestured with his handgun, motioning for his partner to take the lead. They took a short path down to Kal Jova's outer boundary. There might've been a wall there once, but Carson couldn't be sure anymore. He stepped onto a debris pile, the crunch of the rubble replacing the squish of jungle mud. His boots left caked soil across the refuse.

Once they were inside the ruins, his partner checked his wrister. "Looks like Emil wants us to go investigate the old spaceport. We're headed to the west." Carson looked over his shoulder at the other two-man teams as they fanned out, each one investigating a different part of the city.

In another minute, they were out of visual range from the other Offspring. Bradley had never been much of a talker, although this might've been the first time Carson wished he was. The dead streets were eerie enough that he could almost feel his hair rising beneath his brown enviro-suit. They walked through a tunnel of carved-out buildings, past buses with their roofs blown off, past decrepit streetside food stalls that were almost indistinguishable beneath a thick coating of moss.

It was a rare dry day. Except for the wind whistling low through bombed-out buildings, everything was silent. Until he heard a hiss and a loud snap from his left. He almost jumped in fright, but it was just a snapping vine he hadn't noticed. It was too easy to be distracted by the mesmerizing ruins. Carson sidestepped as the end of the vine snapped harmlessly at him.

They came to an intersection, where Carson saw the remains of a holo-billboard. Corkscrew vines hugged the poles in interweaving spirals. The light photons were still flickering. The message was advertising a new holo-tech start-up, promising long-lasting holo-projections with a self-generating power source. "How long ago did you say this place got bombed?" he asked Bradley.

The other man scratched his head. "Was late 2394, I think...so what is that, twelve years ago?"

Carson looked at the holo-advertisement and grinned. Whoever made the new tech clearly knew what they were doing. He caught up to his partner, and they proceeded onward.

Carson looked around at some of the gaping holes in the building.

Wouldn't be that hard for a rebel sniper team to hole up in one of those, then take us out before we knew what was happening. Another one of the many common thoughts he had now that he'd never imagined having back when he was a therapist.

A fearful chill passed through his chest. Every time he'd left intel for the rebels, he'd never left his name. He'd figured it would be too risky to do so—after all, what if the Offspring found them? After a while, making the intel notes anonymous became a habit.

Didn't seem so smart anymore. If he encountered a band of Ashkagi rebels, how would they know who he was? And if they really were using Kal Jova as a supply depot, he figured it was reasonable to assume they had at least *some* kind of presence on site. He might be in real danger of getting shot by a rebel who assumed he was just another Offspring.

Carson tightened his grip on his handgun and moved closer to Bradley. For so long, his fears had centered solely around the risk of detection from his new companions. It felt strange relying on another Offspring to keep him safe. The idea of seeing the others as a source of safety caused a spectacular kind of cognitive dissonance, one that he'd need to work through next time he was alone.

He pictured Juliet Lessitor leaning against one of the nearby building husks, regarding him with an amused look. *Getting pretty deep now, aren't we?* he imagined her saying.

After another few blocks, they reached the spaceport. It looked like a giant pit, a circular hole in the ground extending dozens of stories down beneath the surface. Multilevel, circular hallways lined the rim all the way down. Stepping over the tall grass that had swallowed the edges of the spaceport, he peered down into the center. It was hard to tell with the vines and the grass and the moss, but he thought he could make out a handful of wrecked starships.

"It looks like they were in the middle of an evacuation," Carson said.

He thought about the individuals who'd boarded those doomed ships during the bombardment, for whom escape to safety would've felt like almost a sure thing—only to be whisked away. He was glad the bottom of the spaceport was too far down for him to spot ossified remains.

"Someone really did a number on this place," Bradley agreed. "Come on. Let's see if we can sniff out any signs of rebel activity down there."

They trudged their way through thickets of tall grass until they found a descending ramp that led to the first circular rim walkway. Or at least, they found the remains of it. It looked like a sizable chunk of the walkway had fallen to the ground long ago. And the distance was too far to jump.

"Okay then," Bradley said. "Grappling hooks."

They unhitched grapples from their suits' utility belts and lowered themselves down to the first walkway. Carson retrieved his device as soon as he heard his boots hit the walkway.

"Looks like a control station up ahead," he said, gesturing toward a room several hundred feet ahead of them. "Could be a good place for stockpiling supplies." Bradley shrugged, and the two headed for the control room.

Heights had never bothered Carson before, but he couldn't help but feel a nauseating sense of vertigo every time he looked over the railing. Maybe it was amplified by the eeriness of the destroyed city, or his anxiety about being mistaken for some regular Offspring.

They reached the control station, prying the door open until both of them could squeeze inside. As soon as he was in, Carson saw dozens of supply crates stashed in the room. He barely even noticed the long-depowered computer terminals and control consoles that had once guided the flow of air and space traffic.

He walked over to the first stack of crates and inspected the contents. Most were filled with non-perishable foodstuffs like corn and beans, along with plenty of pre-packaged nutra. A couple of supply crates had built-in cooling systems and contained fruit. "Looks like food, mostly," Carson said. "But I'm guessing this confirms rebel activity."

Carson looked over at Bradley, who was rummaging through a few crates on the far side of the room. He pulled out a couple plasma handguns. "Weapons too," he said.

"All right. I guess we should radio this in," Carson said.

"Will do."

His partner pulled up his wrister, typed a few buttons, and spoke into the microphone. "This is Brad and Carson, checking in. We've just discov—"

The sound of a low whistle cut him off.

A long-tailed plasma bolt—a sniper's discharge—sliced through the outer window and cut through Bradley's head. He went limp immediately and crashed to the ground.

Carson dove for the nearest terminal station as fast as he could. A flurry of sniper bolts whistled by overhead, striking the back wall.

Once he'd gotten his breathing under control, Carson assessed his options. If he was pinned down by rebel sharpshooters, he was stuck in the control room until the Offspring dispatched reinforcements.

If they dispatched reinforcements. He had no idea if Bradley's message had gotten through, and he wrestled with the idea of dispatching his own message. Although they were trying to kill him, Carson had to remember that he was technically on the rebels' side. Siccing the rest of the Offspring on them didn't square right with him.

He could try dispatching a message to all local frequencies, explaining how he'd been passing along intelligence to the rebels for months. But if any other Offspring patrol teams were in the area, they'd pick it up as well. It'd put his cover in serious jeopardy.

He looked down at his utility belt. He had two smoke grenades. That gave him an idea.

He loosed the first grenade from his belt, crawled along the perimeter of the room until he reached the other side, and tossed the grenade out the door. Sure enough, the sharpshooters began shooting wildly at the smoke, probably assuming he was making a break for it in that direction. Carson grinned and crawled back.

He threw his second grenade out the opposite door, onto the other side of the walkway. With the snipers' attention drawn elsewhere, hopefully he could make a quick escape. He darted out through charcoal clouds of smoke, coughed, and sprinted forward.

He pulled his grappling device out of his belt as soon as he was past the smoke plume. But just as he was about to launch it back up to the surface, he noticed a squad of Ashkagi rebels on the walkway below him, rifles raised. Plasma fire streaked toward him.

Sheer panic took Carson. Logic failed him. He had no plan, other than running. Fast. He tore down the walkway, back to the control room, heart racing. Burst through the other side of the control room, not even caring about the sharpshooters.

If he'd been more in control of his faculties, he might've noticed that the sharpshooters had stopped firing as he sprinted toward an elevator about fifty feet in front of him.

When he reached the lift station, the door slid open and revealed a hooded figure standing in the doorway. Carson stuck his feet out in front of him to bring himself to a halt. He spun around and ran back in the other direction. But the figure was on him before he could get much further.

The hooded man sent a swift uppercut toward him, which Carson blocked with his forearm. But faster than he could react, the hooded man grabbed his wrist and twisted it behind his back. He tried steadying himself by throwing his left leg wide, but he was already too off-balance.

Carson liked to think he was decently proficient at unarmed combat, but the encounter—calling it a *fight* might've been generous—quickly humbled him. The hooded figure forced him to the ground and pressed his arms and legs beneath his torso, so he couldn't resist.

He waited for a delayed onset of pain, sure that his opponent had broken something. Or at least twisted a joint. But nothing came. His opponent had subdued him with minimal injury in the time span of a few seconds.

The other man stood up, pulling the hood away from his face. The man had shoulder-length hair, equal parts black and grey, with warm beige skin. Carson thought he looked familiar—not someone he knew personally, but someone he'd seen on a newscast somewhere.

"My name is Noah Tasano," he said. *The rebel leader.* "And I know who you are, Carson Erlinza. I've been wanting to thank you for all the help you've provided us."

He pulled Carson to his feet. "Now, let's talk about what comes next."

CHAPTER 11

E ven with the help of the *Caretaker*'s automated systems, keeping the ship running over the last month had been a lot of work. Especially now that it was down to Tanner and eight of his brothers.

Basic upkeep for a warship was more intensive than Tanner had ever imagined. The nine of them were spending most of their waking hours making sure the ship's systems were running smoothly, the air recycling systems weren't about to malfunction and kill them all, and that the weapons were serviceable. After a month in, they were all worn out.

And yet, energized.

The end of their long crusade against the invaders was so close to its endgame. If it hadn't been for the newars' untimely completion of their laser defense matrix—a move that had thrown a wrench into

Tanner's plan to nuke the *Preserver*—it would already be over.

Every night, before turning out the lights in the captain's cabin where Tanner had taken up residence, he stared at the blip of light orbiting Bitanu on his holo-projector. The *Preserver*. Destroying it would make all the yawns and the coffee and the monotonous days of running diagnostics checks and scrubbing air filters worth it.

A couple of his followers were taking point on the deception project. They'd constructed an artificial holo-program that looked and spoke just like the dead Junta captain. It was all too easy to program the hologram to read whatever text they inputted. Every time they got a request for a report from Junta command, they fired up the hologram and made it read a fake report.

So far, it didn't seem like anyone had caught on. When messages from family members down on Enther had come in, Tanner had ordered them to create fake holo-programs of the rest of the dead crew to respond to their unsuspecting and unknowing widows or orphans.

And then, during Tanner's "breaks" from upkeep and maintenance duties, he coordinated a planetwide counterinsurgency campaign from his quarters.

Although it was hard to care about that. Technically, rooting out the Ashkagi rebels was the entire Offspring's responsibility per the terms of his deal with the Junta. Especially with the bulk of the military now redeployed to Ikkren, they were reliant on the Offspring to keep the home front safe.

Tanner absent-mindedly dispatched orders for a unit to raid a nearby village. It didn't really matter at this point. He really couldn't care less if the Ashkagi rebellion got crushed or not. He already got the Junta to start its war with the Horde and blockade the asteroid belt. And he'd used the chaos to seize control of the *Caretaker*. He had everything he needed.

He also supposed that made the hundreds—almost a thousand, in total—Offspring down on Enther's surface somewhat superfluous. Countless hours spent recruiting them, bringing them to Enther, and training them had become meaningless.

Or maybe not. In chess, sometimes it only took a single piece to checkmate the enemy king. So would it be with the Offspring. The *Caretaker* was now the most vital piece on the board. But that didn't mean all the other pieces were worthless.

Expendable, maybe. Just like everyone in the Offspring, including Tanner. But he'd never seen any reason to treat the rest of his followers cruelly, superfluity or not. The Offspring had set up the entire board to be just the way it needed to be.

If only the winning move weren't so elusive.

The blip representing the *Preserver* seemed to taunt him. If only he'd seized the *Caretaker* a month ago, before the newars had finished setting up their defense matrix...

Tanner rubbed his temples with his fingers. This routine couldn't be healthy for his sanity. Not that it mattered. Seeing the cause through to the end was everything.

He leaned back in his chair and let his thoughts drift to Rebecca. It'd been a while since he'd allowed himself to think about his little sister. Even longer since he'd seen her. Had it really been almost two years? She'd be seventeen soon.

He could send her a birthday message. But by now, he figured she knew what he was up to, and the Union's security services would intercept any message he dispatched to the core worlds. Ever since the encounter with Nadia Jibor back on Enther, Tanner had seen his name and face rise to the top of the Union's most wanted lists.

Rebecca would surely have seen the news.

Tanner liked imagining that she was proud of him. That she'd forgiven him for striking her all those years ago. That she understood the Offspring existed to protect her, to keep her safe from the newars. He liked knowing that no newar would ever bother her after he'd finished his work.

His work. He took a deep breath, refilled his coffee tumbler with a canister he kept at the back of his desk, and departed the cabin.

The ship was empty now, far quieter. Even though most of the *Caretaker's* bulk came from its missile silos at the rear, the crew decks were still big enough that he spent his entire waking hours alone some days. He'd taken to talking to himself just to fight the silence.

Tanner arrived at the meeting room. It was the first time he'd seen the other eight Offspring aboard at the same time. They all sat straighter as he walked in. His mind returned to his old job at Veltech Colonial Supply. It was almost like a return to his past, to stupid, inane meetings where everyone feigned respect for Tanner's dipshit of a boss.

But looking around at the eight Offspring, there was nothing feigned about the respect they showed him. Just genuine loyalty. Devotion.

"I'm glad we could all be in the same room for once, brothers. Thank you for taking the time out of your days to come here," Tanner said. He sat down and took a long drink of coffee.

"We're here to discuss the problem of getting around the invaders' defense matrix on Bitanu. Right now, we cannot launch a missile strike on the *Preserver* until the matrix is down, but we suspect that the facility will be well-guarded by newar security forces. Since I've been tied up with managing the counterinsurgency down planetside, I've asked you all to come up with ideas. What do you have for me?"

"We could redeploy enough of our brothers on the planet's surface to Bitanu to storm the matrix," Claude said. "We have the numbers to overwhelm their security."

His suggestion would draw the Junta's attention for sure, if they took Offspring away from the counterinsurgency campaign. From there, it'd be all too easy for the Junta to figure out what they were up to, which would lead them to the *Caretaker*.

The objections were immediately obvious, but Tanner kept them to himself. These men were all loyal Offspring. He saw little benefit to berating them publicly.

"I'll consider it," Tanner said. "Anyone else?"

"Mercenaries," another Offspring said. Tom—a former drug addict Tanner had recruited from a rehab clinic on Sarsi. "We have the funds to pay a private security firm to attack the matrix for us."

Which sounded nice, of course, except for the fact that most mercenary troops were located on the sunward side of the belt, and the Junta blockade would stop them from reaching Bitanu. And Tanner had a feeling that the Union could trace any communications between their ship and a core world private security firm, which would— again—lead back to the *Caretaker*.

"We could bait the *Preserver* out," a third member of the crew suggested. This was Cole, who'd been in and out of jail his whole life. He'd been searching for a purpose, until the Offspring had finally given him one. "If we attack one of their settlements and send out a distress beacon, the newars might dispatch the vessel to check it out."

Relies on the newars being incompetent morons, Tanner thought. Unfortunately for them, the invaders were evil, not stupid.

The others went through their suggestions, none of them workable. Tanner felt a sinking feeling in his gut. He'd chosen the Offspring for the *Caretaker* mission based on their unquestionable loyalty and resolve. He'd never imagined that he'd need a brilliant problem-solver.

"What about an underwater raid?" the last of the eight suggested. Austin, a man with relentless energy, who'd been desperately trying to get off the Union's basic income program with a series of failed start-up companies.

The fact that none of them had worked out was more of a testament to economic stagnation under Prime Minister Favan than anything about him. Maybe that creativity and vision were just what the Offspring needed right now.

"Sorry?" Tanner asked.

Austin cleared his throat. "There are oceans underneath the surface glaciers on Bitanu, and the *Caretaker* is equipped with submersible craft. We could outfit the submarine with ice-breaking technology and launch it at Bitanu with a small strike force inside. Then, it could tunnel up through the ice and lodge against the underside of the newars' defense matrix. We could cut through the floor panels, bypass security, and sneak inside before they even knew they were under attack."

Tanner blinked rapidly, his heartbeat quickening. Austin was right: they had a craft on board they could use to traverse Bitanu's subsurface oceans. In all the chaos of the war, no one would notice a tiny blip as it traversed the empty space between Enther's orbit and Bitanu. It wouldn't even register on the Junta blockade's scanners.

And it'd let them sneak past whatever security the newars had set up around the defense matrix. It'd still be a tough fight once they got inside, but they had a chance with the element of surprise. Hell, more than a chance.

"That's it," Tanner said, the raw conviction in his voice silencing all further discussion. "I want this to be our new priority. Any free time will be spent working on getting a submersible craft ready for launch. Let's get to it."

The meeting concluded abruptly, with his eight followers standing up in unison and departing the room. Tanner looked at the empty meeting table and grinned.

The *Preserver*'s blip on his holo-projector might just start taunting him a little bit less now.

·   ·   ·

It took almost three weeks, but the submersible was finally ready for launch. They'd upgraded the entire bow end of the vessel with ice-breaking technology. Additionally, they'd outfitted a small spacefaring capsule so that it would break apart upon impact with Bitanu's oceans.

The capsule had an automated piloting system that would take them from the *Caretaker* and safely through Bitanu's atmosphere, and it could reposition for a braking burn as they reached their destination. They'd also dispatched drones to survey the newars' defense matrix, which would automatically forward all data collected to the submersible.

Tanner stood on a catwalk at the top of the hangar bay, his arms crossed over his chest as he overlooked his eight followers while they completed final checks of both the submarine and the capsule.

It was going to be a rough few weeks. The craft was far from a standard military submarine, and he could only take along two additional crew members. Even then, it'd be cramped. They'd had plenty of nutra or non-perishable foodstuffs aboard the *Caretaker* to stock the submarine, but it wasn't going to be a comfortable trip.

Tanner paced along the catwalk. He'd picked Claude and Austin to join him for the operation. Even with the submersible allowing them to sneak past the matrix defenses, he knew there would be security forces inside the complex itself.

A thin smile spread across his face. He'd personally killed Russ Kama, who used to be the security chief for the entire newar operations. It stood to reason he could handle Russ' subordinates.

He took a lift down to the hangar bay floor. "Everything is ready for departure," Tom said. "We have linked the capsule's controls with the *Caretaker*'s systems, so we can manually plot a trajectory for you. And Brothers Claude and Austin are already inside, waiting for you."

"Excellent," Tanner said, resting a hand on the other man's shoulder. "You've done well. You've *all* done well," he added, turning his attention to the other five who would stay aboard the warship.

"Keep this ship operational," he said. "And keep our ruse up with the Junta. We'll still need this vessel's weapons capabilities once we bring the newars' matrix offline."

"We will," Cole said. "Be careful out there. And give these invaders the wrath they deserve."

Tanner said his goodbyes and entered the submersible. He latched the outer airlock door closed behind him, and heard the six Offspring back in the hangar seal the space capsule.

Behind the insulation of two thick vehicle walls, everything seemed to go silent. Tanner had never imagined himself to be claustrophobic, but the sudden silence and the way the tight corridors of the submersible felt like they were clamping down on him were uncomfortable.

They'd have to preserve the submersible's power for when they breached Bitanu's atmosphere. The only thing they'd powered on were red emergency lights. Tanner worked his way through a maze of tight rooms—a single bathroom the size of a closet, a canteen the size of most *normal* bathrooms, and a dorm room that could barely fit a three-tiered bed unit—until he reached the cockpit. The glass jutted out like a bubble over the pilot station.

Claude and Austin were already strapped in. "Ready to bring our righteous struggle to a close?" Tanner asked. He strapped himself in over their conveyances of enthusiasm.

One of the six Offspring still aboard the *Caretaker* messaged Tanner on his wrist terminal, letting him know they were about to fire the capsule's engines. Tanner gave them the go-ahead. A minute later, he felt his back sink into his chair as they blasted off from the hangar.

In another half-hour, they'd reached optimal burn speed, and the engines cut out. Now, it would be a slow drift across the vacuum of space. Followed by a violent descent through Bitanu's atmosphere and an icy plunge into Bitanu's depths.

And after that, victory.

CHAPTER 12

*T*he *Chamber of Parliament.* Isadora had seen the chambers at least a dozen times in her tenure, but only as an observer. Never as a speaker.

It was less grand down below. Speakers came up via a circular platform lift that would take them to a central hub, while rows of elevated parliament members would all be facing them. That meant Isadora was effectively pacing around in a glorified basement cellar, waiting for her turn to address some of the most powerful people in the system.

"Nervous?" Valencia Peizan asked.

She'd been rehearsing her talking points with her chief of staff for the past half-hour, while Tricia Favan was addressing Parliament and taking questions from the opposition. Once she was done, she'd invite

Isadora up to give her speech.

"Naturally," Isadora said.

It didn't matter how comfortable she'd become in her position, the set-up made her feel like a zoo animal in a cage. She guessed that was the point. The MPs represented the Natonese people, so having them tower over whoever was speaking at the central hub—usually the prime minister—was a reminder that the people were, ultimately, in charge.

Valencia shrugged. "Just picture them all naked."

"Why is *that* the universal advice for public speaking nerves?" Isadora asked. "I'm not sure I like the idea of picturing a bunch of aged career politicians' naked bodies."

Valencia flashed her a toothy smile. "Of course not, but if you're revolted, how can you be nervous?"

Isadora gave her a glare and returned her attention to her wrister, reviewing her speech notes. A pop-up at the top of the screen reminded her of her most recent message: another entreaty from Vincent, asking her to find some way to visit him on Bitanu.

She still couldn't fathom what he needed to talk to her about so badly. Especially if it was something he didn't feel comfortable sending over the system's net. Was he just being paranoid about the Union net's security infrastructure? That didn't seem like Vincent.

Still, she had a couple of ideas for how to arrange safe transport to Bitanu. If the speech went well, she might even—

"I'm getting a notification," Valencia said, urgency in her voice. "Looks like they're ready for you."

"I thought Tricia still had fifteen minutes left," Isadora said.

Valencia just shrugged. "Guess she talked fast. I dunno."

Either way, it was time for Isadora to go address Parliament.

Maybe it'd be better to just get up there and start talking. The anticipation was always worse than the actual experience.

"Okay. Wish me luck," she said. She straightened her blouse and stepped onto the circular lift. Valencia waved at her as the lift hummed and hovered off the ground. Slowly, she rose into the air.

The lift came to a halt at the chamber's central hub. The first row of Parliament members' desks was a couple dozen feet away from her, at about the same elevation. From there, the seats went up for dozens of rows.

The full count for Parliament was 1,882 MPs. Collectively, they represented every populated district across Union space. There were individuals from northern Zoledo, Haphis, all of Obrigan and Sarsi, Rhavego, and even a handful of MPs representing a Union research base all the way out on Bitanu.

But from Isadora's perspective, they looked like a single, amorphous tapestry of faces. Each one sat at a desk with a built-in holo-projection terminal. The vast majority had their screens activated, although she couldn't see what was on them.

It looked like many of them were taking advantage of the brief break between Tricia and Isadora's speeches. Isadora wondered if the majority of the MPs were going to spend their time during her speech perusing the net. Then wondered if that'd make her more or less nervous.

"Are you just gonna stand there, gaping?" the hoarse voice of Tricia Favan whispered from her left. "Usually, we expect guest speakers to, y'know, *actually speak* at some point."

Isadora looked over to the creased face of her friend. It always surprised her that someone who'd once been on the other side of a battlefield from her was now one of her closest confidants in the whole system. Then again, her position had thrown all kinds of surprises at her. Becoming close with Tricia might've been one of the more normal ones, even.

"Sorry. Just threw me off a bit when you finished your own speech so early."

"Yeah, well, I accidentally deleted some of the notes on my wrister beforehand," Tricia said gruffly. "I figured they'd be more enthusiastic to hear from you than listen to me prattle on, anyway."

It always secretly delighted her that Tricia called wrist terminals *wristers* now—the Earthborn term for it. Although Isadora had never been able to understand how something as clunky as *wrist terminal* had become standard usage among the Natonese.

On the other hand, Meredith was picking up enough Natonese slang from her classmates that Isadora was glad something from their culture had imprinted on their hosts in return.

And although Isadora was pretty sure Tricia was just being self-deprecating in order to make her feel more comfortable, she appreciated the gesture nonetheless. She walked up to the podium at the center of the hub and cleared her throat.

"Esteemed members of the Union Parliament," she began, keeping her voice low and grave. "I come before you to discuss the threat my people face. As long as the outer rim is at war, as long as the Junta navy has a blockade around the asteroid belt, and as long as the Offspring are still active behind the smokescreen of war, my people trapped in cryo aboard the *Preserver* will never be safe. I am here to ask that our people work together to end this destructive war—one that the people of this system do not want."

Valencia had been conducting opinion polls ever since Isadora's speech back on Sarsi. She'd won major accolades from all major media outlets for her decision to open her own people's settlements to Natonese war refugees, spiking her already-high approval ratings from the public.

And as she'd continued using her platform to speak out against the war, the Natonese public had started responding in kind. Major cities across Union space and each ward of Obrigan City had seen growing anti-war protest movements. Now, it was her job to harness that grassroots energy into actual policy goals.

"I realize the Union is not a participant in this war," she continued. "And I believe I speak for all of us when I say no one wants a destructive military intervention. Sending the fleets in would only make an already-volatile situation worse. But there are still things we can do."

Isadora looked to her left for a second and received a supportive nod from Tricia. She appreciated the gesture, but she hadn't felt as nervous as she thought she would. Assuming and deploying the trappings of political power had stopped feeling so unnatural to her. Her political persona was more an extension of herself, than a guise.

"I am here to ask that you impose sanctions on the Junta until they agree to lift the blockade and allow a limited number of medical and trade vessels through, focus your diplomatic corps' attention on getting the Horde and the Junta to negotiate, and freeze the Junta's bank assets in Union space until they agrees to these terms."

It was a measured list of objectives—she'd dropped any reference to the settlement charter ban when Tricia had insisted revisiting that topic simply wasn't in the cards—but it seemed effective. It at least got her a decent amount of polite clapping. Isadora was fairly sure that implied a similar level of enthusiasm as the shouts and cheers of the Sarsi crowds.

Or, if not enthusiasm, political necessity. One way she'd deployed her newfound favorability with the Union citizenry was encouraging them to begin a massive letter-writing campaign to their individual MPs, asking them to take anti-war stances and support the same legislation that Isadora was now formally calling for. Thereby pressuring Parliament from all sides.

Isadora cleared her throat and continued with her speech.

.   .   .

"That really was something," Tricia said after Isadora had finished. The two women were in a bathroom just outside the Chamber of Parliament, which Tricia knew the codes to lock. "Otherwise," she'd told Isadora, "we'll never be able to have a conversation without a dozen ambitious fucks looking to get a photo op with you."

"I felt pretty good about that," Isadora said, resting her hand on the counter. "You think any of those reforms will pass?"

Tricia paused. "I wish I could say there was a good chance." She frowned. "Everyone in my caucus is running scared with the election coming up. With Justin Hacelo running Reform, who fucking knows what they're up to."

Tricia's governing Workers' Party was opposed by a large, minority coalition of parties both big and small. The largest among them was the Reform Party, running on a platform of social liberalism and fiscal moderation. "Boring, in other words" was how Tricia had described them once.

Now that it was mid-2406, a Parliamentary election would be coming up in about five months. The Reform Party had put up a young, dynamic ex-banker named Justin Hacelo as their leader.

"Are you still sure you're comfortable with me meeting with him?" Isadora asked.

Tricia's party had won comfortably back in 2396 and 2401, so there was little reason to think she'd lose. But it was common knowledge that the two women had become incredibly close, and Isadora didn't want that to harm her people's political prospects should she actually go down in defeat. It made sense to establish a relationship with the leader of the largest opposition party.

Tricia shrugged. "Of course. It makes sense. If you want to go hang out with some slimeball, be my guest."

"You know I'd never side with anyone else over you, right? I'm not really in the political backstabbing game."

"You should try it sometime. Just, preferably not with me," Tricia said.

"Okay," Isadora said. "Well, I guess I should head out to my meeting with him."

"Thank goodness. I actually really have to pee. Was holding it in the whole time during your speech."

Tricia promptly rushed over to one of the stalls and closed the door. On the way, she pressed a button on her wrister and the door to the bathroom unlocked.

Isadora departed, where a crowd of MPs were waiting for her. Each was clamoring to tell her how much they sympathized with her people's plight. Or how they were all intending to vote in favor of the policies she'd proposed. Sure enough, most of them were hailing down the nearby media drones for a photo op.

Isadora adopted a serene, congenial expression and expressed gratitude that they were planning to vote her way, trying to forget Tricia's doubts. *They just want the fame of being associated with me, but they don't want to stick their necks out.*

Sho apologized, noting that she was running late for another meeting, and gracefully excused herself. She gently worked her way through the throng of MPs.

Getting to Justin Hacelo's office was a relief. She pressed open a mahogany door with an ornately carved door knob and walked inside. The office was smaller than Tricia's, naturally, but still had beautiful reddish-brown wood furniture and a ceiling-high bookshelf, stacked with financial management texts that'd probably put her to sleep within a page or two.

"Welcome!" a bright, eager voice came from the office's occupant.

Justin Hacelo looked young, especially for someone aiming to become the most powerful politician in the Natonus System. Isadora had read his file and discovered that he was a few years older than she was, but he'd seemed to age more gracefully. Or maybe he just dyed his hair to keep all the grey out.

His hair was jet black, visibly gelled and slicked back in a way that made his forehead look a little bit too large. His skin was a balanced shade of warm brown, not particularly pale nor dark. He stood up, gave her a wide grin, and shook her hand. "Thanks for taking the time to meet with me," he said, gesturing toward a pair of recliners facing his bookshelf.

Justin crossed his legs. "Coffee?" he asked, pouring himself a cup from a cylinder press sitting on a nearby table.

"Always." Isadora gratefully accepted a mug.

"So," Justin began, "if you don't mind, I'd like to get straight down to business."

Isadora found that refreshing, since she'd become accustomed to the usual politician thing of spending ten minutes on idle chitchat before getting to the meat of whatever issue they wanted to discuss.

"First off, I wanted to say that the Reform Party is fully in line with your proposals," he said. "I have no qualms with letting a bill like that pass, even if it comes from the prime minister. But I believe that we can—and should—push further. Specifically, I see no reason to uphold the settlement charter ban on your people."

It was so unexpected Isadora hardly knew how to react.

Within months of her people's arrival in the Natonus System, a series of referenda had denied her people settlement rights on any Union-controlled world. They'd skirted the ban on Bitanu with a legal technicality, and the Sarsi planetary government had later overruled the charter ban. But that still meant there were a lot of planets where the refugees had no right to settle, including the all-important Obrigan.

"In her thirteen-year tenure, Tricia Favan has frequently ignored previous legal rulings on financial law," Justin said. "The courts have struck some of her most egregious bills down, but the precedent still stands. Executive power gives you the power to pick which laws you want to enforce, and which ones you want to ignore. And besides, most polls show that if the referenda were held again, the bans would be overturned. If I become prime minister, I would ignore the charter ban."

"I—sorry, I'm finding myself at a loss for words," Isadora said. "That would allow my people to empty the *Preserver*'s cryo bays in short order."

It'd mean the end of the resettlement project: something she'd imagined would still take years, even if it hadn't been indefinitely put on hold by the war in the outer rim and the Junta blockade.

"The way I see it, gravity wells are artificial boundaries. Which planet you come from shouldn't determine where you get to live. My party's platform has therefore called for the uninterrupted flow of capital and people across space."

Isadora studied him. Justin seemed eager, excited even, as he talked about the prospect. Given his financial background, she wondered if he just saw her people as a possible labor force. She returned her attention to the bookshelf, full of economics texts where real people got portrayed as little more than productivity automata. Did he really want to help her people, or did he just want anything to spike gross solar product?

Capital and people, he'd said. *Interesting which one came first.*

"That's an incredibly generous offer," she said, taking a sip of the coffee he'd given her. "I assume there's something you want in return."

Justin smirked. "That *is* the normal politician way, isn't it? Maybe I simply think getting the rest of your people out of cryo would be best for everyone. Maybe I genuinely feel it's a win-win."

Isadora nodded, waiting for the inevitable *but*.

"But," he said—*so predictable*—"I could only enact this agenda if my party manages to capture the most seats in the election. And given current opinion polling, an endorsement from yourself would be a major asset in the campaign."

Isadora coughed on her coffee. "You want me to publicly endorse you instead of Tricia?"

Justin spread his hands. "Why not? Look—I know you and the prime minister are close. But we both know she won't go further than piecemeal reforms. She's used up so much capital on her economic reforms that she's lost the political will for a real fight."

"One might say that Tricia's economic agenda has improved a lot of Natonese lives," Isadora said carefully. In politics, *one might say* was always a good way of weaseling out of giving your real opinion.

"Sure, she's kept the bottom from falling out for some people. But at the cost of a stagnant, undynamic economy that hasn't experienced any real growth in a decade. The thing is, the Union was never supposed to operate like a system-wide government. We were supposed to be a *trading bloc*, giving individual member planets autonomy wherever possible. But under Tricia Favan's watch, the Union has grown into an overbearing monstrosity that strangles the solar market.

"The crux of the matter is this: I want to unleash our system's economy in a way that hasn't been done in decades. And I think having all hands on deck—and by that, I mean every single one of your people still on the *Preserver*—is necessary. But none of that will happen if Prime Minister Favan wins again. And I think your endorsement, given your popularity, would upend this election.

"So tell me: are you comfortable with the status quo?"

No, Isadora wanted to say. Ideological disagreements with Justin's financial agenda aside, a world where the *Preserver* was empty would always be preferable to one where it wasn't.

And it made sense that he was hungry for her endorsement. The media consensus was that Tricia would win again easily, that *of course* Isadora would support her, given their friendship.

She'd promised Tricia only minutes earlier that she'd never side with anyone over her. But from a selfish perspective, Justin was inarguably offering the better deal.

"You've given me a lot to think about," she said finally, setting her empty mug back down on the adjacent table. "But I would need to consider your offer at greater length, and consult with my staff."

"Of course," Justin said. The two stood up in unison as Isadora prepared to leave. "Just don't take too long. If you want to go ahead with endorsing me, it would make sense to do so before the election really heats up. So that we can maximize impact, naturally."

"I understand. But as I said, this isn't a decision I'd like to make lightly. I'll get back in touch once I've made up my mind."

Justin waved politely at her as she departed the office. Isadora let out a sigh and headed out to the helipads outside the Government-General. All she wanted right now was to get back to her people's embassy and get input from the rest of her staff. Hopefully, they'd be more clear-headed than her.

CHAPTER 13

Nadia had never imagined that her first time visiting Heykan, the biggest settlement on Ikkren, she'd be arriving in a grain sack. But Gus Pallek had told her the colony was Tori Hyrak's last known location, and landing the *Exemplar* just outside would have been a dead giveaway to the Junta occupation, even with its new stealth tech.

They could've landed the ship well away from the settlement and walked, but a few miles' worth of hiking through the Ikkren tundra might've been even less preferable than a bumpy ride in a transport rover.

Gus had put Nadia in touch with a grain farmer sympathetic to the resistance, who lived in one of the agricultural co-ops outside Heykan. Someone who made semi-regular trade shipments into the settlement. He'd agreed to smuggle Nadia and her crew in with little hesitation.

Meanwhile, thanks to her and her crew's intervention in Lethock, Gus Pallek's renegade faction had rejoined another Horde resistance cell. Together, they'd opened up new fronts against the Junta. Pulled off a couple of operations inside occupied zones, even.

They'd slowed the rate of the Junta advance, although the occupation had not yet been fully stalled out. They'd need Tori's unifying leadership to really start turning things around.

For most of the journey to Heykan, Nadia hadn't hidden inside the grain sack. She looked out of the rover's windows at the Ikkren landscape, as ice and mud gradually gave way to the outskirts of civilization.

First came the massive growing fields and granaries, then came the water tanks and the insulated irrigation units, then came outlying dwellings. As soon as they arrived at the first Junta checkpoint, Nadia figured it was time to get in her sack.

She, Boyd, and Derek each hopped into their respective grain sacks at the back of the rover's rear hold. "This shit is way too itchy," Boyd said, followed by an exasperated grunt.

"If you concentrate on other physical sensations, you won't notice the itchiness," Derek said.

"Great. I'll just think about how damn close I am to frostbite. I'm sure that'll help."

Nadia shook her head and grinned just as the compartment hold opened. It was hard to hear with the grain sack and the fierce howl of Ikkren's wind, but she could make out the voice of the farmer who owned the rover, plus a couple of deep voices. Junta soldiers.

The closer she listened, the better she could make out phrases like "just my usual shipment, sir" and "routine inspection" and "thank you for your cooperation."

Nadia gulped. Their sacks were at the back, so the only way the soldiers would find them was if they searched the entire hold. And with almost three dozen sacks inside, she'd assumed they'd be safe. But assumptions had gotten her in trouble before.

Each time she heard the rustling of a bag in front of her, her heart moved another few inches up her throat. She was pretty sure she could hear the sounds of the soldiers' breathing. Slowly, she inched her hand over till it was resting on the grip of her handgun.

And then, she heard one of the soldiers say, "Looks good. You're cleared to proceed."

Nadia let out a long exhale as the soldiers left the vehicle and the engines roared back to life. After another few minutes, they came to another halt. The rear hold door swung open once again, and the driver gave them the all-clear. She loosened the internal drawstring and emerged from the empty sack. Boyd and Derek followed suit.

"We're in an unloading depot on the southwestern side of the settlement," the farmer told them. "But you should hurry. More occupiers will be here soon to process my shipment."

Nadia ducked under a low-hanging roof and used a ramp to cross onto the dock. "Won't they compare your hold to your official manifest?" she asked, furrowing her brow. "You'll be three sacks short."

The farmer grinned, pulled up the mat on the floor, and twisted open a handle. Which revealed a secret compartment, too small for even a single person to fit, but with three extra sacks of wheat inside.

"This isn't my first rodeo," he said. Nadia was pretty sure the first Natonese colonists hadn't brought horses or cattle with them, so it amused her they still used the word *rodeo*.

She looked around the depot. The dock was made up of three connected platforms, forming a makeshift vehicle berth perfectly sized for the transport rovers they used on Ikkren. There were a couple of carts and hand trucks scattered over in the far corner.

She scanned the area, looking for an exit, but only found a single set of turbolifts on the far side of the depot. "I figure that way's a no-go," she said.

"There's a grate down there we can use to get inside the settlement," Derek said. He jumped down to the ground. When Nadia followed him, she spotted an exhaust grating along the inside edge of one of the platforms.

"Lemme guess: some kind of sewer system?" Boyd asked. He walked forward and took a long whiff. Nadia wasn't sure how effective that was. Ikkren's cold had always numbed her nose, rendered her sense of smell almost null.

"Good guess, but no," Derek said. "They're raiding tunnels from the pre-Horde era." He walked forward. His hands found a latch hidden behind a loose metal flap on the edge of the grating, opening up the pathway. Nadia flipped on her wrister's light beam function and followed Boyd in.

"How'd you know about that?" Boyd asked once they were all inside.

"I spent a summer here back when I was a teenager. It was a good place to drink grain liquor after hours."

Boyd and Nadia exchanged incredulous glances. "Okay, there's *no* way young Derek was sneaking off to get drunk. Come on, man. We know you."

Derek shrugged. "It sounded better than saying I wanted a nice quiet place to read."

"You said the tunnels were used for raiding?" Nadia asked.

"Back in the early days of Ikkren colonization, the settlements used to fight each other for resources," he explained. "Heykan was always the most productive settlement, making it an easy target for raiders. But soon into colonization, the Heykan colonists set up watchtowers and patrol teams. Hence the need to tunnel underneath the settlement."

In normal times, Nadia might've liked to hear more about Ikkren's history. But while the war was on, and while her people were in constant danger, her curiosity always took a backseat to her work ethic. "So," she said, turning to face Derek, "now that we're here, do you have any idea where Tori might be hiding out, if she's here like Gus said?"

Derek looked thoughtful. "Not for sure, but I *do* have a hunch. Again, back during the early settlement years, raiders would some-times sneak inside the settlement, disguised as traders. They'd hole up in one of the settlement's bookstores, wait for cover of nightfall, and then head out to steal from the local inhabitants. So I wonder if she might've returned to that same bookstore."

"That's...not the first place I would've imagined as a meeting site with the Horde allchief," Nadia said dryly.

"I'm more interested in the fact that they still have *bookstores*," Boyd said. "Back on Calimor, we never had anything like that. Not that we ever did much reading back then. Mostly just e-manuals you could download from a communal data pool. But even on Obrigan, hell, I dunno if I've ever seen a physical bookstore."

Nadia continued down the ice tunnel. The walls felt like they were tightening: a sign, she hoped, that they were getting closer.

"Physical books were one of the few sources of entertainment we had back in the early days," Derek continued. "We didn't have satellites back then, so we couldn't access the Union net to download e-files. Things have changed nowadays, but there's still a strong culture of reading physical books here."

Nadia finally saw a ray of natural light cast down on the tunnel floor. Small, jagged shadows formed in the thin grooves carved in the ice walls.

"I think we're in," she said. She walked up to a grating leading into the settlement and pressed a button on the underside. She peered as far out into the alleyway as she could. Once she couldn't see any boots going by, she pressed the grating open and stepped out.

Sure enough, the alleyway was empty. She extended a hand and pulled Boyd, then Derek out of the tunnel.

"I'm surprised the Junta didn't notice the tunnel network. There's no way this is the only one leading into the colony, right?" Boyd asked.

Derek shook his head. "No one really uses them anymore. They're just a relic, commemorating our past. The Junta probably didn't even think about the importance of securing the tunnels."

Nadia shrugged. "Let's just focus on getting to the bookstore."

Her teeth chattered violently as they walked. She'd been outside for only fifteen minutes, and the warming features of her enviro-suit were barely adequate in the severe cold of Ikkren.

They stepped across snow-covered cobblestone, moving cautiously. No one was in sight, but Nadia half-expected a patrol to round the corner. From what she knew, Heykan was the most heavily occupied settlement on the planet.

No one appeared, but Nadia still kept her hand on her handgun. When they reached an intersection, they emerged into a much busier street. There were hundreds of pedestrians walking around, strolling between shops and restaurants.

And there were Junta patrol teams. She spotted at least three: one on the far end of the street, two on either side of the middle. Nadia figured the Junta would be on the lookout for her, Boyd, and Derek, but they had no reason to suspect they'd arrived in Heykan.

The closest patrol was also a good fifty feet away, and with plenty of other pedestrians wandering by—and without Nadia or her crew wearing anything distinctive—she hoped they could blend into the crowds without attracting too much attention.

The trio moved over to a larger group of colonists, gathered outside a hot cocoa shop. Most of the businesses looked like small snack or drink venues, not full restaurants. One was selling wheat protein skewers, another was advertising stir-fried noodles with carrots, turnips, and potatoes. A few of the shoppers sneered at the Junta patrols, although most just ignored them.

At least it was warmer here, and not just because of the crowds. There were heat lamps strategically placed along the street, each one casting a faint orange halo on the ground.

Nadia thought it warmed up the area in more ways than one. The Ikkren settlements had always looked colorless to her: white plastic prefab shelters, light grey cobblestone, and a dark, overcast sky the Natonus sun barely penetrated. Even a few spots of orange glow breathed life into the district.

Nadia snuck a glance at one of the patrol teams. Anger lodged in her gut. Some of it was misplaced, she knew, since what she *really* wanted was to search for the Offspring. To bring the fight to Tanner Keltin directly.

But with the Offspring going dark, the only way to get to them was through the Junta. Still, there'd been times when she'd been frustrated that all she'd been doing was chasing the elusive Tori Hyrak—when the stakes of the conflict were so much higher.

All she could do was hope that finally finding Tori was going to be worth it. "Derek," she said, "mind telling us how to get to this bookstore?"

"Unfortunately, it's down that alley right there," Derek said. He pointed toward the mouth of a street where one of the patrols was stationed.

Of course it is, Nadia thought, rolling her eyes. She was fairly confident that walking around was low-risk, but passing right by one of the patrols was almost asking to get spotted.

"All right. Ideas?" she asked.

Derek frowned. "As far as I know, that's the only entrance to the bookstore's street. It's something of a back alley."

"Seriously? That's some horrible urban planning right there," Boyd said.

Derek shrugged. "We weren't really thinking about that back when we were setting everything up."

"We need a distraction," Nadia said. Fighting wouldn't be a smart choice, and sneaking by didn't sound like a reasonable option either.

"All right," Boyd said, and then drew in a deep breath. "BOMB!" he shouted at the top of his lungs. Nadia clutched her ear, sure that Boyd's shouting had nearly ruptured her eardrum. "There's a bomb over here! Everyone get out!"

Everyone on the block went silent. Turned to stare at the three of them for a half-second. Then, screaming. Running. Silence and stillness devolved into abject chaos. Half-eaten snacks and skewers flew through the air, the contents of half-finished drinks suddenly coated the street.

At first, Nadia had thought it was an absurd diversion tactic, but the more she thought about it, the more she could see the logic. The Junta had presumably been suppressing news about the Horde resistance, but even then, the populace would know there was a war going on.

It wouldn't have been out of the question for a resistance agent to plant explosives on a busy street of the planet's most heavily occupied settlement.

Those closest to them split up, each running in a different direction. Nadia looked up to see two of the Junta squads making their way toward her crew, but a stampede of people separated them. She grabbed both Boyd and Derek's forearms, then muscled her way through the rampaging crowds.

By the time they'd reached the other side of the street, the Junta soldiers had already lost sight of them. They'd set up a perimeter around the cocoa shop, keeping their distance and trying—failing, really—to direct the flow of foot traffic. Nadia gritted her teeth and tried to hold her ground as more people surged by them.

Finally, they reached the back alley leading to the bookstore. The crowds thinned out, and Nadia looked over her shoulder to make sure the Junta hadn't followed them. It seemed like they'd lost their pursuers in the chaos.

From the outside, the bookstore looked like it could've been any other kind of shelter, although Nadia noticed a staircase along the side that led down to a subterranean cellar. It was warm inside, with a gentle, dim yellow light welcoming them. It looked like a cavern of dusty books, each one with a title she didn't recognize. She coughed almost immediately after walking in.

The bookshelf closest to the entrance was advertising various histories of the Junta or the planet Enther more broadly. She guessed from the titles—*The Rise of Michael Azkon and the Stabilization of the Enther Crisis* or *Counterterrorism on Enther: A Concise History of the Junta* or *The Theocracy's Successors: The Triumph of the Junta State, 2394-2403*—that they were more like propaganda than accurate accounts.

There was something pernicious about walking into an Ikkren bookstore only to be greeted with information on the Enther occupiers. *Imperialism...imperialism never changes.* She doubted the bookstore stocked—much less advertised so prominently—any of those texts willingly.

As far as Nadia could tell, the bookstore was eerily empty. That was probably a sign they were on the right track. She couldn't hear the Junta patrols outside, so they'd at least bought some amount of time to search the place before their enemies returned.

Boyd began strolling up and down various aisles. Derek, on the other hand, was pacing around the far end of the bookstore, tentatively testing the wooden floor with his foot.

"Derek?" Nadia asked.

He ignored her, suddenly pivoting around and returning to where he'd just been standing. He tested a floor panel once more, then bent down and pulled up a wooden slat. "Trapdoor," he explained. "This might be nothing, but if Tori or another ranking Horde member is here, I'd bet they're holed up down there."

Nadia exchanged glances with Boyd, waved him over, and headed to Derek's position. She cast her eyes down a dilapidated stairwell, musty concrete and peeled plaster everywhere. She drew her handgun in case the Junta occupiers had somehow figured out about this particular hiding spot, then started descending slowly.

When she got to the bottom, she saw almost a dozen gun barrels pointed at her.

Nadia lowered her weapon and raised her arms. No use fighting back against those kinds of numbers.

It was only after the others lowered their weapons that she realized they weren't Junta. She'd spent enough time negotiating settlement rights or hashing out trade policies with the Horde leadership team that she recognized a handful of them.

And, emerging from the back of the crowd, was the pale face of Tori Hyrak.

"Nadia Jibor," she said, her voice quiet in surprise but no less stern than usual.

She grinned. "We've been looking for you." She gave a hand signal to let Boyd and Derek know everything was okay. Cautiously, the others joined her.

"And," she continued, "we're here to help you win your planet back."

CHAPTER 14

So this is how it feels to be around people who don't want me *dead*, Carson thought. He'd been undercover with the Off-spring for so many months that it was past feeling like the new normal. Even sitting in a room with a handful of Ashkagi rebels felt like a strange return to another life. One where he didn't have to always watch his back.

Technically, they'd taken a few shots at him before they'd been able to identify him. But the sharpshooter who'd shot his patrol mate had already apologized, and Noah Tasano had explained that he'd issued a stand-down order as soon as they'd confirmed Carson's identity.

The rebels all wore jade-colored armbands with some kind of spiral symbol on it. The same kind Carson had seen in all the Ashkagi temples he'd been hiding intelligence in. Come to think of it, he was pretty sure he'd seen the same symbol on Riley Tago's neck trinket over a half-year ago, back when she'd first brought him out of cryo.

Other than the armbands, the rebels looked how Carson had expected a jungle guerrilla group to look. Drawn, ashen faces and scraggly, patchy facial hair abounded. Noah himself was clean-shaven, however, and adopted the posture of someone for whom hardship was no longer an irregularity. He leaned against the room's outward-facing window, his arms crossed.

"Riley Tago got in touch with me several months ago," he explained.

They were in one of the many control stations on the circular hallways of the decrepit Kal Jova spaceport, which the rebels had repurposed as a supply depot. Carson sat on top of a three-box-high stack of weapon crates.

One of the rebels—the sharpshooter who'd shot at him earlier—offered him his canteen. He drank gratefully. Water always tasted better the thirstier you were, somehow.

"Riley filled me in on your situation," Noah continued. "So I had my people surveil various Offspring attack groups, hidden unseen in the jungles, until they finally spotted you. And then they started shadowing your unit's movements. Which in turn led them to find the information you've been hiding."

"I was worried no one was getting those," Carson said.

Considering that was the most significant intel he'd gleaned, he'd be crushed if it was useless. He took another long drink of the sharpshooter's canteen. He drank too much at once and issued a series of violent coughs.

The rebels let him finish coughing before anyone said anything. It was a good time for Carson to work through his feelings about Riley telling Noah everything about him.

It made sense: Juliet Lessitor was supposed to be his handler, and she was dead. The only way for him to be valuable to his people was to have someone who could report back to the refugee leadership, and Noah might've been the most logical choice. It was still dangerous, however—if one of Noah's rebels had been captured and tortured, they might've given away Carson's cover. But from Riley's perspective, it was probably the only option. A calculated risk.

"On the contrary," Noah said once he'd finished coughing. "Your intel was invaluable. It allowed us to evacuate the villages the Offspring were targeting well ahead of the actual attacks. Your actions have saved a lot of lives, Carson."

He let out a relieved sigh.

"Riley's been eager for me to make contact with you, actually," Noah continued. "She wants to hear what intel you've discovered."

Carson didn't have anything particularly spectacular, but even the minutiae—Offspring camp locations, weapons shipments, unit movements, size and organization of various detachments—could be useful. Noah had one of his followers record all the intel Carson spat out.

Noah nodded along while he spoke. "All that will be extremely helpful. But what about Tanner Keltin? What do you know about what he's planning?"

Carson's face fell. "I...I haven't been able to find out anything about Tanner," he mumbled.

Noah blinked rapidly. "What do you mean?"

Carson wanted to protest that he'd only been with the Offspring for about three months. These sorts of things were supposed to take time, he thought. Or figured.

His growing friendship with Emil Gurtrin seemed promising enough. Maybe in another few months, Carson could get some real valuable information out of him. "I need time," he said, gritting his teeth.

"My understanding is that your people don't *have* time. Riley's been urging me to find you for this very reason. They're so bogged down responding to the war that they have little time to figure out what the Offspring are up to. And especially with what happened at Bitanu..."

Carson lifted an eyebrow. "Bitanu?"

Noah shook his head. "Not enough time to explain. Suffice to say, Tanner Keltin, his capabilities, and his plans present a real danger to your people."

Carson didn't know what to say. He wanted to argue that he still wasn't the perfect spy—his trainer had died before he'd been fully prepared, after all—and that pushing Emil further could expose him.

But if Juliet were here, she'd call that a lame excuse. She'd died to protect him, and then Russ Kama had died to get him behind enemy lines. Along with a spec ops team from Calimor. So many people had given their lives, hoping he could deliver.

And right now, he had nothing to offer. "I...I don't know," he finally managed.

Noah lowered his face and rubbed his forehead with his thumb and index finger. "Well, I will let Riley know the next time she gets in touch," he said, deflated.

"We should talk about what happens now," one of the other rebels interjected. "Carson is going to have to report the stockpiles here. Otherwise, the Offspring would suspect him."

"True," Noah said. "Normally, I would say that it would be better for you to lie to your overseers to keep our stockpiles hidden. But I have a feeling that our secret supply depot might not matter for much longer."

Carson looked up at the rebel leader. "You're planning something."

"Yes." Noah hesitated, struggle written across his face. "I'm not sure we can tell you everything. There's still a risk that the Offspring may figure out who you really are. And then extract information from you."

Nice way of saying, "Torture me until I start talking."

"But we believe there may soon be an opportunity for you to help us. You will know when it happens. We think our odds of success would be better with someone helping us from the inside. I wish I could tell you more, but I fear that could come back to bite us."

"Gotta protect op-sec," Carson blurted out, nodding. *Now I'm starting to sound like Russ.*

"Precisely. Anyway, we should get moving. Once we're gone, you should get in contact with your superiors."

The rebels took whatever crates of weapons or food they could carry. Come to think of it, it was surprising just how *much* the rebels had stockpiled. Guerilla movements required a vast quantity of arms and material, but this was beyond what he'd imagined.

He wondered if they'd gotten an influx of arms from somewhere.

After the rebels departed, Carson returned to the upper level of the spaceport, where his dead patrol partner was still lying on the floor in one of the control rooms. He looked out the window at the retreating rebels as they worked their way to the top of the spaceport pit, then out into the surrounding jungles.

Please don't go, a part of his mind said. He wished Noah had told him more. Whether there were any new developments in the war. What Nadia Jibor was up to. How Stacy was doing, and would he mind telling him that his big brother was still out there, trying his best to keep him safe?

Don't be stupid. There was no way Noah knew the answers to all those questions. Hell, he probably had no idea who Stacy Erlinza was. What Carson really wanted was to feel like every single action he took wasn't laced with danger. To feel like a normal person again.

He closed his eyes, swallowed the lump in his throat, and contacted Emil.

He explained the situation, doing his best to sound panicked. He told a story about how he and Bradley had fallen under rebel sniper fire, about how he'd been holed up in the control room ever since. It was the best kind of lie: one that was based in the truth.

Emil sounded worried, promising to dispatch several patrols to investigate and provide support. Carson might've felt touched by his concern if it weren't just another part of the ruse. If he knew who Carson really was, he'd probably leave him to die. Or worse.

Carson rested his head against a wall, trying to ignore the worsening stench of Bradley's corpse. He felt a surge of heat rise in his cheeks. White hot embarrassment. Embarrassment that, after so much blood had been spilled to get him inside the Offspring's ranks, he still hadn't gotten any closer to discovering Tanner's plans.

He'd been playing it too safe. Cultivating a relationship with Emil had only gotten him so far. Maybe if he had more time, his approach would've made sense. But everyone on the *Preserver* was vulnerable as long as the war went on.

Carson needed to take more risks, accept more personal danger. When millions of lives were on the line, it was irresponsible *not* to stick his neck out a little further to figure out Tanner's plans.

He was in the middle of figuring out how to do just that when he heard shouting from above. He stood up, walked out of the control room, and waved his arms at the other Offspring gathered at the spaceport rim. They acknowledged him and worked their way to his position.

Once they were there, Carson went through his story again. A handful of Offspring went to retrieve the body of their fallen comrade. A few others worked to secure the supply crates abandoned by the rebels.

Emil arrived minutes later. The two of them stood along the railing of the uppermost perimeter hallway, looking out over the subterranean pit while other teams combed through the area.

"You had me worried there for a minute, brother," Emil said, clasping Carson's shoulder. "And I'm sorry to hear about Brad. But the best vengeance is accomplishing our agenda. Finding this hidden cache of supplies will be a major step forward for us."

"I'm surprised to hear you say that," Carson said. *Time to make a push.* "It's always seemed like you weren't very happy with our ongoing campaign against the Ashkagi rebels."

Emil opened his mouth to speak, but he didn't say anything.

Carson berated himself inwardly—he wasn't sounding like someone who had supposedly just survived a harrowing experience, nor whose patrol partner had just died in front of him. He still needed to act the part.

Before Emil could respond, one of the scout teams walked up from their left. It was Marcus and a quiet member of their unit named Harry Klim. Carson was pretty sure Harry had been Marcus' patrol partner for a while.

"We've just finished going through the spaceport," Harry reported. "We've recovered a large quantity of rebel supplies. It seems they've been using Kal Jova for a long time."

"Good," Emil said. "I radioed in our findings to the higher-ups. They're sending more transports to help us secure the supplies. Until then, let's set up a perimeter, in case the rebels try to retake this place."

Marcus cast a withering stare toward Carson. "There's something else, brother. I think we should talk about it in private." .

Carson felt his stomach drop. *Did they find something?*

"Anything you want to say to me can be said in front of Carson. He is our brother, too," Emil said.

Marcus' eyes again darted over to him. "We found an unsent message on Brad's wrist terminal. It looks like he started recording about twenty minutes ago."

His stomach twisted. Bradley had been in the middle of dispatching a message right when he'd been shot. And it would've been logged a while before Carson sent his own message, since he'd taken the time to talk with Noah and the rebels.

"I panicked," Carson blurted out. "I'm sorry. I-I wasn't thinking straight. I should've just sent a message when Brad got shot. But this was my first time in combat, and I could barely think straight."

There was a thin line separating the stammer of someone trying to cover his tracks, and the stammer of someone reliving a traumatic experience. He tried to modulate his voice to resemble the latter.

"I don't think anyone can blame you for that, brother," Emil said.

Marcus was still glaring at him. "It just seems funny, don't you think, brother? After all, it's always felt like the rebels have been one step ahead of us the entire time. And that only started after *he* showed up."

He jabbed an accusatory finger in Carson's direction. Harry looked back and forth between the two of them, but he seemed more fascinated by the conversation than eager to partake.

"No one gets to question my loyalty to the cause," Carson hissed, feigning righteous anger. "I didn't get invited by a recruiter. I made my way to Enther on nothing but willpower and determination. And I came with the kinds of skills that the rest of you had to practice."

Harry shrugged. "It's true. He always cleaned up at the shooting range." A furious look from Marcus shut him up.

"You have to admit that it's a pretty convenient set of circumstances," Marcus said.

"That's because the campaign against the rebels only *started* after Carson showed up," Emil said, his voice quickening in frustration. "And if you seriously think our brother's loyalty is in question, then you're a fool. He's been one of our best."

Carson was pretty sure Emil was just biased. But having a well-respected, established Offspring leader like Emil in his corner bolstered his credibility. Far more, probably, than anything he could say.

"I remember talking to Brad before he died," Marcus continued. "He said Carson was always going off on his own during the village raids. And I checked with the requisitions officer back at camp—do you want to hear what's been on his shopping list?"

Carson tensed up. He was surely about to reveal his acquisition of the flameproof chemicals he used for his intel drops. Emil would surely put the pieces together and—

"—it's some kind of strange, luxury food item. He could be hiding someone, giving them food!"

Carson wasn't sure whether to laugh or breathe a sigh of relief. Marcus had discovered the birthday ice cream he'd given Emil a few days ago.

Emil, who'd grown red in the face. Who then shoved Marcus back aggressively. "That was for my *birthday*, you fucking dimwit! You're making wild, unfounded accusations, and *this* is the proof you've brought me? This conversation is over."

Marcus bowed his head. "My apologies then, brother. I do not mean to question your assessment of Carson's character." He cast one more suspicious look at Carson, then turned around and headed toward the far rim of the spaceport.

Carson and Emil walked along the perimeter hallway. "I'm sorry you had to hear that, brother," Emil said after a few minutes had passed. "Tensions are just high. Most of us haven't been in a gunfight before. So now that you experienced contact with our enemy, I think it's become a lot more real for many of our brothers.

"And," he continued, "I imagine they're frustrated that we're still bogged down with these damn rebels. Or maybe I'm just projecting. Anyway, take some time for yourself. It isn't easy to recover from what you just went through. Come find me and we can talk, if that'd help. Until then, I'll make sure the others give you space."

Carson thanked him, and he placed a comforting hand on his shoulder. Then, he headed for a ramp leading back up to the surface, leaving Carson alone. The starship wreckages below seemed to look even more ominous now than when he'd arrived.

It was time for decisive action, for taking risks. He knew that now. But it sounded like some of the others were starting to view him with suspicion, which meant he might already be in danger. Despite the fact that he'd been playing everything safe so far. He had a feeling that, soon, he might look back on this moment with fondness.

Because he also had a feeling that things were only about to get more dangerous.

CHAPTER 15

M aybe it was because Isadora had only recently visited the Union Chamber of Parliament, but it seemed funnier than usual that her people's own legislature met in a basement. It wasn't how things were supposed to be, but the war on the outer rim had upended almost everything.

Technically, the refugees' legislature was called the Consultative Committee, and they lacked the full power of the Union Parliament, where the political dynamics meant any bill passed immediately became settled law. Although the Consultative Committee could pass legislation, Isadora had supreme veto ability on any bill they sent her. To be fair, she almost never did. Wasn't worth burning bridges, especially now.

She'd had relatively little influence on choosing individual legislators. Especially after her reelection had focused, in part, on her tendency to centralize power, she wanted to decentralize the process. Each colony across all three outer rim planets—and now Sarsi as well—had come up with individual plans.

Sometimes, that meant a standard election. Other times, that meant a mayoral appointment. And a handful of colonies had opted for an in-between approach, where elected local officials convened and voted on who to send. Most of the Consultative Committee's work in recent months had been standardizing governmental procedures and legal codes, and coordinating with local officials to develop planetary-level decision-making bodies.

The complications hadn't ended there. Given that each Consultative Committee member was representing a colony—defined as any concentrated grouping of at least a thousand refugees, although remote work settlements could vote absentee at their primary settlement of residence—there were significant population differences in terms of each member's constituency.

By nature, a one-representative-per-colony approach gave unfair weight to the smaller, less populated settlements. But when the bigger ones had protested, calling for each member's vote to be weighted by constituency size, the smaller ones declared that they would refuse to send their representatives unless Isadora promised to uphold the one-representative-per-colony principle.

Apparently, there was only so much mileage you could get out of *don't you know there's a war for the rest of our people's survival going on, and wouldn't you please just figure this shit out yourselves?*

Eventually, a handful of mayors, representing an equal mix of large and small colonies, had convened a mutual task force to overcome the question of representation. They'd eventually come to a mutually agreeable solution: Consultative Committee members who represented more populous colonies would receive speaking priority during quorum, and therefore get more time to make their cases or advance legislation. But voting on resolutions would still occur on a one-representative-per-colony basis.

And then, when the committee members had traveled to Obrigan for their first full session, the Junta blockade of the outer rim had gone up, and now they were effectively trapped. Hence sticking them in the basement.

But that also meant Isadora felt her duty required her to attend more quorum sessions. She sat at the front of the basement auditorium like a professor in a lecture hall, sitting with one of her cheeks in her palm, while dozens of committee members argued back and forth.

She'd already told the entire legislature about Justin Hacelo's offer—endorse his party in the upcoming Union parliamentary election, and he'd rescind the settlement charter ban. Isadora continued to feel deeply conflicted about the offer, not just because she was loath to betray Tricia, but also because removing the charter ban would do next to nothing with the Junta blockade still in place. They couldn't bring a single refugee out of cryo, even if they were allowed to.

In hindsight, telling the Consultative Committee about the offer might've been a mistake. Then again, it at least provoked fiery debates. Which kept things interesting.

"I move that we immediately begin consideration of a resolution calling for an endorsement of Justin Hacelo's Reform Party!" one legislator declared loudly, pointing his finger in the air theatrically.

Isadora stifled a grin. *Immediately* was always a bad word to use in politics, especially in the context of starting debate on a resolution that would be revised heavily, before being submitted to her, which she could then legally veto if she felt like it.

"You're just saying that because you want to turn us into Union colonies!" another legislator thundered back.

Another round of shouting followed. Turned out, stuffing almost a hundred legislators into a basement *wasn't* the most stable way to run a government. Still, Isadora didn't mind letting them scream their hearts out in the basement while she and her executive cabinet did the real work upstairs.

She supposed, however, that it was her duty to keep things relatively professional. She cleared her throat, and the pitched debate died down almost immediately.

"I appreciate your candor regarding this issue," she said quietly. "But there are real stakes at play here. Stakes that should be debated with the dignity they deserve. Let's keep the debate calm, rational, and civil."

The arguing continued, but at least no one was trying to shout over each other anymore.

Isadora grinned. With everyone's attention mostly focused on each other, she figured she could sneak a couple of glances at her wrister. From the corner of her eye, she saw Valencia give her a glare that was equal parts reproachful and understanding.

She pulled up her most recent messages. She had three new ones. The first was a security briefing from Riley, outlining the progress of the war. The Junta had now occupied about 76% of the original Ikkren settlements, placing about 89% of the Horde population under their authority. But they'd still been ignoring the refugee settlements.

Then there was a message from Meredith. Things had slowly been getting back to normal between them, especially after she'd returned to going out with Rebecca. They'd been spending most of their free time together, attending art galleries or museums or theater productions from a local playwright Rebecca adored. The more time Meredith had been spending with her, the less standoffish she'd become with Isadora.

Which made it easier to process the third and last unread message on her wrister. It was a note from Tricia, letting her know that Parliament had approved the deployment of a humanitarian convoy to the outer rim to distribute medical supplies, food, and other basic repair supplies.

Tricia had let the Junta know that the entire convoy was under the Union military's protection. If they drew fire from the blockade, the entire Union war machine would come down on the Junta. Michael Azkon had pledged to allow the convoy through.

Isadora was glad to hear about the convoy, but it was still a far cry from the sweeping measures she'd called for in her speech to Parliament. But at least it gave her the opportunity to personally board one of the ships and disembark on the planet Bitanu.

Vincent had continued to ask her to make a trip whenever she could. Now, the humanitarian convoy had given her the chance to do so safely. She keyed in a quick request, letting Tricia know that she wanted to book passage on one of the vessels.

And then returned her attention to the ongoing debate. "I don't see what there isn't to like about Justin Hacelo's offer, personally," a voice said from nearby.

The speaker was none other than Alexander Mettevin, her chief financial adviser. Her cabinet didn't have to attend Consultative Committee meetings, but she'd asked that they go whenever possible. She couldn't recall an instance where one of them had spoken up before, except to testify regarding an ongoing issue.

"I've looked over the Reform Party's financial platform," Alexander continued. "His calls to liberalize solar trade would be a massive boon to our frontier settlements. Shipping costs from the core worlds make the price of imported goods from Union space prohibitively high. Even disregarding the question of the settlement charter ban, Reform's political positions are more beneficial to us than the Workers' Party."

"Justin Hacelo sees us as little else than a source of cheap labor," another voice nearby said. Katrina Lanzic, this time.

It was already rare for a cabinet member to speak up during quorum, but having *two* argue was unheard of.

"His only interest is in solarwide economic growth," Katrina continued. "I've looked at the numbers, and they've been stagnant for a decade and a half. I'm betting he thinks he can spike them by unfreezing 30 million new workers. Maybe even in our gratitude, we'll let him slide on applying normal Union labor laws."

"Solarwide economic growth is...an unambiguously good thing?" Alexander said, slack-jawed. "If we're growing the economy, plenty of our people will get lifted along with it."

"You know, as well as I do, that the primary beneficiaries will be the Union financier class."

Isadora rubbed her temples. She'd brought Justin Hacelo's offer to her cabinet because she hoped they'd provide clarity. But it sounded like her internal debates had just carried over.

It was also the most spirited debate between her cabinet members she'd ever seen before. Her schedule, jam-packed with attending rallies, giving speeches, and meeting with community anti-war activists—had torn her away from cabinet meetings.

"I concur with the chief diplomat's assessment," another representative said. "The Reform Party's economic plans will bulldoze our colonies' autonomy."

"Yes, well, we all know you're just a rabid isolationist!" a representative in the back shouted. Another all-out war of words ensued.

Isadora cleared her throat again. Eventually, the auditorium settled down. "I appreciate that there are a diverse array of passionate views on this subject," she said. "I promise that I will continue to study the issue, and will respond appropriately."

That seemed to get the representatives under control. To her left, Riley spoke up: "Ma'am, if you wouldn't mind, I'd like to give a security assessment on Justin Hacelo's offer."

Isadora gave her a go-ahead gesture.

"To state the obvious, we won't be able to bring anyone else out of cryo until the war winds down," Riley began. "But even if we get the Junta to back down, the threat of the Offspring is still very much real. We know they've gone dark in recent months, but there's nothing to suggest that the Offspring haven't been continuing to plan future operations or recruit more members.

"And if we bring everyone out of cryo at once, we'll open ourselves up for potential high-casualty attacks from them. Lastly, I would add that we have generally enjoyed a friendly relationship with the Union's security services under Tricia Favan. If the prime ministership changes, we could lose that relationship."

Good points, all of them. Back when Isadora was sitting in Justin Hacelo's office, his offer had seemed too good to be true—the only downside had been turning her back on Tricia. But after hearing out Katrina and Riley, she had to admit that there were actually good arguments against bringing everyone out of cryo right away.

Or at least, as long as the Offspring were still functioning. If they could make a decisive strike against their enemies, maybe that calculation would change. Perhaps she'd been so desperate to empty the *Preserver*'s bays that she hadn't properly assessed the downsides.

She was also concerned about the growing factionalism in the Consultative Committee. They seemed almost split down the middle, half supporting Alexander, half supporting Katrina. Had they gotten so bored being holed up in the embassy basement that they'd subdivided into proto-political parties?

The thought exhausted her. Factionalism was the last thing she needed right now.

"I want to repeat my gratitude for everyone sharing their views," Isadora said, wearing a congenial smile that was the polar opposite of how she really felt. "For now, however, we should recess. After the break, we will continue to discuss and debate security issues regarding the *Preserver*. In the meantime, I'd like to consult with my staff."

There were mutterings of discontent, but the Consultative Committee members finally picked up their belongings, stood up, and headed out to the waiting rooms. Katrina and Alexander left too, each one following their respective backers.

Isadora glanced over at Valencia and gave her a *go figure out what the hell that was* look.

"On it, ma'am," Valencia mouthed, then retreated outside.

Once everyone had departed, Isadora was alone with Riley and Gabby Betam. She summoned them over. "I'm getting the feeling that there are problems in my cabinet I'm not aware of," she said.

Riley and Gabby exchanged glances. "There have been...some recent divisions between Katrina and Alexander, ma'am," the latter said.

"Honestly, we wanted to keep this off your plate, ma'am," Riley said. "You've been busy enough managing the war that we didn't want to trouble you with party politics."

Party politics? That implied a level of formalization to the factions' disagreements that Isadora feared. "I think it's time that I know the full extent of what's going on," she said.

Gabby cleared her throat. "Well, it started with the issue of long-term residence passes at our settlements. Since so many of our colonies depend on solar trade, a couple local governments were pushing to extend residence passes to Union merchants, so they could extend their stays. It would drive up local spending, in addition to incentivizing more trade activity."

"Of course, all residence pass holders would be subject to extensive background checks," Riley interjected.

"Seeing as this was a legal matter, I was about to approve the usage of merchant residence passes at a select number of colonies. But Alexander wanted to push further, making them the default for any merchant, Union or not, at any colony. He made convincing arguments that it would drive up our revenue across the board. Katrina pushed back, arguing that we should be aiming for self-sufficiency instead of further integration."

"Things mostly stalled out after that," Riley continued. "And then things...got unfriendlier at our meetings. That's why we haven't brought the residence pass issue to you for a final decision."

Isadora thought about reprimanding them, but she second-guessed herself almost immediately. She'd been running from one end of the core worlds to the other over the past month, trying to drum up anti-war sentiment wherever she could.

Hell, the last time she'd even attended a cabinet meeting in person was at least five weeks ago. Her success relied on having her cabinet keep things running smoothly in her absence. Riley and Gabby had been trying to do just that.

"I'm guessing their debates eventually trickled down to the Consultative Committee," Isadora said.

"Yes," Gabby said. "A bloc of representatives formed in support of Alexander, supporting trade liberalization and promoting more ties between our colonies and Natonese settlements. They started calling themselves the Integrationists. In response, a second bloc formed in support of Katrina, arguing that we need to maintain our identity as Earthborn and preserve our cultural heritage. At first, the Integrationists called them Isolationists in derision, but they adopted the label as a marker of pride."

"Ah," Isadora said. "So when that representative called the other one an Isolationist..."

"...yes," Riley said. "It was with a capital I."

Isadora placed her forehead in her palm. During her first year, she'd felt so uncomfortable in her role, uncomfortable taking charge. But back then, everyone always did what she asked them to and hardly made a fuss.

Now that she was finally comfortable in her position, her people's unity was splintering. The universe sometimes played the cruelest jokes.

"For now," she said, "this stays between us. But I'm about to depart for the outer rim. The Union is sending an aid convoy past the Junta blockade under the navy's protection. I'm going to board one of the vessels and inspect our defenses on Bitanu."

Gabby looked at Riley, who nodded in confirmation. So far, only Riley and Valencia had known about her plan.

"Can you two keep these divisions from paralyzing the rest of the government while I'm gone?"

"Of course, ma'am," Gabby said.

"Certainly, ma'am," Riley said.

"Okay," she said, grinning. "I'm relying on you two to be the adults in the room while I'm gone. Dismissed." The two women bowed their heads and departed, leaving her in the auditorium by herself.

She exhaled slowly. The humanitarian convoy would be leaving soon, so she'd need to return to her residence and pack. She knew she was going to miss Meredith, but she also knew that her daughter could take care of herself, and a combination of Riley's agents and Union security services kept watch on her at all times. If anything, she might enjoy concentrating on her relationship with Rebecca.

Isadora stood up and stretched her shoulders. It was time to go find out what Vincent wanted to tell her so badly.

CHAPTER 16

A fter a few days mostly spent in the basement of the Heykan bookstore, Nadia had stopped coughing so much from the dust. It was colder down here than on the main floor, but the walls were insulated enough that it wasn't unbearable.

Nadia, her crew, Tori, and the rest of the Horde leadership were huddled around a meeting table. They didn't even have holographic projection technology, so they were looking at a printout map of the Heykan colony and the surrounding tundra.

Tori cleared her throat and brushed one of her light blond braids away from her face. "Everything is ready. Ever since the occupation began, we've been planting the seeds for an underground resistance here. We've been very disciplined. I find it unlikely that the occupiers have caught wind of our plans."

Nadia measured her words before responding. The Horde had splintered into various factions, with some of Tori's longtime followers blaming her for the Junta occupation. A challenge like that would throw off any leader, but there were times when Nadia wondered if Tori wasn't being as meticulous as usual in her planning.

Her logic was that a dramatic operation would rally the rest of the splintered Horde around her. Affirm her right to rule. The more spectacle, the better. Nadia understood the argument, but she wondered if a more calculated, incremental strategy of wresting territory away from the occupiers would work better.

"Even with numbers, I'm having a hard time seeing a mass uprising work," she said cautiously.

Tori turned her head and stared at Nadia. The emotions behind her hawkish face were harder to read than usual. "The uprising is just a distraction. The biggest power mismatch right now is the Junta's air superiority. They have eight warships in orbit, while we don't have a single one of our own.

"But we *do* have a sizable number of gunships we could use to fly teams into orbit. Enough of them could take down an enemy capital ship. Unfortunately, the interlopers have placed our gunship hangar outside Heykan on lockdown."

Nadia returned her attention to the printout map. Sure enough, there was a hangar facility to the north.

"I see where you're going," Boyd interjected. "You want us to get a bunch of pilots into the hangar."

Derek, meanwhile, wore a skeptical look on his face. "Junta security will be thick around the hangar. We would need a significant distraction to draw the Junta's attention away."

Nadia was impressed that Derek was confident to at least push back, gently, against Tori's plan. The Derek she'd first met on Calimor never would've been so bold.

"Our people are fighting for their homeland," Tori said, gritting her teeth. "They will resist with a ferocity that will catch the Junta off guard." Her voice was declarative and flat, cutting off discussion. Nadia searched the faces of the other Horde leaders, but none of them registered any doubts.

"Starting early tomorrow morning," Tori continued, "while Junta patrols are lighter, resistance members are going to stage a series of coordinated protests around Heykan. Concurrently, an infiltration team is going to sneak a group of pilots into the gunship hangar and combat the Junta guards while the pilots enter their gunships, override the lockdown measures, and take off into orbit."

Nadia could understand the logic behind the plan, and she knew Tori had been spending most of her time underground trying to sow the seeds of a mass resistance movement. That was why she'd disappeared in the first place—it was a desperate gamble to both flip the table on the Junta, and to serve as a dramatic display of her leadership to the splinter factions. But that didn't mean her plan was any less risky.

Isadora had sent Nadia all the way to Ikkren to coordinate with her, hopefully to alter the course of the war and rob the Offspring of the smokescreen they'd engineered. But now that she was here, she wondered if Tori's head was really in the right place.

With the Horde as splintered as it was, however, Nadia wasn't sure they had any other choice than working with Tori. No matter how impulsive the leadership challenge had left her, she was still their best choice for coordinating a resistance movement against the occupation.

With all her options bad, Nadia had to go with the least problematic one. Didn't mean it was any less frustrating.

"What do you need us to do?" she asked, fighting to keep the resignation out of her voice.

"I want you to go in with the infiltration team," Tori said. "I will need to direct the uprising personally. And you three have considerable experience fighting the Junta. If I can't go to the hangar, I want you three there."

Experience fighting the Junta. Nadia almost wanted to laugh. She was supposed to be the refugee settlement surveyor, but that'd been on hold ever since Boyd had gotten kidnapped. Then, indefinitely postponed while the outer rim war raged on.

Now, she was just someone who showed up. Did the things that were necessary. Hopefully, that ended with Tanner Keltin in her sights.

"Okay," she said. "Sounds like a plan."

·   ·   ·

The gunship hangar was on the other side of a large lake. Nadia, Boyd, Derek, a dozen Horde fighters, and a cohort of trained pilots worked their way down a winding path along a cliff face before skirting the lake's perimeter.

They could see the hangar in the distance, and Nadia feared they were too exposed. If any Junta soldier peeked their head out of the facility, they'd be spotted. Hopefully, the protests back in the Heykan were drawing everyone's attention.

Nadia, Boyd, and Derek brought up the rear. She paused as a speckle of reflected sunlight shimmered across the water's surface, nearly obscured by billowing steam from the underwater geysers. For the first time since arriving on Ikkren, she felt a powerful, aching sense of loss.

It was just so damn *beautiful*.

Back when she was running point on the settlement surveying operation, she'd loved how her job always led her to gorgeous vistas like this. Coupled with the practical objective of figuring out how to create conditions for improving people's livelihoods, it was practically her dream job.

Where had that gone? It was like the Offspring attack on New Arcena had abruptly closed that chapter of her life. Her days had been consumed by violence and anger ever since.

Hell, it was the first time she'd been on the same planet with her parents all year, and she hadn't even contacted them, much less made plans to visit. Her work had been all-consuming. The rage inside her had cannibalized all other facets of her personality.

"What am I even doing here?" she whispered, her voice disappearing into the wind. She wasn't some commando. The *Preserver*'s computer didn't pull her out of cryo to carry out operations like this.

She liked imagining Russ' voice telling her that it was okay, that no one knew what they were doing, that everyone was just figuring things out one step at a time. And insisting that she use the word *operator* instead of *commando*.

It'd almost been half a year since he'd died to save her, and she still felt guilty. Inadequate. Imagining him talking to her, reassuring her—that always calmed her down.

"Nadia?"

She turned her head and saw Boyd giving her a concerned look. The rest of the infiltration team was a few dozen feet ahead of them.

"Sorry. Just trying to get my head on straight," she said, falling into step behind Boyd as they sped up to catch the rest of their companions. "I'm worried this isn't going to work. I'm worried Tori is too disoriented to see the risk in her plan."

Boyd nodded. "She's angry about the occupation, about the Horde infighting. Justifiably so. But it seems like she's letting her anger blind her, turn her into something she isn't."

By the time he finished, Boyd was giving Nadia a piercing look. *Just like you*, he didn't have to add.

They reached the outskirts of the hangar before she figured out how to respond. They still hadn't encountered any resistance. Once they reached the facility, they'd need to circle around back.

The previous evening, Nadia had asked Derek whether there were any security features they'd need to bypass. Derek had explained that the Horde had never really cordoned off military installations from the public. The people who needed to access the bases would, those who didn't have any business going there could be trusted not to bother. Nadia was mystified, but at least it made their jobs easier.

The infiltration team peeled around the wall of the hangar and entered. There were about a dozen Junta soldiers on guard. One of the soldiers raised her head, pointed at them, and shouted.

There was only an infinitesimal lag time between the soldier's shout and the air filling with bursts of plasma fire or the suffocating smell of ozone. Nadia's instincts sent her sprinting over to a crate along the far edge of the hangar before she'd even processed the start of the battle.

It was just the latest instance of a long series of firefights she'd found herself in since arriving in Natonus. First there was the fight to take Calimor from the Junta, then there was the all-out brawl at Kal

Mekan on Enther, followed by the assault on the Offspring hideout deep in the Enther jungles. The inner terror was still there, of course, but there was also a new, added terror at how increasingly *normal* it felt.

Nadia raised her weapon over her crate, fired off a few salvos to cover two of the Horde resistance members as they moved up. Ducked just in time as a flurry of plasma bolts lunged toward her. Kept her head down as the bolts sheared metal off the wall behind her.

There was a numbness, too. A numbness that'd been built up every time she found herself in a firefight. The shouts, the screams, the frantic stuttering of guns and the awful smells of battle felt like a routine. The only difference was the setting.

From the maelstrom of violence, a voice called out to her: "You see those catwalks up there? We can get a height advantage over them!"

Boyd's voice. It was faint at first, but the more she focused on it, the duller the din of battle became.

Her head shot up. A series of catwalks on the upper levels of the hangar caught her attention. Returning her gaze to Boyd, the two exchanged nods before simultaneously using their suits to jet up into the air.

Nadia hurled toward the ceiling, faster even than the misplaced shots that tore through the empty air below her. Her outstretched hands found the railing. She cut her suit's mini-thrusters and pulled herself onto the catwalk.

A handful of soldiers exited a room on the other side of the hallway. Nadia and Boyd reacted faster, firing rapidly until their pursuers retreated inside. Then they ran down the catwalk until they stood over the middle of the hangar. A perfect vantage point to fire on their opponents, for whom cover was now no longer sufficient.

They rained plasma fire down on a huddled group of Junta troops. Boyd's went wide, while one of Nadia's struck a Junta soldier in the leg. He tumbled to the floor as the squad retreated. One of the soldiers went back for the injured man, only for incoming fire from the other Horde resistance fighters to cut both of them down.

It looked like most of the Junta forces had departed the main bay. From below, Nadia heard the call to advance. A handful of resistance fighters, along with Derek, set up in the middle of the bay.

The pilots rushed for the gunships. Another team went to work on a control terminal on the other side of the hangar. Probably to override the lockdown.

"Seems like a full retreat," she said.

"They could be regrouping for a counterattack," Boyd said.

The two of them knelt down on the catwalk, each one swiveling their weapons from side to side as they surveyed the battlefield. Nadia tensed up, expecting to hear the swish of a door as more Junta troops spilled into the bay. Nothing happened.

The gunship's engines howled to life, and still, there was no response. "Something's not right," she said, squinting. "I wonder—"

She almost didn't hear it over the engines. But eventually, she could make it out. A long, slow whine that got incrementally louder. An explosive sound rocked the hangar. When she looked up, there were three gaping holes in the ceiling.

"Railguns!" Boyd shouted, grabbing Nadia and diving downward. Both of them collapsed on the catwalk.

The railgun salvos struck the floor, leading to plumes of fire and rended metal and bodies. The gunships—along with all the pilots inside—disappeared in the explosions.

Everything happened so fast Nadia barely had any time to worry whether Derek was okay when the catwalk came loose from the wall. She and Boyd were airborne, tumbling toward the ground. She slammed into the back end of the hangar and rolled to get up, but her whole left side ached.

She glanced at Boyd, saw that he was okay, and screamed "Derek!" out into the chaos. Another railgun blast hit the hangar. This time, snow, ice, and dirt from underneath the hangar floor was part of the resulting plume.

Vague silhouettes stumbled toward them, nearly obscured by the smoke. The surviving resistance fighters. Derek was carrying two wounded comrades out, one on each arm.

Nadia's relief at seeing him alive was quickly replaced with dread. There could be another blast any second. They had to get out of the hangar. *Fast.*

It was only after they were outside that she let herself contemplate the utter failure of the operation. All the pilots had died, the gunships had been destroyed, and over half the infiltration team members were dead. And with the Junta now on high alert, she had a feeling they couldn't sneak back into Heykan even if they wanted to.

"Stay close to the hangar edge!" Boyd said. "We don't know if the Junta is surveilling the area. If they spot us, they might launch another salvo."

As soon as he finished speaking, the wall behind them caught flames and exploded, sending slats of plastic and metal in every direction. Nadia tucked her neck beneath her hands to protect herself from the rubble raining down on her.

After the rubble shower ceased, they proceeded onward. Her

heart fell further with every step along the rubblized edge of the hangar. The operation had come tantalizingly close to succeeding, but it felt like there was little they could do when the Junta controlled the skies.

Which meant they could stop the resistance every time the Horde tried to neutralize that advantage. What could you do when there were eight enemy warships orbiting a planet you were trying to liberate?

"Okay," Boyd said. "We all have enviro-suits. It'll be cold, but we can swim across the lake for cover. Especially with those geysers heating the water up. Once we're on the far bank, we split up. The rest of the infiltration team returns to the city, we double back and head for the *Exemplar.*"

Nadia was impressed that he'd taken charge so effortlessly, keeping everyone's heads on straight. She then steeled herself for an icy plunge into the lake, followed by several miles of hiking through the tundra. But even when they reached the *Exemplar*, she had no idea what to do next.

· · ·

Nadia and her crew were all quiet when they got back to the ship. Derek had retreated to his cabin. Boyd was mechanically going through the motions of pre-takeoff maintenance checks. That left her sitting dejectedly in the vessel's canteen.

The only way to distract herself from the despondency was to refocus herself on the problem she'd been considering earlier. About how to possibly neutralize the Junta's air advantage on Ikkren.

Reduce the number of enemy warships was the obvious solution, but Nadia had no idea how she could possibly accomplish that. To make the Junta withdraw some of their vessels, you'd have to force them to focus on a bigger threat elsewhere. That could only mean threatening them on their home planet.

And, to be fair, there *was* an ongoing rebellion on Enther. Except the Junta's partnership with the Offspring allowed Tanner's forces to cover the home front.

But if that balance of power on Enther could be altered...

A plan started to form in Nadia's mind. It was desperate, maybe even more so than Tori's plan to seize the gunship hangar. And it would require her to get back in touch with the rest of her people's leadership, which was impossible at the moment.

She shook her head and turned her attention to her wrister. She needed to compose a message to Tori, let her know how things had shaken out.

But the first thing that popped up was a message from Riley Tago. Isadora herself was on her way to Bitanu right now. Considering that Nadia was still supposed to refrain from directly communicating with her, Riley wondered if it could be an opportunity for the two of them to meet up discreetly.

Nadia's heart leapt. The last missing piece in her plan clicked into place. She began typing a brief report to Tori, but her thoughts were racing.

She needed to get to Bitanu. If she could meet with Isadora, she was increasingly certain she'd thought of a way to bring the war to an end.

CHAPTER 17

Reentry couldn't come soon enough for Tanner. He'd been in a cramped submersible with Claude and Austin for almost two weeks. Only the first one was remotely bearable. He got through it with a grim determination to see his titanic crusade finally come to a close, but even still, breaking Bitanu's atmosphere was a relief. So relieving that he hardly cared as his body shot in every direction while he was strapped to his chair.

Just before splashdown, he heard the capsule detach from the outside of the submersible, followed by another agonizing few seconds of feeling like his chair straps were about to slice through him. And then, finally, the plunge. The submersible was finally in its natural environment.

Tanner's hands couldn't undo his chair straps fast enough. From the looks on Claude and Austin's faces, they were equally relieved. He followed the two of them to the helm. The piloting station was a night sky of buttons, levers, and switches. Tanner had told the other two to take the lead on reading the manual and actually figuring out how to drive the damn thing during their transit from the *Caretaker*.

He pulled up a holographic navigational chart as well as the surveillance data they'd gotten from the *Caretaker* drone. They were still several days out from the newars' defense matrix.

Several days too many. He'd played a careful, calculated chess game for years, bringing him to the present moment. Every betrayal, every alliance, every recruitment had led him here. But the destruction of the *Preserver* and the cleansing of the newar threat was still days away. And feeling cramped didn't help with the impatience.

An idea struck him. Just as Claude was about to pull the piloting lever, Tanner said, "Stop. I want to surface briefly."

He supposed there was some risk of surfacing, but considering how lifeless most of the planet was, Tanner figured the threat of detection was microscopic. Still, Claude and Austin exchanged glances.

"We've been cooped up so long," he continued. "We could all use an invigorating breath of fresh air. And it will give us the motivation to continue."

The two Offspring nodded, and pressed another series of buttons. Tanner felt the submersible lurch beneath his feet as they climbed through the Bitanu depths. He wished the submersible had some kind of viewscreen where he could see what was going on outside, but there was little else but machinery and bare metal walls.

They leveled out. Tanner could feel the vessel bobbing on the water's surface. Grinning, he retreated into one of the rear corridors, squeezing his shoulders together to avoid brushing up against the walls. He activated his suit's helmet before arriving at the airlock ladder. Twisting the rotary wheel until the hatch opened, he emerged into open air for the first time in months.

The view almost caused him to stumble.

The oceans below were an enchanting shade of deep blue, while vast chunks of ice floated around them, extending beyond visual range. If he squinted, he could make out a glacial shelf large enough to form its own landmass.

Bitanu was also home to the tallest mountains in the Natonus System. Even if the mountains were nothing more than hazy silhouettes from his vantage point, he felt like he was in the shadow of mythical giants.

It was only the third planet he'd ever been on in his life. Tanner became aware of a sense of sadness inside him, that he'd never spent the time to take in all the beautiful, natural vistas that Natonus had to offer. The Enther jungles had been a welcome change of pace from a lifetime spent in Obrigan City, but Bitanu put them to shame.

He also felt a sense of pride swelling in his breast. These vistas were part of what made the Natonus System such a special place. Something worth defending, worth fighting for. They were a reflection of the hardy character of the Natonese people.

Cautiously, placing each step to make sure he didn't slip off the wet hull, Tanner walked to the front end of the vessel. He felt so small. Miniscule, even, in contrast to the oceans and the mountains and the titanic glaciers. It was a feeling he'd never gotten before, one that made him forget, momentarily, why he was here.

One that made him wish Rebecca was by his side.

He heard his two followers working their way up the vessel's ladder, and they emerged soon after. "This is...wow," Claude said.

Tanner nodded in agreement, but wished the other man hadn't said anything. There were some views that were just too transcendental to accurately put into words.

He turned his head back to face the closest glaciers. As their submarine had drifted closer, he could make out a light band of teal-colored ice that ran along the surface of the water.

According to a datapad he'd read on the flight from the *Caretaker*, Bitanu had always been the least populated planet in the system. It had once been the site of the Outer Development Project—a Union initiative that had tried to set up a sustainable trading ecosystem, which collapsed shortly after the Union's war with the Horde. The former ODP headquarters had downsized to a small research base.

Most of the planet was protected land under the jurisdiction of the Solar Park Foundation, but they'd given some of it away to the invaders so they could set up colonies.

Traitors, Tanner thought with a scowl. Natonese natural beauty should be preserved only for Natonese people.

Other than the research base, the parks, the sparse newar colonies, and now the defense matrix protecting the *Preserver*, the only other inhabitants were desperate water haulers trying to sell melted Bitanu ice at a markup.

Tanner took a deep breath, wishing that the planet had a breathable atmosphere that would allow him to take his helmet off. Maybe someday in the far future, with enough terraforming. Or maybe not. Tanner liked the purity of the Bitanu landscape.

Then again, it wasn't *entirely* pure. It was the Offspring's job to eliminate the imperfections: the cancerous polyps of the newar colonies. Now, it was time to make sure the planet stayed pure.

.   .   .

Tanner knew from the surveillance data that the defense matrix facility was ugly, and it didn't disappoint. The structure was a giant, rectangular box made of cheap steel with a glossy veneer. Then there was a perimeter of large laser batteries that were taller than some office buildings he'd seen.

There was also an outer ring of fortified security checkpoints staffed with newar militia personnel, one they bypassed with the submersible. He'd worried they might have sonar detection capabilities, but the newars hadn't reacted to their approach. He figured it was safe to assume they'd overlooked this particular security contingency.

Tanner continued to monitor the surveillance footage as his followers steered the submersible onward. The complex covered a vast swath of land. They were well beyond the security perimeter by now, with the ring of laser turrets probably hundreds of feet away from them.

The actual control building looked smaller than the cannons. Tanner had his followers hold position for about fifteen minutes, wondering if newar militia forces would patrol the area in rovers. Nothing came.

During the few days' worth of travel from their initial landing spot, he'd learned that a convoy of humanitarian aid vessels had arrived in the outer rim. While most of them were delivering food and medical supplies to Ikkren, a small handful had come to Bitanu. Two had even landed just outside of the complex.

He had no idea if he was going to survive the operation—the primary objective was taking the defense network offline, while his and the others making it out alive was a distant secondary one—but if he did, the aid ships would be their escape route.

Tanner ordered his followers to approach the main facility. They proceeded onward, slowly breaking through thick glacial ice, until they were directly beneath the defense matrix.

The ice was so thick that it took over half an hour for them to approach the underside of the facility. Once they were there, Tanner had them use the submersible to create a vacuum-sealed latch onto the bottom of what the surveillance data suggested was a supply closet.

The three of them retrieved plasma cutters from a gear locker. Then opened the top hatch and got to work. It was another ten minutes' worth of plasma cutting until they'd sliced a hatch-sized hole through the floor. A thick circle of steel fell with a loud clang.

Tanner unholstered his plasma weapon and worked his way up the ladder, beckoning Claude and Austin to follow him. He peeked out cautiously once he was inside the facility, but there was no one around. Sure enough, they were in some kind of supply room. He pushed himself up and out of the submersible.

The room was a labyrinth of wire shelves, each filled to the brim with plastic crates containing a variety of cables, connector devices, and defunct computer terminals. Large coils of wires were scattered across the floor.

Tanner and his two followers approached the far door cautiously and silently. Given how the room was so full of junk and tech, he feared that a single misplaced step could bring the shelves crashing down. Which would then give them away.

They reached the exit without incident. "Move fast," Tanner breathed to Claude and Austin. "If we are under fire when we step through this door, get to cover immediately. If not, we need to upload our virus program into their servers."

He'd previously designed a program that would disrupt all out-going communications from the facility, preventing the newars from radioing the perimeter personnel for backup once they realized they were under attack.

The two Offspring nodded in acknowledgment just before the door swished open. They entered the main room. Tanner found an unoccupied workstation to the left and hid behind a row of terminals. No one had fired at him yet.

He raised his head slightly out of cover. His two followers had moved into cover as well—Austin behind a turbolift shaft, Claude behind a pillar. Dozens of catwalks crisscrossed the room in a gridlike pattern. Each one dead-ended at a control station instead of crossing to the other side of the room.

There were a handful of security guards, but the room was so large that Tanner wasn't surprised they hadn't spotted the three of them. Most of the room personnel looked like technicians. About a dozen individuals with utility belts were patrolling the catwalks, usually stopping by a control station to run a diagnostic.

He figured that each station must link up with one of the laser cannons outside. Which was smart—that way, a single station mal-functioning wouldn't lead to a system-wide shutdown.

But it made things harder on them. If he wanted to disable the laser turrets to allow a nuclear strike on the *Preserver*, that meant he and his followers would have to turn off each control station individ-ually.

But first, they had to upload the virus. Considering that Tanner was closest to a computer terminal, he figured he should be the one to do so. He gave hand signals to Claude and Austin, telling them to line up shots and cover him as he moved forward. They nodded in acknowledgement.

He crept forward, ducking behind crates or workstations whenever possible, moving quickly but silently when it wasn't. He made it to the closest computer station without incident. Hid behind a counter and waited a few seconds, just in case.

When he peeked out of cover, no one was paying any attention to the ground floor. He grinned, withdrew the uplink drive from the folds of his suit, and crawled toward the terminal. Thereby exposing himself to detection.

He held his breath as he inserted the drive into a slot on the back of the terminal. A pop-up showed that it was downloading the virus. Just as the download progress approached 80%, he heard a shout above him: "Hey! Who are you?"

Tanner turned around with his gun already drawn. The man's shout had given away his location. He pulled the trigger gingerly. A newar security guard on one of the nearby catwalks took his plasma bolt straight to his chest. He staggered before flipping over the catwalk's railing and crashing to the floor.

A beep behind Tanner let him know that the virus had been successfully uploaded. The newars' comms were now offline. He looked over to his companions and signalled them to fire. Then dove back into cover.

Claude and Austin picked their shots well. Five technicians went down in the first few seconds, their plasma-riddled bodies hurtling toward the ground floor. The guards responded quickly, but the element of surprise was on their side.

Tanner shot another technician before the first salvo of plasma fire rained down on him. Then leapt over the counter and sprinted out into the open, staying beneath one of the overhead catwalks to make it difficult for the guards to get him in their sights.

When he looked up, he saw a technician sprinting down the catwalk to the control station at the end. Two plasma bolts from Claude and Austin struck his body, sending him skidding across the grating until he lay lifeless.

By this time, one of the security guards had repositioned to get a better shot at Tanner. A plasma bolt landed uncomfortably close to one of his feet. He ran toward the closest pillar he could find. Another plasma bolt, this one from one of his companions, whizzed by the back of his head. He could feel the heat of the blast on his neck.

As his followers continued to trade fire with the rest of the newar personnel, the sound of a door opening caught Tanner's attention. Probably a dormitory. A group of groggy technicians stepped out, eyes still squinting from the bright fluorescents. Tanner gunned them all down before they had a chance to react.

In another few seconds, the room fell silent. No weapons fire, and more importantly, no alarms. He looked at his two followers and saw that they were unharmed. As he circled around the ground floor, surveying the carnage, it looked like they'd taken out every single guard and technician.

Tanner's knees shook from excitement. They were, at last, in the clear to disable the laser turrets outside.

CHAPTER 18

Back on Earth, Isadora had never been able to sleep on airplanes. She was sorry to see that her misfortune carried over to space travel in the Natonus System. The flight from Obrigan to Bitanu aboard a humanitarian convoy vessel had taken almost a month, and she was pretty sure the most sleep she'd gotten at night had been five hours.

When the vessel finally landed outside her people's defense matrix installation, she yawned as soon as the landing gear touched down on the ice. *Appropriate.*

From there, it was a short rover ride to the actual facility. Vincent Gureh greeted her after the rover rolled into a bay, and they'd sealed the outer door. Isadora shook his hand—Vincent had never been a big hugger—and they walked into the facility proper. The crew that'd piloted the rover began refueling the vehicle and doing maintenance checks.

"I wanted to thank you for finally coming," Vincent said. He handed her a thermos. "I figured you'd be wanting some coffee at the moment."

He'd once promised to devote a considerable amount of his time watching Meredith while she was still in cryo, and Isadora had left the *Preserver*. But except for that, this was the most amount of gratitude she'd ever felt for him. She took a long drink from the thermos, hardly even caring when she scalded her tongue.

Vincent's voice had always been warm, soft, and quiet, but Isadora thought she could detect an element of anxiety today. Then again, that might not have anything to do with him asking her to come visit him in person. Setting up and maintaining the laser defense matrix had been a lot of work, and the stakes were enormous. She could empathize.

"I'll always have time for my people," she said. "But I should apologize for taking so long. My schedule's just been packed the last few months. More so than I ever could've imagined." She yawned again.

Vincent shook his head. "There is no need for an apology. I understand you have important work to be doing."

The two of them walked into a large room with at least two dozen walkways intersecting at right angles. "Each catwalk leads to an individual control station for one of the laser cannons outside," Vincent explained. "That way, if one fails, it doesn't bring down the entire network."

Isadora nodded. "I can see the logic behind that. I don't suppose we've had to use them yet?"

Vincent shook his head. "Space is big, of course. And I have a hard time believing a stray missile from a Junta vessel would strike the *Preserver*. The larger threat, in my view, is if the Offspring convince their allies to fire at us. But if that were to happen, we'd be ready."

They walked over to a turbolift that took them to the topmost level. They then strode down the catwalk at a leisurely pace, giving Isadora time to take in the full view.

There were at least eight security guards, and the number of technicians dwarfed that. One worker was walking straight toward them. Isadora and Vincent politely stepped to opposite ends of the catwalk, letting the woman pass. She gave her a warm smile as she walked by.

"It helps me sleep at night knowing how hard you and your staff are working here," Isadora said.

Vincent nodded, but his attention strayed. His eyes seemed fixed on the other side of the room. He moved his lips, mouthing something indistinguishable, as though he were trying to figure out how to word something.

"How are the others?" he said at last, although Isadora got the feeling that wasn't what he *really* wanted to say.

She took another drink from her thermos. "Good," she said. "Nadia's been helping the resistance on Ikkren, but from what I understand, she's been stalled out. In fact, according to Riley, she's on her way here to discuss future options."

She'd been surprised that Nadia had left Ikkren, although it sounded like her efforts against the occupation weren't going well. And knowing Nadia, she probably needed a change of scenery and someone to bounce ideas off.

"It would be good to see her again," Vincent said, the distracted look on his face unchanged.

"Are you...all right?" Isadora asked.

"Hm?" Vincent shook himself out of his stupor. "Yes. Sorry. Nadia. I was surprised to hear you publicly denounce her for aiding the Horde."

"Yes, well, I have to play the political angle, and that means neutrality. Nadia knows I support her in private, of course. And I imagine our Junta foes know that too, but my facade at least gives us plausible deniability." She sighed. "Sometimes, the political theater has really been getting to me."

"It seems you've handled yourself well."

"I certainly *hope* it seems like that from the outside. But I'm growing weary of it all. It doesn't matter how many anti-war rallies I go to, or politicians I urge to help us, it feels like I'm not doing enough."

"I suspect the end of the current crisis may be closer than you think. In fact, that is related to what I wanted to discuss with you."

That certainly piqued Isadora's interest. Had Vincent concocted some sort of ace in the hole? Something that would bring an end to the Offspring threat and draw down the war? She couldn't imagine what that might be, but then again, her sleep-deprived brain was not functioning optimally.

He led her to his private office at the end of the walkway and gestured inside. Isadora sat down in a chair facing his desk and crossed her legs.

It might've been the most depressing office she'd ever seen. The walls were completely bare, and there was no furniture besides the two chairs and the desk. No table ornaments, no pictures, no anything. It was like living in a small metal box.

Vincent crossed to the other side of his desk, sat down, and leaned forward. "What I'm about to tell you is invaluable information," he said. "It could alter the course of the war, maybe even the political situation in this entire system. I could not risk it being intercepted, even via encrypted wrister communication."

Isadora scrunched her eyebrows. "You can always tell me anything. We know each other."

Vincent let out a sharp laugh. "That's exactly the issue. The problem is, I am not at all who you think I am."

.   .   .

If there were a mirror in Vincent's office, Isadora was certain she'd look a shade of ghostly pale. "I'm...sorry," she whispered. "Can you repeat that?"

"A Hegemony agent," Vincent said. "I was at the head of the fleet that drove your people from their home. From Earth."

A series of still frames flashed through Isadora's head. Satellite images of ominous, lumbering warships bearing down on Earth. A holofeed relating the nuclear annihilation of Mars. Her and Meredith, racing to pack everything they could in their Seattle condo before fleeing to the *Preserver*.

Vincent sighed and lowered his forehead. "It all came down to the work my team did for them. I swear, I didn't know what they were planning. Or how they would use what we developed."

"I...don't understand," Isadora said, her voice still a whisper.

"How do you think the Hegemony was able to conquer so many colonized star systems? My team and I had been experimenting with using antimatter to construct solar relays that would greatly speed up transit times in space. *Wormholes*, if you will. When we presented our findings to our government, we were thrilled when they offered to bankroll us. We never stopped to ask what they would do with it if we successfully constructed an antimatter relay."

Isadora's tired mind was spinning so hard that focusing on any single part of his story was difficult. But now that she was thinking about it, one of the more mysterious facets of the Hegemony invasion was how their fleets had showed up without triggering Earth's long-range scanners.

Their usage of wormholes cleared that particular mystery up.

"They used our technology to return to humanity's outlying star systems. When we could drop fleets on their capital worlds in an instant, they quickly surrendered to us. And before long, the vast majority of the colonized galaxy had fallen under our heel. We started calling ourselves the Hegemony. And before long, with the resource bases of a dozen conquered star systems in our grasp, we sought to return to the motherworld. To finish our conquest of our own species."

Isadora couldn't think of anything to say. Her ears were comprehending what Vincent was saying, but her head and her heart insisted none of it could be true. It was a bad dream. She pinched her wrist to make sure. Nothing.

"We knew, of course, that the Natonus System was the crown jewel," Vincent continued. "That was partly why the military wanted to conquer Earth. But after the invasion began, the UN must've wiped all data files containing the coordinates of the Natonus System. After Earth fell, we could find no trace of information about the system or its location. And without knowing where Natonus was located, we could not construct a wormhole that would lead here.

"On the eve of Earth's fall, our fleets detected two cryo vessels departing Earth. The *Anointer* and the *Preserver*. The military assumed that the two ships had been programmed to retreat to the Natonus

System. That's where I come in.

"Hegemony command dispatched me to infiltrate the *Preserver*, while the other millions of inhabitants were sleeping unaware in cryo. But command saw little utility to letting the *Anointer* escape. The fleets destroyed the other vessel."

The *Anointer* had been carrying the top political and military officials from Earth. Everyone who would've gotten Isadora's job, in other words. The only reason she, or Nadia, or anyone else in her government was even awake was because of the *Anointer*'s destruction.

Because of Vincent's mission.

"For years after we departed the Sol System, I worked in complete solitude to upgrade the *Preserver*'s systems in secret," Vincent said. "An antimatter relay that would connect Natonus to Sol would require a massive power spike, one that could only be generated by a vessel the *Preserver*'s size. So I programmed the various ship's systems—life support, engines, the like—to execute a simultaneous energy burst needed to transform the entire vessel into a relay gate.

"And then, I wiped the ship's computer so that it would have no memory of my tinkering. I examined its directives and ensured that I would be among the first awakened from cryo upon arrival in the Natonus System. And then, it would be a simple matter of dispatching the others, beginning the *Preserver*'s transformation protocol, and waiting for the fleets to pour through the newly opened gate. The last free system would fall."

Vincent stood up and paced around the room, hands clasped behind his back. Isadora could see the tears welling in his eyes.

"But I...I couldn't," he continued. "Not after the carnage I'd seen across the galaxy. The conquests were brutal. We depopulated entire cities, entire *planets*. All because of the technology I gave them. I...am a murderer, Isadora."

She pictured Vincent, alone for years aboard the *Preserver*, surrounded by frozen refugees, haunted by the conquests he'd borne witness to. She found that her overwhelming emotion was not anger, not even confusion—but sympathy.

"Those months—those *years*—when I was working alone on the *Preserver*, I told myself I had to figure out some way to make it stop. To save lives. And so I used the computer to send out a fake message back to Hegemony command, stating that the *Preserver* had been destroyed in transit."

"You wanted to keep the location of Natonus secret," Isadora said mechanically. Any emotional processing of Vincent's story would only come much later, she was certain.

"Yes. But the effects of my lie were more far-reaching than I had anticipated. The issue was, the Hegemony had staked its conquest agenda on eventually finding and subduing Natonus. Even if it took a century. But with the promise of finding the lost system withdrawn, factions within the Hegemony turned on each other. I discreetly sent out drones from the *Preserver* to monitor the state of the galaxy.

"Only a week before the war began, the last drone returned. I understand you may not believe the information I'm giving you, but I hope you will at least believe the recordings from these probes."

He walked over and slid a small data drive across his desk. Isadora picked it up, unable to take her eyes off it.

"I can say with certainty that the Hegemony has collapsed after several rounds of civil strife and uprisings," Vincent continued. "Our species is now spread across isolated, leaderless star systems. Waiting for someone else to come along and pick up the pieces."

Isadora had never really thought much about the other humans spread across the stars. The Immediacy of her own people's problems had never given her much time to speculate.

She couldn't deny an instinctual yearning that rose within her. Humans were a social species—they belonged together. The great human diaspora was a tragedy.

When she looked at Vincent's face, such romantic notions ceased. Suspicion replaced them. She'd only ever thought of him as an absent-minded intellectual. Clearly, she knew even less about him than she thought.

But his actions had also helped save their people, and possibly even the Natonese. She shuddered, imagining an alternative reality— one where she'd never woken up, where the *Preserver* had transformed into some antimatter relay before anyone had come out of cryo.

One where Hegemony ships suppressed the last free system in the galaxy, one where she and Meredith had never been reunited. A lump caught in her throat.

"You saved us," Isadora said eventually. She stood up and walked to Vincent. The man's head drooped low. She placed a comforting hand on his shoulder. "If what you have told me is true, your...people used your research for their own twisted ends. That is on them. Not you."

Vincent blinked several times. "Your words are kinder than I deserve," he said. "But I'm surprised you aren't already capitalizing on the political implications."

Isadora had been so focused on somehow trying to wrap her mind around the revelations that she hadn't even considered the implications. *It could alter the course of the war, maybe even the political situation in this entire system*, Vincent had told her.

Indeed. If she could persuade the Union that opening a solar gateway back to Earth was a noble goal, it would incentivize them to empty the ship's remaining 30 million cryo pods.

And it would place the *Preserver*'s survival within the direct interests of the rest of the solar system. Parliament might take real action to force the Junta to back down.

Isadora's tired head spun, pondering the various ways she could reveal what she now knew. She pictured the headlines. It would completely upend the coming parliamentary elections. How to manage the *Preserver* would become *the* defining political issue at hand.

And it might mean an end to her job. If the *Preserver* were emptied at long last, and if the ship itself were repurposed into a new structure, what need was there for her, anymore?

"The implications are...staggering," she said at last. "Of course, I would need to get your probe data out. I can't imagine anyone would be enthusiastic about transforming the *Preserver* if they fear an invasion would follow."

Vincent nodded. "Of course. All the files you need are on that drive. Everything. You can access them at your conven—"

Violent thud-pings from right outside interrupted them. Isadora's overwhelmed brain took seconds to realize that it was plasma fire.

She turned back to face Vincent, who looked more confused than terrified. He rushed back to his desk and tapped a series of buttons, playing a camera feed of the main room.

Isadora watched with horror as three armed individuals—all in brown enviro-suits—methodically shot each one of their security and technical personnel.

Vincent froze. "The Offspring are here." Chills writhed their way up Isadora's spine.

He dashed toward the door. "This room is not safe. They will trap us in here and kill you. Our only hope is to leave right now. There is a turbolift at the end of this walkway that will take us to an airlock leading to the rooftop."

A political mind was a natural compartmentalizer, and Isadora was grateful for that now. She placed her panic on the back burner and foregrounded her logic. Vincent was right. Running was risky, but not as risky as staying put. She followed him to the door.

It swished open. "Run!" he said.

They sprinted down the walkway. Plasma bolts screamed at them. It was damn unnerving how loud they got as they slammed into the wall right next to her.

Vincent positioned himself so that his body was between Isadora and the edge of the walkway. The exit was in sight now. Just a little bit further.

She heard a sharp grunt from her left. Turned, only to see Vincent stumble. A plasma bolt had cut a diagonal swath through his torso.

Adrenaline surging, she grabbed his forearm and pulled him the final few inches into cover. When she cupped his face, he coughed blood on her blazer.

"Please..." he gasped. "Please."

Violent coughs erupted from his throat. His head leaned forward, and his body lay still.

Isadora couldn't even focus on that. She could still make out one of the three Offspring infiltrators on the far side of the room.

For a split second, all she could see was the face of her daughter's girlfriend. Or a masculine version, rather. Confusion and anguish and grief gave way to terror.

Tanner Keltin was here to kill her.

CHAPTER 19

It was Nadia's first time seeing the laser defense matrix on Bitanu. From the look of it, everything seemed just fine. Derek had radioed over the *Exemplar*'s approach, which had been received and acknowledged by perimeter security. They quickly received permission to land at the helipad atop the installation itself.

Nadia spent the last few minutes of their flight enjoying Bitanu's untapped landscape. The first time she'd visited the planet, she'd wondered if it would be almost indistinguishable from Ikkren. Both being frozen worlds that looked mostly white from space. But now that she'd made plenty of trips here, there was no way she'd ever get them confused.

Ikkren was dry, with very few natural bodies of water, and little snowfall. Permafrost was more common than accumulated snow. The planet was also mostly flat, with only a few mountain ranges in the northern hemisphere. And she didn't need a helmet to breathe Ikkren air.

Bitanu, on the other hand, was almost entirely oceanic under its glacial surface. Blizzards raged on the regular, gigantic mountain ranges slithered across the surface. The largest peak in the Natonus System, Mount Sorjen, sitting at twenty-six miles high, was located in the Bitanu wilderness. And the atmosphere wasn't oxygenated.

But for Nadia, natural beauty was easier to appreciate when she wasn't addled by stress and frustration and pent-up anger. She wondered how long it'd be before she could go back to the Nadia of her first two years in the system. The Nadia who'd gleefully pranced across the Natonese frontier, fueled by optimistic visions of peaceful settlement.

Could she? Would the bitterness of xenophobia and terrorism and war last forever?

She turned her head and saw Boyd looking at her with a concerned glance. She felt for him—she knew that both she and Derek had been absolute chores to be around during their flight from Ikkren.

Both of them became detached when they were unhappy, while Boyd had always been the most social. They'd spent most of the trip ruminating alone in their respective cabins. Boyd had tried to get both of them to open up—and failed.

Derek, at least, could translate his anguish into art. Nadia had spied him writing in the blank pages of his book of Ikkren poetry.

She didn't even have that. Victory or death were her only releases.

Maybe today would push her a little bit closer to one of those. The fight against the Junta occupation on Ikkren was hopeless as long as the enemy could keep the bulk of their fleet in orbit. Which meant that the path to victory on Ikkren ran through the Ashkagi rebels on Enther.

If Nadia could persuade Isadora to covertly funnel aid that would bolster the rebels' chances, that might force the Junta to relocate at least some of their warships. Then, the resistance on Ikkren could actually pull off operations like the failed one at Heykan.

The *Exemplar* descended further as they approached the matrix control facility. A circular helipad atop the building welcomed them with blinking lights. A light snow was falling, not heavy enough to impede visibility. They touched down without incident.

Nadia sent a message to Isadora informing her they'd arrived. When she didn't respond, she sent one to Vincent Gureh, who also didn't respond.

Which wasn't like either of them. Nadia briefly wondered if something could be wrong inside. But then why did perimeter security act like nothing was out of the ordinary?

The concern must've been obvious in her face. "Maybe they're in a meeting?" Boyd offered.

Nadia shrugged. "Maybe. Either way, I'd like to see for myself. Let's head indoors."

The three of them suited up and exited the *Exemplar*. A thin metal slab along the rooftop opened as they approached, leading down to an airlock. Once the outer door was sealed, their helmets folded back into their enviro-suits. They took a turbolift down to the main facility. Nadia checked her wrister on the way down. Still nothing from Isadora.

The door slid open, and Nadia watched Vincent get shot.

The man stumbled before collapsing. Isadora pulled him into a corridor, barely avoiding a flurry of plasma bolts that slammed into the nearby wall.

Back when Russ had died, Nadia hadn't reacted fast enough. She'd frozen when Tanner Keltin drew his gun on her.

This time, she'd learned her lesson. She activated her suit's thrusters and sped past Isadora and the downed Vincent. Isadora called her name out, a mix of incredulity and gratitude in her voice. When she landed, she was in the middle of a catwalk spanning the upper floor.

Some part of her knew *exactly* who was shooting at Isadora. Three brown-clad men were stationed at various points on the other catwalks, spread out across the room. Nadia's attention was focused on the one at the far end.

Tanner Keltin. The leader of the Offspring, the man who'd kidnapped Boyd and killed Russ. Probably just killed Vincent, too.

Nadia's arm swung up in an arc, unholstering her handgun in a single, fluid motion. Bolts screamed out at Tanner, each one an expression of rage. For a moment, she convinced herself that all her problems would evaporate if Tanner was dead.

Three weapons' worth of plasma bolts responded. She activated her suit thrusters again, landing on a parallel catwalk about ten feet lower.

Two more plasma bolts sped by from behind her. Struck the two Offspring accompanying Tanner with artful concurrence. Nadia turned her head, saw Boyd and Derek with their own weapons raised.

"Get Isadora to safety!" she shouted. "I can handle him!"

With almost a dozen dead refugee security guards, Nadia figured Isadora lacked any personal detail. Perimeter security, judging by their reaction when Derek had radioed the *Exemplar*'s approach, might not even know what was going on—all the more likely, given the lack of any alarms going off.

That meant Boyd and Derek were Isadora's last line of defense if there were other Offspring infiltrators in the area. Nadia heard the clank of their boots from above as they extracted Isadora.

She turned and exchanged plasma rounds with Tanner. Both of their shots either went wide, or the other sidestepped. Tanner's suit must not have been equipped with thrusters, but he was close enough to a couple of control stations to easily use them for cover. After another salvo from her, he disappeared behind a station.

"I'm starting to see a pattern here," Tanner shouted at her, his voice reverberating in the empty room. "You seem to be there every time I put another one of you animals in the ground. Except you're always too late—or too slow—to do anything about it."

If he was trying to piss her off, then it fucking *worked*.

She took a running leap and jetted to another catwalk to get a better vantage point. Sidestepping a light barrage from Tanner, she tugged viciously at her weapon's trigger, spewing waves of plasma fire down at him. He ran for a lift, firing wildly over his shoulder.

None of the bolts hit, but one ripped through the supports at the far end of the catwalk. Nadia cursed as the walkway jerked to the side. She tumbled over the railing, her body going into freefall. Then activated her thrusters before she could hit the floor, landing gracefully. Just in time to see Tanner's lift come to rest.

The two exchanged fire almost immediately. But without any cover on the ground floor, both had to be more concerned with dodging each other's shots than lining their own. Plasma fire flew in every direction—except toward each other.

Deep scores marked the room's walls, a testament to their rage.

To their mutual hatred. Tanner sprinted for a supply closet while Nadia used her suit to jet around his gun blasts.

He ducked behind the wall. She fired a couple of rounds off, knowing full well that they wouldn't hit anything. Sure enough, all they did was rip through a couple of wire shelves. Severed cables and equipment boxes spilled out over the stockroom floor.

It was the first time she'd had Tanner in her sights since he'd killed Russ, and she wasn't able to do anything.

"I've got to hand it to you," he called out from behind cover, "at least you *tried* this time." She half-considered sending another pointless volley of fire into the stockroom.

"You failed," Nadia sneered at him. "Whatever it was you were planning to do here." It was a weak retort. And she couldn't even be sure she was being truthful—after all, who knew why Tanner had attacked the facility?

He responded by dropping a smoke grenade. She fired into the smoke cloud blindly, but by the time the smoke cleared, he was gone. She ran inside, where she saw a missing hole in the floor and a long cavern of ice that'd been carved out beneath the facility. It went deep enough that Nadia saw water.

She nearly threw her weapon against the wall. Nearly screamed in rage. Given what'd just happened, it was a miracle that all she did was collapse to the floor and hang her head.

.   .   .

If there was a way for a ship to fly despondently, Nadia was pretty sure the *Exemplar* was doing just that.

She'd barely said a word to Isadora after Tanner escaped. Barely paid a moment of respect to the fallen, to Vincent. She'd marched off back toward her ship with Boyd and Derek as soon as the rest of the perimeter security guard arrived. Then blasted off to scour the area for Tanner.

Scour unsuccessfully, apparently.

They'd figured Tanner must've been using some kind of submersible craft—how he'd bypassed the facility's perimeter, presumably— but they lacked sonar detection capabilities.

Boyd had managed to jury rig a weak sonar device with a few of the transducers in the *Exemplar*'s control system, but actually finding Tanner was still a long shot.

It'd been over an hour when Boyd and Derek had tried to convince Nadia that they weren't going to find Tanner. And with a blizzard coming in, they needed to make it back to the facility before flying conditions turned truly dangerous.

Nadia had protested with tear-stained eyes, which was how they ended up spending another half-hour flying around, trying to ping Tanner's submersible.

The half-hour ended with them returning to the defense matrix, sheets of snow falling all around them. She could barely see the landing lights by the time they approached.

Boyd laid a comforting hand on her shoulder. "I'm sorry. We've done everything we could."

Nadia wished she could draw comfort from his gesture or his kind words. In reality, the anger felt like it was consuming her. The more she could focus on Tanner, on everything he'd taken from her, the longer she could put off having to reckon with everything that happened back at the defense facility.

Nadia's shoulders slumped as the *Exemplar* came to a rest. The trio unbuckled from their seats in silence. It was a far grimmer entrance than before.

The facility felt surreal to Nadia. Medical and maintenance teams must've already come through while she and her crew had been searching for Tanner. The bodies were gone, the damage from all the plasma fire repaired. Like nothing had happened.

Nadia stood on the upper catwalk, surveying the room alongside Boyd and Derek. Isadora was down below, thanking the stragglers from the maintenance team and talking to the new security detail that'd transferred over.

"I should talk to her," Nadia said finally.

"We understand," Boyd said. "Take all the time you need."

She took one of the lifts down to the ground floor. Leaned against the wall while Isadora finished talking to the crews. After she finished making her rounds, she caught Nadia's eyes. It almost looked like her chest deflated.

"We couldn't find him," Nadia blurted out as she walked over.

Isadora nodded. "It's strange...with everything that's happened, it was hard for me to remember that a manhunt was still going on. It was easier to think about the human cost of what Tanner did. Of what he was *trying* to do."

There was only one reason Tanner would be at their defense matrix: he was trying to destroy the *Preserver*. He'd come perilously close to succeeding. A shiver passed through Nadia's body when she thought about what might have happened if she'd arrived even a few minutes later.

Isadora rubbed her forehead. "And despite all of that, I can't stop thinking about Vincent." For the first time since coming out of cryo, Nadia thought she looked truly exhausted. Drawn. On the verge of collapse.

She didn't want to think about Vincent. Couldn't *let* herself. It was a cruel joke of the universe that someone so awkwardly charming, so quiet, so helpful had his life taken by a monster like Tanner Keltin.

She gritted her teeth. "We'll get justice for Vincent."

Isadora looked at her, her eyes reddened by stress and lack of sleep and sorrow. "I can't stop thinking about our first few days in the Natonus System. Back when it was just me, you, Russ...and Vincent."

Nadia's jaw clenched. Now half of the original four were dead, and the same man was responsible for both.

But maybe dwelling on Tanner so much had hardened her. For a moment, Nadia admired the genuine, human sorrow on display. She forced herself to stop thinking about him.

Forced herself to remember Vincent: his awkward smile, the way he always stroked his chin when he was deep in thought, the efforts he'd made to upgrade the *Exemplar* with its missile scrambling system.

She looked at her feet. "Vincent was a good man. Straightforward, honest."

The pause from Isadora was almost unsettling.

"He was a good man," she repeated, finally. Nadia arched an eyebrow. She then gestured toward a lift. "We should talk in private."

The two rode the elevator back up to the upper level, entering Vincent's office. The only way Nadia had known it belonged to him was because of the nameplate. The room inside was totally bare.

As soon as the door was closed, Isadora looked at her with renewed vigor in her eyes. "Nadia," she said severely, "there's something I need to tell you about Vincent."

CHAPTER 20

I t'd been almost thirty hours since the Offspring attack on Bitanu, and Isadora had probably been asleep for half that time.

To be fair, there was little she could do at this point. Nadia's best efforts hadn't turned up Tanner or any other Offspring personnel in the area, security personnel had ensured that the defense matrix was protected, and the maintenance staff were repairing any damage to the laser batteries protecting the *Preserver*.

For the moment, the crisis had ended. And they were still gathering information before the decisions needed to be made. Isadora thought resting up—so she could have a clear head to make them— would be the best use of her time.

Before going to sleep, she'd sent Riley a transmission detailing everything that had happened. With the time delay to Obrigan, the chirp from Isadora's wrister announcing Riley's reply had been her alarm clock.

After dressing and a quick vapor shower, she was back in Vincent's office, reviewing Riley's after-action report. Isadora had read countless of these kinds of things since the beginning of her tenure, and rarely had the clinical, dispassionate language in which Riley or her staff wrote them felt so uncomfortable.

Even reading about the Offspring attack on New Arcena almost a year earlier hadn't struck a nerve like this. Isadora could only conclude that it was just different when she'd been on the scene, when one of the victims had been a close friend.

One who she apparently hardly even *knew*.

She pushed thoughts of Vincent's revelation from her head and continued to read the report. Riley acknowledged that sonar detection had been a major oversight, one that they were working on correcting. However, a team of security analysts suggested it was unlikely that Tanner would attempt a follow-up attack. His offensive patterns suggested adaptability, a never-try-the-same-thing-twice attitude.

As for the probable objective of Tanner's attack, the report was more chilling. By itself, the facility made little sense as a target. The number of security and technical staff was nowhere close to the population of any single one of the refugees' settlements, and the facility was so far from civilization that it wouldn't attract media spectacle.

Destroying the *Preserver* was the only plausible explanation.

That only confirmed what Isadora and her advisers had been thinking. The cryo vessel being in mortal danger wasn't *news*. But it confirmed their worst fears, and it was chilling to think how close Tanner had potentially come to annihilating millions of lives.

The report turned more speculative from there. It was difficult to know exactly *how* Tanner planned to destroy the *Preserver*. Perhaps he'd convinced the Junta navy to strike the vessel, or perhaps the Offspring had somehow taken control of a few asteroids in the belt to launch at the vessel.

Both would require cooperation with the Junta military, however, and no intelligence so far suggested that they were interested in a literal genocide of the refugees. Michael Azkon was hostile to them, sure, and the Junta were at war with their allies. But acquiescing to an attack on the *Preserver* seemed unlikely.

More plausibly, Tanner had been planning to use the laser defense matrix *against* the *Preserver* itself. The report was inconclusive on how much damage the lasers could do, however. They were equipped to destroy incoming projectiles, not entire starships. In theory, if a vessel remained in range long enough, the lasers could probably do decent damage.

And the *Preserver*, being the size that it was, would've been cumbersome to move out of the way quickly. But the report suggested that it was unlikely that lasers alone could've destroyed the vessel entirely. Significant damage was, however, possible.

Unfortunately, other than doubling down on securing the defense matrix, there was little they could do without actionable intelligence on Tanner's capabilities and plans. With Carson Erlinza being their only field operative embedded in the Offspring, and without him having provided anything yet, they had nothing.

Isadora closed the file on her wrister, dug her elbows into Vincent's desk, and leaned forward until her forehead rested on her knuckles. *Little they could do* felt like such a long-running, frustrating summary of her tenure.

It'd always felt like she'd been scraping by. Every time it looked they might be past the worst of things—right before the New Arcena bombing, or right before Russ' death in the Enther raid—reality had come crashing down on her.

But the whole time, she'd done what she could. Even if it felt small, irrelevant, inadequate. That was all she could do now.

She pressed another few buttons on her wrister, forwarding Riley's report to Nadia and inviting her up for a meeting when she'd finished reading it.

She arrived about a half-hour later. Her face still seemed frozen in anger from her confrontation with Tanner. Isadora felt for her—what would it be like to have confronted her greatest enemy *twice* now, with nothing to show for it?

But with Vincent's death, Nadia was the closest confidant Isadora had on this side of the asteroid belt. She needed someone to help her formulate their new strategy.

Even after catching up on sleep, she still felt numb and half-delirious from everything that'd happened. She tried to give Nadia a smile intended to be warm, but one which she feared would just look loopy.

"Why don't you sit," she said. Nadia eyed the chair sullenly, then finally sat down. "How are you doing?"

Nadia closed her eyes, took a deep breath, and let it out slowly. "I'm angry and confused and ashamed and hopeless and scared and frustrated. All at once. I'm not sure it makes sense." Her chest seemed to deflate as she went on.

Isadora gave her a sad grin. "All that is perfectly understandable. Did letting that out help?"

"Y'know...it actually kind of did." Nadia mustered a smile. "Thanks. What about you?"

"I'm still trying to process it all. I think my logical side has only barely caught up, but my emotional side hasn't at all. Honestly, I was hoping we could talk through some of the political implications. I like input, and you know I've always valued your insights. And I know you had a proposal you wanted to run by me."

Nadia nodded. "Of course. Go ahead."

Isadora leaned back in her chair, crossed her legs, and folded her hands in her lap. "The intelligence from Vincent changes everything on one hand, and nothing on the other. That is, the Offspring are still clearly the biggest threat to our people's livelihoods, and defeating them must be our priority.

"But on the other, I've been coming up with ways that Vincent's information about the *Preserver* could help us do just that. Right now, the biggest hurdle I'm running up against is that there just *isn't* any political will in Parliament to intervene and stop the conflict.

"But if the public knows that the *Preserver* could open up a wormhole to Earth, that could put pressure on Parliament to intervene. Vincent's information might very well be the missing piece of the puzzle we've been searching for. But there are problems with convincing the Union and the Natonese people that unleashing the *Preserver*'s full capability is a wise move."

The longer she went on, the more fidgety she got. Her hand moved to the desk, where her fingers gingerly flicked a data drive with Vincent's probe data back and forth. "Especially because the original plan was to use the *Preserver* as a conduit for an invading fleet to attack the system."

"Can I interject?" Nadia asked.

There I go rambling. She'd invited Nadia up to get input, and then she'd talked at her for the first few minutes. She waved her hand in a go-ahead gesture, nearly dropping the drive. "Always."

"Humans have been here before," Nadia said. "Every time the possibility of new exploration has come up, there were people who said it was too dangerous. Crossing the oceans, leaving Earth, leaving the Sol System...there were naysayers the whole time. And they always lost out."

Isadora's heart swelled at her words, and not just because she was making a case that Isadora's job might be easier than she'd thought. Nadia sounded more like her former self. The one Isadora had met after coming out of cryo originally.

But then again, she was essentially *also* saying that people were naturally dumb and took risks they probably shouldn't. Which was more in line with what Russ might've said if he were here.

Maybe there was space inside her for both ideas: that most people yearned to explore and to touch the stars, *and* that people's risk assessments were tragically misinformed. Maybe she could find a natural synthesis of her old idealism and her newfound cynicism.

Isadora refocused on the problem at hand. "That's very true. Another problem: I fear that if I take this to the Union government directly, they'll just classify everything. Even Tricia doesn't have that kind of pull over the bureaucracy, and it would be much more *convenient* for them to just sweep everything under the rug. Nothing would change at that point."

Nadia leaned forward in her chair, a newfound energy in her eyes. "Then *don't* take it to them directly."

Isadora's mind went through the possibilities rapidly. She pushed herself out of the chair and paced around the office. "You're saying that, if we decide to get out the information on the *Preserver*, I'd have to leak it. Have to seed the rumor into the general public first. Wait for it to spread like wildfire. That way, the Union government wouldn't be able to just put a lid on it and make it go away." Isadora mused for a moment, then added, "I bet Tricia might be upset with me when she finds out."

Nadia looked like she was about to jump out of her chair. "The Syndicate," she said breathlessly. "It's the answer to both of our problems."

Isadora cocked her head.

Nadia explained the situation on Ikkren: the search for Tori, the Horde leadership crisis and fracturing, how a raid on an occupied gunship hangar had failed. "Back during our last meeting on Obrigan, we came up with a plan to attack the problem from different angles," she continued. "You handle the politics, I try to win the war, Carson looks for the intel. But I think we need to reexamine that strategy. Because I don't know if I can make a dent in the Junta occupation without assistance from you.

"After seeing the situation on Ikkren, I've concluded that the only way to make the situation winnable is to force the Junta to withdraw at least some of their ships to Enther. And we know the Ashkagi rebels can put up a fight, but they're outgunned by the Junta's superior arsenal.

"That's where the black market comes in. If we can convince the Syndicate to funnel more weapons and ordnance to the Ashkagi rebels, in exchange for the information on the *Preserver*, we might tip the balance against the Junta on the home front. Then, the Syndicate could leak the *Preserver* intel to other information brokers at a profit."

Isadora found Nadia's idea darkly ironic. She stared at her for a long time until a single laugh escaped her. "It's funny. A long time ago, it was *Russ* urging me to get in bed with the black market. Giving him the go-ahead didn't help the spiral toward our near-conflict with the Union."

"I realize the irony, but things are different now," Nadia pressed. "Hell, *I'm* different. Tricia Favan trusts you, and our position is not as fragile as it used to be. Our one major vulnerable point is the *Preserver*. If we can find some way to turn the tides of the war *against* the Junta, and if Parliament comes to see an intervention as necessary, that could help protect the ship."

Isadora sighed. "I've been trying really hard to put the heat on Parliament to act. I've been racing from one end of Union space to the other, trying my best to grow the anti-war movement. But none of that has moved the needle."

"The information from Vincent will change that. If the Natonese public sees the vessel as a gateway to expansion, then I bet the anti-war movement will increase tenfold overnight. Giving the intel to the Syndicate is the best way to seed it out to the public—and it might just open up the possibility of pushing the Junta off Ikkren."

Isadora gazed downward. "I will need to give this a *lot* more thought," she said finally. "But I see the merits of what you're suggesting. And...and I think you may be right."

The two women stood up in unison and embraced. The enormity of everything that'd happened in the last two days had left so much unresolved, so much unprocessed, that Isadora didn't know where to start. Maybe embracing her friendship with Nadia was all she could really do.

A thought struck her. A half-remembered approval order she'd signed years ago, bringing one Leila Jibor and one Rashad Jibor out of cryo. "Your parents are on Ikkren, right?" she asked softly.

"...yes," Nadia said. "I haven't really gone to see them. Not with everything that's been happening. It didn't feel like the right time."

Isadora couldn't help but think of Meredith. Of her little baby girl, who was, somehow, almost an adult in her own right. "You should go see your mom and dad, Nadia. They want to see you. Trust me."

Nadia tensed up in her embrace. After the two broke apart, she said quietly, "The thought of taking time off to go see them doesn't seem fair. Not while so many lives are hanging in the balance."

"I've always hoped to be someone who would be there for Meredith in her darkest moments. There are times when this job hasn't allowed me to do that—and it's been one of my biggest regrets. I'm sure your parents want the same thing."

Uncertainty clouded Nadia's eyes. "Maybe. We'll see. If I have time. But I guess I should head out. We need to get back, need to catch up on the war effort. Really, the only reason I came to meet you in person was to run the Syndicate idea by you." She let out a hollow laugh.

"As always, I'm eternally grateful for all the times you've saved me. I owe you my life," Isadora said gently. "And be careful out there," she added as Nadia moved to the door.

This time, unlike when she'd departed Obrigan months ago, Nadia lingered. Smiled. "You too," she said warmly. Then departed.

Isadora let out a long sigh and returned to Vincent's seat. The room's emptiness felt more oppressive. Her confused muddle of emotions returned. Along with her unshakeable anxiety in the face of a chaotic universe.

But that wasn't all. There was a comfort, too. A comfort in the strength of her bond with Nadia. And the certainty that, despite the brave new world Vincent's revelations had unleashed, no matter where their divergent paths were leading them, the two of them would meet their challenges together.

CHAPTER 21

Something had changed in the Offspring camp, deep in the Enther jungles. Carson could feel it every time he went to the ideology sessions, where others talked over him or ignored his contributions. Every time he went to the canteen and no one bothered sitting with him. Every time he ran drills with the others and no one wanted to be on his team.

At first, Carson had been terrified his cover was about to be blown. But as the pall of suspicion followed him around for weeks, and nothing else happened, he'd realized something else was going on.

Almost everyone recruited into an organization like the Offspring had doubts. They weren't always as vocal about them, as Emil had been, but leaving your life behind for a meager existence never came without reservations.

For most recruits, voicing any of those doubts could lead to ostra-cization or worse. And with radical organizations preying on the so-cially isolated, doing anything to risk your standing in your new group was a nonstarter. Many recruits dealt with their repressed doubts by casting suspicion on their peers. Like Marcus had with Carson.

It was a process he could understand perfectly from a clinical per-spective, but watching it happen to him felt different. At least their unit hadn't deployed anywhere recently, so there was no reason to put himself in risky situations where he might get discovered. Then again, that meant there hadn't been any opportunities to prove his loyalty, either.

It also didn't help that he'd been feeling an increasing amount of pressure on him ever since his meeting with Noah Tasano. He'd eventu-ally gotten Emil to explain what Noah had meant about "Bitanu," about how Tanner had nearly succeeded in an operation to destroy the *Preserver*.

Knowing Tanner, he wouldn't stop at *nearly succeeded*. Time was running out for Carson to figure out exactly what he was planning.

Even with all the suspicion on him, he'd managed to sneak out at night and see what he could find on the camp's computer terminals. Russ had taught him a few rudimentary hacking skills in their time together, but unfortunately, that hadn't come to anything.

Nothing valuable was on a single camp's terminal stations, espe-cially not a camp without any major leadership figures. That left him back at square one: leaning on those higher above him in the hierar-chy for information. Except he needed to accelerate that process.

From Carson's perspective, that left a single option.

"People are looking at me all different now," he complained as he sat down next to Emil in the supply depot canteen. There were no rules regarding newer Offspring recruits eating with older ones, but it still seemed that his friendship with Emil was unusual. And useful, he hoped. He caught a half-dozen recruits at the other end of the table, giving him a dark look. Marcus caught his eye and sneered at him.

Emil shrugged, picking at the rations on his tray. "It's like I said back in Kal Jova. They're just frustrated. It doesn't have anything to do with you. It's shitty, but just ignore it, brother. It will pass in time." The man's lack of concern was all the more apparent since he didn't seem to care about being seen with Carson.

Carson picked at his rations. "If it's all the same, I'd like to talk to you," he murmured.

"Of course, brother. But really, you have nothing to worry about."

"Does now work?"

Emil chuckled and finished the rest of his rations. "I can tell you're taking this too seriously. Let's walk and talk. I promise, you should calm down."

Carson left the rest of his rations untouched and followed Emil out of the canteen. They passed through decrepit, bare concrete hallways where most of the light fixtures were hanging down by a single wire. They then took a handful of stairwells down until they exited the facility, heading for the surrounding jungle.

It hadn't rained in almost three days, a rarity on Enther. But the sky had been dreadfully overcast the whole time, and a thick layer of humidity had settled on the area.

Carson almost wished it were storming. The sweltering humidity made it feel like he was swimming as soon as he stepped outside. And despite Enther's temperate reputation, it was hot enough that he was almost always sweating. He wished the Offspring suits had temperature-regulating features. No such luck.

He and Emil talked absentmindedly the deeper they went into the jungle. It was avoidant small talk: how Emil still hadn't gotten used to all the trees on Enther, even after almost a year with the Offspring, having spent his whole life in Obrigan City.

Carson rattled off some of the fictitious stories about his past he and Juliet had made up long ago. Lying about his past came so easily now that he hardly even noticed it.

They arrived at a clearing with a downed tree. Emil sat down on the trunk with a grunt. "All right, brother," he said. "What did you want to talk about?"

Carson wiped his brow and inhaled. Back in his old practice, he'd tried something like this with a trio of particularly difficult ex-Primordial members. He'd exposed them to a widow of a solar panel worker who'd been killed by their group.

With the first patient, it was the breakthrough Carson had been waiting for. He'd been reading about the potential for restorative justice in cases of radicalization, and in that instance, it'd worked. The patient went on to stay in touch with the widow for years afterward.

Then Carson had tried it with the other two, and it backfired. It'd collapsed whatever relationship he'd built up with them. He'd come to think of restorative exposure to a victim as a sort of Hail Mary, a last-ditch attempt with a patient if nothing else was working.

And now, he was about to gamble everything on a tactic with a 33% success rate.

He looked up at the canopy far above, half imagining the ghosts of Juliet and Russ looking down on him. He wondered what they'd say if they could be here now, see what their sacrifices had come to.

If your instincts are telling you this is the right thing to do, then go for it, he imagined Juliet saying. *After all, your instincts are why we put you in this position in the first place.*

He almost chuckled. *You fucking idiot, what the fuck do you think you're doing, you're about to get yourself killed* was just as likely.

He liked imagining that Russ would be more supportive. *I hope you know what you're doing, son,* he'd say, an expression equal parts skeptical but kindly on his face.

Carson finally let out the breath he was holding. *Here goes nothing.* "Honestly, I'm worried about what everyone is saying about me because it's *true.*"

Emil blinked several times, then cocked his head.

"My name is Carson Erlinza, but I'm not at all who you think I am."

He was so nervous he hardly had the courage to look at Emil's face. The other man's visage was blank, incredulous. He continued. "I'm a refugee. I was born in Vancouver, on Earth. I boarded the *Preserver* along with 50 million others when the Hegemony attacked our home and forced us here."

"This is a joke, brother," Emil said. "A bad joke. I don't understand."

"You want to know what I did back on Earth? I was a *therapist,* Emil. I worked with former members of a group called Primordial. That's why my people's leadership chose me. They wanted someone who knew how to pass as an Offspring. I snuck into your ranks during the raid four months ago. The one where," Carson paused to swallow the lump in his throat, "the one where Tanner killed Russ Kama. I inputted my identity—my fake identity—into the recruits' shuttle databanks during the raid."

Emil's expression was still blank, but Carson saw an eruption of cognitive dissonance bubbling behind his pupils. Right now, he had three beliefs in his head: (1) the newars were subhuman vermin, (2) Carson was his closest friend at the moment, and (3) Carson was a newar.

Either the first belief had to go, or the second.

"But I want to let you know that the other things I've said to you *haven't* been lies. I believe you're a good man, Emil. You've never killed anyone. Never even *hurt* anyone. You're here because you were mistreated by your parents. Mistreated by your own government. I see you, I hear you, I get you. I'm not here to hurt you."

Carson thought he could see Emil's mouth quiver, but he couldn't tell whether it was coming from wrath or cathartic release. Right now, the most important thing was to establish that a *dirty newar* could in fact be a real person, with a real family, real hopes, real fears, real goals. That had to be the first step in deprogramming Emil's mind.

"Remember what you said to me?" he pressed. "That you wanted to be somebody who would stand up and defend your fellow Natonese people? That's the same thing I've been doing. You and I are in the same situation.

"I have a brother, Stacy. My parents adopted him when he was seven and I was thirteen. He's all I have out here. I'm *scared* for him. Everyone's scared. We were chased from our home by people who wanted us dead. We just want a chance to live our lives. We're not invaders. We don't want to harm anyone."

Carson held out his palms in a gesture of peace. "My people's leadership wanted me to come here to find something, *anything*, that would keep more of us from dying. That's it. I'm not here to hurt anyone. I'm here to find information that I can use to save my people."

When he met Emil's gaze, he saw only disbelief and anger. Hard to tell which emotion was stronger. "This can't be true," Emil growled.

"It is. All of it."

Emil pushed himself to his feet and stepped toward him, a dark look in his eyes. "Don't" was all Carson got out before he lunged at him.

"I hate you!" he screamed as he tackled Carson. He fell to the ground with a hard thud. Emil pummeled the sides of his head with his fists. He raised his forearms to block the blows, but one of them still got through. His right temple throbbed violently.

Carson twisted underneath Emil until his hips were free. He rose with a sudden force and thrust the other man off him. His head still felt like it was spinning, but at least he wasn't trapped. Emil pushed himself up and swung at him once more. It was easy enough to duck. Then he shoved Emil back.

"I don't want to fight you," he said, keeping his voice steady despite the adrenaline surge of combat, the humidity, the wound on his head.

"I hate you!" Emil repeated, although this time there were tears intermingled with the rage.

That meant the cognitive dissonance was working. Like a vaccine, the revelation had to worm its way through Emil's body until it entered the bloodstream, where it could inoculate him from Tanner Keltin's brainwashing.

He lunged at Carson once more, who placed his hands on Emil's shoulders to keep him at bay. Emil clawed at his eyes and neck.

The harder he tried to get at him, the more fatigued his movements became. At last, the man shrunk back wearily and began to cry. "I hate you," he whimpered.

"I *don't* hate you," Carson said. "I believe in you. And I trust you. That's why I'm telling you all this. If you want, we can go back to base and you can tell everyone else about me. About who I really am.

"But I'm betting you won't. Because you've been wondering for weeks now whether this has all been worth it, and you know, somewhere deep down, that I care about you."

Emil brushed the mud and moss off his suit slowly. The man looked utterly crushed. His shoulders slumped, and he couldn't take his eyes off the ground.

Carson had just done a number on Emil's psyche in the time span of a few minutes. It was the time for gentleness now. And hope—hope that Carson's instincts were right, that the cognitive dissonance was now shaping new pathways inside his mind.

Without saying anything, Emil stood up, turned around, and started walking toward the depot. Carson fell into step behind him. Probably best not to talk to him. To let him really sit on the revelation, linger on it.

And then decide what he was going to do about it.

In another fifteen silent minutes, they were back at the stairwell leading inside the facility. The sounds of excitement rushed toward them as soon as they reentered the canteen.

In another few seconds, almost a dozen Offspring sprinted over to meet them. "Did you hear?" and "Have you checked your wrist terminal?" and "Were you two talking about the news?" all spewed forth in a jumbled mess.

Emil didn't make eye contact with Carson. He furrowed his brow and checked his wrister. Carson looked down at his own device. Sure enough, he'd gotten an emergency notification. He guessed it must have gone off while they'd been grappling.

Apparently, the Ashkagi rebels had launched a major offensive on the planet's capital city of Caphila. During their talk, Noah had told

Carson he'd been planning something big. This must be it.

Assaulting the planetary capital was a brazen move, but with most of the Junta military off-world, it wasn't purely suicidal. Still, an attack on the capital implied the rebels possessed a far greater supply of weapons and ordnance than they knew about.

"We're gonna go squash those motherfuckers, right?" Marcus asked Emil eagerly. Then he turned to Carson. Must've registered a bruise on his face, because next came: "What happened to *him*?"

"Tripped on a log," Carson said quickly. Marcus' eyes shot to Emil, who hesitated, but eventually nodded in confirmation.

Carson studied Emil's face. Uncertainty clouded his eyes—he'd always been skeptical of their participation in Enther's civil war, after all—but Carson couldn't figure out whether it was uncertainty about going to Caphila, telling everyone else about Carson's real identity, or his entire justification for the Offspring cause.

More likely, his mind was simultaneously going through all three issues at once.

"We struck a deal with the Junta," Emil said finally, adopting a deathly quiet voice. He still hadn't looked up from his wrister. "Tanner would want us to go aid them."

"What were you two talking about, by the way?" a voice came from the back of the crowd.

Emil turned and looked straight at Carson for the first time since they'd left the forest clearing. He raised his chin to meet Emil's gaze.

In reality, the pause might've only lasted a second or two. To Carson, it felt like a lifetime.

Images flashed through his brain: his old practice in Vancouver, hiking the mountains of British Columbia with Stacy, boarding the *Preserver*, working with Juliet, flying with Nadia Jibor and Russ on the *Exemplar* before the latter's ultimate sacrifice. Everything had brought him to this moment. To this one desperate gambit.

"Nothing," Emil said. The tension oozed out of Carson's body. "We were just catching up. Now come on. We need to get ready to move out. We're going to Caphila."

CHAPTER 22

The whirlwind that Isadora's life had become showed no signs of slowing down. If anything, it was only getting more intense.

She'd spent over three weeks on a transport from Bitanu back to Obrigan, mostly sleepless, her mind constantly switching between grief at Vincent's murder, disbelief at his revelation, and trying to figure out what the hell to do next.

The more she'd been ruminating on Nadia's proposal to give Vincent's information and probe data to the Syndicate, the more it felt like the best option. Or, perhaps, the least bad one. It was always damnably hard to tell the difference.

Which was how Isadora found herself on a private yacht orbiting Obrigan. It was something of an open secret that one of the major fronts for the Syndicate's operations on Obrigan was the seedy world of high-end art collectors, the kind who flew around on private luxury yachts in orbit, avoiding both the hustle and bustle of the capital city as well as the largely undeveloped hinterland. That, at least, was the takeaway of the research her staff had done for her.

As soon as Isadora had stepped aboard the yacht, she'd been handed a complimentary glass of champagne by a man in a tuxedo. Then been told that a meeting would soon be arranged with a high-level Syndicate representative—high-level enough that Isadora had felt going in person would be the best sign of respect, rather than dispatching Katrina—and urged to make herself comfortable in the gallery while she waited.

She sipped her champagne and strolled across the lush, carpeted floor, looking at the various paintings hanging on the wall. There were a handful of other patrons in the gallery, each clad in a synthetic jacket or a high-necked sweater. All looked elderly and effete. Isadora contemplated whether they didn't know that the yacht's ownership was in bed with the black market, or whether they knew but didn't care.

As she moved down a row of paintings, she received a short art history of the Natonus System. The first paintings were rough, rugged depictions of frontier life in the 2310s and 2320s, back when the first settlers arrived in Natonus.

She was amazed at the portrayals of early Obrigan City as nothing more than a chaotic blend of prefab shelters, not too different from the colonies her people had set up along the outer rim. Rough, taut lines defined these paintings. Although few depicted people, the human subjects that appeared looked equal parts tough and shrewd.

Isadora moved on to a series of paintings she was pretty sure were from the middle of the last century. She'd picked up a decent amount of second-hand knowledge of Natonese art from Meredith, who'd in turn picked it up from Rebecca, who was into that sort of thing.

She'd expected these paintings to be triumphant, depicting the success of the settlement project as haphazard colonies transformed into glistening cities. Instead, a series of gritty portraits greeted her: the haggard beggar in the shadow of a corporate skyscraper, the emaciated frontier settler suffering from a poor harvest, the mercenary looking out at a hapless colony with predatory eyes.

She even saw a painting that depicted New Arcena, with individuals from all corners of the Natonus System coming together to help Isadora's people get the settlement set up.

Well. At least I've got the wealthy art snobs on my side. Then again, she supposed having the well-connected, right-thinking clientele of a private art yacht was, in fact, a promising sign. Elite public opinion was a powerful card to have in your hand.

Isadora strolled forward, coming to a long viewscreen that gave a breathtaking view of the Obrigan planetscape. The night lights of the capital were sparking to life as sunset descended on the city. The surrounding space was dark enough that she could make out her own reflection in the viewing panel.

She looked powerful. Regal, even. Far more than she felt on the inside. She'd been doing her job for so long that the little things—how to carry yourself, how to square your shoulders, the proper facial expression to wear in each setting—had become second nature. Her eyes looked darker, somehow more secretive than she'd remembered. Like they'd retreated into the hollows of her face.

She looked like a political animal. *Was* a political animal. She was here, aboard a private yacht with powerful elites, ready to meet a representative of the most notorious black market organization in Natonese space.

Earlier, she'd attended a security briefing analyzing the Offspring attack on Bitanu. Later, she'd booked an appearance on a media station to make her case against the outer rim war.

Earlier in her tenure, power had been something she'd either faked, or hadn't bothered thinking about. Now, her working definition of *power* was that it meant learning how to assert control over society in multiple ways, pulling whatever levers were available to her.

Mobilizing public opinion, rubbing shoulders with the powerful, strategic planning, embracing the dark side of politicking—all were different facets of the same job. Because at the end of the day, millions of lives were depending on her, and *that* was what mattered most.

Often, she'd regretted the last time she'd worked with the Syndicate. Or rather, sent Russ to deal with them on her behalf. It'd backfired when the weapons he'd bartered for hadn't made them any safer, and then the Syndicate may have played a minor role in smuggling the explosives used by an Offspring operative to attack New Arcena.

This current endeavor probably had a number of unintended consequences waiting for her down the line, too. Whatever they were, Isadora had a feeling they wouldn't be as severe as the consequences of *not* bringing a swift end to the war.

And if working with the Syndicate again truly was a disastrous decision? Well, then her successors could sort it out. Moral judgment was a luxury afforded to historians sitting in the comfort of dusty offices.

Really, the only person likely to pass moral judgment on her that she cared about was her daughter. Isadora saw the break in the facade of the powerful woman staring back at her in the viewscreen. Meredith would be eighteen in a little over half a year. It felt like she'd just turned seventeen. *That's just how it's always going to be, moving forward.*

Isadora heard footsteps behind her, and turned to see two well-dressed, burly men approaching her. "She's ready to see you now," one said. She wondered who, exactly, *she* was, but followed the two men politely.

The two enforcers led her down several hallways, each one lined with paintings Isadora wished she had longer to examine. There were a couple of absurdist statues erected at the hallway's termini, the kind that she didn't have any hope of understanding without a thorough reading of the associated description plate.

They arrived at an office with gold-crusted door handles. She got all her eye rolling done by the time the two enforcers pulled the doors open for her. They beckoned her to enter. Isadora finished the last of her champagne. One of the enforcers took the empty glass from her.

The meeting room itself was mostly bare, with a lush carpeted floor and a pair of recliners facing each other. Two gold statues of naked human bodies adorned the far wall, on either side of a viewscreen that spanned the entire exterior.

Isadora had assumed she was in the room by herself until she heard a hoarse voice clear its throat from behind her.

Skulking in the shadows of the far corner was another woman. Shorter than her, she sported a violet suit, composed mostly of various plastic shell pieces on top of mesh fabrics. Half her head was shaved, while the other half was combed to the side. Her skin was a leathery shade of mahogany.

Isadora recognized her instantly. Lena Veridor: the head of the entire Syndicate.

It took a real effort not to keep her eyebrows from raising. When she'd had her staff set up a covert meeting between her and the Syndicate, she'd assumed she'd be meeting with someone relatively powerful, but not the woman sitting at the apex of the entire criminal empire. The impression she'd gotten from her previous dealings with the Syndicate was that Lena preferred to work through intermediaries, at least at the outset of a negotiation.

"Isadora Satoro," she introduced herself, sticking her hand out.

Lena just eyed her coolly. "You look like a serious person," she said at last. "I, too, am a serious person. So I don't expect you requested this meeting to waste my time." She jerked her head over to the recliners—presumably, her way of asking Isadora if she'd like to take a seat.

She walked over, sat down, crossed her legs, and let a thin smile spread across her face. "Does that line work on a lot of people?" she asked, using a tone just innocent enough to be incredibly snarky.

Lena looked at her coolly. "Worked on the last one of you people who came to see me."

Grief gripped Isadora's heart for a fleeting instant as she contemplated the time she'd dispatched Russ to Zoledo. His proposal to work with the Syndicate had been part of why Isadora had fired him. And now, she was doing the same thing, after dumping all the blame on him.

It was just another entry in the endless list of apologies she'd never get to make to him.

"I suppose it *would* be relatively easy to intimidate a newly arrived refugee, back from when we only barely had a single colony established," Isadora said. She knew enough from Riley's reports on working with the Syndicate that staying composed in the face of their intimidation tactics was paramount.

Lena continued to study her with predatory eyes. "Wasn't under the impression that your people's number of settlements had any bearing on our interaction."

"You know as well as I do that power gives people options," Isadora countered.

A quick flash of a sneer from Lena was the best indication yet that she was successfully testing her patience. "Obviously," she said. "But now, you're on my turf."

Another conclusion of Riley's report was that the Syndicate respected raw strength first and foremost. If politics and charm couldn't do the trick, hardball aggression *might*. Isadora decided to shift tactics.

"Let me be *absolutely* clear about this," she said, her tone darkening. "My staff knows exactly where I am. I've got a nano-tracking beacon sitting in my gut, relaying this yacht's location to our embassy. If I don't report back in the next half-hour, those coordinates get forwarded to the Union military. I'm sure they'd happily jump at the chance to wipe out the head of the solar black market in a single missile strike."

She studied Lena, whose poker face was legendary, according to Riley. "So. What do you want?" she finally said.

"Weapons," Isadora said. She didn't get the feeling Lena was particularly interested in playing political games. Might as well get straight to the point.

"Seems to be a common request every time one of your people comes to me for help."

"These aren't for us," Isadora clarified. "We want the Syndicate to smuggle weapons to the Ashkagi rebels on Enther. Enough to help turn the tide of the civil war."

Lena nodded. Isadora figured explaining herself would be an insult to her intelligence. It was relatively common knowledge that the Junta and the Offspring were working together. Same with Nadia's ongoing participation in the resistance movement on Ikkren. Even with Isadora's disingenuous public denunciations of Nadia's actions, she imagined it wouldn't be difficult for Lena to connect the dots.

"And your plan to pay for the weapons shipments?"

Isadora leaned forward. "Information."

"You people never want to just pay for things, do you?"

"Trust me. This information is worth more than whatever sum I could hope to fork over. I know the Syndicate has worked with high-end information brokers all over the core worlds. They'll pay you handsomely for the intelligence I'm offering."

Lena's face remained unchanged, but she paused before responding.

Isadora's own thoughts shifted to Vincent, now that she was essentially going through with his exact proposal: get the intel about the *Preserver* out, which could eventually make defending the vessel a top priority for the Union, and force them to intervene and end the ongoing war.

She'd wondered whether her fondness for Vincent was clouding her judgment, made all the worse by the way he'd died. Her various emotions surrounding the man she'd thought she knew—grief, guilt, disbelief—had made it necessary to get a second opinion.

But she'd brought the intel to Riley, who'd combed through his data drive and had come to the same conclusion: the Hegemony had collapsed in the century while they were in transit to the Natonus System. Opening a wormhole back to the Sol System wouldn't lead to a sudden invasion.

"I want to know, exactly, how valuable your information is before I begin smuggling weapons to Enther," Lena said at last.

Isadora leaned back, placed her hands in her lap, interlaced her fingers, and grinned. "You can't expect me to hand over everything I have before you've sent over any weapons at all. Making, say, 20% of the total shipment in advance would be a sign of good faith. I'd feel comfortable sharing my information after that, at which point you would complete the remaining 80% of the order."

"10%," Lena said flatly. "Don't push it. And I want to know the general topic of the information."

"15%," Isadora countered. "And all I can say is: my information details new options for high-speed space transport."

"You mean, schematics for new thruster technology?"

"I mean something that would open up new options for extrasolar exploration and development."

Lena went back to her blank expression. An exaggerated rise and fall of her chest was the only sign that internal contemplation had resumed. "15% is still a lot," she said finally. *At least it wasn't a no.*

"May I remind you that the last time we dealt with your organization, you betrayed us and helped smuggle explosives for the Offspring?" Isadora said. She kept the thin smile on her face, but narrowed her eyes.

Lena shrugged. "Business."

"15% is a gesture of goodwill from you. An apology, if you will, for stabbing us in the back after we generously allowed you to set up operations in the outer rim."

Isadora looked at the crime boss' face, and couldn't decide whether she'd already made up her mind and was toying with her, or whether there was genuine contemplation going on behind her stony visage.

She'd been fond of drawing out the silences between her responses, but this one seemed to last longer than any of the previous ones. Isadora liked interpreting that as a positive sign.

"Okay," she said at last. "You have a deal."

CHAPTER 23

Nadia hadn't decided yet whether *emotional train wreck* or *adrenaline-fueled blur* was a better descriptor for the last few weeks. After a solemn flight from Bitanu back to Ikkren—where she'd spent most of her time in her cabin cycling between mourning Vincent and trying to wrap her head around his revelations—she and her crew had gotten back in touch with the Horde leadership.

Tori had dispatched them on a few information runs, where they slipped past Junta security checkpoints in the *Exemplar* to deliver intelligence to resistance cells across the planet.

And then, several weeks later, the tides turned.

Four of the eight Junta warships had departed Ikkren orbit and were on a trajectory back for Enther. Two others had risen to high orbit, perhaps to be recalled soon. Whatever Isadora was doing to funnel support and funds to the Ashkagi rebels on Enther was working. That gave Nadia and the Horde resistance their opening.

The only problem was, they still needed a way to actually hit the remaining Junta warships. And with the bulk of the Horde's gunship armada destroyed, that meant they had to think of something else.

Eventually, Boyd had come up with an idea. There was a defunct missile battery located in the ruins of the original Modrin colony, destroyed back during the war with the Union a decade earlier. Boyd felt confident he could repair the turret and get it back to working order.

But repairing the weapon was only half the problem. The other: the turret possessed no real ordnance. Which led to Nadia, Boyd, and Derek heading into the Ikkren wastelands to find the wreckage of a Union frigate from the last war. The plan was for them to scour what warheads they could find within the wreckage.

Nadia took her first steps onto the frigate's decaying hull. It seemed like the entire ship groaned under her weight. Snow and ice had crept up the sides as the hull had slowly slipped further into the ground.

"All right," Boyd said from behind her. "Shouldn't be too hard to get to weapons control. Then we just need to override a decade-old security system and withdraw their warheads."

"And hope their missiles are still functional," Derek added grimly.

"Optimistic, aren't we?" Boyd said.

Nadia opened her mouth to respond, but the wind chose that moment to hurtle across the early morning sky. Her teeth just chattered instead.

Normally, sunrise was one of her favorite times of day, but the cloud cover on Ikkren was so intense, and the size of the Natonus star so small, that none of the orange or pink rays she'd seen on the

Natonese core worlds were visible. Instead, it was just cold and windy.

As the wind continued to howl, the decrepit warship groaned once more. She placed her footfalls carefully. "At least the Horde had the good graces to shoot this ship down in the middle of the tundra," she said, "as opposed to nestled against the edge of a cliff, or something like that."

The others chuckled, and the trio pressed onward. After about a hundred feet of walking along the top of the engine section, Nadia finally got used to the creaking of the metal.

And then a chunk of the vessel disappeared beneath her.

Nadia opened her mouth in surprise, but her body staggered violently before she could let out a cry. Her exposed foot fell forward.

Falling.

Further.

She was fairly sure she could hear Boyd and Derek calling after her as she fell into the dark, cavernous interior of the warship. *Use your thrusters*, she tried to tell herself, but her head was disoriented from the wild spin of her body. When she finally pressed the button on her wrist, her thrusters fired unevenly.

Which only worsened the vector of her fall.

The light beams on either side of her helmet danced wildly across the dim interior. As she continued to fall and her head swiveled to face the floor, it looked a lot closer than it had a fraction of a second earlier. She frantically jabbed at her thruster controls to execute a deceleration burn.

It only partially worked.

She avoided slamming into the ground with full force, but landed awkwardly on her side. For all of two seconds, she thought she was fine. And then a sharp pain emerged from her left hip, its intensity growing with each passing second.

Boyd and Derek called after her. Nadia turned—painfully—onto her back, just in time to see the two of them use their own suit's thrusters to land gracefully. *Way to rub it in.* What was almost a laugh instead became an agonizing, stabbing pain from her lower extremities.

When she tried to push herself up, her left leg couldn't move.

She looked down. Her legs resembled a number four, and her left foot was completely numb. "Okay, *that's* dislocated," Boyd said as soon as he got close.

Thanks, asshole, she wanted to say. The injury couldn't be that bad if her desire to banter with her crew was still in place. And then a flash of white-hot pain coursed through her. A reminder that, okay, maybe it *was* that bad.

Boyd took a deep breath. "Okay. Checklist. Back when I used to visit construction sites in my old job, we had procedures for injuries like this. Not that they were particularly common, or anything, but—"

"—Boyd," Derek interjected, "maybe it would be better to figure out how to help Nadia instead of giving us a history lesson."

Nadia winced. "My vote's with Derek."

"Right. Of course." Boyd stood up and surveyed the surroundings. "First, we need to keep the injury site as warm as possible."

"It's Ikkren," Nadia and Derek said at approximately the same time. "Safe to say we're gonna have to skip that step," she added.

"Fair enough. Step two: we need to reset the bone as fast as possible. It'd be a hell of a lot easier to do this back at the *Exemplar*, but we'd have to use our jets to carry Nadia out, and that'd just make things worse. So we need to do it here. The few times I did this at my old job, we'd use anesthesia to help. Because otherwise, this is gonna *hurt*."

Boyd searched a first aid kit strapped to the back of his utility belt. "Nothing on hand. But this is a warship. I figure it shouldn't be hard to find the old med bay. Might even be some old painkillers and anesthesia in there, if we're lucky."

Nadia tried to remember the last time she'd gone under. Her mind came up blank. Was it really getting her wisdom teeth removed as a teenager? But she had an even greater concern than that. "This warship's been dead for over a decade," she protested. "Won't any meds have expired?"

Boyd gave her a reproachful glance. "This is the *twenty-fifth century*, Nadia. We've figured out how to make anesthesia that doesn't expire. And trust me, I won't reset your leg until I'm sure you're out."

She winced. "How comforting."

"If it doesn't work, I could always go fetch some of the Ikkren grain liquor we have on the *Exemplar*," Derek said. "Enough of that, and she'll be out cold."

Her wince deepened. "Honestly, I think I'd rather take a chance on potentially expired anesthetic than drink any more of that stuff."

Derek shrugged. "Your loss."

He helped Boyd scan the area. "There's plenty of scrap metal we can use as a makeshift stretcher. That way, we can keep her stable while we search for the meds."

"Good idea. Let's go scrounge something up. And," Boyd said, turning to Nadia, "don't, uh, go anywhere," he added weakly.

"Wasn't planning on it." Side-splitting stabs of pain returned as her two crewmates retreated from her field of vision. Leaving her on the floor, shivering in agony.

Now that she could finally pay attention to her surroundings, it looked like she'd fallen into some kind of engine control room. There were a few ruined control terminal stations scattered around, along with a handful of crashed maintenance turbolifts and railing units.

If she hadn't gotten injured, it would've been an easy walk to weapons control. Most Union warships' weapons systems were just ahead of the aft engine section.

But now, Boyd and Derek would have to journey deeper into the heart of the old vessel to find the med bay. She let out a frustrated sigh. She wanted to find the weapons, get the old Modrin turret set up, and launch the operation *now*. Patience had never been one of her virtues.

How *could* it be, after all, when so many people had died? At first, it was just the victims of the Offspring bombing at New Arcena. Then it was Russ, who'd given his own life to save hers. Now Vincent. So many people who'd placed their hopes on Nadia were gone.

Time was running out to stop Tanner from expanding that list. And all she had to show for it, at the moment, was lying crippled in the belly of a decade-old crashed warship.

At least Boyd and Derek returned soon, a large piece of rended metal in tow. "Your stretcher," Boyd said with a weak grin.

They slid Nadia under the metal sheet carefully. Even the gentle movement produced a boiling pain that spread through her lower body. When they got her loaded on the metal sheet, Boyd and Derek departed once more, with a promise that they'd be back soon with anesthesia. Hopefully.

While they were gone, she tried to distract herself from the pain by examining the ship more closely. In a way, the decrepit vessel looked beautiful. The way the ice and frost had infiltrated the peeling metal, had collapsed the pipe system, was mesmerizing. Like it was an infectious growth that'd reclaimed the ship.

The sound of Boyd and Derek's voices echoing in the halls announced their return. Boyd walked over with a bottle and an injector in hand. "Let me look up your vitals. I'm syncing my wrister to the *Exemplar*'s computer, getting your numbers from the med bay so I can prepare the right dosage. I don't need long—just enough to reset the hip bone."

"Honestly, I'm just glad we didn't see any bodies in there," he continued, while reviewing the stats on his wrister and preparing the syringe. Nadia knew he was just trying to distract her, but she appreciated the effort nonetheless. "Watched too many horror vids as a kid. Crawling through a derelict starship, bodies everywhere...no thank you."

"Most likely, the crew would've jettisoned in the escape pods during reentry," Derek chimed in. "And after the war, Tori allowed the Union military to reclaim any of their dead still left on the planet."

"Generous. But I guess she told them not to pick their wreckages clean for parts or weapons, right?"

Derek let out a deep laugh. "No. Not *that* generous."

"Okay," Boyd said, approaching Nadia with a partially filled syringe. He pulled her left glove off and gently slid the tip of the needle into a vein on the top of her hand. "Want to count to three for me?"

She took a deep breath.

"One," she said, but her teeth chattered violently. "Two." She tried to ignore a growing anxiety about letting Boyd and Derek take the reins for the rest of the operation. Unloading her burdens on them seemed neither fair, nor right.

She didn't even make it to three.

.   .   .

The world seemed funny to Nadia when she woke up. She was in a strange ship she didn't recognize, and she felt groggy. She blinked several times. The silhouette of a man appeared in the doorway, who she recognized as Boyd after several seconds.

"She's up!" he called over his shoulder.

"Hi," Nadia said, flashing what surely must've been a dumb smile. "Is everything okay?"

"Guess you're feeling all right," he said, walking to her stretcher. "I reset your hip bone while you were out. Then we injected you with regrowth gel and made you a makeshift cast."

Nadia looked down at a haphazardly constructed plastic shell that enveloped her left leg. "Oh, and I gave you some mild painkillers too," Boyd added. "You should be fine in a few weeks, but until then, we're gonna need to keep your hip immobilized."

A few weeks? she thought, despairing. She needed to push the Junta off Ikkren, needed to put the squeeze back on the Offspring, needed to find Tanner Keltin and finish the fight once and for all.

Hard to do that while immobilized. "So...you want me to stay here while you two fly around Ikkren?" she asked, her words coming out choked up.

"Hardly. Derek!"

Derek appeared behind him. He was dragging a cargo net full of inert warheads inside. In his other hand, a small, egg-shaped capsule. About three-feet tall, it looked almost equivalent to the size of Nadia's upper body.

He handed the capsule to Boyd. "We found this in the warship's emergency stockpile room while you were out."

"It's a hoverseat," Boyd said, setting the contraption down next to Nadia's stretcher and pressing a button. The device hummed and rose a couple of feet off the ground. "I realize it's not ideal—"

"—it's exactly what I need," Nadia said, as the other two helped her into the capsule. A control panel on the interior made it easy enough to operate. She practiced moving the hoverseat in a small lap.

She then looked at Derek with his haul of warheads in tow. "I'm guessing the mission was successful."

"Boyd hacked the old Union security system and depowered the projectiles," he said. "They're safe to transport to the Modrin ruins."

Nadia was both impressed and taken aback. They'd hardly even *needed* her. They'd reached the med bay, retrieved anesthesia and painkillers, given her the correct dosage, treated her, then figured out a way to acquire the mission objective on their own.

All she'd done was get hurt and make everything harder.

Somehow, that relaxed her. She thought back to her frustrations from earlier, about how so many people who believed in her had perished. Maybe she didn't have to put so much weight on her own shoulders. She'd put together a good team, one that knew how to adapt on the fly. How to push forward, even when she was incapacitated.

She sank into the recesses of her capsule. Her heartbeat slowed, for what felt like the first time in years. Boyd and Derek went back to casually conversing as they made their way toward the vessel's exit.

Nadia stayed silent, appreciating their company, enjoying taking a backseat for once. And wondering—for the first time since she'd woken up in the Natonus System—if not everything depended solely on her.

CHAPTER 24

They were getting closer to Caphila. The loudening sounds of battle—the thud-ping of plasma fire, the hiss of missiles, the sharp boom of flak cannons—were a dead giveaway. Carson couldn't see out of the windowless interior of the Offspring transport, but he figured the planetary capital was probably in visual range.

Sure enough, they touched down within the minute. One of the Offspring lieutenants—one of the ones from another regiment, who Carson had never met before, with a thick mustache and angry eyes—was giving them orders. Orders that he was only half paying attention to.

When he'd talked to Noah Tasano, he'd been told the Ashkagi rebels were planning something, something that he could help with. Noah must've meant the attack on Caphila.

This was his moment. He'd need to sneak away from the Off-spring—he wasn't ready to break his cover, not yet—and figure out some way to assist the rebel fighters besieging the city.

Carson's eyes flickered to where Emil was standing, behind the mustachioed lieutenant. He leaned against the bulkhead, his eyes fixed on his feet. The two of them hadn't spoken since Carson had told him who he really was. From what he'd seen, Emil had hardly spoken to *anyone*.

Which was fair. After a tough session, it wasn't uncommon for some of Carson's patients in his old life to need some alone time. Some needed more than others. And what he'd sprung on Emil was far tougher than anything he'd ever put a patient through.

But as hard as he wanted to analyze Emil clinically, he could never truly see the other man as *only* a patient. He was both far more dan-gerous—given what he knew about Carson's real identity—and, inex-plicably, his *friend*. On some level.

Emil looked up and caught Carson looking at him. He averted his eyes immediately. He didn't want to pressure Emil, not in any way. The only thing to do was wait for all the logical contradictions he'd ingested as part of his radicalization process to come crashing down.

Or not. It could all still result in an utter failure and a summary execution.

The door to the Offspring transport swung open, and the others filed out in a chaotic mess. Carson waited for most of them to exit before unstrapping from his seat. He checked to make sure his hand-gun was properly holstered and followed the rest of them out.

A fierce storm raged outside. Torrential, angry rain pummeled the ground while flashes of lightning illuminated the air battle. Rebel gunships dove for the city in attack runs, usually chased away by the dark emission of a flak cannon.

The angry-looking lieutenant shouted at them that they were headed to one of the forward guard outposts inside the city, where they'd report to the local Junta commanding officer.

The fight must've been coming from the other side of Caphila. The sounds of battle were loud, but Carson couldn't make out any actual troops or weapon reports in the vicinity. The Offspring hustled toward the outer wall of the capital. The battlements were entirely made of stone, a large guard tower every few dozen feet.

A wooden gate swung open as they approached. A squad of Junta soldiers, clad in green combat armor, met them. "This way! Hurry!" one of them said, and led the Offspring regiment toward the base of one of the nearby towers.

Carson wiped his brow as he ran in formation. A mixture of sweat and rain coated his palm. Then he looked skyward. More flashes of lightning. More frantic exchanges of plasma bursts and missiles, more cannon roars. More screams and fiery crashes and death. His body seemed to shake—violently, briefly, uncontrollably—with every shattering cannon blast.

As they continued to run through the city streets, they passed by a golden statue of none other than General Michael Azkon, the head chairman of the Junta. Carson remembered that the planet used to be ruled by a theocratic Ashkagi government, and that it was common to see statues of religious iconography spread across the capital streets. After the fall of the old Theocracy, the general must've melted down the old statues and refashioned them into likenesses of himself.

The capital city's skyline felt dystopian. Giant holo-billboards reported exhortations to the populace to watch for rebel activity: REPORT ANYTHING SUSPICIOUS TO THE AUTHORITIES, one said;

KNOW THE SIGNS FOR SUBVERSIVE ASHKAGI ACTIVITY, another said; SUPPORT THE AUTHORITIES, KEEP OUR PLANET SAFE! read a third.

Just as Carson finished reading all of them, a rebel gunship swooped in low. A flurry of plasma fire ripped through the second one, so that it briefly displayed only SUBVERSIVE ASHKAGI ACTIVITY, before the holo-emitters completely shut off and crashed to the ground.

The irony got a chuckle out of him.

The Offspring regiment reached the guard tower and began climbing a spiral, stone staircase up to a small command center. A handful of uniformed Junta officers paced around anxiously, looking at a variety of holo-screens and datapad reports.

"They shouldn't be doing so well," the commander said in a crass voice. He was thick-bodied, with the deepest dimples Carson had ever seen on a person's face before. "Where did the rebels get this kind of firepower?"

"We're here to help," the mustachioed Offspring lieutenant announced.

"Finally," the Junta commander grumbled. "Somehow, the damn rebels have access to targeted artillery batteries. Their gunships are painting targets and lining them up for precision strikes from beyond our ground forces' striking range."

"You want us to take out their batteries?"

"Precisely. We're short-staffed with most of our fighting forces bogged down on Ikkren. This is your people's responsibility." The sneer in the large Junta commander's lip seemed to suggest his personal opinions on the Junta's partnership with the Offspring.

"We've had to pull back some of our fleet from Ikkren to deal with the intensified rebel threat," he continued. "Our flagship, the *Sancti-tude*, should be arriving soon and will dispatch fighters to regain air superiority. It's your job to make sure they haven't taken out all our defenses by the time the *Sanctitude* arrives with air support."

"Understood. We'll work our way through the jungles and assault the rebels' line. Let's move out!" the Offspring lieutenant said.

Carson turned back around and descended the staircase, along with the others. He was thankful to get back outside, despite the storm and the terrifying proximity of the battle. It was damn stuffy in that command center.

The more he thought about the Junta commander's orders, the more it sounded like he was throwing the Offspring into a meat grinder. The Ashkagi knew the territory better than they did, and a head-on attack on their position would lead to massive casualties.

Considering that so few of the Offspring were actually battle-tested, Carson was fairly sure it'd be a slaughter. And given how na-ked the commander's contempt for them had been, maybe that was the point.

So he had to get away, but for more reasons than to just save his own skin. The commander had sounded worried that the Ashkagi re-bels could actually *win* the fight for the capital.

Carson wasn't quite sure how the rebels had gained access to ad-vanced firepower—enough to decisively turn the tide of the civil war—in such a short amount of time, but he decided not to spend too much time questioning his luck.

If the rebels could take Caphila, that could alter the balance of power in the civil war, and potentially change the course of the larger outer rim conflict. And it'd be a major setback to the Offspring, to presumably whatever Tanner Keltin was planning.

Seeing as he hadn't made much headway on figuring out those plans, stalling out the Offspring seemed to be a wiser short-term goal. And assuming he could help the rebels without blowing his cover, it'd still leave open the possibility of continuing his spy work.

He looked up as a cannon burst took out a rebel gunship. The flaming wreckage careened until it took out a chunk of the outer battlements. If the arriving Junta fighter squadrons could turn the tide of the battle, he had to find a way to nullify that advantage. The easiest way to do that, he realized, was turning the city's air defenses against the reinforcements.

Most automated military ordnance ran on some kind of IFF system. If he could find the controls for the turret network, he could make them target the arriving Junta fighters and allow the rebels to maintain aerial dominance.

Considering that the city's defenses were probably controlled at a central location, Carson figured his best bet would be in the city's spaceport, since identifying incoming vessels' transponder codes was as much a civilian problem as a military one. Hopefully that'd make it easier to infiltrate.

Just as he was trying to figure out how to slip away from the other Offspring without being noticed, another rebel gunship broke apart in midair. This time, the burning hull came screaming down right on top of the regiment. More than a few cried out, and they all scattered in every direction.

My lucky break.

It was easy enough for Carson to break off from the rest of his regiment. The gunship came down and crashed hard. Shredded metal and bursts of fire spread in every direction. He forced the fear out of his mind and sprinted for the nearest building across the block, hiding behind the outer wall. He didn't bother checking over his shoulder to see if any other Offspring had noticed his departure. Just kept his head low, then headed for the spaceport.

The twisting cobblestone streets of the city began to blend together, as a dozen different chaotic scenes blurred to become one. Junta soldiers were running in every direction. Civilians were scrambling to get into cover. Although Carson hadn't seen the Ashkagi rebels inflict any damage on civilian targets. If anything, they seemed to be carefully taking down government and military facilities.

He pulled into view of the Caphila spaceport. Most likely, the military would've locked down the area at the outset of the battle. And despite his Offspring garb, Carson had a feeling the Junta soldiers on guard wouldn't just let him walk in. He approached a control tower on the side of the port and readied a grappling device he took from his utility belt.

The tower itself was made of stone, with uneven ledges the whole way up. The structure ballooned at the top, where the main offices were probably located. Where he needed to get to, in other words.

Carson shot his grappling device up as far as it would go until it latched onto a ledge about halfway up. Then he pressed a button on his belt. The wire began to automatically retract, pulling him up the outside of the structure.

He kept his legs out, essentially walking up the wall of the tower while his device pulled him. The wind and rain smacked him about as he ascended. Heights had never particularly bothered him before, but in the middle of a rainstorm and with a deadly battle less than a mile away, it took the entirety of his self-control to not look down.

He'd watched plenty of spy thrillers back on Earth. The real thing had way less mingling in fancy casinos, dressing up in classy suits, flirting with rich and dangerous socialites, or spewing out suave one-liners than he'd been primed to expect. His job had mostly involved a lot of haphazardly trying to figure out the best thing to do in any given moment, all while a crippling fear of death and failure hung over him.

Then again, he was currently scaling a building with a grappling hook. Maybe the thrillers weren't *always* wrong.

Little by little, he worked his way up the control tower until he was at the base of the uppermost section. Pulled himself onto a wet ledge until he could see in through the windows. There was a room full of eight technicians, each absorbed by their own terminal screens. Luckily, there were no Junta soldiers on patrol.

He only had a few seconds to think of a plan. It was desperate and might not work, but he felt he had a good chance if he moved fast enough. He drew his handgun from his holster, placed his forearm over his eyes, and shot the closest window pane out.

He hopped through the hole and pointed his gun at the nearest technician. Eight pairs of eyes darted toward him, a mix of surprise and fear in all of them.

He clenched his jaw, raised his weapon toward the ceiling, and fired off several rounds. "You have ten seconds to get the hell out!" he barked, trying to make his voice sound as deep and intimidating as possible. As though he were the kind of person who could gun down unarmed civilians without a care.

His ruse worked. The technicians promptly pushed themselves to their feet and ran for the door. Carson followed them over, and input an Offspring encryption protocol into the door's controls.

He figured the technicians were running to get whatever soldiers they could find to retake the control room. To get in, the soldiers would either have to get in touch with someone else who knew the

Offspring codes, or blast their way through. Either way would delay them.

Carson got to work on the closest terminal. He'd navigated through the root menu and found the IFF system before he heard the door unlatch. Two figures in brown combat armor rushed inside.

Carson's mind went through a series of realizations in a matter of seconds. First, that he must've been followed after the gunship crash. If a couple of other Offspring had pursued him, it made sense that they'd be able to get to the top of the control tower faster than it had taken him to work his way up the exterior.

Second, that one of them was Emil.

"*You*," the other Offspring hissed. Marcus. The one who'd been suspicious of Carson ever since Kal Jova.

He pulled his gun out. "I always figured you for a coward and a rat. Glad to get some confirmation." He walked forward, circling around Carson, while Emil hung back.

It was the first time since Kal Jova that Carson had a gun trained directly on him. His chest contracted rapidly. If he went for his own gun, Marcus could shoot him faster. That meant he only had one hope of survival.

Emil had to save him.

Carson looked at him. Pleadingly, desperately. They'd moved beyond the level of abstract principles—whether he wanted to be a party to a genocidal terrorist organization, whether it changed things to know that Carson was a refugee—and to the concrete: did Emil want Carson dead in this moment?

It was now a binary choice.

"Put your weapon down," Emil urged his companion. "He should be disciplined formally. Not like this."

"Why?" Marcus asked incredulously, cautiously turning his head over his shoulder but keeping his eyes on Carson. "We know he's been sneaking around behind our backs. He must be working for the Ashkagi. The rebels planted a mole in our organization. And there's a real easy way to deal with traitors."

Carson found it vaguely amusing that Marcus had realized he was a spy, but that he was so incredibly wrong about *who* he was secretly working for. But there were more important things to do than correct him.

He locked eyes with Emil. *So,* he was asking with his glance, *what are you going to do about this?*

"Put. Your. Weapon. Down," Emil repeated.

Marcus raised his gun so that his arm was fully outstretched. Still, his finger hadn't moved to the trigger yet. "No, I don't think I wi—"

The sound of a plasma blast cut him off. Carson closed his eyes on instinct. Wondered if he'd miscalculated, if Marcus had actually fired on him. But the fact that he could think about all that was a decent enough sign that he was, actually, alive.

When he opened his eyes again, Marcus' body had crumpled on the floor. Emil, meanwhile, had a weapon outstretched. The barrel glowed yellow-orange: an indication that it'd just gone off.

Pale and wide-eyed, Emil turned to face Carson. "What do we do now?"

CHAPTER 25

Isadora couldn't remember the last time she'd worn a pair of jeans. Certainly, it had to have been back on Earth. And yet, here she was: clad in a pair of denims, a white T-shirt, and a bandana wrapped around her neck to keep the sun off. Ready to attend what all the media outlets were calling the largest protest in Obrigan City's history. The anti-war movement was coming into its own.

When she walked into the living room of her private residence, Meredith did a double take. "You look...normal?" she said, placing down the datapad she'd been reading. Her feet were at the edge of the couch, her knees raised close to her face.

Isadora grinned. "Thanks. You look lovely too."

Meredith's chuckle warmed her heart. It'd been over three months since Rebecca's house arrest had ended, and their interactions were finally getting around to going back to normal.

Whatever *normal* really meant, anymore.

Isadora gave her a sympathetic look. Meredith was never supposed to be the daughter of their people's preeminent politician, never supposed to have a war with genocidal terrorists disrupt her dating life. And now, just as she was finally learning how to be a normal *Natonese* young woman, Isadora was making plans to reopen a galactic channel back to Earth. From her perspective, did the word *normal* have any meaning left?

"I guess you're going to the protests?" she said.

Isadora sighed. "My staff and I think it's the best way to leverage public opinion against the Union government, which might just convince them to intervene in the war."

She looked up, saw that Meredith had raised a curious eyebrow. "I'm not sure about that, but I *do* know it seems like the right thing to do."

Isadora paused. She'd been so deep in politics that it was hard to tell the difference between attending a protest and negotiating with the literal black market. Both were political ploys, part of her larger toolbox. Morality seemed so hazy that there were days when it faded from view entirely.

But Meredith's easy grin had a way of making her calculating side rest. "I'm *proud* of you, mom. I know we had that spat last year, but...this is a good thing. A noble thing."

Despite all that, one look at Meredith's penetrating eyes suggested she knew, very well, that political theater determined all of her moves. "I think it's important to have a presence there," she said at last.

Meredith nodded in acceptance, even if she knew it was just a nicety. She looked old, Isadora thought—not elderly, of course, but mature. A woman in her own right. Everything that had happened in the last few years had forced her to grow up far faster than she had a right to.

"Things will get better soon," Isadora said gently. "After my work is done. I promise." She headed for the exit.

As she reached the door, Meredith said quietly, "What do you mean *after*?"

Isadora paused, her hand on the door controls. She'd told Meredith everything that Vincent had said to her. After all, it was a secret she was trying to get *out*. No sense in keeping it from her daughter.

"You mean, after the outer rim war ends?" she asked. "Or..."

Meredith took a long, thoughtful breath. "Or *anything*, really. When the Offspring threat goes away. When you get all our people off the *Preserver*. When you reestablish a connection back to Earth. The thing is, there will always be another crisis. There will always be another problem you have to run away and go fix. *San neomeo san*."

San neomeo san: over the mountains are mountains. Or, more literally, mountains beyond mountains. It was one of the few Korean phrases Isadora still remembered from her parents, and probably the *only* one Meredith knew. The idea being that problems never went away, really. Passing one set of obstacles had a way of putting you square in the next set's path.

And it was, depressingly, accurate. Isadora could see her life stretching out before her, one consumed by the theatrics of politics, one that saw her aging and isolated from normal human behavior, the cruel realities of politics slowly draining her of her moral integrity.

One that would continue to rob Meredith of any real normalcy she might have left.

It'd be so easy to say she'd be done when the *Preserver* was empty.

But figuring out how to manage the opening of the gateway back to the Sol System would be equally monumental. As would figuring out how to not just make homes for her people, but actually *integrate* them in what was, possibly, about to become a truly galactic civilization.

"I don't know," she said quietly. It was the truth, and Meredith was old enough to deserve it.

"I was just curious," she said with an accepting nod. One that sent a chill down Isadora's spine. The kind that told her she was talking to an equal, or someone becoming an equal.

"Anyway," Meredith continued, "I wouldn't want you to be late. I asked Rebecca if she wanted to go, by the way, but she doesn't like loud noises or crowds, and, well, protests..."

"...are all about loud noises and crowds?" Isadora offered with a smile.

"Exactly. So she's gonna come over to work on some homework. But she wanted me to tell you she's 100% behind you, of course."

"I understand. And I appreciate that. You two have fun."

Isadora headed out of the residence. Left her people's embassy, where two plainclothes security guards met her. After what had happened to Vincent, Riley wouldn't let her leave without a security detail. The trio headed for the nearest airbus terminal outside.

It was late fall in Obrigan City, but the weather was uncharacteristically warm. So much so that it reminded Isadora of the sweltering summer when the outer rim war had begun. She was thankful she'd dressed appropriately, even more so after she boarded a crowded airbus. The quantity of passengers made the transport all the stuffier.

She wondered if anyone would recognize her. Maybe, but even Isadora had to admit that she was easy to miss in a crowd. Especially when she was dressed so casually, or when she'd tied her hair back into a ponytail instead of letting it fall down straight. She was not especially tall, nor particularly striking.

It'd been so long since she'd been able to get lost in a crowd. So long since she didn't have a legion of staff constantly waiting on her. Her heart ached for the absence of these normalities.

The airbus arrived at the downtown plaza at the epicenter of the anti-war protests, and Isadora pushed those thoughts aside. The only way back to normalcy, to personal obscurity was *through* her current predicament. And the more public pressure she could generate, the faster that would come.

She wasn't prepared for the size of the crowds. The media had been claiming it was the largest public protest since the Union's founding back in the 2360s, but an academic description like that didn't do justice to the actual scene. The gathered crowds nearly stopped her in her tracks. The plaza split off in six different directions—it would look like a giant asterisk from above—and the gathered crowds stretched as far as she could see down every block.

As Isadora and her two security guards walked closer, she could make out the closest signs. Some protesters held up the same slogans that the anti-war movement had been pushing the entire time: calling for the Union to force the Junta to back down, reiterating support for Isadora and for the refugees more broadly, that kind of thing.

But now, there were new signs as well.

THE *PRESERVER* IS OUR WAY OUT, one read, while Isadora caught the phrase END THE WAR, SEE THE GALAXY on a handful of signs. She even saw a few that read END THE SETTLEMENT CHARTER BAN NOW, which caused her heart to swell.

She'd never really pushed the Union government to reconsider the charter ban with much intensity, given that the Natonese public seemed conflicted on that issue. Part of her appeal came from her pragmatism and relatability. Coming off as a transformative radical wouldn't help her image.

But if actual Natonese people were calling attention to the issue, that could change things. She hadn't endorsed Justin Hacelo of the Reform Party, even though the Union parliamentary elections were heating up. His promise to end the ban was tempting, but she couldn't betray Tricia Favan. On the other hand, if ending the ban had genuine public support, that could reshape Union politics.

And it was all because the real truth about the *Preserver* was seeping into the public realm.

The ploy with the Syndicate had worked. Isadora had her staff discreetly keep tabs on at least a dozen information brokers in the city, and all of them had started selling a supposed bombshell to their highest-paying corporate and political clients. The rumor would spread like a virus, so much so that even protesters in the streets had probably heard at least *something* about the *Preserver*. Even if they weren't sure what was true yet. And now, the secret was too big for the Union government to contain.

Isadora thought back to the last conversation she had with Nadia on Bitanu. She'd predicted that the anti-war movement would increase by a factor of ten if the Natonese people knew the truth.

Next time Isadora saw her, she'd have to tell her just how excellent of a prediction that'd turned out to be.

She finally approached the back of the gathered crowds. The sound of various chants—all disorganized and chaotic, too much so for Isadora to make out what anyone was saying—the smell of body odor, and the raw force of human energy all threatened to overwhelm her. And above it all, a groundswell of gratitude: a thankfulness that so many people were showing up because they believed her people were worth helping.

As she slowly meandered her way through the gathered crowds, people began to take notice. Eyes moved in her direction, followed by double takes. People's attention slipped away from the organizers at the plaza center. It was hard to tell through all the shouting and the cheering, but Isadora was pretty sure she heard at least one "Holy shit, I think that's *her*" from behind her.

One utterance turned to many. She drew stares from all sides, and people parted for her. People pumped their fists or waved. She congratulated herself at keeping her composure in the face of an odorous wave of sweat. Then smiled warmly and waved back as best she could.

She hadn't planned it this way, but the crowds were pulling her toward the center of the protests. Toward where the event organizers were all located, giving short speeches or leading chants through voice amplification functions on their wristers. Perhaps seeing the crowd surging for them, the organizers slowly turned their attention toward Isadora. A handful of them looked at her in surprise. All she could do was shrug back and wink.

The organizers exchanged glances, came to a nonverbal agreement, and gestured for her to join them. Everyone who could see her began cheering even louder. She walked up the steps to the central platform slowly, giving the other organizers a gracious smile.

She shook all their hands. The last one offered Isadora his wrister for voice amplification purposes. "Uh, I guess maybe you have one of your own," he realized belatedly.

She stepped to the front, activated her own wrister's loudspeaker function, and waited for the noise to die down. "My friends," she said at last, "my fellow *Natonese.*"

The crowd erupted at this. It was an intentional phrasing, one that negated the Offspring's old assertion of *Natonus for the Natonese.* Maybe it was because Isadora had been thinking so much about the idea of returning to the Sol System—to Earth, whatever it would look like in the twenty-fifth century—but she'd recently realized how much of an outsider she'd feel. She'd only been in the Natonus System for a little over three years, but it was already feeling like home now.

One where she'd fight for her right to belong.

"I feel overwhelmed by all your support," she said, trying to improvise a speech on the fly. A good handful of rules for doing so in politics: keep it short, keep it simple, don't use any complex language. "My people—everyone that's awake, as well as every single person on the *Preserver*—owe you a debt of gratitude."

Deafening claps and cheering. Apparently, "Natonus means all of us!" had become the chant of choice. The crowds went on long enough for Isadora to slip in a natural pause, considering how best to proceed.

Part of her political brand had always been her warmth, her congeniality. Her maternal side. She wasn't the kind of politician who could use soaring rhetoric to convince a crowd to march on the government district, arm-in-arm, demanding that the Union convene a peace summit immediately.

So Isadora decided to be herself.

"The road here has never been easy," she continued. "Forces from one end of the system to the other have opposed us every step of the way. Today, we are facing our most dangerous challenge yet. And it means more than I can express that we have our new neighbors at our backs for this fight."

After another round of reactions, she continued: "I ask that we go forth, to every politician that will hear us, to every journalist that will listen to us, to every organization that will fund us, and declare a simple truth. That every single one of us—all of you, and all of my people—has value. Has the right to a fulfilled life, one unthreatened by war and chaos.

"One," she added, allowing for a faint grin to spread across her face, "where we can explore the stars as a single people, as a *united* people." Half the crowd responded enthusiastically, the other seemed confused.

Perfect. She'd alluded to the *Preserver* rumors without declaring them true outright. But everyone who was already in the know would realize what she was implying.

"So thank you," she concluded, her voice rising as she waved to the crowds. "I look forward to everything the future will bring, and I am confident we will meet these challenges together."

The crowd gave her a thunderous response, one that reverberated across city blocks and skyscrapers. Reverberated in her own chest as she waved and grinned.

She never imagined she'd be in a position like this, speaking to a gathered assemblage of what must've been hundreds of thousands, when she'd won some small-scale city councilor election back home in Seattle.

And yet, here she was. The stakes had changed, but politics hadn't. Looking out over the crowds, she became increasingly confident that she'd created a tide of activism that would flood Union politics until the government could no longer afford *not* to act.

Once the Junta was ready to come to the negotiating table, Tricia would have to send the fleets in to secure the outer rim. And under the protective blanket of Union guns, whatever Tanner Keltin was planning couldn't succeed.

Isadora had done her part. All that they needed now was for the tides of the war to turn.

CHAPTER 26

"Okay," Nadia said to Boyd and Derek as they rode in the interior of a rover bound for the trading outpost of Ubhasa, "after the first time, I was willing to write it off. But I'm starting to think that hiding in a grain sack must be some kind of official way of sneaking into cities here on Ikkren."

They crossed over a rough patch of ground, and the hoverseat adjacent to her went airborne for a second. On cue, she felt a sharp pain from her hip. She'd gotten to the point where she could walk, but she was still trying to stay as immobile as possible to facilitate a smoother recovery. Still had a ways to go.

Across from her, Derek shrugged. "Grain is a major source of trade here. And it's a relatively easy way to sneak past Junta security checkpoints. Honestly, it's a time-honored tradition...there are

stories about explorers and outlaws sneaking around in trading shipments from the early years of colonization."

"All I'm hearing is, this whole deal's gonna go tails up once the
Junta learns to check rover compartments more thoroughly," Boyd
said.

"Well, with any luck, this'll be the last time we have to do it," Nadia said.

The trio's plan was well underway. Boyd had programmed the
warheads they'd retrieved from the downed Union warship to fire
even if the *Exemplar*'s missile scrambler had been activated. That
meant they could have the ship's scrambler active in the vicinity of
the missile turret they were planning to use, diverting incoming Junta
fire while shooting back at them with impunity.

The only remaining problem was manpower. Nadia figured that
as soon as the Junta realized they were getting shot at—and once they
discovered they couldn't fire back without their own projectiles going
well wide of the target location—the most logical follow-up would be
to dispatch ground troops. Which meant Nadia and her crew needed
to defend the cannon until it did enough damage.

That meant recruits. Tori Hyrak herself was traveling from one
end of the planet to the other, trying to piece the Horde back together
under her leadership. She'd dispatched the *Exemplar* to recruit from
wherever they could get numbers. They'd already pulled in a few hundred to defend the turret.

Now, they were headed to Ubhasa. Tori had brought Nadia here
years earlier to hash out the details for settlement and trading rights,
but she'd never imagined she'd return. Much less in the present circumstances. But with plenty of hardy traders inhabiting the settlement—the kinds of people who had no love for the occupation—she

figured they could clean up with a recruiting drive. Tori was hoping they could get at least another hundred.

When Nadia leaned back into the rear hold wall, her hip continued to ache. A loud banging sound distracted her from the pain. It was the sound of the rover driver knocking on the rear hold. Which meant they were coming up on the Junta security checkpoint outside Ubhasa, and that it was time for them to hide. Boyd and Derek both helped Nadia into her sack. They passed through the checkpoint without incident.

After about twenty minutes, Nadia heard the engine die. She pushed herself out of the grain sack, trying to keep her left leg as immobile as possible—and failing, another sharp jab told her—and pulled herself into her floating capsule.

Once the rear hold door swung open, she activated the hoverseat's thrusters and moved the device forward until she was resting comfortably about three feet off the ground. She was just a tad bit taller than she'd normally be, and found the contours of Boyd and Derek's faces to be just so slightly *off* from what she was used to.

"Poor you," Boyd said as they headed away from the rover. The driver had already gone to work unloading various grain sacks into one of the receptacles. The whole supply depot had a pleasant musky smell pervading the air.

They exited the depot into the crowded colony interior. Back when Nadia had first visited Ubhasa, Tori had explained it had been constructed haphazardly, when the volume of trade between settlements grew so large that waypoint stations became necessary.

The crowd inside certainly looked younger and hardier than the general population, and the blocks were so crowded that it was hard to move freely. The trio only made it a few feet before they were caught in a pedestrian traffic jam.

She figured someone wandering the colony streets in a hoverseat was unusual, since people kept bumping into her. She liked to think she'd gotten good at correcting her steering when someone ran into her, but Ubhasa was keeping her on her toes.

To her sides, Nadia saw dozens of traders wrapped up in insulated sleeping pods, usually made through some brightly colored combination of nylon and polyester. "Hostel space is so limited—and so highly priced—that sleeping on the streets is a more affordable option," Derek murmured.

Even still, the settlement didn't look like a shanty town. Nadia had spent plenty of time perusing the market for high-end outdoors gear to keep the *Exemplar* stocked. She recognized the traders' sleeping pods as some of the priciest models.

Derek led them deeper into Ubhasa. They were moving a lot slower than normal thanks to Nadia's hoverchair, making her paranoid that they'd be easily spotted. But they hadn't even seen a single Junta soldier on patrol yet. The crowds were thick enough that she wondered if it'd even be possible to spot one.

They stopped at a streetside vendor, where Derek ordered, and then distributed, three wheat protein skewers. She bit into one of the cubes, finding it tough, sinewy, but flavorful. "These used to be a lot blander," he said. "That is, until your people started growing spices on Calimor and shipping them here." Sure enough, the cubes exploded with flavor after taking a bite.

They entered a drinking den. The door was just wide enough that Nadia could fit her capsule through without assistance from either of her companions. It'd been ages since she'd tried any of the grain liquor that Ikkren was famous for, but just seeing bottles of the clear venom sitting on the shelf made her stomach lurch.

The establishment was tiny, cramped, with overhead heating units blasting out waves of hot air at intermittent bursts. The floors and walls were all aged wood, presumably from the planet's massive everblue forests. There were at least three dozen people inside. Most had lined up empty shot glasses of grain liquor—*how?* Nadia wondered incredulously—but a few nursed beers.

The bartender at the far end of the establishment made eye contact with them. Then scratched his upper lip in an obvious fashion. A resistance sympathizer, according to the information Tori had given them.

Nadia, Boyd, and Derek worked their way across the tavern. "Thanks for coming," the bartender said as he wiped down a set of empty shot glasses. "I've been rounding up some folks I think might be sympathetic to the cause. Already vetted their backgrounds, made sure they aren't undercover with the Junta or anything like that. Problem is, I think word of our gunship raid must've dampened enthusiasm for the movement. I got less than a quarter of what I was hoping for." He indicated a back room, where there were eight individuals waiting for them.

Eight? Nadia's heart sunk. She'd felt Tori's estimate of about a hundred was unrealistically high, but eight was so far off from the goal that it was almost laughable.

The assembled recruits looked young and hungry for a fight, but scared too. And given how badly the last operation had gone, who could blame them? The trio thanked the bartender, then headed into the back room.

Nadia forced her mouth to contort into a shape she hoped was equal parts resolved and reassuring. Eight skeptical faces turned toward her. "We've asked you here because we're planning a major operation to hopefully take out a Junta warship," she said.

"Isn't that what you told everyone who died back in Heykan?" one of the potential recruits asked.

Saying *yes* would probably be in poor taste. "Things are different now," she said instead. "Back then, the Junta enjoyed such over-whelming air superiority that they could dispatch a warship to our location almost immediately. Now, with the situation changing back on Enther, the Junta had to recall the bulk of their fleet."

"Plus, we're covering our bases better," Boyd said. "Our vessel has a missile scrambler that can block incoming enemy projectiles while letting our own warheads through. They won't be able to hit us back while we're blowing them up."

"The issue is, the occupiers *will* attack our position with conven-tional forces," Nadia said. "Which is where you all come in."

"The eight of us against a battalion of trained soldiers?" another asked.

"Technically eleven, counting us," Boyd said with a grin. No one laughed. "In all seriousness, we've assembled recruits in all the major settlements. And Tori Hyrak's been busy as well. We'll be going in with an army, don't you worry."

Nadia shot him a disapproving look. Gallows humor probably wasn't ideal, given the circumstances. "What my friend meant to say is, it *won't* just be the people in this room. But we need everyone we can possibly get to make sure this works."

A back-and-forth ensued, most of the recruits expressing some degree of doubt about the operation. Not that she could blame them. Doubt slithered through her head, and she retreated into the recesses of her capsule.

Derek must've seen the dejection in her face, because he strode over to talk to her. "I have an idea," he said. "Follow me."

Yes please, Nadia thought. "We're gonna step out for a minute," she muttered to Boyd. "I trust you can keep the fort down?"

"I...sure?" Boyd said, his brows furrowing.

Nadia pressed a button on the interior of her capsule, floating out after Derek. They returned to the main area, where there were still a few dozen people gathered. A loud belch came from the table to their right.

Derek looked nervously from side to side before closing his eyes, taking a deep breath, and clearing his throat. It took a few seconds, but eventually, everyone quieted down and turned to face him.

"I'm not going to insult you or waste your time by introducing us," he began. For good measure, Nadia leaned forward to expose her face. The two of them and their exploits had been covered heavily enough in the Natonese media that anyone who hadn't been living under a rock should've probably figured out who they were.

"I'm here because I used to be just like you," Derek continued. "After the war with the Union, the only way to get out of our settlements was to join up with a trading crew, and the only way to get off planet was to join the Horde's expeditionary forces." A handful of loud agreements confirmed the story. "I chose the latter. And I'm back because I want you to know that there's more out there."

Nadia instantly figured out what he was talking about. During the flight back from Bitanu a month ago, she'd finally told Boyd and Derek about the full functionality of the *Preserver*. They'd mostly ignored the issue—they had far more pressing matters to attend to, after all—but Nadia had made sure they felt free to confirm the rumors swirling around the Natonese media sphere. She figured Isadora would see that as congruent with her goals.

"I know many of you have been reading about the refugee cryo vessel," Derek said. "Wondering if it's true, wondering if there really could be a way out of this system. Well, I'm here to tell you that everything you've heard is accurate. I was there when it was confirmed."

Nadia heard a handful of gasps. She turned to look at Derek again, seeing him in a new light. For most of these people, he was probably the first person they knew from Ikkren who'd ever received positive media coverage from Union journalists. To have someone of his stature confirming wild hearsay must've been an epochal moment for these traders, most of whom probably saw a bit of themselves in Derek.

"Our parents and grandparents came out here because they knew that they'd never be content, hemmed in on the core worlds," he said. "Soon, the next frontier will be open. And I believe it is our people's birthright to be at the forefront of the new era." More than a dozen patrons voiced some kind of agreement.

Nadia was surprised at how eager the Ikkren population was to explore beyond the wormhole, but she supposed it made sense. The planet was far from a paradise, and these settlers had stomached it all to evade Union expansionism. They were a hardy people—people who wanted to live away from the ever-encroaching grip of an interplanetary empire. Seeing the rest of the galaxy was just a logical extension of that, she supposed.

"But the first step in our new odyssey is before us," Derek concluded. "The war is threatening the very existence of the *Preserver*: our one and only path out of this system. And as long as the Junta occupies our planet unchecked, the war will continue. We must strike back against the occupiers to ensure the safety of the refugee vessel.

We have a plan to do just that, but we need volunteers. I'm asking for help to secure our people's future."

Almost fifteen people immediately stood up to come talk to him. And Nadia knew that not everyone who volunteered to fight represented only a single person—some of them might bring along family or friends.

And it had all been because of Derek.

He'd leveraged his symbolic status almost perfectly, made a convincing argument that might just help change the course of the war. Maybe more than that. She couldn't help but smile as he shook hands and talked with everyone personally. He'd grown into so much more than the withdrawn pilot from the beginning of their travels.

It was just like when Boyd had taken charge back at the downed Union warship. She increasingly felt superfluous, but what surprised her was how *okay* with that she'd become. Once, a long time ago, she'd vociferously denied she was a miracle-worker, or anything like that. Her biggest claim to fame was that she'd assembled a good team.

It was true, but somewhere along the way, she'd forgotten that. She'd let herself get consumed by the image of herself, the woman who could end wars and settle millions with a cheerful, unending optimism. When she failed to meet her own expectations for herself— when she'd unwittingly caused the Enther civil war to reignite, when she'd failed to stop Tanner, when Russ had died to save her—she'd collapsed. Turned into a shell of her former self.

Maybe literally, she thought, casting a glance at the egg-like medical capsule that surrounded her. Maybe she had to relearn the old truths that used to guide her. Maybe only then could she finally become the savior her people needed her to be.

CHAPTER 27

C arson knew it was coming. He was only off by about thirty seconds. "Fucking hell," Emil said, staring at the body of Marcus.
The Offspring he'd shot to save Carson. "What have I done?"

Carson had successfully deradicalized patients before, but always
from the comfort of an office. Emil's process was deradicalization by
fire. Which meant he really had no idea what to say. Backsliding was
inevitable in any therapeutic process, but he didn't have time to be
completely patient and understanding while a battle was raging. Literally outside.

He walked toward the other end of the air tower control room and
locked eyes with Emil. "You saved my life," he said. "I would have
done the same thing for you. This isn't about my identity, it's about
whether or not you wanted me to be shot dead. And I'm grateful."

Emil returned his gaze to Marcus' corpse. He slumped to the ground, placed his back against a terminal, and hugged his knees. "I've ruined everything."

Carson didn't think it was particularly likely that he'd turn around and shoot him, but he still checked to make sure he'd holstered his plasma gun. Then he went to the doorway and put in another security code. There were still Junta soldiers in the tower, presumably, and they'd still very much want the infiltrator in their midst dead or disabled.

As soon as the terminal chirped an affirmation, Carson evaluated his position. The Ashkagi rebels were locked in a pitched battle with the Junta for control of the planetary capital, and now, the city's defenses were taking out the arriving Junta air support. Only problem was, the Junta's available manpower could almost certainly overwhelm his position and reset the city turrets' IFF.

If holding the control tower was a losing game, that meant he had to act fast. Change the stakes of the battle, so it no longer mattered if the Junta held the control tower. That meant he had to open the city gates to the rebels outside, letting their fighters flood the streets of Caphila.

All while trying to figure out what the hell to do with Emil.

On cue, the other man groaned again. "I'm hoping the security lockout might slow them down, but no matter what, Junta soldiers are gonna be flooding this room in a few minutes," Carson said. "I'm genuinely sorry for the position I've put you in. This was never what I wanted. But we have to act.

"The whole time, you've been telling me you don't have a stake in the civil war. I'm suggesting we do something about that. What if we turned control of the capital back to a group of people who've done nothing wrong, whose religion has been brutally suppressed by the Junta? That's the choice in front of us. Help the rebels, or let ourselves get captured and maybe worse."

Emil banged his forehead on his kneecaps. He couldn't help but sympathize. "It's okay if you're angry with me right now," he said softly. "Or confused, or hurt, or scared. Whatever you're feeling—it's okay. All I'm asking right now is we do the bare minimum to keep us alive. And, if possible, help the rebels."

That, at least, got Emil to stop banging his head on his knees. "Okay," he said at last. "Let's get out of here."

Carson stifled a grin. "I'm glad to hear you say that. Only problem is, we can't do it the conventional way." He tilted his head toward the shot-out window he'd used to enter the tower. The two of them used grappling devices and cables to carefully lower themselves down the building's exterior.

As soon as they were outside, the sounds of battle loudened. The city seemed even more chaotic, with Junta fighter jets screaming by, only to be taken out by one of the defense turrets soon after. Carson looked toward the stormy sky as they descended, where a Junta warship had moved to high altitude to stay outside of the turrets' range. Most of the fighters had stopped doing attack runs.

Which meant he'd successfully bought the rebels time, but only a little.

When they hit the ground, they immediately started sprinting for the nearest building. They hadn't been shot at, but Carson was almost certain that Junta troops were bypassing the lock he'd left on the tower control room by this point. They might even try to take potshots at them from the window.

"So I'm guessing you and Marcus were the only Offspring sent after me?" he asked Emil once they were safely out of the tower's sight.

He nodded. "After that fighter crash barely missed us, I was the only one who saw you running away. I figured you were up to something. I grabbed the closest brother I could, who happened to be Marcus, and pursued you. We followed you to the control tower, but once the soldiers inside realized you'd used Offspring encryption to lock down the top level, they sent us ahead."

It worried Carson that he was still referring to Marcus as his *brother*. Then again, his mind was probably racing in so many directions, simultaneously, that falling back on learned behaviors made sense.

Still, Carson was glad to know that there weren't more unaccounted Offspring pursuing them. But once the Junta was back in control of the tower, it stood to reason that they'd dispatch information about a rogue infiltrator in Offspring garb. "I think we need to lose these suits," he said.

Emil agreed. They stripped down to their plain clothes, tossing their Offspring suits to the side of the closest curb. It should've felt like a weightier moment, since he'd been wearing the Offspring browns for most of the last half-year. Emil probably went through an even more poignant concoction of emotions. But the boom of a nearby cannon made both of them jump, and they proceeded onward without comment.

The streets looked little different from earlier. Hundreds were still rushing in every direction, military and civilian alike. No one seemed to notice them, much less the fact that they were in plain clothes but still carried handguns.

"I know some people," Emil said as they rounded a street corner.

"I know it might seem like everyone in the Offspring is completely committed to the cause, but there are others who've been having doubts."

Carson thought about saying that the signs of doubt from other Offspring members had been fairly obvious. But he let him continue without comment.

Emil pulled up his wrister and began typing frantically. "I'm not telling the doubters anything about you," he said. "Just that I'm putting an end to this stupid war. None of them care about the Junta's problems. I'll let them know we need to meet them at the city's main gate."

After another few minutes, they arrived at a Junta military fortification just outside the city's entrance. The area was barricaded off with concrete barriers, overlaid with particularly painful-looking barbed wire. A large artillery blast took out an entire chunk of the outer walls, sending pulverized stones and Junta troops flailing through the air.

"We may have to fight our way in," Carson said. Emil just nodded in response.

He turned his attention to an unoccupied security station. Whatever soldiers had been guarding the checkpoint were probably needed more elsewhere. He crouched low, drew his handgun, and used his hands to communicate with Emil.

Both of them stayed as low as possible, slowly crab-walking their way past a screening station with a still-flickering holo-terminal nearby. The screen flashed red as they crawled past. Sirens blared. Five Junta troops stormed out of the gate control room on the other side of the checkpoint, took one look at Carson and Emil, and opened fire.

They dove for opposite ends of the station as plasma fire streaked through the open doorway. Carson took an explosive device out of his utility belt, fastened it to the wall next to him. Then tossed a smoke grenade out to cover the checkpoint entrance, sprinted over to where Emil was hiding, and pressed the button on his detonator device.

The wall blew out. He placed his hands on the back of Emil's shoulders, urging him on. "Go now," he said. "Fast."

The two men raced out while blind Junta plasma bolts tore through the station. They found refuge behind a pile of crates. By the time the Junta squad had realized they'd moved, they were already in cover again.

Still, that hardly improved their position. Bolts tore through the sides of the crates. Carson scanned the area frantically, but there weren't any other obvious cover spots.

Which was when he heard a chorus of shouting coming from the other side of the perimeter. Followed by a violent exchange of plasma fire. He looked over to see a dozen Offspring charging forward through the checkpoint station. Two went down almost immediately, but all five of their Junta opponents did as well.

Carson found it deeply ironic that a bunch of Offspring showing up was a relief. All he had to do now was get to the gate controls.

"Shit," Emil muttered. "One of the two men who died was the brother I got in touch with. I don't know if the rest of his regiment will be as—"

"—why did we just do that?" one of the other Offspring exclaimed. "Tanner Keltin has told us to trust the Junta. Coming here was a mistake!"

Three others voiced their concurrence with the speaker. Carson's heart dropped. But Emil took that opportunity to stand up, his arms outstretched in a calming gesture. "Brothers," Emil said. "I promise this wasn't a mistake. I'm asking you to trust—"

"—why aren't you in uniform?" the speaker barked.

Carson feared where this was going. He grabbed Emil's sleeve. Pulled him back into cover before any shots could go off.

Emil looked at him wide-eyed. "I don't know any of these people personally. I don't know what to do."

"But you *do* know them," Carson said. *Because radicalization requires a certain set of personality traits already in place. No, scratch that. Too clinical.* "You came out here for a reason, just like them. There was something you were looking for, something you thought you could find with the Offspring. They were doing the same thing. You *know* how to appeal to them."

Emil cast his face downward, doubt written all over his expression. "All you need to do is convince them to let us open the gate," he pressed. "You're not trying to tell them to give up the cause. It's just baby steps."

Emil raised his head to look at him, first with incredulity, second with acceptance. "Brothers!" he shouted, louder than before, louder than even the thunder and the rainfall.

"I am the same as all of you," he continued, his head darting nervously over to Carson for confirmation. He just closed his eyes and nodded. "We all came here because we wanted to belong to something. Wanted to believe we were about to embark on some great crusade to protect our fellow people.

"Well, I'm asking you now: is this it? Is fighting and bleeding and dying in someone else's civil war, on a planet far from home, what we signed up for? We were here because we believed in defending and supporting the Natonese people. Well, those Ashkagi rebels outside the gates are Natonese too. And I say we have no business—no right—fighting them."

Carson found his tactic clever. He wasn't focusing on Tanner Keltin, nor on anything about the refugees. He was doing exactly what Carson had done to him: focusing on the absurdity of the task they'd been given. His speech was still dripping with nativist sentiment, sure, but it was the best place to start.

Circumstances had, once again, forced Emil into a binary choice. He either had to convince his brothers to stand aside and let the rebels take the city, or most likely get shot. *Deradicalization by fire, again.*

"All I'm asking is that you let us lower the gate," Emil continued. "If you want no part in what comes after that, I understand. But we have a chance to let this war-torn, cursed planet finally start healing. To let our fellow Natonese people get back some semblance of a normal life. On some level, that's what we all want. So please...just don't fire on us."

Silence. Then, after a few seconds: "Okay. Go."

Carson needed little encouragement. He sprinted toward the gate control room as fast as he could. Emil right on his heels.

The control room was deserted. He identified the main computer station, began running a bypass on the Junta security system. In another few seconds, he'd navigated to a screen giving the option to open the city gates. He pressed the button without hesitation.

And then slumped over and collapsed. Emil followed suit. Outside, they heard chaos as the Ashkagi rebels charged into the city. Once they were inside, Carson was confident they could take control of the capital. And with Caphila and its defenses under their control, they could drive the Junta reinforcements back.

It was probably too early for Carson to get optimistic, but he felt a certain sense of satisfaction in creating what might end up being a pivotal turning point in the planetary civil war.

He looked over at Emil. The two men grinned, then started laughing.

Carson stopped first. Turning Caphila over to the rebels was a major victory, but it barely changed the situation for his people. What he *really* needed was actionable intelligence on Tanner Keltin's plans. He could only hope that an opportunity to find just that would occur in the certain chaos to come.

But he had one thing, now, that he hadn't when he'd started his undercover assignment. Emil had just laid his own life on the line to help him, and he'd even started *other* Offspring down the path of de-radicalization.

For the first time since Carson had infiltrated the Offspring, he had a real in.

CHAPTER 28

I t took two weeks for Tanner to fly a hijacked aid freighter from Bitanu back to Enther. Back to the *Caretaker*, where his six surviving brothers had kept the ship running in his absence. And then it'd taken two months for anything else to happen.

It had been a frustrating interim. Tanner had gloated about killing the chief newar engineer, but in reality, the Bitanu operation had been a humiliating failure after Nadia Jibor's vessel had showed up unexpectedly. If it hadn't been for her timely arrival, the *Preserver* would be a debris field by now.

Once again, the work of maintaining the *Caretaker* and keeping up their ruse took precedence. When he wasn't helping his brothers with maintenance duties, Tanner sat in the captain's office. Brooded.

He wasn't going to get another chance to attack the newars' laser defense matrix, he was fairly certain, and he couldn't nuke the *Preserver* with the matrix still operational. He was still in the same quandary as before, except two men short, and his most promising course of action rendered moot.

As the days dragged on, he'd become engrossed in reading net stories. That was how he learned that the Enther civil war had shifted dramatically in favor of the Ashkagi, who somehow seemed to have access to far better military equipment than they'd ever owned before.

The talking heads had various opinions and theories on that, but Tanner was almost certain it was the Syndicate. A mass movement of weapons to the outer planets on that scale wouldn't just *happen* without the black market being involved.

And then he'd started seeing strange rumors about the *Preserver*.

At first, he thought they were just wild delusions. But then these stories began gaining traction, sometimes even from respectable media outlets. More concerningly, all the stories were saying the same thing: that the *Preserver* was, in addition to its cryonics functions, able to transform into an antimatter gateway leading back to the Sol System. To Earth.

Tanner was surprised at how *little* the revelation affected him.

If anything, it only reinforced his sense of purpose. Before he'd become a full member of the Offspring—back when he was still blind—he'd speculated that the wave of Earth refugees might be tolerable on their own, but future waves of migration would be unacceptable. How naive he'd been then—*any* invasion was an affront, and had to be met with force.

But the principle still stood. Suddenly, the *Preserver* was more than just home to 30 million invaders. It represented a literal infinite stream of hostiles into his people's home. The Natonus System was not—would *never* be, he was determined—the place for the huddled masses, the wretched refuse of the galaxy.

They were just fine on their own. Destroying the *Preserver* would affirm that to an even greater degree.

Finally came the developing news about an Ashkagi attack on the Junta capital. General Michael Azkon himself, along with the majority of the occupation fleet at Ikkren, had rushed back to defend the home front. But armed with Syndicate weapons, Tanner assumed, the rebels had breached Caphila. Taken control of the defenses before the returning ships could deploy their full air support.

With the capital in rebel hands, most major cities had revolted. The Junta had been nearly pushed off its own planet in a matter of weeks.

Of more concern were the reports that the Offspring members sent to help defend Caphila had defected, had helped turn control of the city over to the rebels. Not that Tanner cared very much—he had few tangible opinions on whether the Junta or the Ashkagi rebels were preferable—but that meant there'd been dissent in the ranks.

Then again, he'd promised his followers a great crusade against the newars, only to force the overwhelming majority—the Offspring had grown to a little over a thousand, before he'd suspended their recruiting drives—to help clean up the Enther civil war. Maybe the frustration had finally gotten to some of them.

That was when his wrist terminal chirped a notification at him. Now that Michael Azkon had returned to Enther, only to see his planet taken by the rebels, he was requesting a meeting with him.

He arched an eyebrow. Was the general going to rage at him?

Tanner keyed back a message, saying he'd contact the general via holo-emitter in a few minutes. Then he sat back in his chair and considered his options.

As far as Michael knew, the *Caretaker* was still under control of his officers. The other Offspring had kept up the ruse, piecing together recordings from the dead Junta captain's logs to make fake holo-recordings they dispatched to his superiors. If the general was planning on retaliating against Tanner, he could send messages to the long-dead Junta crew, asking them to incarcerate the Offspring. Which would give away the game for sure.

That meant it was of vital importance that Tanner *not* aggravate the general. He had to keep their partnership alive in order to preserve his people's duplicity. But when the general had just lost his own capital, soothing words probably wouldn't calm him down. He needed to offer him something.

What would mollify Michael Azkon? He considered what he knew about the general. He was driven, it seemed, from little other than a massively inflated ego and a burning desire to be regarded as one of the major players in the Natonus System. Before the arrival of the newars, he'd had his sights on Calimor—and then the invasion had started, whisking the planet right out from under him.

Above all, he suffered from some crippling sense of emasculation, a feeling that the system had surpassed him, that he was entitled to far more than he'd gotten. Tanner could work with that. Perhaps more so than winning the war against the Horde, what the general really wanted was respect. Prestige. To be seen as an equal to the other political powers.

Tanner had it. An idea crystallized in his brain with dizzying speed, staggering in its implications. And one that would require making sure his six surviving shipmates could accept.

He nearly ran out of the captain's cabin, using his wrist terminal to call for an all-crew meeting in the CIC. One by one, the other six accepted.

Tanner was the third one there. The other four trickled in over the course of the next five minutes. "Brothers," he began immediately after the last one had entered. "All of us have borne incredible hardships just to get here. I've put you all in danger countless times. We've risked our lives over and over. Now, I have a plan to destroy the *Preserver*. But it will require the ultimate sacrifice from all seven of us."

The six Offspring exchanged glances, but none of them hesitated in agreeing. A grim smile appeared on Tanner's face. He wasn't really worried that any of them would refuse. Still, asking some of his most trusted comrades to accept certain death for the cause was a weighty ask.

And maybe hard to contemplate, personally. Tanner had always known coming back from his war against the newars was unlikely, but he'd never come up with a plan like this before. One where he would die, no matter what. He'd accepted that he was unlikely to return during the Bitanu attack, but his current plan went beyond even that.

Almost no fear crossed his mind. Only a twinge of regret that he'd never get to hold Rebecca again. That he'd never hear her thank him for how much he'd sacrificed to keep her safe.

He pushed thoughts of his sister from his mind. "That is all. Thank you for all of your bravery," Tanner said. "I promise, I would never spend our lives in vain. This will ensure our final victory over our enemies."

He dismissed them, allowing his shipmates to return to their maintenance duties, then proceeded to a nearby meeting room. He entered, composed himself in anticipation of Michael Azkon's wrath, and set up a channel to the Junta flagship *Sanctitude*.

"Tanner," Michael said, almost as soon as the holo-projector spat out a simulation of the man's grizzled face, "what the hell? We had a deal, and—"

"—I realize how this looks, General," Tanner interrupted. "I promise, I had no forehand knowledge of my regiment's plan to defect. I am working right now to identify and correct the problem," he lied.

What could he do, after all? The defectors were now with the Ashkagi, presumably, and the remaining hundreds of loyal Offspring on the planet couldn't retake the city by themselves. All that really mattered was concealing the fact that Tanner had commandeered the *Caretaker*—a secret that was locked away in only a single Offspring database down on Enther.

He searched the general's face for any signs of frustration. He'd interrupted him, and he knew his protests were likely to fall flat, given that the man might've just lost his planet. To his surprise, however, he seemed more annoyed than irate.

"Although this is a setback, I don't think it necessarily complicates our long-term goals," Tanner continued. Better to shift the parameters of the conversation before he had time to dwell on the Enther situation.

The general stroked his chin. "Enlighten me."

"Call for a peace summit. The situation on Enther is...complicated, sure. But your forces still hold a considerable amount of territory. And you've placed Ikkren under occupation and nearly dismantled the Horde's power base. Beyond that, your ships' blockade of the asteroid belt has squeezed the newars' finances. Your negotiating position is quite strong. The war has solidified the Junta as a great power, nearly on an equal footing with the Union."

Michael nodded along. Tanner found it difficult to keep his dismally low assessment of him off his own face. He seemed so entertained with delusions of power and prestige that he was blind to Tanner's manipulation.

Then again, he'd convinced the general to start a war that would only ultimately benefit Tanner and the Offspring. Every conversation with him made him just seem all the more pathetic.

"I suppose you're correct," he said. "We still have a lot of cards in our hand."

Tanner stifled a grin at his usage of *we*. He was so painfully ignorant that he thought Tanner cared about him at all. They were allies of convenience, little more. "Call for a peace summit at a good neutral ground. Like, say...Bitanu. The planet has seen little fighting so far, and its orbital path has lined up almost perfectly with Obrigan. It'd be the shortest trip for Union ships."

And the location of the *Preserver*.

"I see the logic," Michael said. "Still, I worry that suing for peace, at this juncture, would still be interpreted as a sign of weakness. And Tricia's always had it out for me. She'd try to finagle the situation so the damn rebels get a decent chunk of territory on Enther."

"I'm sure the prime minister would, but you have enough assets under your control to keep her from getting her way. The Union's economy is tied up with the newars' colonial expansion. Trust me, I used to work for one of the biggest supply megacorps in Union space. They've been bleeding during the entire duration of the war. I guarantee the Union's corporate sector will be lining up, begging the prime minister to do something, *anything*, to secure a quick peace deal."

"Another good point. I'll need to give it some thought, but

tentatively, setting up a peace summit at Bitanu makes sense. And you are correct that we have accomplished a lot through our partnership. The recent events notwithstanding."

"I'm glad you agree. I suppose that means we'll be joining you. It would be good to have your full fleet at Bitanu. As a show of strength."

"Naturally. When I make my decision, I'll be sure to get in touch with Captain Jonchi. I hope he's been treating you okay," Michael added, smirking. "He always had a reputation for being a hardass."

Captain Jonchi. It'd been so long since Tanner had ordered his followers to knife the man to death that he'd almost forgotten his name. "The captain has been nothing but hospitable," he said with a wide grin.

"Good. I'll be in touch. Azkon out." The holographic image fizzled and died.

Tanner replaced the likeness of the general with a projection of the planet Bitanu. He had a good feeling that he'd soon be returning to Bitanu for the second time in the last few months. The planet's orbit looked so empty on the projection—other than for the blip representing the *Preserver*—but soon, it would be flooded with vessels from all corners of the system.

And that would give Tanner his chance. He'd been so focused on the question of how to nuke the *Preserver* to realize that a missile strike was not truly necessary.

Not when the *Caretaker* itself could be a projectile.

The newars' laser defense matrix could destroy missiles, but not entire ships. Tanner pressed a few keys on the input terminal, and the holo-emitter showed a projection of the *Caretaker*'s probable velocity if it used Bitanu's gravity well to slingshot to the other side.

The peace summit would occur, bringing him within striking distance of the *Preserver*. At that point, keeping up his ruse would hardly matter. He would order his followers to bring the warship out of formation. Slingshot around Bitanu on a collision course for the newar cryo vessel.

There were other logistical items he'd need to figure out—how to make sure they didn't get fired on, how to disrupt communications so that the newars couldn't be warned in time for it to matter—but he was confident he could make the plan work.

He and his six shipmates would die in a spectacular blaze of glory, ramming into the *Preserver*. But they'd take 30 million invaders with them.

Rebecca would never get to see him again, but she could know that he'd sacrificed everything for her. Tanner surprised himself as his eyes grew misty thinking about her. It didn't matter. Any sacrifice would be justified to bring the war against the newars to an end.

And with his death—and theirs—maybe the Natonus System could finally know peace again.

CHAPTER 29

It was the second time Isadora had entered the situation room, situated in the basement of the Union Government-General. This time, she felt far more confident.

She and Riley had been invited to brief the joint chiefs on the *Preserver*'s newly revealed capabilities. Now that the intelligence had gotten out, now that the rumors were flying from one end of the system to the other, the Union could no longer ignore the issue.

She lingered at the threshold to the room—a steel door that looked heavier than some airbuses she'd traveled in—and looked inside. The deep blue lighting and the holo-projector of the Natonus System were familiar sights, as were the dozen military officials and intelligence officers inside. Last time, they'd mostly stared at her with hostility. Now, it was more a mix of curiosity and suspicion. She supposed she could take that.

They walked in and took seats off to the side. Tricia stormed in soon afterward, letting the door shut with a loud bang. "All right," she said, an edge of harshness in her normally croaky voice, "what—and I cannot stress this enough—the *fuck*, Isadora?"

"It's nice to see you too, Tricia," she said with a warm smile. To her left, Riley suppressed a grin. The nearest general seemed to flinch at her use of the prime minister's first name.

"Very cute," Tricia said, crossing her arms as she sat down. "No, seriously. Did you know about this the whole time?"

Isadora shook her head. "I was only informed about the *Preserver*'s true capabilities less than two months ago." She used her wrister to tap into the central projector's controls, then displayed a simulation of the *Preserver*'s transformation process that her staff had retrieved from Vincent's cabin.

A looping video played, showing the cryo vessel collapsing in on itself until it was subsumed by a ball of light. At the end of the video, a series of emitters emerged from the sphere and formed a circle. Then the video restarted. One of the admirals let out a low whistle.

Tricia, meanwhile, was anxiously pinching her lips with her thumb and index finger. "And if we send ships through *that*, we'll show up at Earth?"

Isadora shrugged. "Presumably. I've never used one before."

"It would be the Sol System, not Earth," Riley interjected. "We can't be exactly sure where. As the chief coordinator implied, this isn't our technology."

"Right," a general said, "this experimental wormhole technology was made by the people who conquered your home—along with every other colonized star system in the galaxy, other than ours—and we're just supposed to trust it will work?"

"I have already passed along the full trove of survey data collected by my late chief engineer, indicating the Hegemony collapsed within the past century," Isadora said. Mentioning Vincent caused a twinge of sadness to course through her. A phantom wound.

"My team has reviewed the report extensively," Riley interjected, before anyone had the chance to question her. "We understand that you may have concerns about the fact that a Hegemony affiliate was responsible for collecting the intelligence used in the report. However, he used *Preserver* probes to do so. Furthermore, he uploaded the survey data to secure servers within the ship's systems that were regularly monitored by the computer, which show no signs of tampering."

A few of the joint chiefs opened their mouths to respond, but they all closed them promptly when Tricia spoke up. "I'm inclined to believe you," she said. "But here's what I'm wondering: by all accounts, it looks like you *gave* this information to the Syndicate, who then sold it to information brokers, which is how the public finally became aware. If you found out a few months ago, why didn't you bring it to me first?"

"Because I knew you would just classify everything immediately, and it wouldn't see the light of day for years. Decades, maybe," Isadora said.

Tricia muttered something under her breath that sounded awfully like *probably true*.

"For my people, this is not just a military issue," she continued. "After the Offspring raid on Bitanu, we know for certain that Tanner Keltin is using the war as a distraction to plot the destruction of the *Preserver*. Thus far, the Union has been unable to bring the war to an end. The most logical course of action, for me, was to raise the value of the *Preserver* to a level that would force you to intervene."

Isadora sat back and studied the faces of the joint chiefs. Their reactions all seemed to fall somewhere on the spectrum of uneasy to horrified. She'd been intimidated by the power of the situation room once, but now, she was arriving as someone who was, quite possibly, the most popular politician—maybe even the most popular *individual*—in the whole system, who'd built a vigorous anti-war movement from the ground up.

Was her gambit to seed the *Preserver* intel into Natonese society nakedly political? Obviously. But her job was to do nakedly political things all the time, and she liked to think she'd gotten pretty damn good at it.

Tricia sighed, closed her eyes, rubbed her temples. "Okay. Let's hear them out."

Riley launched into an explanation about the probable effects of beginning the *Preserver*'s transformation functions. "Even if there are active Hegemony forces waiting on the other side, our projections of the resulting wormhole make it look like a bottleneck," she explained. "A full flotilla of ships stationed just outside could easily defend the system from an invading fleet."

"I should add, of course, that all available data suggest that an invasion is eminently unlikely," Isadora interjected. No one looked particularly reassured.

"I'll forward all available data we have pointing to the Hegemony's collapse immediately after this meeting. My team has also been running projections on the probable tech level of Hegemony warships," Riley said. "Obviously, it's extremely rough, given that the little data we have is over a century old, and extrapolating based on a single invasion is difficult. Nevertheless, the projections we created indicate a high likelihood of parity between Union and Hegemony vessels."

"Which is all hypothetical, of course, since you think the Hegemony has collapsed," Tricia said.

"You took the words out of my mouth," Isadora said.

Riley continued, while she scanned the faces of the joint chiefs for clues. A sea of furrowed brows and hands cupped over mouths greeted her. But there was something else too: a sense of resignation. Shoulders slumped, eyes heavy.

Isadora knew how these things worked. Knew that all kinds of lobbying and interest groups had been pressuring Tricia and the rest of the Union government to open the wormhole to Earth: corporations that wanted to expand to new markets, explorers who wanted to see new sights—including those who wanted to see the long-abandoned birthplace of their species—and workers who wanted to seek new opportunities. Staying put had never been humanity's strong suit.

By the end of the briefing, she didn't need any of them to confirm that the decision had already been made. "Thank you," Tricia said wearily. "I promise to give your proposal a good deal of thought." Isadora considered it a good sign that she was speaking without her trademark snark or profanity.

"If you wouldn't mind," the prime minister continued, turning to face her, "I'd like to speak to you privately."

Isadora looked to her left. Riley shrugged. "I've got plenty to do back at the embassy."

While the joint chiefs turned around and began talking to each other, Isadora, Tricia, and Riley all departed the situation room. Riley headed to the front of the building, out to a nearby helipad. Isadora followed the prime minister.

It was the middle of the day. A flurry of bureaucrats, legislators, and aides rushed around, each one seemingly late for wherever they were headed. Isadora was surprised so few people tried to talk to Tricia. Maybe they assumed she wouldn't want to talk to them if she were tied up in a conversation.

Which, knowing her, probably explained why she wanted Isadora to accompany her.

They made it to the prime minister's office, where Isadora fixed herself a cup of coffee and Tricia collapsed into one of the recliners. "Holy fuck am I *tired*, Isadora."

Isadora took a sip of her coffee, winced when it scalded her tongue, and sat down in an adjacent chair. "I can empathize."

"This is the third parliamentary election of my career," Tricia said. "Somehow, it's been way more exhausting than the first two. And that was before you dropped the biggest fucking bombshell possible in my lap." Tricia shot Isadora a glare that was half-joking, half-serious.

"I understand I've put you in a difficult position. But I'm sure you understand why I did what I did."

"I do. And you're going to get what you want. We both know that I won't have any choice but to open up your ship. Gateway. What-the-fuck-ever. Plus, your timing couldn't be better—we just got an official communication from Michael Azkon. The Junta is suing for peace. You're the first person outside of my inner circle I've told, so keep this one to yourself."

Isadora's heart leapt. She'd read about the sudden capture of the Enther capital by the rebels. Had hoped that might accelerate the end of the war. If the Junta was ready to come to terms, then Tanner Keltin's smokescreen was about to fade away.

But that wasn't all she felt. "I appreciate you sharing that with me,

even after I kept something like the *Preserver* data secret from you,"
she said solemnly.

Tricia shrugged. "You did what you had to do."

The foundation of their relationship had always been that they
were both friends and politicians. Keeping secrets from each other
wasn't something that friends did, but politicians? It was just a fair
part of the game.

Isadora could see the conflict in her eyes between the hurt and the
respect—the acknowledgment that Isadora had played a good game,
that she probably would've done exactly the same thing if their roles
were reversed.

"So," Isadora said, "have you made plans?"

"We're moving forward with a peace summit around Bitanu. I
wondered if you would want to attend. Don't worry, I'll send plenty of
warships to keep the peace."

"If there's a way to bring the war to an end, I will be there."

"I suppose it's only fitting. After all, you kickstarted the anti-war
movement, got the information out about the *Preserver*, and made
some kind of backroom deal with Justin Hacelo."

Isadora had been nodding along until Tricia got to the last detail,
at which point she went still. "I have not come to any formal agreement with the Reform leader."

Although Tricia had given Isadora her blessing to talk to the opposition leader, she hadn't told her about Justin's offer: endorse him
over her, and he would end the settlement charter ban on the core
worlds. No need to make Tricia paranoid over something she was unwilling to do. Probably.

"Well, you'd be stupid not to," Tricia said. "Especially if I'm not
going to be on the ballot."

Isadora froze as the edge of her coffee mug touched her lips. She almost dropped the cup. "...excuse me?"

"Look. Almost three years ago, I was thinking about resigning. And then, some snot-nosed asshole shows up with a readout of our long-range satellite scanners showing an approaching object. Your *Preserver*. So I convinced myself that our first encounter with our long-lost brethren needed an experienced hand at the helm. And then, I convinced myself that seeing that through meant rooting out the Offspring."

"And now, I'm putting another once-in-a-generation crisis on your shoulders," Isadora said, not without sympathy.

"Exactly. This morning in the shower, I almost convinced myself that I had to stay on until we figured out the wormhole situation. That was the moment when I decided I had to resign. Because I'd just get sucked into another crisis after that."

"*San neomeo san*," Isadora blurted, recalling what Meredith had told her a few weeks ago.

Tricia shot her a bewildered look. "Do I need to get my translator out of whatever dusty fucking hole I stuck it in?"

"It's an old Korean expression," Isadora explained. Which didn't seem to clear up any of the prime minister's confusion. "One of Earth's nation-states. Where my parents were from, originally. It translates, roughly, to 'over the mountains are mountains'—the meaning being that, as soon as we solve one major problem in our lives, another one crops up."

Tricia nodded. Looked uncharacteristically reflective. The winter sun outside was glaringly bright, casting a beam onto one of Tricia's cheeks, making it look especially sunken. "Seems fitting."

Not the least, because Isadora had been thinking the same thing.

Even if she could successfully bring the outer rim war to a close, thereby neutering the Offspring, and bring the rest of her people out of cryo—and those were *big* ifs, she feared—more crises were on the horizon.

Figuring out how to jointly manage control of the *Preserver* wormhole. Deciding her people's place in the Natonus System, whether that meant further integration, or going it alone. Creating contingency plans for whatever they found back in the Sol System.

Her respect for Tricia's decision grew.

"I'm going to announce my intention to step down by the end of the week," Tricia continued. "I'll serve out the end of my term, since there's less than two months left, then I'll resign after the parliamentary elections. If the Workers' Party wins, someone else will have to take the reins on the shitshow. So what I'm really saying is: go endorse Justin Hacelo. It's too good of an opportunity to pass up."

Isadora looked at her, seeing more of the friend than the political counterpart. "Are you sure?"

"My party's still up in the polls. Don't expect it to be a cakewalk for your guy. But yes, I'm giving you permission. And don't go yapping about my intentions to the media just yet. You're the only one I've told."

"Of course." Given all the times Tricia had complained about the younger generation in her party, as well as the lack of extreme polarization in Union politics, it didn't fully surprise her that she was giving her blessing to endorse a rival.

They sat in silence for another few minutes, basking in the warmth of the sun coming in through the window. "Maybe after all this is over, you and I can take a vacation together," Isadora said. "We damn well earned it, after all this. And you've been in office far longer than I have."

"I'd genuinely like that," Tricia said. "Not even shitting you. Let's plan on it."

Isadora chuckled. But she also got a feeling the prime minister wanted some time to be by herself. She finished her coffee and stood up. "Let me know when the details are finalized for the peace summit."

"You'll be among the first to know."

Isadora left, walking through halls just as packed and hurried as earlier. But she was lost in her thoughts. Lost imagining a future beyond the confines of politics. Lost envying the weighty decision Tricia had made, admiring the firmness with which she'd come to it. The future felt pregnant with possibilities for the first time since Isadora had woken up, shivering and alone, back on the *Preserver*.

But that could wait just a little bit longer. For now, she had a Union Parliamentary candidate to officially endorse. And a war to bring to an end.

CHAPTER 30

Nadia and her crew had gotten the go-ahead order from Tori. Soon, they'd begin shelling one of the Junta warships orbiting Ikkren—one of the last two remaining. If they could severely damage the vessel, maybe even take it out, that could force the entire occupational forces to surrender. All the ground forces had to do was protect their anti-air cannon from a near-certain response.

The problem was that Tori and the main Horde fighting force had been delayed. They'd had to go around a Junta military encampment, but if Nadia didn't start firing the anti-air gun ASAP, the whole operation was in danger of getting spotted by Junta orbital surveillance. Hopefully, Tori and her troops would only be delayed a few minutes.

At least Nadia could walk again. Sort of. Running at a sprint still hurt, but she could move briskly. She tried telling herself she would be fine, but with their attack on a Junta warship about to commence, and a shootout certain to follow, she knew she was just lying to herself.

She, Boyd, Derek, and almost two hundred armed volunteers from all over the planet had arrived at the ruins of the original Modrin settlement in the far northern hemisphere. It was there that they'd repaired the colony's old anti-air turret back to functionality, then loaded it with the warheads Nadia and her crew had recovered from the crashed Union vessel.

Despite the looming fight, she'd been feeling superfluous. Boyd had been rushing back and forth between the *Exemplar* and the anti-air gun, making sure the warheads were programmed to ignore their ship's missile scrambling frequency. Derek, meanwhile, was busy giving last-minute speeches to the volunteers and scouting out the best defensive positions.

The ruined colony was in the middle of a mountain caldera, with the ridgeline serving as a natural defensive point. Derek had parked the *Exemplar* right in the middle of the dead settlement, meaning the entire depression was blanketed by its protective scrambling systems.

And they had the numbers to set up a full perimeter along the edge, meaning that if the Junta wanted to land troops in the middle of the colony, they'd be under fire immediately. Hopefully, that'd mean they'd be forced to land at the base of the mountain far below, where they could be easily picked off from above.

It was while Nadia was pacing the caldera perimeter that she heard her wrister scream out the phrase "comms check" at her. Boyd's voice.

"You're as loud as an engine whine," Derek said in their shared comm channel. At least a dozen of the volunteers murmured their agreement.

"Yep. Right. Sorry. Accidentally hit the speaker volume knob while I was, y'know, handling a deadly explosive," Boyd said, his voice returning to normal volume.

Nadia grinned. Before she got a chance to reply, however, a massive boom echoed throughout the icy mountain range. A plume of fire and smoke escaped the barrel of the anti-air gun. A trail of smoke led up to the atmosphere, where a missile disappeared past the cloudline. The Junta warship they were targeting was holding orbit thousands of miles away, which meant that they would be unlikely to hear so much as a faint echo of the resulting explosion. They all cheered anyway.

They launched another three warheads over the next half-hour. Hopefully, at least one had made it through the enemy warship's defense systems and inflicted some serious damage. But with the Junta's tracking abilities all focused on the source of the attack, that meant every hostile gun barrel on the planet was now pointed toward them.

On cue, a Junta projectile came whistling through the cloudline. It arced downward toward the ruined colony, until it veered sharply and suddenly to the left, disrupted by the *Exemplar*'s active missile scrambler.

The projectile's flight path went haywire as it careened in every direction, finally landing in the ice plains to the east. The explosion was hardly visible from Nadia's vantage point. All she saw was a plume of orange fire and white ice chunks, muddled in the blue haze, until it evaporated in the wind.

Fifteen minutes later, Boyd's voice came through the comm

channel: "Picking up something on the scanners."

Nadia reached for her earpiece with renewed urgency. "Is it Tori's strike force?"

"Negative. Junta signatures. Looks like we have at least fifteen incoming troop transports."

"All right everyone, this is it. Look alive," Derek said.

Their volunteer force split up, taking position at the edge of the caldera. A small number hid out in the bombed-out ruins of the colony, on the off-chance that the arriving Junta soldiers attempted a landing behind their defensive perimeter.

In another few minutes, faint dark specks materialized out from the blue haze of the atmosphere. The sound of engines followed. The Junta gunships grew larger and larger until they descended, latching onto the sides of the mountains with their landing gear.

Shit. Nadia hadn't realized that they could do that. This fight was about to get a lot harder.

She, Boyd, and Derek had split up to each take one section of the ridgeline. A couple of the more trigger-happy volunteers began firing plasma rounds at the troop landers. A few bolts chipped away at the enemy gunships' plating, but most of them just ended up scraping the rock and ice along the slopes.

Junta troops filed out of their gunships. A flood of plasma bolts streaked up at their position, forcing Nadia and the others below the ridge for cover. When she popped up to return fire, she got a better look at their enemies' equipment. Each Junta soldier was outfitted with crampons to help ascend the steep slope, and many of them had already used grappling devices to pull themselves up.

"Take out their grappling hooks!" she shouted to the other volunteers. With crampons affixed to their boots, the Junta troops could still reach their position eventually, but it'd be much slower and difficult without ropes. And it'd give them time to lay down a withering screen of fire.

It was harder than it looked. The hooks were embedded in a band of ice only a little more than a dozen feet below the ridgeline. And every time one of them took aim at the devices, a flood of enemy fire greeted them. It didn't help that the Junta troops were professional soldiers, while Nadia's team was made up of volunteers.

And most of all, she didn't want any of them to resort to unnecessary heroics. They won just by staying alive and preventing the Junta from destroying the anti-air turret. There was no need to make risky, sacrificial pushes. She didn't hold it against anyone if they retreated into cover when faced with an overwhelming barrage of Junta plasma bolts. Even if that meant they were giving their adversaries free rein to advance.

Nadia stood up, ignoring a quick spasm of pain from her leg. She laid down a screen of covering fire before taking aim at one of the grappling hooks. It was so close, so *agonizingly* close. She narrowed her eyes, lined her shot, squeezed the trigger. The device snapped in two, the rope slid off the mountain, and the attached soldier stumbled and rolled down the slope.

A sharp cry from her left kept her from celebrating.

Her head snapped over to see one of the volunteers sprawled out on the ground, a deep wound in his shoulder. Two others were huddled over him while the rest were laying down suppressing fire.

Nadia crawled over as fast as her recovering leg would take her. When she got close, she could tell the shoulder injury was serious—probably painful as hell—but not fatal. "We have teams with medical supplies back in the colony proper," she said. "I'll take him."

The other two volunteers nodded and returned to the firing line. She scooped up the injured man, draping him around her shoulders and trying to stand. Her hip protested violently, so she had to emit a small thrust from her enviro-suit's propulsion device for assistance.

In hindsight, sending the person with the most combat experience—and the one with the injured leg—to carry back the wounded probably wasn't the smartest choice. *Too late now.*

Walking was hard, but she eventually staggered her way back to the center of the destroyed settlement. As soon as she arrived at the half-destroyed prefab shelter they'd converted into a field hospital, Derek's voice came over the comms: "We're taking a lot of incoming fire. Falling back."

Nadia didn't have time to worry about the collapse of his team. A pair of volunteers with medical experience ran over to help her ease the injured man onto a bed. They applied healing gel to the man's shoulder and began tying a tight bandage around the wound site.

"You're gonna be okay," she said, locking eyes with the injured volunteer. "But I need to get back to the ridge."

When she turned and left the bombed-out shelter, however, all that greeted her eyes was the rest of her team barreling toward her. "They took the perimeter!" one shouted.

Nadia looked on in horror as Junta troops appeared at the edge of the mountain, working their way down into the crater. Deadly flashes of fire streaked past the bodies of retreating volunteers. One received a blast directly to his back and crumpled down. Two others went back to retrieve their fallen comrade, only to take plasma bolts to the face and arm, respectively.

Nadia pulled her handgun out and fired wildly at their attackers, hoping to give the survivors time to get to safety. Then she ducked behind a wall of rended plastic and metal alloys before the enemy soldiers could line up shots on her.

"This is too much!" Boyd's panicked voice came from her earpiece. "We've got to relocate to the Modrin ruins!"

"I'll put my team in position to cover your retreat," Derek said.

"The Junta has breached the ridge on all sides," a third voice said. "They've got a clear shot at the turret." He sounded crestfallen.

The ground shook beneath Nadia's feet as the anti-air turret fired off another salvo into the atmosphere. She couldn't help but wonder if this was the last one they'd get off before their enemies destroyed the gun. *No*, she told herself, *I can't think like that. I just have to figure out—*

She heard a deep thud, followed by a deadly hiss. The wall in front of her exploded. *I guess they brought a grenade launcher along* was the only thing going through her head as slats of plastic and metal flew in every direction. As one particularly heavy chunk of the wall came crashing down on her.

She heard two volunteers nearby shout her name. Footsteps followed. In another second, a pair of hands were tugging her, one under each of her armpits.

Or at least, trying to. "You're stuck," an exasperated voice told her.

Nadia wanted to say that if she could just get her hand down to her wrister controls, she could fire her suit's thrusters, giving them momentum. But a dozen thud-pings of incoming plasma fire cut her off. When she looked down, she saw dozens of Junta soldiers advancing on them.

"Just go," she grunted. The two hesitated. "Go!" she repeated more forcefully. They exchanged glances and fled.

Nadia fought tears stinging the edges of her eyes as she

desperately reached for the handgun. If she was going to go down, she wanted to go down swinging. Preferably in a blaze of glory that might even make Russ proud if he'd been here to see it. Her fingers stretched out, agonizingly close, but still too far from the grip of her weapon.

And then felt the ground vibrate beneath her.

Nadia was so mesmerized by the sensation that she almost couldn't concentrate on Boyd's triumphant voice: "It's the Horde! Tori's strike force is here!"

Nadia craned her head to look over the debris pinning her down. It was like the advancing enemy line had caught fire. Plasma bolts were flying in every direction, but mostly coming from the sky. A gunship shot out from the edge of her peripherals and unleashed a barrage on the advancing Junta troops.

Cheers and joyful cries erupted over the comm channel. Nadia's adrenaline surge must've subsided, because the rubble on top of her suddenly felt more painful. She tried to wiggle free, but only got her right arm to move a few inches before it got stuck again.

She looked up to see one of the Junta troop transports taking off. At least, until Horde gunships swooped in to blast apart the transport's hull. Chunks of hull plating spat out, and the husk of the transport spun toward the mountain ridgeline. It scuffed the edge and disappeared beyond her view.

Nadia tried to be happy. *Really* tried. This might've been the second time in her career since arriving in the Natonus System that she'd kicked the Junta off a planet. But she just wanted to get out from under the wreckage. Celebrations could come later. She cleared her throat and pressed her mouth as close to her earpiece as possible. "Once you all are done," she said, "would someone mind getting me out from under this thing?"

．　　　●　　　●

Nadia's body was sore and cold, but the giddiness made it all fade away. Volunteers and professional Horde fighters alike were celebrating nearby. Boyd and Derek had joined them, while she and Tori had stolen off to the edge of the ruined settlement.

"When I first directed my raiders to assist you on Calimor, I had hardly imagined it would culminate in this," Tori said. Her words sounded grateful, but her tone of voice was, as always, cold and reserved. Nadia wasn't sure she had any other mode.

"I'm still trying to process it all," Nadia muttered.

Per Tori, the warheads they'd fired had taken out one of the two remaining Junta warships orbiting Ikkren. The other warship had retreated to high orbit to evacuate as many of the occupation force as possible, before burning for Bitanu. The remaining Junta forces had surrendered unconditionally.

And it was more than that. Apparently, the situation on Enther had turned dramatically against their enemies, forcing Michael Azkon to sue for peace. The Junta fleet was speeding for Bitanu orbit, where the upcoming peace summit would supposedly take place. Nadia knew she and her crew would need to attend. If Michael Azkon was proposing something, that meant he had some kind of agenda.

And assuming Tanner Keltin was still pulling the Junta leader's strings, that meant he, too, had an agenda. The war may have been coming to a close, but the real threat was still out there.

She turned to face Tori, who wore not even a faint grin. "I thought you'd be happier."

Tori paused and looked out over the ice plains. "We may have our planet back, but we will soon lose it forever. Looking out over this expanse feels like saying hello to an old friend—and goodbye. It's true, isn't it? The rumors about what your *Preserver* can do?"

"They are. But I don't see how—"

"As Union merchant and military vessels travel from the core worlds to the outer rim, the flag will follow. It is the way it has always been. Extrasolar explorers, corporations, migrants will come. In a world where our system is connected to the rest of the colonized galaxy, Ikkren will not be the *frontier* any longer. Development only goes in one direction. At the end of it is the final disappearance of our independence."

That gave Nadia pause. She looked back toward the ruined village, where Boyd was busy chugging a beer. He made eye contact with her, raised his canister. All she could do was wave weakly. Her and Isadora's ploy to convince the Union to activate the *Preserver*'s wormhole function might've doomed the Ikkreners and their fierce desire for sovereignty.

"I don't know what to say," she said quietly.

Tori cast a smile toward her that seemed equal parts genuine, angry, and sad. "You did what you had to do. And you've done more for my people than any outsider ever has. We all knew that someday, the jig would be up. And besides, we are explorers. We might be on the verge of the largest age of exploration in human history. I'd like to be there for that."

"I'd be honored to survey the galaxy alongside you and your people."

"And we will help see this thing through. Our flotilla has been badly damaged, but I will send our surviving host of gunships to Bitanu to help secure the peace summit. I imagine you've had the same suspicions about our mutual foe as I have."

"I have."

"Good," Tori said, her emotionally ambiguous smile returning. "Well then. I will begin preparations immediately. I'll be in touch."

"I look forward to it."

"I suppose you'll be heading to Bitanu soon."

"Soon, yes," Nadia repeated, a soft grin spreading across her face. "But I had one more quick stop I wanted to make on Ikkren first."

CHAPTER 31

Just like that, Carson was a therapist again. Not by choosing, but by necessity.

The Ashkagi rebel takeover of Caphila was quick and relatively painless. A testament to the popularity of the rebels among the populace, he figured, although by this point, the word *rebels* was probably no longer appropriate. With the Junta fleets retreating to Bitanu, that gave space for the Ashkagi to seize control of most of the planet's major urban areas. And they were already popular in the countryside.

Immediately after the fighting, Emil had volunteered as much information about the Offspring's Enther operations as he knew to Noah Tasano's forces. A list of hideouts and secret bases, mostly. But it allowed Noah to send a series of rapid deployment teams to each of the locations Emil gave him. Carson wanted to go with them, but it would be a better use of his time to wait until they'd reported back to Noah. Then, he'd infiltrate the most promising sites.

That left him, suddenly, with an abundance of free time until the teams' reports started coming in. At first, he'd volunteered for everything the rebels needed—cleaning up rubble, distributing essential supplies and medical equipment to the war-weary populace, helping high-ranking rebels get set up in transitionary roles—but Noah had eventually suggested that a better task for someone with his talents was working with the captured Offspring.

They had almost a hundred Offspring under incarceration in the city's detention facilities, with hundreds of others at regional facilities. Right now, they'd estimated the remaining Offspring at large on Enther at less than two hundred.

At least a couple dozen prisoners had expressed interest in deradicalization. Well, Noah had called it *adjustment therapy*, but deradicalization was what he meant.

Carson wasn't sure how to feel about this. On one hand, he was so far removed from his old life that he wasn't sure how good of a job he could even do anymore. Made all the worse by his personal connection with the cases. On the other, any conversation with Offspring prisoners could yield intelligence.

It was that last point that had encouraged him to go through with Noah's plan. And then he'd felt vaguely uncomfortable since. Going into a therapy session with an ulterior motive—with the intention of actually trying to *use* his patients—violated just about every ethical norm he could think of.

Desperate times.

The deal the rebels had given the Offspring who agreed to participate in therapy was an exercise in carrots and sticks. Those who agreed to participate in Carson's program would be moved to a luxury condo the rebels had seized from a coterie of high-ranking Junta officers. They'd still be under house arrest, but they'd be able to live in far better conditions than their comrades.

Carson strolled through Caphila's streets, heading toward the convention center that'd been requisitioned for his therapy sessions. He nursed a coffee that was still steaming at the top. It was early morning, the sky still dark with rain clouds. Every time a raindrop landed in his coffee, concentric ripples formed.

The streets felt less dangerous than when a battle had taken place, but only slightly less frantic. There were still civilians constantly on the move, too many probably displaced. Carson was impressed at how little damage the Ashkagi had inflicted on the city, but a siege was still a siege. Everywhere he looked, there were buildings with the top few floors blown off.

He arrived at the convention center and paused. When he'd first agreed to conduct therapy sessions with willing Offspring, he'd debated whether to tell them he was, in fact, a refugee. Revealing his Earthborn identity would be naturally triggering to someone inculcated with radical nativist ideology, but establishing trust with patients was one of the first vital steps in any therapy program. If he didn't tell his new patients who he was, he'd have to construct a new backstory and continue to deceive them.

Luckily, the Ashkagi had taken the decision away from him.

Noah had disseminated information on Carson's real identity to all Offspring interested in therapy. In some ways, that gave him more confidence that those who had volunteered *really* wanted it by weeding out anyone still unable to face a refugee one-on-one. But the revelation would set the tenor of the first session in a way he wasn't entirely comfortable with.

Maybe there weren't any good choices. Carson opened the door to the convention center, somewhat grateful for Noah's forthrightness.

The building interior was depressing. Hallways and rooms alike were empty. There were athletic courts and meeting rooms, virtual gaming stations and spin chambers. All rooms had some flavor of cancellation notification on a scrolling holoscreen: INDEFINITELY POSTPONED, CANCELLED UNTIL FURTHER NOTICE, REFER TO [various wrister coordinates] FOR AN UPDATE. The aftershocks of war and revolution.

He walked down a row of deserted rooms and more cancellation notices until he reached a room with an armed Ashkagi outside. "Are you sure you want me out here?" the woman asked. "No one would blame you if you want someone inside with you."

Carson paused for a moment. It was, of course, possible that the Offspring inside might want to attack him, especially given that this was the first time he'd be seeing Carson with the knowledge of his refugee status.

But having an armed guard on duty was a massive breach of trust. He'd thought about taking a handgun with him as well, but rejected that for the same reasons. And he felt confident that he'd be able to fend off an unarmed attack. Long enough to call for help if he was seriously mismatched, at least.

"Thank you, but no," he said firmly. "It's important for this to feel as normal as possible."

The rebel nodded solemnly. "I understand. Good luck in there. May the Ashka light your path."

Carson wasn't really sure how to respond to that, so he thanked the guard again and entered. The room was large enough for a small community meeting, but only contained two chairs. It was almost hilarious how disproportionately large the room looked.

And then there was the Offspring. Harry Klim, according to the file. He'd been Marcus' patrol partner, but he hadn't seemed as suspicious of Carson as Marcus had been. He'd always seemed quiet. Mostly kept to himself, not much of a natural leader. Not like Emil.

Harry's eyes stared back at him with a mixture of suspicion and curiosity. But it was an *othering* curiosity, the kind that Carson suspected a zoo animal would see when it gazed up at its onlookers.

He sat down, gave Harry a small grin, and sat back in his chair. It reclined slightly. He crossed his legs and looked at his file. "It's good to meet you in this context," he said, trying to keep his voice as congenial as it could be, given that Harry belonged to a group that wanted him dead. *This is going to be a first.*

Well, there was Emil, but that was more of a calculated gambit that'd paid off than an actual therapeutic experience.

"What's it like, being one of them?" Harry blurted out.

Carson rubbed his lip with his index finger. *Well, at least the curiosity is winning out over the suspicion.* "Have you ever had an experience where you were facing a tremendous amount of uncertainty?" he asked.

That seemed to take Harry aback. He looked up and to his right as he considered his response. "Well...I guess I was kicked out of secondary school for plagiarism," he said at last. "My parents kept trying to sign me up for every extracurricular they could. I was so busy, and it seemed like the easy way out. Basically ended any chance I had of going to university."

Carson appreciated that he was already communicative. He'd remembered him as somewhat quiet, but it didn't surprise him that he was suddenly talkative. Sometimes, naturally quiet people were the most chatty in the one-on-one environment of therapy.

"Well, it's a little bit like that," he said with as disarming of a smile as he could muster. "It's been a lot of uncertainty, a lot of future plans that are having to get rewritten. And there's certainly a lot of pressure, too—like the kind your parents put on you. Why don't you tell me more about that?"

Days passed, filled with countless circular back-and-forths, before Carson got his answer. "I can count the number of times my parents told me they loved me on both hands," Harry finally revealed during a session six days later.

"Wow," Carson said, genuinely horrified. He hadn't necessarily been as close to his parents as he could've been—leaving them behind on Earth had been hard, but not paralyzing—but Harry's experiences sounded extreme. Ripe for Tanner Keltin's manipulation.

"They just always forced me into stuff. Never asked me whether it was what I wanted. And then after the plagiarism thing came out and I got expelled, they shunned me. Practically didn't talk to me for months. They told me I had to pay them rent to live with them—and they're both old money, so I know it wasn't really necessary—so I had to get this real shitty delivery gig."

"That must've been really challenging."

"Yeah. I began poking around on the dark net, since most of my secondary school friends stopped talking to me. Eventually got to talking to Tanner, although I didn't know that's who he was at the time. Shit...he was the first nice, approving person I'd met."

A natural older brother figure. Carson had developed the sense that the Offspring would never have become what it grew to be without him at the helm.

"So tell me," he said, "you signed up for this willingly. That means there's something going on, maybe beneath the surface, that made you come to therapy. Even though you know who I really am."

"One of the enemy, you mean?" Harry asked.

"A refugee, yes," Carson said, although not in a corrective way. Telling Harry he was wrong would certainly backfire.

"I...don't know. The stuff Emil was saying always made sense to me. I came out here because I believed in Tanner, but his vision wasn't anything like what we ended up doing."

Carson nodded. "And how did that make you feel?"

More days passed. Days filled with therapy sessions, slow progress the norm. Which was to be expected. Carson hadn't gotten any actionable intel out of the prisoners yet, which partially made him feel better. The moment where he had to make that ask would be difficult.

"I never got angry with Tanner," Harry eventually told him, about two weeks after their first session. "Not until the past few months. For a while, I was blaming myself. Saying that, you know, if I wasn't doing what Tanner told me I'd be doing, maybe that was because I'd screwed up. That it was my fault, or something."

Carson took quick notes on his wrister. The tragedy of therapy, sometimes, was how quickly it was apparent what the patient's issue was. Harry clearly wanted a parental figure—maybe even just any authority—to approve of him. Somewhere along the line, that basic impulse had gotten twisted. Corrupted, to the point that he was training to murder refugees.

From Harry's point of view, of course, it wasn't even close to that obvious. It was like he was caught in a deep jungle, while Carson had the benefit of a topographical map. The challenge was to get him to find his own way out.

"I want to ask you something else," Carson said. "It may sound a little strange. I want you to picture a moment where you felt really, genuinely happy."

It'd be an easy question for a lot of people to answer, but it clearly took Harry aback. "I was gonna say the first few weeks after I joined the Offspring, but now, I don't even know anymore. Maybe the time when I helped my netball team win the local championship in secondary school. One of the extracurriculars my parents made me sign up for, you know the deal. But I remember my coach saying how proud she was of me. I remember the rest of my classmates cheering at the school assembly."

Carson made more notes on his wrister. He'd gotten incredibly lucky so far. With most patients, you had to start the first few weeks, maybe months, deprogramming them from whatever radical ideology they subscribed to. Had to disassociate the ideology from what they *really* wanted, but it took time to get there. With Harry, it seemed like they'd breezed through that first step quickly.

"Great," he said with a friendly grin. "Tell me more about that."

. . .

It had been almost three weeks since Carson had started holding sessions. Most of the two dozen prisoners who'd elected to undergo therapy were getting hung up on his refugee status. With more time, he knew he could get to them, but time was running short and his real job wasn't to help these people.

But a few were making some really impressive progress—Harry Klim, first and foremost—which was why he knew he had to stop.

He was approaching the point at which he'd feel comfortable

prodding Harry for information on the Offspring's operations. And he couldn't do it. He'd done so many things—things that felt ruthless in hindsight—that betraying his patients' trust was a step too far.

Which was why, when Emil reached out to him, he couldn't help but get excited. They met at one of the few streetside cafes in the capital left undamaged from the battle.

"Been a while," Emil said with a toothy grin.

"I figured you've had your hands busy," Carson said.

"Sure have. And you're about to, as well. The Ashkagi have been diligently raiding every outpost I gave them, all while tracking any shuttles or transports that got away. Their analysts have found a convergence: an old Junta weapons cache outpost that was supposedly defunct. Hell, *I* didn't even know the Offspring had set up there. Which probably means it's important. Noah offered to send forces, but I figured there was a better way."

"You want to infiltrate them."

"Well...we've still got a couple of Offspring suits lying around. Figure they might as well get some use."

Carson felt a glimmer of anxiety and doubt. What Emil was proposing would put both of them behind enemy lines, where it would be all too easy for him to betray him.

But if they sent in a military force, it'd be too easy for the Offspring to delete any sensitive information stored at the site. And bringing Emil along, considering the other man's prestige in the organization, would make it more likely that the Offspring there would believe whatever story they made up. The only ones who knew that the two of them had defected were currently incarcerated.

Besides, he hadn't given Carson any reason yet not to trust him. "Okay," he said at last. "When do we leave?"

CHAPTER 32

The first normal day of Isadora's life in months was already looking like it was coming to a close. It had started so promising: coffee with her daughter, a half-hour of morning yoga on their residence's balcony, watching the sun rise over Obrigan City, walking to the park with Meredith and Rebecca before the two stole off to meet with an aid organization about their plans for after graduation.

She then headed to her office for the first real cabinet meeting she'd attended since the war began. It was supposed to be like any other cabinet meeting—a glorified status update—but she knew this was going to be a tough one. For at least two reasons.

Per Riley and Gabby, most meetings had devolved into some variety of shouting match or passive-aggressive standoff between Alexander and Katrina. Isadora hoped she could exert a calming presence on her executive staff. Although the announcement she was about to drop on them probably wouldn't help.

She'd decided to hold the meeting in her private office, away from the normal embassy meeting room, located in the thick of well-trafficked hallways and stressed-out executive workers.

And when she entered her office, she found two resignation letters on her desk.

They were paper. Handwritten. Extremely quaint, but for the gravity of the situation, Isadora figured it was appropriate. She skimmed the first one, from Katrina. She expressed her gratitude at having served Isadora for almost three years, and briefly recounted some of the most important diplomatic initiatives they'd accomplished together: winning back the Union's sympathy after the near outbreak of war on Calimor, mediating tensions between the Horde and the Union, encouraging the Sarsi planetary government to overturn the settlement ban.

However, the letter concluded with an acknowledgment that Katrina did not share the goal of complete integration with the rest of the system. Something that seemed inevitable after activating the *Preserver*'s wormhole function.

Isadora figured she should've seen this coming. She'd sought to ameliorate some of those concerns with a slew of new holidays— Founding Day, commemorating the establishment of New Arcena; Unity Day, commemorating the founding of the UN back on Earth; Solstice Day, commemorating what would be the shortest day of the Earth year; Alliance Day, commemorating the upgraded treaty Isadora had brokered with Tricia Favan after the Calimor incident—designed to promote the refugees' shared past and experiences in the Natonus System. Katrina had said it was a good start but—in typical politician language—that it didn't go far enough.

The second letter was from Alexander Mettevin. He recited some of the major financial triumphs of his tenure: promoting a free trade zone on Calimor, securing investment capital from major Union banks, designing a stipend plan for their colonists. But, he continued, all these successes demonstrated that they were on their way to becoming Natonese in their own right. He envisioned the system as an integrated, multiethnic community, where having a formal government controlling the affairs of the refugees would impede social unity.

This, too, Isadora should've anticipated. She'd won major accolades from Alexander with her formal endorsement for Justin Hacelo and the Reform Party, an announcement she'd made on Union media shortly after Tricia announced her intention to step down. In a joint press conference, Justin had promised the same kind of economic and cultural integration Alexander craved. But he hadn't said it out loud, but he might as well have: endorsing the Reform Party was a *good start*, but it *didn't go far enough.*

She'd just finished reading the letters when the door to her office opened. Alexander came in first, followed by Riley. Then Katrina, and Gabby brought up the rear. Alexander and Katrina gave each other frosty glares before turning their heads dramatically and making a point not to look at each other.

Isadora gestured for them to pull up chairs, forming a semicircle around her desk. "Well," she said, raising an eyebrow in amusement, "I suppose this is going to be more of a goodbye than a cabinet meeting."

Katrina spoke first. "I know this might come as a shock, ma'am, but I feel that I would best serve our people's needs in a different capacity than the one I occupy now." Isadora was impressed at how genuine she sounded. To think that, over two years ago, a younger Isadora and Katrina had sat in this very building and exchanged hostile barbs during their first meeting.

Now, there was a warm professionalism to her voice. The kind that showed her respect for Isadora, even if she believed in a different path forward.

"I understand. I can't thank you enough for your service," Isadora said. "Either of you," she added quickly, glancing at Alexander as well.

"Furthermore, I believe I am ending my tenure in a stable position for my successor," Katrina continued. "Our outreach efforts to planetary governments have yielded considerable benefits. And I have cultivated enough goodwill in the Union's Ministry of Diplomacy that we will be fine no matter which party controls Parliament after the elections."

"I am sure your successor will appreciate your dedication," Isadora said.

By now, Katrina had grown her department to include over a dozen subordinates, any of whom could easily be tapped to fill her shoes. How quickly the refugee government had grown, encompassing so many people whose names she didn't know, whose faces were unfamiliar, who she'd never even *met*. Even choosing who to pull out of cryo was handled by mid-level staff now.

"I believe that our finances have never been stronger," Alexander interjected. "Our economy is perfectly positioned to seize upon the opportunities presented by linking the *Preserver* with Earth. We have successfully transitioned all colonies from subsistence production to capital accumulation. Although many settlements are still focused on cash crops, our economy as a whole is remarkably diversified, and should prove resilient in the face of unexpected market shocks. Additionally, much of our surplus has been used to pay back loans from our early months—to the Union government, or Veltech Colonial Supply, for example—which has improved our settlements' credit rating."

Isadora did her best to smile and nod. As mind-numbing as politics could be, it couldn't even hold a candle to economics.

"Little of this will even matter, if the millions still aboard the *Preserver* would rather return to their home," Katrina said. "Think about it: if the Hegemony has indeed collapsed, what prevents us from returning to the Sol System after the wormhole has opened? Why do the economies of a handful of settlements truly matter, when three-fourths of our people have never experienced the Natonus System at all? From their perspective, they'll have just left Earth when they wake up. Why not let them return?"

Isadora opened her mouth to respond, but quickly closed it. She'd thought about returning to Earth plenty of times, but the idea held little appeal for her. Not when all she wanted was the comfort of a normal life in the Natonus System.

Somewhere along the way, she'd stopped considering herself an Earthborn. A refugee, maybe, but a *Natonese* refugee. She'd never explicitly asked Meredith about how she thought about her own identity, but with her deep relationship with Rebecca, it was hard imagining she would think any differently.

But what about the 30 million still in cryo, who'd never *known* Natonus? Had she never even thought about that? *No*, she thought, *too busy running around trying to keep the* Preserver *safe*. She wanted to remind Katrina that the safety of the cryo vessel was not a sure thing until the war had ended and the threat of the Offspring had passed, but it didn't seem like the right time.

"We should let those who come out of cryo go wherever they want," Alexander said. "The fact of the matter is, soon the Union will be the preeminent power in not just one, but potentially two star systems. They will be an economic giant in the galaxy, with the ability to expand even further. As best we can, we should swim with the tide."

"The whole idea of returning millions back to Earth is jumping the gun," Riley interjected. "First, our priority right now is making sure the Offspring don't blow up the *Preserver*. As long as Tanner Keltin is out there, we cannot guarantee our people's safety.

"And, despite Vincent Gureh's assurances, and assuming we actually do manage to bring everyone out of cryo and transform the *Preserver* into a gateway, the security situation in the Sol System is far from certain. We should work with the Union military to send an expeditionary fleet through the wormhole. Any mass-scale civilian traffic between Natonus and Sol is a long way off."

Isadora scanned her cabinet members' faces and caught Gabby's eye. Who just gave Isadora a resigned look. One that said, *yes, this is exactly what I've been dealing with the past few months.*

A strenuous back-and-forth ensued, mostly centered on Alexander and Katrina's continued bickering. Every so often, Riley tried to throw cold water on the situation, refocus everyone's attention on security issues, while Gabby mostly seemed to shy away from conflict.

Isadora pressed her fingertips together, rested her forehead on her index fingers, and let her mind drift for a merciful few moments. She'd focused on little else other than the war and the Offspring for so long that it was easy to forget how much work there was to do. If she really went through with Vincent's plan, she'd be changing everything again.

It'd be a return to when the *Preserver* arrived in Natonese space. When she woke up. Natonese society would be forever changed, as would the lives of the refugees—Earthborn? Natonese? Who could even say anymore?—as would whoever was still left in the Sol System. If there was anyone left at all.

They'd need to figure out how to manage the flow of people between the two systems, while still handling the logistics of bringing 30 million people out of cryo at once, while finding their place in whatever new political realities emerged from the peace summit, from the Union Parliamentary elections.

Well. *Someone* would need to figure all that out.

"I suppose this is probably a highly unideal time to make this announcement," Isadora said, withdrawing a handwritten letter of her own, then placing it on her desk. "Effective as soon as the conclusion of the Bitanu peace summit, I am making plans to step down from my position."

The bickering ceased. Four pairs of eyes turned to face her, each blinking in surprise. Alexander still had his mouth open. "I'm sorry, ma'am?" Riley said weakly.

"When the computer brought me out of cryo, it was ostensibly to handle the initial negotiations with the Union and begin our people's settlement project. That has morphed into much more over the previous years. And now that it appears we have an opportunity to finally bring every single one of our people out of cryo, I believe my tenure should naturally come to a close. Our people will face enormous challenges in the coming years, but I believe someone else will be better suited to managing those obstacles than I am."

Isadora had two basic reasons for resigning. First, she wasn't even sure she had a strong vision for what was supposed to come next.

Assuming she was successful at the peace summit and opened the wormhole to the Sol System. She'd started thinking of herself as Natonese, sure, but she acknowledged that plenty of others might think differently. She saw the logic behind both Alexander and Katrina's worldviews. Maybe integration was the best choice. Maybe maintaining a sense of communal solidarity was.

Who knew? Certainly not Isadora.

But second, and more importantly, was Meredith. She wanted to finally let her daughter live as normal a life as possible. Enjoy whatever their relationship would morph into as she moved into adulthood. The haunting memory of her accusatory eyes back during Isadora's reelection campaign would always return, so long as she remained in her position. So long as she needed to make hard, morally compromised choices.

"I...what should we even do?" Gabby asked.

Isadora felt a pang of sympathy for Gabby and Riley. Somehow, they'd have to keep the whole government running while two of their ranking colleagues—as well as their boss—had resigned.

In the early days, they'd established a clear line of succession: Isadora's position would pass to the chief diplomat, followed by the security adviser, followed by the chief financier, followed by the chief attorney. If Katrina resigned along with her, that would make Riley the official caretaker while the Consultative Committee voted on a proposal for a formal process to replace Isadora.

Probably another election. Somehow, she got the feeling that Katrina and Alexander might end up as the leading contenders to replace her.

"I realize this may come as a shock," she said, "but I've made up my mind. And I wanted to give you all plenty of time to prepare. I imagine the Consultative Committee will have a thing or two to say. And I will continue to stay in office until the peace summit has formally concluded. Although it is my intention to depart for Bitanu within the week."

It was an empty gesture. With Isadora traveling to the far reaches of the system, she'd be out of contact for most of the trip. And when she arrived at Bitanu, she'd have her hands busy. But she hoped at least nominally staying in power would give her staff cover to figure out a game plan for whatever would come next.

Riley was the first to stand up. She pressed her recliner away from her, stood erect, saluted. "Ma'am," she said, tightening her jaw. "It has been an absolute honor and a privilege."

Gabby was next. "Ma'am, it's been a pleasure," she said.

Katrina and Alexander eyed each other suspiciously before standing up in unison. "Ma'am," they said simultaneously, nodding their heads in respect.

Isadora flashed them a warm smile. "The honor, privilege, and pleasure have all been mine. And please," she paused to wink, "you can call me Isadora."

CHAPTER 33

With the peace summit still weeks away, Nadia and her crew had found themselves with unexpected time on their hands. They'd made periodic stops at the various refugee settlements on Ikkren, making sure everything was running smoothly. That'd killed a few days.

Still. Plenty of time for a personal detour.

Cleevan wasn't the first settlement Nadia and her team had founded on Ikkren, but she remembered it well. It was located next to a small lake—"A lake, really? Is that what we're calling that pond?" Boyd had remarked at the time—and a low, rolling mountain range in the southeastern hemisphere of the planet. It was remote, but near enough to a major trading outpost to be viable. The settlers they'd thawed out to fill the colony had mostly focused on growing wheat.

At the start of the first wave of colonization, all that had existed were about a dozen prefab shelters that would serve as multifamily apartment units. Plus two larger buildings that could be used as town meeting centers or community facilities. Now, flying low over the colony in the *Exemplar*, she was treated to a hell of a view.

There were landing pads and docking ports for rovers, amber fields of wheat, genetically modified to withstand the Ikkren chill, that looked strange but beautiful as they emerged from the planet's white permafrost. And there were so many shelters of various types—research labs, markets and commercial food stalls, shipping offices, new housing units—that Nadia could hardly make out the original settlement. There was a massive pipeline running across the nearby lake that distributed water to the wheat fields.

Derek touched the *Exemplar* down on the landing pad closest to a housing unit at the far end of the colony, on the outskirts of the lake. "Thank goodness," Boyd said. "I was getting real sick of nutra and cheap rations. The galley's never fuller than after we pay a visit to Leila and Rashad's."

Nadia and her crewmates headed outside. Took an elevator to the ground. Approached the single housing unit, one registered to Leila and Rashad Jibor.

Mom and Dad.

In another half-hour, the three of them were sitting on her parents' front porch with her mother. Nadia had shed her charcoal-and-teal enviro-suit—it felt like she hadn't taken it off in *years*—and wrapped herself in one of her mother's insulated coats. Her hands clutched a warm mug of tea.

"I can't believe you actually built a deck," she said, laughing in the middle of a shiver. Sitting outside and enjoying the view was one thing back in Kansas, and something entirely different on frigid Ikkren.

"Oh, we adapted after the first year," Nadia's mom said with a smile.

Just hearing her mother again warmed her heart more than the tea could. Both her parents had a way of speaking that no holo-transmitter could adequately capture. They were always so serene, so calm, never raising their voice, even in their moments of greatest euphoria or angst. Listening to them had always made her feel like everything was going to be okay.

She looked up at the night sky, at small, shimmering specks of white and yellow. The sky was clear, cloudless, beautiful. They were far south enough that solar winds, in combination with the polar regions, painted wisps of translucent green and violet streaks across the sky.

Everything felt slower. She wasn't racing to stop a war on Calimor, racing to convene a failed peace summit on Enther, racing to save Boyd from the Offspring, racing to assist the Horde in its war, racing to save Isadora from Tanner. She was just sitting with her mom and her friends.

Her father emerged from the shelter after completing evening prayer. "Hi dad," Nadia smiled.

"Hi Mr. Jibor," Boyd and Derek said in unison.

"Y'know," Boyd continued. "Nadia was telling us a bit about your faith. I've always wondered: how do you figure out what direction Mecca is in?"

"Oh," her father said, a twinkle in his eyes, "I just try to make a good guess." He pulled up a chair to sit down on the other side of her mother.

Of all the colonists they'd brought out of cryo, Nadia's parents had shown remarkably few psychological issues adapting to their new lives. Most of Isadora's advisers didn't, of course, but that was presumably because the *Preserver* computer had selected for the severe workaholics.

That certainly fit Nadia to a T. There were times, in the quiet parts of the night aboard the *Exemplar*, when her mind would drift to the friends and colleagues she'd left behind on Earth. But the truth was, work would always come first for her.

Maybe that was why she'd never had many long-term relationships. It had always been so difficult to imagine that any two people could be more perfect for each other than Leila and Rashad Jibor, so she'd barely spent any effort trying. It was easier to think of work as her forever partner.

"It's so good to see you two again," Nadia's father continued, flashing a smile at Boyd and Derek.

Her parents' relationship with her crew had mostly developed via holo-recording, but she wouldn't be surprised if they'd committed every single factoid she'd ever mentioned to memory. Come to think of it, that probably explained the faint smell of oats and cinnamon she'd gotten when her dad emerged from their shelter: Boyd's favorite type of cookie.

On cue, Boyd spoke up again. "Wait—are those *cinnamon oat cookies?*"

"Just for you," Nadia's mother said with a smile.

"Well, if it's all right then, I'm gonna head indoors."

"I'm coming with," Derek said.

"Too bad. I'm not sharing."

"We left something inside for you too, Derek," Nadia's father said.

"We heard you like poetry. Well, we have a book of poems written by a multinational group of authors from Earth. It's the ragged-looking tome on the central table. You can keep that one. The rest you can borrow, so long as you keep flying our daughter around safe." He winked at Nadia.

"I will. And I look forward to reading the rest," Derek said.

After Boyd and Derek had retreated indoors, Nadia spoke again: "So, how have things been going here?"

"Oh, the irrigation system out there insists on breaking every other day," her father sighed. "I've tried everything, other than maybe a stern lecture. The parts we brought from the *Preserver* just weren't made for these kinds of temperatures. I don't think Cleevan is very high on the government's priority list for the newest colonial tech, and even if we were, the Junta blockade ended all shipping out here."

"Why didn't you mention this before?" Nadia said. "I can send a message to Isadora Satoro personally, and we'll get you parts in no time."

"No, no," her father laughed. "We would never want to take supplies from those who need them more. I enjoy fixing the irrigation system. It's an excuse to get my old, creaky bones out of bed every morning. And besides, I have nothing to complain about. We have everything."

"We really do," Nadia's mother agreed.

"We have our lives, we have our freedom. Our settlement was spared the chaos and misery of the war. We have each other, and we never go hungry," her dad continued. "And of course, we have a loving daughter, who we are very proud of—"

" —but who could stand to send us messages with a little more frequency," her mom laughed. "But your father is correct. We have a supportive community. Life here is idyllic."

Nadia's parents had migrated across the galaxy, fleeing war and destruction. Had been living under the threat of the Offspring and the Junta invasion ever since they'd come out of cryo. How was that idyllic? How was *any* of this idyllic?

As she looked out over the landscape, her mind slowly started to forget the war, the upcoming peace summit at Bitanu, the loose thread that was Tanner Keltin. There was just the colony and the land. Just the *present*. Maybe that's how her parents could find bliss in all this mayhem and danger.

But as much as a part of her wished she could just settle in Cleevan and live a normal life, another part of her knew she'd never actually be able to perceive things like her parents. She'd constantly be rushing around, looking for something to fix. To *improve*. There was so little perfection in the world, which meant there was always more work to be done.

She figured there might be some kind of moral in there.

"So," Nadia's mother said, "do you want to tell us what you've been up to all these recent months?"

Nadia stared at the top of her tea, blowing gently, creating small ripples. The last time she'd brought her parents fully up to speed was when she was still flying toward Ikkren at the outset of the war. Disturbing their peaceful life with all the grisly details of her mission seemed wrong, somehow.

Well, normally.

Tonight, it all came rushing out of her. Her first few unsuccessful operations against the Junta. Her desperate plan to encourage Isadora to smuggle weapons to Enther, forcing the Junta fleet to retreat from Ikkren. The encounter with Tanner and his Offspring agents on

Bitanu. And then, finally, the successful campaign to dislodge the remnants of the occupation force.

It was hard to watch her parents' faces darken when she mentioned Tanner again. They'd always been the ultimate optimists, the kind of people who saw goodness even in the most reprehensible villains. But their faces showed just how irredeemable Tanner was, in their eyes. *Might have something to do with him trying to kill me twice.*

"I am sorry," her father said after she finished. "Sorry that you had to face him again. You've been through so much. It's almost unfair for the universe to ask you to do so much more on top of that."

Her mother, on the other hand, leaned forward. Looked deep into her eyes. "When you were describing your encounter with...*him*, you sounded different. Like there's something new there."

Nadia agreed, but it was hard to name. She stared at her tea once more, trying to focus on nothing but the calmness and serenity of her parents' house. "Vengeance," she blurted out, almost to her own surprise. "I wanted revenge. I wanted to stop seeing his face every time I think about Russ."

Her voice sounded so harsh, so cold. Her mother was right: this was something new. But she also felt an emptiness in her heart. The good kind: the kind you felt after finally shedding some burden that'd been eating you for a long time.

Nadia looked up and saw no judgment in either of her parents' eyes. Just love, just acceptance. "That doesn't sound like you," her mother said. An observation, not a condemnation.

"No," Nadia agreed, "it doesn't. For so long, I kept thinking that there were no evil people. Just misguided people, who I could convince to see things differently."

"And you managed to stop a pointless war between our people and the Union with that philosophy," her father reminded her.

"It is true, though, that there are some evils that cannot be so simply persuaded," her mother said. Her father nodded in agreement. "We know that, on a grand scale, good will always win. The danger is that, in winning, goodness becomes transformed into a mockery of itself."

Maybe it was the joyful emptiness Nadia felt in her heart, but it was surprisingly easy to ingest her mother's words. People always called her a hopeless optimist, naive to the extreme, whatever—but none of those people had ever met her parents.

She came by it honestly, at least.

Her mind then returned to her dark fantasy. Her and Tanner, locked in one-on-one combat, her having the edge at last. Maybe defeating him was necessary, but was it supposed to be her *fantasy*? There could be justice in a momentary, necessary act of violence, perhaps, but there could never be justice in a fit of rageful vengeance.

Some hidden part of her snapped to life. *Russ wouldn't want it to come down to that either*, it said.

"It's getting colder," Nadia's mom said. "Maybe we should go inside?"

Nadia and her dad agreed simultaneously. The living room of their shelter was small, but the epitome of coziness, with a luxurious couch off to the left, a wooden bookshelf nearby that must've been handmade, and the twin smells of spiced tea and cinnamon oat cookies wafting through the air. The soft crack of a fire was their only soundtrack for the evening. A beautiful rug spanned most of the living area.

But all it took was one look at Boyd's pale face to dissipate any notions of comfort.

"Nadia," he said, looking up from his wrister, "I just got a message. Something's gone wrong."

Nadia's heart dropped, but it was hard to take Boyd fully seriously when his entire torso was covered in cookie crumbs. An empty oven tray sat next to him on the couch.

"We just got a forwarded emergency transmission from the *Exemplar*," Derek said. "It was from Noah Tasano."

Nadia exchanged glances with her parents. Then Boyd, then Derek. Hearing from Noah should mean good news, right?

"Long story short: Carson is missing. In his last recorded message, he asked for you by name," Boyd said.

Carson Erlinza. Their hapless spy, embedded in the Offspring ranks for the better part of the last year. Nadia hadn't had any contact with him since the day Russ died. The day she'd first confronted Tanner.

"We can explain more on the way," Boyd said, "but he believes Carson's life may be in danger, and he doesn't have the forces to spare to send in an investigation team. He mentioned Carson was following a major lead."

Nadia looked at her parents, almost as if for permission. "You don't need to ask," her mother said. "We know you need to leave. Just make sure to come back safe. And take some cookies for the road!" she said, retreating to the kitchen and taking a tray of cookies out of the oven.

Boyd nearly sprinted over, packing up the cookies in a hurry.

"I hate to cut this visit short," Nadia said, "but if our friend is in danger, we need to leave *now*." She knew how long a goodbye from her parents could last.

The five of them headed back outside, where she gave both her parents a tight hug. Then followed Boyd and Derek toward the landing pad, while her parents stood on the front porch and waved.

Nadia looked back over her shoulder. "Be safe," her father called out. "We love you. And go do what you were meant to do."

Nadia nodded, turned back around, and headed for the *Exemplar*.

CHAPTER 34

The weapons cache where Carson and Emil were headed was less than a mile away. He figured it'd be a good time to check to see if Emil could get their cover story straight.

Which was how Carson learned his companion was *terrible* at maintaining a cover story.

"Okay," Emil said, panting as he leaned against a large tree in the Enther jungles. "We were part of a detachment sent to Caphila. Most of our regiment defected. We didn't. We headed to the nearest Offspring outpost, but it got overrun by rebels. We eventually picked up a transmission that pointed to the weapons cache out here."

Carson frowned, considering how to be gentle with his criticism. "It sounds very...rehearsed," he said finally. "Which is problematic. A good cover story *should* have plenty of flaws or holes. Misremembered details. You're not trying to concoct an airtight alibi."

Emil nodded. "Sorry. I'm just nervous. And then I get nervous about being nervous."

Carson fought back a grin. He was pretty sure he'd said something almost identical under Juliet Lessitor's tutelage. She'd probably find it more than a little amusing that the shoe was on the other foot now.

"It's actually okay to be nervous," he said. "Thing is, most people have some degree of social awkwardness." *Especially the kinds of people recruited by the Offspring*, he didn't add, figuring it might come off a little insulting. "Being nervous doesn't mean you can't still come off as genuine. That's how normal human communication works."

Emil's facial expression switched from downtrodden to thoughtful. "Huh. Never thought about it like that. You might be on to something. I guess you'd have to be, since you pulled one on us." He let out a self-deprecating laugh.

"Don't worry about that right now. Let's just focus on practicing your cover story."

"Right. So, the thing is, Carson and my unit were at Caphila, which was where most of them defected over to the rebels' side. We just barely managed to escape. We trekked through the night—"

"—what was it like, trekking through the night?" Carson interrupted. "Was it hot? Humid? Raining? Were we fumbling in the dark, or did our wristers still have enough power? You don't need to actually *say* any of this. But it's good to think about. The more you can get lost in this imaginary story you're telling, the more authentic you'll sound."

Emil nodded and paused again to take a few deep breaths. "We were stumbling around in the dark for a while before we made it to the closest Offspring outpost," he continued, sounding almost perfectly natural.

They practiced for almost an hour, with Emil sounding at least serviceable by the end. Hopefully that wouldn't crack when they were actually among the Offspring's ranks.

"All right," Carson said. "I think it'll work."

He wished he could just tell Emil to let him do the talking, but with him being higher up in the Offspring hierarchy, he figured it would seem off for him to do most of the speaking. Few people were as obsessed with hierarchy as the radicalized, in Carson's experience—even the genuine revolutionaries.

The two men took off through the jungle toward the weapons cache. Carson looked down at his brown enviro-suit, wet with moss and rain. He wanted so much to never have to don Offspring garb again, but it was an essential part of the infiltration. And with the outpost secretive enough that even Emil didn't know about it, he had a gut feeling they could discover something valuable inside.

But the operation would be dangerous, even with their disguises and a plausible backstory. He paused next to a sprawling fern and began composing a message on his wrister.

"What're you doing?" Emil asked.

"Sending a message to Noah. I'm telling him we'll send him a check-in in a week. And if we miss that deadline, I'm asking him to radio an...old friend to explain everything." If they got captured or worse, he hoped Nadia Jibor could at least pick up where he'd left off.

"Makes sense."

They continued with their trek until they came in sight of the weapons cache, which was nothing like Carson had imagined. He'd pictured a handful of supply crates with sidearms or assault rifles lying around. Maybe an abandoned barracks, even potentially a garage full of military vehicles.

What he found was a rectangular depression carved into the

ground, leading down into a missile bay. There were over a dozen pencil-like warheads inside—not nuclear warheads, thankfully, but still destructive in their own right.

Carson and Emil turned to look at each other, eyes wide. "What is this place?" he asked.

Emil shrugged. "It's hard to imagine the Junta just giving this over to the Offspring. Maybe they didn't know we took over the base? Or maybe it just fell through the cracks?"

Carson supposed it didn't really matter. What did matter was figuring out what the Offspring were planning on doing with the missiles, how it affected Tanner's larger plan. He couldn't imagine them using the missiles against the *Preserver*, especially with the defensive matrix the leadership had built on Bitanu. But a dozen warheads in the Offspring's hands was bad.

Two Offspring emerged from a bunker on the edge of the pit. They brought their rifles to bear on them. They raised their hands, then said in unison, "Natonus for the Natonese."

The others looked surprised, then grinned and lowered their weapons. "Natonus for the Natonese, brothers!"

Carson fought off a full-body cringe at hearing the word *brother* again. It always made him think of Stacy, no matter how long he'd been undercover.

"We should take them inside," the other said, gesturing for Carson and Emil to follow him.

They entered an elevator shaft inside the bunker. Emil's head shot over to Carson, doubt clouding his eyes. "It's okay," he mouthed. "You've got this." The elevator lurched, and they descended.

When they arrived at the bottom, there were dozens of Offspring waiting for them. "Brother Emil," one said, walking forward and clasping his forearms. "It's been almost a month. We thought you'd been captured for sure."

Carson didn't recognize him, but it looked like Emil did. A decent confirmation that these were ranking Offspring personnel.

"Brother Preston," Emil said. "I'm sorry it took us so long to reach you. Our whole unit defected—or got captured—at the battle of Caphila. We weren't sure about the damn rebels' communications-monitoring capabilities after seizing the capital, so we tried to avoid sending messages on our wrist...terminals."

Carson winced. The slight hesitation between *wrist* and *terminals* was an obvious giveaway that he'd been about to say *wrister*. He must've picked up the Earthborn term from Carson. He looked to the other Offspring, holding his breath in anticipation of the worst, but none of them seemed to notice.

"We made it to Outpost Hargon, but it was already deserted," Emil continued. "Luckily, we found the location of this facility logged in the hangar's databanks. Don't worry—we wiped it clean afterward."

The other Offspring looked impressed. "Thank you. You might've saved us from a rebel attack."

One of the others looked skeptical, however. "Last I heard, the rebels were doing periodic flybys over Hargon. How'd you avoid detection?"

Emil hesitated for longer than made Carson comfortable. "There was only one close call," he interjected. "It was at night, while I was on watch." His mind was racing, trying to paper over the awkwardness. "I climbed up a tree and ripped off one of those giant leaves to cover us."

Emil flashed him a grateful look. "It'd been a long day," he said, his voice regaining some confidence. "I didn't even wake up."

The skeptical Offspring's face returned to normal. The lead one—Preston, apparently—grinned. "It gives me joy to welcome you back into our ranks. Now, I can't say everything about what we're planning, but Brother Tanner has informed us he has a special assignment for our outpost. Although we recognize your bravery in getting here alive, we cannot share information so vital with those who are newer to our organization. As I'm sure you'll understand, we'll need to confine you to quarters."

"Of course. We respect how the Offspring works," Emil said.

"I'm glad you see it our way. Now come. We'll take you there."

·   ·   ·

At least their quarters were comfortable. Every once in a while, one of the Offspring would show up to ask them a few more details about their story, or about the battle of Caphila. Emil's ability to fake a narrative improved with every conversation.

Even still, that left them with ample time without much to do. Early on their second day at the base, Emil spoke up: "How was therapy going? Back in Caphila, I mean."

Carson had already done a thorough search of their dormitory for bugs. Even taught Emil a thing or two about looking for signs of tampering with the walls or ceiling. Satisfied, he'd concluded that the two of them could talk freely—and safely—if they were alone.

He shrugged. "Some progress here and there, but you can't deradicalize people overnight. Or over three weeks' worth of nights, either."

"How does it work? Deradicalizing someone, I mean?"

"It can be hard. So often, it's painfully obvious what the real issue is. People usually don't join groups like the Offspring because they're true believers. It's something else, something that gets tangled up in the group's ideology."

Emil nodded. "Like with my parents. I wanted them to notice me. I wanted to *be* someone."

Perceptive, Carson thought, although he figured he shouldn't be surprised. He'd been helping Emil work through his feelings ever since he'd joined the Offspring. By this point, Emil had been through the equivalent of almost a year's worth of therapy.

Even if it was an especially unconventional version thereof.

"Exactly," Carson said. "But if I point it out, it'll backfire. I have to keep asking questions. Get my patients to figure it out themselves. That's how learning—and unlearning—happens."

Emil let out a sharp laugh. "That's exactly what you did with me. At the time, I thought you were just really curious. But you were getting me to start questioning things. And—holy shit, it's *so* obvious now, in hindsight—it always felt like I was the one putting those doubts in my head."

"Well, sort of. But I *was* genuinely curious. I consider you a friend, Emil."

The words almost surprised him as he blurted them out. Emil had been an adversary, an unknowing informant, a patient, but was now something else. It might be the oddest, most fucked-up friendship he'd ever had, but it *was* one nonetheless.

"You too, Carson. But are you sure? Until a month ago, I might've shot at you if I knew your real identity. Does that scare you?"

Carson shrugged. "Yes." No need to be dishonest with him.

Emil nodded. "Y'know...I've been thinking about what comes

after all this. A lot. I realize what I did—what so many Offspring did—well, we can't just snap our fingers and make it go away. We have to earn our redemption.

"Which got me thinking: everyone back in Caphila was talking about the *Preserver*, how it can serve as a gateway back to Earth. That means they're—*you're*—gonna have to get everyone out of cryo. That means hundreds, maybe thousands, of new colonies are gonna need help. I want to start some kind of relief organization, one where former Offspring can help set up new refugee colonies."

The idea genuinely took Carson aback. He'd never really given a lot of thought to rehabilitation. Figured it was a question for legal theorists and ethicists, mostly. But he supposed that forgiveness without atonement, considering the extent of the Offspring's activities, was an injustice in and of itself.

"That seems...appropriate. And welcome." His professional demeanor cracked for a moment. It'd been the first time he'd heard a Natonese native express a genuine, proactive desire to help his people. And it was coming from an ex-Offspring.

Two more days passed before he decided it was time to make a move. In the meantime, he'd been doing his best to get intel out of the Offspring questioners, but that was a dead end. Every time he was led out of his quarters, he inspected the facility's surveillance capabilities. Studied the Offspring's patrol movements. Memorized as much of the facility's layout as he could. So he knew what to expect.

By this point, considering all the secrecy, he was fairly certain there was at least *some* kind of major intel stored at the base. He'd gladly accept a riskier operation to get at that intel more quickly.

"Are you sure you're ready for this?" he whispered to Emil. They were in the hallway outside their quarters, hiding in a surveillance camera's blind spot.

Emil rubbed his eyes. "I am. Earning my future starts here."

It was a line delivered with such *fervor*. Back in Carson's old practice, plenty of his patients had gone on to channel their energies to a different cause. Sometimes it was a new religion, sometimes it was community volunteering, other times it was an artistic endeavor. Occasionally, it was extreme endurance sports or something along those lines.

There was an intensity to former violent radicals that could not be created or destroyed. Only transferred. Maybe that was why he was able to trust Emil so readily. He matched the profile of his old patients so extensively that it was difficult to believe he was faking it.

Or maybe he just relished working alongside a companion again. He'd been on his own for so long, without even a handler to watch over him, that having someone to watch his back was a relief.

He handed Emil one of the tranquilizer darts he'd stolen from an armory during a previous nighttime excursion. His trust for him notwithstanding, he wasn't about to put him in a situation where he might have to kill his former comrades. Tranq bullets would sidestep that.

"Okay," Carson whispered, "watch me. We want to stay in the cameras' blind spots as we work our way through the complex."

He slinked down the hallway, keeping his back pressed against the wall, until he reached the other side. He'd identified the surveillance cameras as dilapidated models. One time, Juliet had made him memorize every single kind of security camera employed in Natonese space, along with their capabilities.

Emil followed him, more awkwardly than he would've liked. But no alarms sounded, nor stampede of Offspring boots coming to seize them. "Nice work," he said. "We'll take the stairwell down to the lower levels. There should be some kind of database center down there."

The two crept down the stairwell, taking each step as lightly as possible. When they exited, they found themselves in another corridor. Only this time, there were two Offspring on patrol.

Carson almost leapt back into the stairwell to stay out of sight. Emil shot him a quizzical glance. He held up two fingers in response. Emil nodded and readied his handgun, slotting a tranq dart into the barrel.

Based on their mutual training, they could operate based on a shared set of hand signals. Carson communicated that he would take the one on the left, while Emil would shoot the one on the right.

He readied his own weapon and spun back out of cover. A surprised glance from one of the patrolling Offspring met him. Before he could raise his weapon, Carson already had his handgun outstretched, his sights lined, his finger on the trigger. All it took was a gentle squeeze. The dart shot through the air and buried in the target's neck.

Emil followed suit. The other Offspring had managed to unholster his weapon by this point. Emil hesitated a fraction of a second. Enough for Carson to wonder if he could really pull the trigger. Enough for Carson to wonder if he'd have to shoot the Offspring dead himself.

A tranq dart sailed through the air and struck the Offspring. He crumpled to the ground. Both bodies had come to rest outside the range of the surveillance cameras. Carson turned to Emil, gave an approving nod, and proceeded down the hallway.

He and Emil needed to get into the database center, get whatever intel they could find, transmit it to the refugee leadership, and make their way back outside. From his previous observations, they had about fifteen minutes until the incapacitated patrol team would miss their check-in. It'd be tight, but doable.

They reached a door at the other end. As it slid open, images from the past year flashed through Carson's mind. His training with Juliet. The sacrifice of Russ and the other militia members. Infiltrating and ingratiating himself with the Offspring. Turning Emil. Helping the rebels retake the planetary capital.

Everything had led to this moment. To the hope that there was something in the room in front of him, on one of the computer terminals that were now close enough to *touch*, that would help save his people. That would stop Tanner Keltin.

He shook out his nerves and went to work on the closest terminal station. As his fingers danced across the input board, long lists of arcane files and operations names scrolled across the screen, arranged alphabetically. Every time he hovered over a file, it displayed a brief summary. He skimmed through dozens of them.

And then the first entry in the C-range was a file named *CARE-TAKER* OPERATION.

The first paragraph alone lowered his body temperature by a few degrees. Tanner Keltin wasn't on Enther at all. He'd seized one of the Junta warships in orbit.

Carson read the rest of the file, until he reached the final addendum, added only about a week earlier: Tanner was planning to ram the *Caretaker* into the *Preserver* at the upcoming peace summit. The surviving two hundred Offspring on Enther would be mobilized, using captured Junta codes to sneak aboard as many warships as possible. They'd then commandeer them at the onset of the peace summit in order to provide cover for the *Caretaker*, allowing it to complete its suicide run.

Carson was numb. This was it. The reason so many people had died to get him where he was. He'd done it. All he needed to do was send this information to his people, and it would be over. No matter what happened to him.

He was so busy typing that he didn't hear the boots behind him.

Didn't hear when Emil shouted to him.

He was only vaguely aware of the sounds of others entering the room behind him. When he turned, a half-dozen Offspring had their weapons raised. None of it mattered. All he had to do was send the message. They could do whatever they wanted with him after that. He'd have done his job.

Carson was so focused on finishing the message that he could barely process what happened. One of the Offspring tackled Emil. Another one approached him, arms outstretched. He felt his legs give, felt the back of his head hit the ground.

Felt his wrister get ripped from his arm.

Watched it get smashed by an Offspring boot.

That was it. All the death and hardship that had brought Carson here would come to nothing. He looked up at the face of his tackler and slowly raised his hands.

He had failed.

CHAPTER 35

The political perks of her job were one of the few things Isadora would miss when she officially resigned. One of the small ones was the ability to access a high-end restaurant at the edge of Obrigan City's government district.

It was close enough to the Union Government-General—and popular enough with its inhabitants—that the owners had agreed to allow for a full security detail to protect and monitor the building every day around lunchtime, so that Parliament members could eat. Tricia Favan had invited Isadora once, and she'd been a regular customer since.

Today, she'd invited Meredith and Rebecca here.

It was a beautiful, clear, mid-spring day in Obrigan City. Isadora was comfortable in a cardigan, the sky was cloudless. The restaurant

Itself encompassed dozens of small eating terraces, each one stacked on top of the previous one. They were on one of the uppermost terraces, with a view of the entire district on one side, and the bustling metropolitan downtown on the other. Traffic was heavy, but airbuses ran quiet. The smell of fresh pasta wafted through the air.

The sun from overhead illuminated Meredith's face, making her glow in a way Isadora hadn't seen in a long time. At first, she'd only seen Meredith's frozen face from behind the covering of a cryo pod. And then, she'd watched as her face grew more sullen and gloomy during her reelection campaign. And especially after Rebecca's arrest.

It was the happiest Isadora had seen her daughter look in a long time, but she also looked noticeably older. She'd been through more than any teenager rightfully should've, with a front row seat to the kinds of difficult choices and stresses constantly preoccupying her mother.

But there was growth in that. There was a quiet confidence, a sharpness, to Meredith's every word and action. She'd moved across the galaxy, made new friends, started up a successful, against-the-odds relationship, developed a burgeoning worldview to call her own.

Soon, she'd turn eighteen and would graduate from secondary school. She'd always be Isadora's daughter, but she was practically a woman now.

Her eyes grew misty. *My little baby's all grown up.*

"So," she said, trying to distract herself, "I want to hear all about this project you two have in mind."

"Right," Meredith said with an eager grin. "Well, based on what we know, there are going to be hundreds, maybe even thousands, of new colonies. That means there will be a lot of demand for colonial supplies and traded goods. Rather than let each colony try to figure out everything on their own, we want to start a nonprofit organization that works as a sort of middleman. We'll negotiate on behalf of the new colonies and secure the best deals we can get."

Isadora knew that Meredith and Rebecca both wanted to do something related to community service after graduation, but the scale and elegance of their idea took her aback. It was a good idea, after all, and she knew just how much work and research were necessary to create good ideas.

"The problem is, when you first showed up, you kinda got dicked around by predatory corporations like Veltech," Rebecca said. "Trust me: I got a close enough look at how they ran things back when Tanner was worki—"

She paused, and her eyes widened for a moment. She'd mentioned her brother in passing. Probably without even thinking about it.

Isadora remembered the feeling. Even after Meredith's father had left them, after she'd mostly stopped pleading with him to come back, she would sometimes surprise herself with how casually she would bring him up in conversation.

It was the awkward phase of recovery: the phase where you were starting to heal, where everything had just become another part of your life story, but that no longer defined you. Isadora shuddered to think how long she'd been trapped in that stage, and felt for Rebecca.

She must've become aware of both Isadora and Meredith looking at her. "It's okay," she blurted. "Don't worry. I know I need to move on."

Isadora gave her a soft grin. "I'm proud of you, you know," she said. "Both Meredith and I appreciate just how strong of a person you are."

There was a moment where the snarky facade cracked, and

Isadora saw the young woman—the real Rebecca Keltin—underneath. The woman whose parents had passed away before she really knew them. The woman who'd been raised by a brother who turned into a monster in front of her eyes.

The woman who was alone in the universe—except for Meredith. And now Isadora. She was infinitely grateful that Rebecca trusted her enough to be open with her.

And then the facade came back up. She rolled her eyes. "I'm okay. Really. Thanks."

"So anyway," Meredith said, a little more forcefully than was probably necessary, "we're ready to hit the ground running."

"Yes. Please. Tell me everything." Isadora took a bite of her salad, then sat back in her chair and crossed her legs.

Meredith grinned slyly. "Well, it wouldn't have been possible without your political connections. We knew exactly which Union MPs would be most likely to support our idea. And being the daughter of a major politician didn't hurt either."

Isadora raised an eyebrow. After Meredith had castigated her for how easily she'd adopted the usual dirty political tricks during her reelection campaign, she was surprised at how easily she was playing the nepotism card to her advantage.

Then again, she was playing it to start a nonprofit, to help people. Isadora had always felt that the biggest joy of being a parent was watching her daughter use her lessons to grow beyond her.

"Honestly, it wasn't even that hard," Rebecca said with a shrug. "If you want to get your way in Obrigan City, having a lot of money helps. But having connections to the powerful helps even more."

"I agree, that was the easy part. Easier than we'd planned on," Meredith said, exchanging a weary glance with her girlfriend. The kind that hinted at how much time they'd invested into this idea. Isadora would've been impressed if one of her staff had brought this idea to her, but the fact that her own daughter had sunk so much time and effort into this project warmed her heart.

"Everything after that has been a lot harder. We've been trying to shop around, figuring out which suppliers would be willing to give future colonies the best deals. Problem is, everyone has different policies depending on which planet you're shipping to, and we don't even know where all our people are going when they come out of cryo, so..."

"It was easier figuring out what we'd need to get," Rebecca said. "I told Meredith to impersonate you and get your staff to hand over their requisition forms from the past few years. She went with the considerably more boring option of just asking nicely. But yeah, we eventually got Alexander Mettevin to give us copies of all his old receipts."

"We didn't stop there," Meredith said. "We figured that most of the early settlements had to take what they could get. We'll have more flexibility in the future, so we tried sending a message to the *Exemplar* to see if they had any ideas about what kinds of non-essential supplies they thought could be useful for future colonies."

Isadora winced. She figured Nadia was probably a little too busy to send her daughter a wishlist.

"Someone named Boyd Makrum actually got in touch with us," Rebecca said, then rolled her eyes again. "With a *two-hundred page report*. Including whole chapters about architectural considerations based on local geography. If you ever talk to him, tell him thank you for helping with an insomnia episode I was going through a few months ago."

"And that we're grateful, of course," Meredith added hastily.

Isadora felt a big grin spreading up into her cheeks. "I can't believe how much you two have done already. This is amazing."

A part of her still wanted to advise caution. As someone who'd once let a toxic relationship govern her life, she almost thought it was irresponsible not to throw cold water on the two of them banking so much on their relationship.

But the truth was, she *really liked* Rebecca. It was hard imagining a better companion for her daughter.

Maybe the tragedy—and the beauty—of humans was their ability to throw caution to the wind. To acknowledge the mistakes of the past, and then to get up and try again. Because that was all you could do.

"Thanks," Meredith said, grinning. "It was a lot, especially on top of keeping up with schoolwork—"

"—who said anything about keeping up with schoolwork?" Rebecca said.

"—but really," Meredith continued, "we should be ready to start things up right after graduation."

"Well, after everyone starts coming out of cryo," Rebecca added.

"Ah," Isadora said. "That's where I come in." She leaned forward and took another bite of her salad. Meredith turned to her pasta, while Rebecca kept playing with a spoonful of her squash soup before finally taking a bite.

"I'll be departing for Bitanu tomorrow. By the time I get back, the Union parliamentary elections will be over, and we'll see if the Reform Party is in power. Either way, my tenure as chief coordinator will be effectively over. So make sure to use those political connections while I still have them," Isadora concluded with a wink.

"I've gotten used to you saying you need to leave for some planet or another by now," Meredith said. "Honestly, it's going to be weird having you around all the time." She'd said it as a joke, and all three of them laughed, but Isadora could hear the echoes of a real critique in there.

In truth, nothing would make her happier. But only after one last, vitally important foray past the asteroid belt. One that would hopefully restore peace to the Natonus System and pave the way for emptying the *Preserver*'s cryo bays.

Isadora caught Rebecca looking at her feet. She wondered how much Meredith had told her about the last time Isadora had traveled to Bitanu, about how she'd come face-to-face with Rebecca's brother. About how Tanner had shot Vincent in front of her and almost killed her.

From the look of it, Rebecca at least knew parts of the story.

This time, Isadora hoped her trip wouldn't involve a deadly confrontation with Tanner. But he was still out there, and any trip to the outer rim put her in his general proximity. Isadora saw, in Rebecca's eyes, an understanding of the possibility. Maybe even a complicated mix of feelings about how the conflict with the Offspring might be resolved.

"So, how long are you going to be gone?" she said.

"Almost two months," Isadora said. As much as possible, she tried to ignore the dread of flying in a small shuttle for that long. *Just a little bit longer*, she told herself.

"Oh wow," Meredith said. "That means you'll get back right around the time of our graduation."

"Don't worry. I fully plan on being there."

Really, the only possible delay would be if the peace negotiations took longer than anticipated—she'd budgeted about two weeks' worth ot time for the actual summit, in addition to travel time—which, knowing how politics and diplomacy worked, seemed unnervingly possible.

But she wasn't above lighting a bit of a fire underneath a few asses if it meant getting home in time to watch her daughter graduate. And with her public approval at its zenith, she figured she had the political capital to speed things along if necessary.

"So," she said, "tell me what you two are gonna get up to while I'm gone."

Meredith sighed. "Well, I figure we'll be busy. Gotta make sure we study for exams, on top of getting everything ready for our organization's rollout...that reminds me, we need to pick some kind of name."

"Yeah, scratch the whole studying for finals thing," Rebecca said.

"Oh, one more thing," Meredith said, reaching into a satchel at her feet. She withdrew a small data drive. "Rebecca and I recorded an elevator pitch for our organization and its mission. When you get a chance, we'd *love* some constructive feedback."

Isadora beamed, taking the data drive. "I'd love to. I don't know if I'll have time to get to it today, but I'll review it during the flight to Bitanu and send you my notes."

She had a busy day left on her schedule: she needed to return to the embassy in the afternoon, review and approve a couple of last-minute proposals, then pack for her departure early tomorrow.

But for now, she could enjoy a simple, easy lunch with the two of them out on the terrace of her favorite Obrigan City restaurant. The day was beautiful, stirring anticipation within her for what the weather would be like when she finally returned. It'd almost be summer by that point.

There really was a light at the end of the tunnel. Everything that'd happened since Isadora first woke up on the *Preserver*—the deals she'd struck, the decisions she'd made, the structures she'd set up, and the political changes she'd wrought—was leading to the peace summit.

And after they were done, they could finally bring the remaining 30 million refugees off the *Preserver*. Then, the question would change from how to bring people out of cryo to how they would integrate in whatever Natonese society looked like after they opened a wormhole back to Earth.

It'd be the end of the beginning. And, for her, the beginning of the end.

CHAPTER 36

It was Nadia's third time approaching the planet Enther. The first
had been to mediate a ceasefire agreement between the Junta and
the Ashkagi rebels, which led to a pitched battle and Boyd's kidnap-
ping. The second had been to rescue Boyd and insert Carson Erlinza
in the Offspring's ranks, which led to the deaths of the entire militia
team that'd accompanied her—and Russ' sacrifice.

She didn't see how this time could get any worse, but she wasn't
inclined to tempt fate. Especially not with Carson in danger.

She was in the *Exemplar*'s cockpit by herself, watching the planet
grow larger in the viewscreen to distract herself from worrying frantically about him, when she heard Boyd clear his throat behind her.

She swiveled in her chair to see him and Derek standing at the
edge of the hallway. Boyd's hands were behind his back, holding

something out of sight. "We wanted to talk to you about an idea," he said.

Nadia tried her best to push thoughts of Carson out of her head. At this point, there was nothing else for her to do. Worrying wouldn't help him. And she could appreciate her crew—her *friends*—providing a distraction, at least.

"We've been thinking about what comes after," Boyd continued. "Because one way or another, this war is gonna come to a close."

One way or another was another way of saying they could all still die. Noah's transmission had indicated Carson might've found some kind of actionable intelligence before he dropped off the map. Nadia had a hard time seeing that as anything other than a bad omen.

"Even in a best-case scenario, millions of refugees will be coming out of cryo, and they'll need a place to call home," she said. "I've made it clear I don't expect you two to stay on longer than you want, but it's my duty to see the settlement project through."

"I'm surprised you're not ready to move on to bigger and better things. Your boss sure was," Boyd said.

Nadia had still been trying to process the message she'd received from Isadora, detailing her plans to step down. The story had hit the news during the flight to Enther, so now everyone else knew, too. All she'd known since arriving in the Natonus System was Isadora at the helm. Even when she made mistakes, Nadia could never hold it against her. Nothing would be the same after the peace summit.

Again, assuming we don't all die to some Offspring plot.

"You're also assuming that your people will want to settle the Natonese outer rim," Derek said. "But this entire region of space will look different after this war is over."

Nadia paused, remembering what Tori Hyrak had told her: how

kicking the Junta off Ikkren didn't mean things were returning to normal. If everything went right, and the *Preserver* transformed into a conduit back to the Sol System, the Natonese outer rim would be transformed forever.

Boyd, his hands shaking in excitement, brought his arms in front of him. Revealing a poster. Specifically, a diagram of the Sol System Nadia used to keep in her cabin.

She couldn't help but flash a surprised smile when she saw it. She'd spent so many years staring at projections and maps of Natonus that the Sol System looked strange.

So much so that she got lightheaded. Maybe she finally knew, on an emotional level, what it had meant for her grandparents to move across Earth in their youths. For what used to be *home* to now be something else, something strange. Nearly unrecognizable.

"We want to be the first ones through," Boyd said giddily.

"I—what?"

"We're surveyors, but we're also *explorers*. And wherever we go—the Sol System, maybe beyond—there will be places to discover, to map out. I know we have no idea what your home system will look like a century after the invasion, but regardless, there's work we can do to help repair the damage. Facilitate exchange between us Natonese and everyone—anyone—who's still left in Sol. Derek and I have been talking, and we want to take the lead on that project. With you."

Nadia felt a pang of elation in her heart, the kind she hadn't felt since first touching down on Calimor for the very first time, so long ago. The very idea of it was romantic: slowly drifting across the galaxy, traversing the stars, seeing sights that no human had ever seen, all while blazing a trail of hope and life in their wake.

Was she that person anymore?

"This feels like a big change for both of you," she said, sidestepping that question entirely.

Boyd laughed. "I have no illusions. I'm not an architect anymore. I'm the *Exemplar*'s mechanic."

Derek had a thoughtful look in his eyes. "Back when we first touched down on Ikkren, I thought I was coming home. But the planet was different, and even with the Junta gone, I don't think it will ever be quite the same again. My home is here. I'm the *Exemplar*'s pilot."

Nadia's eyes got misty enough that she had to turn around and face Enther once more. It was a good reminder of the task ahead, one whose success would determine whether it was even worth considering the fantasy her crew had proposed.

And still, she couldn't help but chuckle. "All right, you two. Instead of making me cry, why don't you focus on getting us down there in one piece?"

·   ·   ·

"So," Noah began, "what do you think?"

Now that she wasn't getting shot at—yet—Nadia had to admit that Enther was actually kind of nice. The trees really *were* magnificent, she had to admit, with lush vines and ferns that she could imagine getting lost in. The forest was equal parts foreboding and beautiful.

She was standing on the battlements of the capital city with Noah Tasano while Boyd and Derek were getting the *Exemplar* checked out and downloading the latest geographic data on their target: an old abandoned Junta weapons cache believed to be a secret Offspring base.

It was where Carson—with a turncoat Offspring in tow,

apparently—was headed. Before he stopped sending check-in messages.

Nadia also supposed she shouldn't call Noah's followers "rebels" anymore. Then again, they weren't a government either. She asked him what his plans were, now that the majority of the planet had declared loyalty to his people.

"Our goal was always to restore the old Theocracy," Noah continued. "But it's been almost thirteen years. An entire generation has grown up with little memory of the old ways. Those who remember it clearly have turned old."

Hearing out his plans was one way of drowning out the gnawing impatience to go chase after Carson. But she knew without a firm plan in place, and a solid understanding of the situation, they'd be inviting catastrophe. And she'd already experienced enough catastrophes on Enther.

"The truth is, our faith is about *pathways*. Fluidity, chaos, impermanence. We tried to institutionalize that in the form of a strong, central planetary government. And it slowly collapsed over the course of three decades, leading to a military coup. Now that the question of *what do we do next* is actually in front of me, I find myself with less certainty than I once did that simple restoration is the correct answer."

Nadia thought she could see where Noah was going. "If you're talking about pathways opening..."

"Yes, I am talking about your *Preserver*. Ashkagiism grew in the first decades of Natonese colonization because of the devotion and energy of our earliest missionaries. And then, in our darkest moment, the gods saw fit to guide your people here. I think that was a reminder of where our real priorities should lie. Adaptation, not reconstruction, must be our guiding tenet."

Nadia was struck by how similar Noah was sounding to Tori. She felt a twinge of guilt, wondering if the various peoples she'd met in her travels might've been able to maintain some sense of normalcy if the *Preserver* had never shown up. She'd never intended for it to end this way, but all of her actions over the last three years had led to this.

"I want the Ashkagi to be at the forefront of galactic exploration, as traveling missionaries," Noah said. "Those who would prefer can stay on Enther. But I am not sure that I belong here anymore. All this being said, I am well aware that we owe the liberation of our planet in part to the heroic actions of yourself and Carson. Every Ashkagi in the system owes you a debt of gratitude."

Noah turned to face Nadia, an uncharacteristic grin on a face that was usually grim and somber. "I suppose I was right when I said you were the herald of divine grace. And we intend to repay our debt to you, in full. Now that we have seized most Junta ordnance stockpiles, we have found ourselves in possession of a sizable number of space-faring vessels. Not advanced warships, but a handful of light cruisers and gunships. I intend to send as many as we can to the Bitanu peace summit. To help protect against any Junta trickery or Offspring sabotage."

Nadia smiled. She was racking up quite the collection, having acquired supplementary fleets from both Ikkren and Enther to accompany her to Bitanu. She could only hope they wouldn't be necessary.

"You have my thanks," she said. "As well as Isadora's, and every one of us."

"You can keep your thanks," Noah said. "You have done enough for us already. But I suspect you are anxious to search for your friend Carson—and it looks like your companions are ready to depart."

Nadia turned to see Boyd and Derek—along with a third man she couldn't identify—walking toward the two of them. "Good news and bad news!" Boyd said. "Which one do you want first?"

"Considering that the bad news is contingent on the good news, saying it out of order doesn't make sense," Derek said.

"Right. Whatever. The good news: we have a pretty solid plan in place and are ready to depart," Boyd said.

"Okay," Nadia said, scrunching her eyebrows in confusion. "What exactly is the bad news, then?"

Boyd and Derek exchanged glances. Derek grimaced, Boyd grinned. "You're gonna hate the plan," they said in unison.

·   ·   ·

Yep. She hated it.

Nadia's companions had informed her that the third man with them on the Caphila battlements was named Harry Klim, and that he was Offspring. Ex-Offspring. Whatever. Nadia was immediately suspicious of the distinction.

Apparently, before Carson had departed for the weapons cache where they were now heading, he'd been doing deradicalization therapy sessions with volunteer Offspring prisoners. Harry had been his most enthusiastic patient, and had even coordinated group therapy sessions after Carson had left, including about twenty others.

The plan was to have Harry and a small group of seven other ex-Offspring join them on the *Exemplar*, radio ahead to the weapons cache base that they'd lured Nadia and her crew into a trap, and use that as a cover story to bring in the *Exemplar*.

Once there, they'd fight their way in and, in a best-case scenario, find and rescue Carson. Or in a worst-case scenario, at least figure out whatever he'd been on the verge of discovering.

When Nadia had brought up that the plan meant trusting almost a dozen *Offspring*, and even setting them against their former comrades, Boyd and Derek had acknowledged her worries. But if they wanted to bring the *Exemplar* in close to the Offspring base, they'd get shot down for sure. Or the Offspring might just execute Carson, if he was their captive, then wipe their local data drives to boot.

There was only one way to approach the site, and that was with the cover story in place. That meant working with Harry Klim and the rest of the converts.

Nadia had insisted on a variety of protocols: their weapons were stashed in a bio-printed locker that would only respond to her or her crew, and the ex-Offspring had to stay next to the airlock under the watchful eye of either her or Boyd. They weren't allowed onto the rest of the ship, even for bathroom breaks.

She surveyed the eight of them, her palm resting on the grip of her handgun, as if willing them to *just try it*. Most of them averted their eyes when she looked at them. Probably plagued by guilt. *Good.* These people might not have done anything personally to hurt her people, but they signed up for a genocidal, nativist terrorist organization. Every time she looked at one of them, all she could see was Tanner.

"We're almost there," Boyd called to her from the hallway behind the airlock. "I'll take watch. Why don't you join Derek in the cockpit?"

"Just keep an eye on them," Nadia said.

It took all her effort to not add *and shoot them if they so much as look at you wrong*. She had to remind herself of her talk with her parents, of the futility of vengeance. Maybe she'd be able to appreciate the lesson better when she wasn't staring at twenty of her would-be murderers.

Boyd gave her a reassuring nod. "Don't worry. I'll make sure things stay under control."

Nadia thanked him, shot one final scowl toward the closest ex-Offspring, and headed back to the front of the ship. When she got there, she saw trees all around them. They must have breached the cloudline, meaning they were only a few minutes out from the weapons cache.

"We aren't getting a landing confirmation from the base," Derek said. "But I'm not too worried about it—I have a hard time imagining these Offspring types sticking to military protocol—but I thought you should know."

"Maybe they're having some kind of comms issue?" Nadia said, frowning. She was uneasy enough that anything going slightly wrong felt like a potential emergency.

"Could be—wait." Derek had never sounded panicked, exactly, but his tone suggested a deep level of concern. Nadia's heartbeat accelerated rapidly.

"I'm reading a missile launch," he said.

"At us?" she blurted out. Then realized it was a stupid question. *Assume the answer is yes first, ask questions later.* "I'll go start up the missile scrambler."

Derek furrowed his brow. "Wait...I don't think that's necessary. I'm getting a trajectory analysis from the computer."

He swiveled around in his chair and looked at her in confusion. "They're not heading for us."

CHAPTER 37

Now that he was spending most of his days in an Offspring cell, Carson wished jail-breaking had been a bigger part of his training regiment. Or rather, part of it at all. The unspoken assumption between him and Juliet had always been that if his cover ever got blown, the Offspring would probably just execute him on the spot.

Which would make sense, if they knew he was a refugee. But from the perspective of the Offspring at the weapons cache, Carson was a rebel sympathizer. He'd been interrogated almost a dozen times, and he'd been careful to only reveal the clandestine actions he'd taken to help the Ashkagi. Never anything about his real identity.

They kept Emil away from him, presumably interrogating him separately. Every time Carson got questioned, his interrogator told him he could restore his standing in the Offspring by informing on

Emil, blaming the other man for everything.

Carson never did. And considering that he hadn't been taken out and shot—the only reasonable conclusion to a scenario where Emil betrayed him—he assumed Emil wasn't telling their captors anything about him. Said a lot about his mental resilience, in the face of possibly the most dangerous backsliding threat imaginable.

Sitting in a cell most of the day got boring, but at least Carson got in a few laughs, here and there, about people who used the prisoner's dilemma to explain everything.

He spent the days doing calisthenics—push-ups, crunches, strengthening yoga poses. During all his interrogations thus far, he'd been escorted to a room by two armed Offspring. He could go for one of his escort's weapons, but it'd be too easy for the other one to just shoot him.

And now that he was the only refugee in the entire system who knew that Tanner Keltin was on the *Caretaker*, he no longer felt expendable. At the very least, he needed to survive to get to a comms terminal, or find someone else to give the information to.

Today, he was in the middle of a yoga flow when his usual two escorts came to get him. To his surprise, they led him to the right after exiting his cell, not the left, where the interrogation room was located.

"I'm guessing the plan changed?" he asked. Neither Offspring responded.

Hearing his own voice speak was strange. He didn't undergo an interrogation every single day, which meant there were sometimes entire days that went by without hearing himself talk.

As much as Carson didn't miss the near-constant fear and stress during his first few months undercover, he almost preferred that to now. Humans were social creatures. They belonged together. Even if that meant being around people who unknowingly wanted you dead. Anything was better than utter isolation.

That was when he heard something. An explosive sound—loud enough to shake the entire base—followed by a fading, stuttering staccato. Like a vessel launch, only far faster.

"What was that?" he blurted out. As expected, his escorts didn't respond.

They brought him to a large assembly area. It was devoid of anything, but Carson figured it would normally be some kind of armory. He spied a few gear lockers and empty weapons crates along the far walls. In the center was an interrogator.

As well as Emil.

Seeing the other man brought up a curious mix of emotions. The first was relief at finally seeing another person who wouldn't immediately execute him if they knew the truth about his identity. The second was happiness to see that Emil was unharmed. The third was a detached sense of irony that he was now relieved to see someone who used to be a ranking Offspring.

Emil looked at him, but stayed silent. The two escorts lined up behind them, keeping their weapons at their waists. That gave rise to a fourth emotion: for the first time since being taken into captivity, Carson and Emil were now together, and they were currently only being guarded by three armed individuals.

"Both of you have been recalcitrant," the questioner said with a sneer. "That is unbecoming of two Natonese men. Here in the Offspring, we are supposed to be true to ourselves, to our Natonese virtue first and foremost. Or have you forgotten Tanner Keltin's teachings?"

Carson had been in so many deeply ironic situations in his time undercover that he should've gotten used to them. Maybe it was just because he was out of practice, but refraining from laughing was harder this time.

He distracted himself by trying to get Emil's attention. Both of them had their hands cuffed, but if they made a simultaneous movement against their two guards, they might be able to catch them off guard and break free. It'd be risky, but this might be their only chance.

And with what he knew about the *Caretaker*, every second counted.

Before the interrogator continued, the same sound Carson had heard in the hallway outside reverberated through the area. The Offspring's eyes briefly flickered to the ceiling, but his expression registered neither surprise nor discomfort.

This time, another sound followed.

It started the same, although instead of a loud stuttering, there was a low, steady hum. Engines, Carson assumed.

"You're launching transports," Emil observed. "What's going on?"

"Tanner is forgiving," the questioner continued. "In fact, he has something magnificent planned. And it will take all of us to ensure his plan's success. He is willing to overlook your misguided fondness for the Ashkagi rebels, so long as you recommit to our true cause: the defense of our system from invasion. He understands that even the righteous might stray from the cause. But now is the time to return to the fold."

Carson looked at Emil once more. Saw a flicker of doubt pass across his eyes. Emil's progress had been so astounding—probably one of the most effective cases of deradicalization he'd seen in his career—that it was hard to remember that he still had a ways to go. And considering that he'd joined the Offspring because of his need for others' approval, for a sense of meaning in his life, the interrogator's line of reasoning could be unnervingly effective.

As if looking for reassurance, he turned his gaze toward Carson, who frantically tilted his head at the guards behind them.

In unison, they tackled the escorts.

Their movements were so sudden that neither got a shot off. Carson pushed the Offspring to the ground and pressed the chain of his cuffs down on the man's neck. His hands naturally let go of his sidearm as he struggled to push Carson off him.

The interrogator, meanwhile, was going for his own weapon. Carson pinned his opponent's arms down with his knee, worked his hands around his head, and snapped his neck.

He grabbed the gun and turned to face Emil, who'd been less successful. His opponent kicked Emil in the gut, then went for his gun to finish him off. Carson shot him in the face before he got the chance.

But when he turned around, the interrogator had drawn his own weapon. Was pointing it straight for his chest. He didn't have time to react.

And then Emil came barreling for the man. The interrogator's gun went off, but the bolt went well wide of Carson. Emil punched him in the face, wrestled the pistol away from him, and shot him. They then helped each other out of their cuffs.

And despite all that, there were no alarms. Nothing—other than the sound of two more launches. One loud and violent, one followed by a low hum. Just like before.

"What should we do now?" Emil said.

"We need to get to a comms terminal," Carson said. "Do you have any idea what those sounds are?"

They sprinted for an adjoining hallway, one leading to a turbolift shaft. "That second sound is a transport taking off," Emil said. "I'm sure of it. As for the first one…could it be those warheads we saw when we first arrived?"

Carson's blood went cold. There'd been at least a dozen projectiles at the weapons cache. Come to think of it, the stuttering sound seemed nearly identical to the sound of a warhead's thrusters. That meant they had to hurry, regardless of the risk. But when they entered the adjoining hallway, it was completely empty. Not an Offspring in sight.

Carson hadn't been able to get a perfectly accurate count of the Offspring stationed at the base, but his observations had suggested there were about sixty personnel on site. More than enough to station a patrol to guard the area, in other words.

Something was *very* off.

The elevator led to an unoccupied control room overlooking the assembly area. Emil took position next to the lift door, in case anyone followed them up. Carson ran over to the closest terminal station.

He was in the middle of inputting the comms frequency for his people's Obrigan embassy when he got an error message. One stating that the terminal had been shut down. The same message flashed on every other terminal screen nearby.

Shit.

It made sense. The Offspring knew he'd been going through a database of their secret operations, even if they didn't know exactly what he'd found. It made sense that they'd cut power to the command room to make sure he couldn't get any communications out.

Carson walked over to Emil. "The Offspring cut off power to the terminals in here," he said. "New plan: we need to find another terminal. Then we send a message to my people's leadership."

"When we arrived, there was a bunker on the top of the facility," Emil said. "Why don't we try there? They might not think to take exterior systems offline."

A decent suggestion. They took the elevator back down to the main level, still encountering no resistance. Carson narrowed his eyes as the two cautiously worked their way through a labyrinth of corridors, heading to an exterior turbolift. Something was wrong—why weren't they getting swarmed?

What were the Offspring doing instead? The sound of two more launches—one possibly a missile, one probably a transport—answered him.

They finally found a turbolift taking them to the base's exterior. The capsule-like lift had a glass cover, giving them a view of the same grid of missiles that had so unnerved him when they first approached.

Only this time, there were four missing warheads. And a fifth was about to launch.

Carson stepped forward and widened his eyes as the missile took off. It rose slowly until it was almost a hundred feet in the air, then abruptly swiveled, and darted off toward the atmosphere. It disappeared above the cloudline in a matter of seconds.

The turbolift came to a halt, and the capsule door slid open. They stepped out into the rain, only to hear another thruster ignition. A sixth missile rose and sped off. This time, heading in a different direction.

A seventh launched, heading in yet another direction. That implied they weren't all aimed at the same target. Carson wondered if it was a desperate move—maybe they were hurtling toward the most populated refugee colonies across the outer rim—but they were well-defended enough that they could shoot down a single incoming projectile. You could probably overwhelm the colonial defenses with a barrage, but each missile was clearly going for a different target.

They ran down the side of the roof toward the control bunker. Just as they reached the door, they saw a Junta troop transport emerge from the underside of the base. It hovered above the facility for a few seconds, then sped off toward orbit.

Had the entirety of the base's occupants already loaded up onto those ships? That would explain why they didn't encounter any resistance inside.

No matter. He had a job—a crucially, vitally important job—to do. He approached the terminal station inside the control bunker. Navigated to the root menu. Only to discover that the communications capabilities of the entire base had been taken offline. He banged the terminal with his fist.

He returned outside. Emil arched an eyebrow. "They turned off all outgoing communications," he said. "We need to go somewhere far away to get the message out."

The sound of another ignition drew his attention. Another missile blasted off. An eighth projectile rose, hurtled toward some unknown target. Still in a different direction from all the others they'd seen.

Between the rain and the sounds of the missile or transport launches, Carson didn't even hear the ship approaching. But there it was, at the edge of the forest: the silhouette of a starship, coming in fast. His heart dropped. After all, who else could it be, other than Offspring reinforcements?

But it wasn't an Offspring dropship. It was the *Exemplar*.

Carson blinked rapidly, nearly forgetting about the missiles. This had to be a dream. A waking fantasy. And yet, the ship touched down. The outer airlock door opened. Nadia Jibor, clad in her charcoal-and-teal enviro-suit, emerged.

And behind her were Offspring.

Nearly a dozen of them. *She's been captured* was all he could think. His mind was still playing that thought on repeat when the Offspring flanking Nadia raised their weapons, then moved into position to secure the turbolift leading down into the facility.

It was only then that he recognized them: the ones he'd been working with back in Caphila. Those who'd made the most progress in therapy, more specifically, like Harry Klim.

"Is that Nadia Jibor?" Emil asked, wide-eyed. Carson figured she was famous enough that any self-respecting Offspring would know her.

"Sure is." And then he rushed toward his old companion.

He hadn't gotten to know Nadia particularly well during their time together, but she might be one of the people closest to him in the entire system. And even though he now felt comfortable with Emil, and had always enjoyed working with the Ashkagi rebels, there was something comforting about seeing a fellow refugee.

The two embraced for only a moment. Before Nadia could explain how she'd come to work with a group of deradicalized ex-Offspring, Carson blurted out that Tanner was on the *Caretaker*.

"It's a Junta warship," he explained. "He's taking it to the Bitanu peace summit, where he's going to ram it into the *Preserver* on a suicide run."

Nadia's eyes widened. "That's where Isadora is going."

"We have to send her a message *now*. But the comms are offline here at the base."

Nadia's companion Boyd Makrum—a man Carson had heard about, but never actually met, considering they'd essentially switched places during the Ruhae operation—emerged from the *Exemplar*'s airlock. Looking pale.

"Comms are offline *everywhere*," he said.

Carson and Nadia turned to face him simultaneously. "Derek and I just ran trajectory analyses on all those missiles. The one we tried to stop on the way in just struck the main communications satellite orbiting Enther. The rest are headed toward other satellites in orbit of every outer rim world. For all intents and purposes, this entire region of space is about to go dark."

The blood in Carson's veins was on the verge of icing over. The Offspring had just cut off any chance of telling Isadora that she was walking into a trap.

Any chance, other than telling her in person.

"Ship-to-ship comms should still work, right?" he asked.

"Yeah," Boyd said. "It'd be spotty, but—"

"—we need to get to Bitanu," Nadia interrupted. "*Now*."

Carson looked at the collection of ex-Offspring, who'd been joined by Emil, and a thought struck him.

"Part of Tanner's plan was to have the rest of his people board the Junta warships en route to Bitanu using military codes," he explained, realizing what all those transports were doing. "They'd pose as Junta soldiers, escaping the Ashkagi takeover of the planet. Then, they'd seize control of whatever vessel picks them up. Since they've already done it once, I'm inclined to believe they could do it again."

"Which means if I race off after the *Caretaker*, they'll just shoot my ship out of the sky," Nadia said.

"Exactly. That means someone else needs to stop them."

Carson turned and looked at the assembled collection of ex-Off-spring. "We can hide out in the jungles and take one of the transports docked here. Link up with the rest of the Offspring shuttles, and hope-fully get picked up by one of the Junta ships. Then we'll make sure it doesn't slag you."

Nadia cast a dark look at the others. "You trust them?"

No, Carson thought. *Not 100%.* "I trust them enough to try to make this work. And I don't know if we have any other options."

Nadia nodded. "Okay. Boyd, Derek and I will get to Bitanu as fast as our ship will let us. See you on the other side."

Carson's thoughts were racing so fast he didn't have any time to regret the fact that Nadia was leaving already. Right now, they had a job to do. As Nadia and Boyd retreated into the *Exemplar*, the assem-bled ex-Offspring turned to look at him. Carson took a deep breath and explained the plan to Emil, to Harry, to all the others.

"You all are here because you're serious about healing. About re-covery, about atonement," he concluded. Then paused to look up at the sky, where even now, thousands were converging on Bitanu, una-ware that Tanner Keltin was poised to deliver a death blow to millions of refugees.

Carson turned back to face the others. "Well, now's your chance to do just that."

CHAPTER 38

The last time Isadora had docked at the *Preserver*, she'd been here to bring Meredith out of cryo. It was like she'd been finally getting a piece of her old life back. Considering that the peace summit would be the last act of her tenure as chief coordinator, she supposed this trip to the *Preserver* was also about reclaiming her old life. In full, this time.

The entire planet of Bitanu was swarming with ships from all over Natonus: Union military vessels, a flotilla of Horde gunships, the remnants of the Junta navy, even some captured Junta ships used by the Ashkagi transition government on Enther. Plus all sorts of media ships. Isadora's transport had passed by hundreds of starships on approach to the *Preserver*. More trickled in every hour.

The *Preserver* dwarfed all the others. She figured you could probably fit at least four entire Union planet-killing warships inside its hull. As her transport eased into one of the cryo vessel's hangar bays, it felt like being swallowed by a massive whale.

It had been an eventful trip. First came the Union's parliamentary election results. Justin Hacelo's Reform Party had been swept to power, deposing the long-reigning Workers' Party. Tricia Favan had already gone into retirement, apparently telling anyone trying to interview her to fuck off. The Reform Party was making good on its promise, scheduling a debate in Parliament to repeal the settlement charter ban.

Second came the complete shutdown of all communications across the outer rim. No one was really sure what'd happened, although they'd picked up a dozen missile launches from Enther right before the comms went down. Isadora had exchanged plenty of messages with Riley, who guessed they were symbolic protests against the peace summit from Junta holdouts. Still, she was concerned the comms disruption could be a sign of Junta recalcitrance.

The disruption had also become a frequent topic of conversation among the summit attendees. Isadora had lost track of all the transmissions she'd exchanged—via radio, tragically, which was always grainy and laggy—with others, many of whom seemed to be genuinely afraid of what the disruption portended.

But there were no follow-up attacks. No claims of responsibility, no manifestos leaked onto the net. The comms disruption would be an inconvenience, but far more of a headache than a serious cause for concern.

The shuttle rattled as a docking clamp seized its hull, and then it went still. The door swung open. Isadora unstrapped herself, walked down a catwalk to the cryo vessel's interior. The hangar bay was massive, big enough to give her a feeling of vertigo. Both the floor and the ceiling were hundreds of feet above and below her, respectively. The rest of her accompanying detail followed her in.

She felt a twinge of sadness as she realized she no longer knew anyone who worked on the ship. Vincent was dead, the other high-ranking members of her staff had all left, and the technicians and engineers who kept the vessel running were all unfamiliar to her. She introduced herself to everyone she came across.

She walked past half-remembered bays of cryo pods with sleeping refugees still inside—people blissfully unaware of everything that had happened around them for the past three years—past the old conference room where she'd held her staff meetings.

Her heart ached at the memories. Now, Tricia was no longer prime minister, and Russ and Vincent were dead.

The peace summit—to be held on the *Preserver* itself, due to the inhospitality of Bitanu—wasn't slated to begin for another couple of days, in order to give the remaining ships still in transit time to reach Bitanu. But Isadora figured she should go ahead and start making calls now.

After all, she was probably the most well-known, prolific politician in the system now that Tricia had gone into retirement. Sure, Prime Minister Hacelo was more powerful, now that he commanded the Union's economy and military, but Isadora had *stature* in the way a newly elected prime minister didn't.

And she still had a job to do. She had to secure the most favorable peace settlement for her people, allowing the 30 million still in cryo to settle across the entire system. She also hoped to limit the Junta's power as much as possible, given their alliance with the Offspring. She wanted to leave her successor with the most favorable playing field possible.

For now, that meant playing politics. Reaching out to the other diplomats, military officers, and politicians in attendance. She headed for one of the *Preserver*'s central turbolift bays, took one headed for the observation deck. She arrived in a comfortable viewing lounge. The same one where she'd first glimpsed the Union navy that had arrived to meet them.

Isadora was alone at last. She filled a tumbler with coffee at a station nearby and sat down in a chair. Then opened up comms channels to a variety of other vessels—Union, Horde, and Ashkagi—to check in. She received warm receptions from all.

At one point, she felt an uncomfortable jabbing sensation from the left-side pocket of her blazer: Meredith's data drive, with the pitch she and Rebecca had recorded for their nonprofit idea. Isadora had listened to it three times during the flight, finding little to critique.

After a half-hour's worth of making calls, Isadora noticed someone was reaching out to the *Preserver*. She flipped a switch on the comms terminal, and heard a familiar voice: "Isadora, this is Nadia."

She felt a surge of joy—but one that quickly disappeared when she realized how frantic Nadia sounded.

"You have to listen to me," she continued. "You're in serious danger."

The rest of Nadia's transmission became garbled—the *Exemplar* must've been too far from the *Preserver* for a stable connection—but Isadora could make out three distinct words.

Tanner.

Caretaker.

Trap.

. . .

Tanner had done it all. Almost.

Thanks to his followers' seizure of a cache of Junta warheads, he'd taken out the communication systems for the entire outer rim. That way, the newars and the misguided Natonese who had rolled over for them couldn't easily coordinate a response when he launched the *Caretaker* on its suicide run.

As for their navigational path itself, it would take place in three stages. During the first, they'd be close enough to the other starships in orbit that no one would reasonably nuke them. Not with the potential for massive collateral damage. During the third, when they'd be close enough to the *Preserver* that nuking them would still send debris hurtling for the cryo vessel, it would be superfluous for anyone to use their arsenal on them.

It was the second stage—where they'd pulled out of formation, but weren't far enough around the planet yet—that would be the most dangerous. Sure, they had a point-defense laser system, but he needed an extra layer of security.

Which was why he'd directed the rest of his surviving Offspring on Enther to board captured Junta transports, broadcast signals that they were escaping Ashkagi rebel retribution, then get picked up by Junta military vessels.

From there, they'd seize control of as many Junta ships as they could. Just like how Tanner and his crew had seized the *Caretaker*. He'd been having the rest of his people study and practice the same tactics he'd employed at the outset of the war.

Most of their attempts would probably fail, but if even a handful succeeded, it could turn the tide. They could cause chaos and protect the *Caretaker* as it hurtled toward the *Preserver*, during that pivotal second stage.

It was time.

Tanner used the central station in the *Caretaker*'s CIC to transmit written dispatches to the transports. The message was simple, straight to the point: *Now is the time. Wrest as many Junta ships from their control as possible. Natonus for the Natonese.*

On the holo-projection, the tiny blips representing Offspring shuttles began moving toward the Junta warships. Like tiny predators coming together to take down a larger prey.

To Tanner, the projection of Bitanu, along with all the various ships in orbit, looked like a giant chessboard. The final one in his long crusade. The enemy king was at last in his sights. A checkmate, nearly inevitable.

A final end to the greatest threat ever to fall on the Natonus System.

He knew it would mean his death, but he'd learned to accept the necessity of his sacrifice. When he imagined a future after his heroic final act, he imagined a system that would come together, united by his example, ready to stand up against all outsiders.

And with Tanner taking out the vast majority of the enemy's numbers, the Natonese people would at last have a fighting shot at reasserting their sovereign right to their own system.

His six remaining crewmates kept going in and out of the CIC. The last few days had been an endless blur to get everything ready for the *Caretaker*'s final voyage. Like performing maintenance checks on the engines to make sure they were ready for a high-burn maneuver. Or analyzing Bitanu's gravitational pull to plot the best path for a slingshot into the *Preserver*.

And now, they were ready.

While his hijacking teams were closing in on Junta naval vessels, he inputted the latest navigational path he and his crew had charted. First, they'd break out of the Junta formation, descend into low orbit, and finally execute a high-burn maneuver.

In just under an hour, the *Preserver* would be nothing more than space dust.

.   .   .

Carson, Emil, Harry, and the other ex-Offspring were huddled around the central terminal in the shuttle they'd taken from the Enther weapons cache. They'd hid in the jungles until the other Offspring had left the base, boarded one of the remaining shuttles, and then sped for Bitanu as fast as possible.

They'd only just gotten in range to use their ship's radio system. When they'd dispatched a message to the *Preserver*, they'd gotten confirmation that Nadia had already gotten in touch with them and explained the situation.

But before they could warn anyone else about the *Caretaker*, their computer logged an incoming message: *Now is the time. Wrest as many Junta ships from their control as possible. Natonus for the Natonese.* It was transmitted by none other than Tanner Keltin.

Carson and the others took turns exchanging glances. They then leapt into action, trying to radio whatever Junta warship they could get ahold of, warning them about incoming Offspring hijackers. Silence was their only response.

Some of the hijacking teams might've already gotten picked up en route to Bitanu, Carson remembered from the files he'd uncovered.

Which meant that some of the Junta warships could already be under Offspring control.

"Okay," he said, drawing in a deep breath. "The Offspring are about to seize control of the Junta fleet. Or they could be partially there already. We need to stop them."

"We're closest to the *Sanctitude*," Emil said. "The Junta flagship, probably the best-armed vessel in their navy. If the Offspring get a hold of it, they'd get their hands on some major destructive power."

"Right," Harry said. "You said Nadia's plan is to intercept the *Caretaker*. The *Sanctitude* would be able to take her out for sure."

"Then it's decided. We're heading to the *Sanctitude*," Carson said, looking around at the others' faces. Faces that had been ready to follow Tanner to the end just a few months ago, but were now risking everything to stop him.

He wasn't sure this was what his people had intended when they'd chosen him to infiltrate the Offspring, but it was the best way he knew how to operate. The *only* way he knew how to operate. You had to believe that people could come back.

The engines to their transport fired, and they dispatched a Junta military code to the nearby *Sanctitude*. They were cleared to approach. But he had no way of knowing whether it was a Junta officer who'd given them clearance, or an Offspring infiltrator.

In another ten minutes, they reached the *Sanctitude*'s docking bay. Once they were clamped in, Carson heard an alarm blaring. That meant the Offspring attack had already begun.

They activated their helmet functions, checked their sidearms. Any use of plasma weapons would depressurize the vessel, requiring them to rely on their own oxygen stores. According to the file Carson had uncovered back on Enther, that was how Tanner had taken the

Caretaker—the Offspring infiltrators had used knives, and the Junta crew hadn't responded quickly enough.

He wasn't sure whether the infiltration plan was the same this time or not. But either way, he figured it made sense for his team to go in with their own oxygen supplies. At the very least, it'd give them the flexibility they needed to use their own firearms.

Carson, Emil, and Harry fanned out while the rest of the ex-Offspring disembarked. Given that all of them were disguised in Offspring brown, and because it sounded like fighting had already started aboard the *Sanctitude*, he figured any Junta personnel would likely shoot them on sight. But no plasma bolts came for them.

"Okay," Emil said. "I'm guessing the plan would be to attack three areas simultaneously: the CIC, weapons control, and engineering. We don't know how many Offspring have boarded the ship, but it's safe to say they'd probably mount a three-pronged attack."

Carson thought through their options. Taking the CIC would be helpful for piloting and navigating the vessel, and engineering would be helpful to make sure no one scuttled the ship. But their job was to protect the *Exemplar*.

"Weapons control is our best bet," he said. "Let's move."

·   ·   ·

The week and a half it had taken for the *Exemplar* to reach Bitanu from Enther was an exercise in patience for Nadia. She'd been nearly exploding with anxiety. Fear for Isadora, horror at Tanner's plan to kill 30 million innocent refugees, a sense of foreboding at the showdown she knew was coming.

Now that they were here, she'd dealt with her anxiety by

constantly checking if the *Preserver* was in range of the *Exemplar*'s radio system yet. She needed to let Isadora know about Tanner's plot ASAP.

It made for an agonizing approach. For almost a day, the white orb of Bitanu had grown larger and larger. The vast multitude of ships and fleets in orbit had grown from microscopic to visible. And even still, there was nothing she could do except wait. She'd hardly been able to sleep, even though she knew she was going to need all her wits about her.

At last, the *Exemplar*'s comm terminal lit up green. They were in range of the *Preserver*.

Nadia grabbed the controls so frantically that it made Derek and Boyd flinch. "Isadora, this is Nadia," she said. "You have to listen to me. You're in serious danger." She outlined Tanner's plan to use the *Caretaker* to ram and destroy the cryo vessel.

"Damn. I think we got cut off," Derek said. "The range is making our comms spotty. And the *Preserver* is still on the dark side of the planet."

Despair surged inside her. "Do you know if any of that even got through?"

"I'm...not sure."

"We need to move *now*," Nadia said. "The *Exemplar* is faster than a warship. We might be able to catch Tanner. We'll slingshot around Bitanu as well, dock on the *Caretaker*, and try to stop it before it can reach the *Preserver*."

Behind her, Boyd nodded. "That'd work. Boarding a ship is risky as all hell, but we know there probably aren't that many Offspring aboard."

Derek grimaced. "It would take everything our engines have.

According to the scanner, the *Caretaker* has already fallen out of the Junta navy's formation. I'd guess they'll collide with the *Preserver* in an hour at the most."

Nadia closed her eyes. "Derek—can we catch them?"

He paused. "Yes. But it won't be comfortable. And we wouldn't have much time when we *do* catch them. Less than a half-hour, for sure. Probably much less."

"Do it."

Nadia thought about reaching for the comms to try Isadora again, but the *Exemplar*'s engines roared with a ferocity she hadn't yet experienced. Her body slammed into the back of her chair. She couldn't even move her arms. Her teeth felt like they were about to snap off and fly straight into her brain.

But none of that mattered. She'd bear all that and more to stop Tanner and save her people.

Assuming she got there in time. And in one piece.

CHAPTER 39

At least a dozen messages from the Junta navy had arrived since Tanner had taken the *Caretaker* out of formation. They were all roughly the same: asking him what the hell he was doing, and commanding him to get his ass back in line. It struck him as wildly amusing that no one had figured out the *Caretaker*'s Junta crew had perished long ago.

He ignored the messages, which soon stopped. He figured that meant that his people had seized the Junta warships, and that the rest of the military had better things to do. Like trying to avoid getting killed.

Tanner also had better things to do. Namely, bringing his long crusade against the newars to an end.

The *Caretaker* entered low orbit around Bitanu. His followers were maneuvering the ship into position for a slingshot directly into the *Preserver*. In just another minute, the warship's engines would fire, and they'd be on their way. Their final journey.

And then the *Preserver* itself moved slightly, forcing Tanner and his followers to rapidly recalculate their navigational path. It also implied someone knew he was in control of the *Caretaker*.

It didn't matter. The *Preserver*'s gargantuan size made it cumbersome, difficult to maneuver. Even a warship the *Caretaker*'s size was infinitely easier to steer. The newars had bought themselves minutes, perhaps, but they hadn't bought themselves a different outcome.

And even if it had gotten out that Tanner was in control of the *Caretaker*, his followers should be in control of at least a few Junta warships by now. That meant they could protect the *Caretaker* from any incoming fire. By the time they couldn't, they would be close enough to the *Preserver* that it wouldn't matter anymore.

Tanner was strapped into a chair next to the CIC's holographic projector, trying his best to ignore the nauseating repositioning maneuvers, when he noticed a lone blip moving on an intercept trajectory toward them. The scanner gave him its transponder ID, but he guessed the vessel's identity before he even read the name.

The *Exemplar*. Nadia Jibor's vessel.

There was a time when he'd been obsessed with ending her. Thinking back made him laugh—how unambitious he'd been!—but now, she was little more than a nuisance. He knew the *Exemplar* didn't have any weapons systems, only an easily overwhelmed missile scrambling system for defense. That meant the ship would be easy prey for the warships his followers had commandeered.

Tanner began dispatching radio messages to all Offspring hijacking teams. After taking control of their assigned warship, they were to move their vessels out of formation. Straight toward the *Exemplar*'s flight path.

They would then fire whatever ordnance they had at the newar ship. With so much incoming fire, he was nearly certain the *Exemplar*'s scrambling systems would fail. It would be the long-awaited end of Nadia Jibor.

And it would finally allow him to turn his attention to the newars' cryo vessel. The *Caretaker* finished its maneuvers. Tanner allowed himself a smile as he felt the warship's massive thrusters fire. In fifty-eight minutes, they would ram into the *Preserver*.

.   .   .

Isadora had been in danger enough to develop a growing affection for the chemistry of adrenaline. There was minimal panicking, some—but not overwhelming—dread over never seeing Meredith again, but mostly planning and action.

Nadia's warning had allowed the crew to move the cryo vessel further away from the *Caretaker*, since the protective umbrella of their laser matrix on the planet's surface was superfluous against a suicide run from a warship. The maneuver had bought precious minutes, but they couldn't outrun their enemy.

The crew aboard the *Preserver* were non-military, so even if she loaded some of them onto a transport and dispatched them to the on-coming *Caretaker*, a boarding operation would probably fail.

She had no military resources at her disposal, and when she sent out transmissions begging the other warships at the summit to destroy the *Caretaker*, their missiles had been intercepted by Junta warships. She soon learned that Tanner's Offspring had commandeered enough warships to effectively protect the *Caretaker* from a Union nuclear strike.

And even if a projectile got through, the *Caretaker* would soon be close enough to the *Preserver* that the resulting debris from its destruction could cause catastrophic damage to the cryo vessel as well.

So, unideal. But not hopeless.

Isadora's first move was to encourage all ship personnel to evacuate. She hadn't contemplated fleeing, but she wasn't willing to ask the crew to go down with her. The ones who'd elected to evacuate were hastily loading whatever cryo pods they could into the shuttles.

It was a pitifully low number. If Tanner's plan succeeded, it would still be a genocide on an unimaginable scale. Heartbreaking and terrifying, she'd find it, if she weren't in the throes of an adrenaline surge. The scale of the impending catastrophe took a backseat to her drive.

Her second move was to mentally catalog the resources at her disposal. After the year she'd had, her first conclusion was that her biggest asset was *herself*. She'd grown to become, apparently, the most popular, widely admired politician in Natonese space.

And the one person who could board and wrest control of the *Caretaker* was Nadia, along with her crew on the *Exemplar*. No other ship would be fast enough to catch Tanner.

Isadora knew how she could help Nadia get there.

The problem was, the *Exemplar* was still on the far side of the planet. Its fastest intercept trajectory with the *Caretaker* would take it through hundreds of ships, including, apparently, several Offspring-controlled Junta vessels. Isadora's best course of action was trying to help clear a path for Nadia.

She began transmitting a radio message to every open transmitter in orbit. "This is Isadora Satoro," she said. "I'm messaging each and every one of you because my people are under threat of total annihilation. The Offspring have seized the *Caretaker* and are piloting it directly into our vessel. 30 million lives are at stake. We need your help at this moment of direst necessity."

Isadora paused, knowing she was about to ask many others to put themselves in harm's way, to fly directly into a flotilla of Offspring-controlled warships, for a desperate chance at saving the *Preserver*. It was different from starting an anti-war movement, where asking people to come out and protest or contact their Parliament representatives was all she'd been asking. She'd hardly ever had to order her *own* people into combat. Asking strangers to do so was harder still.

"The *Exemplar* is the only ship that can catch the *Caretaker*," she continued. "But with the Offspring in control of an unknown number of Junta vessels, they will destroy it for sure. I am asking that anyone—everyone—carve a path for the *Exemplar*. The lives of 30 million innocent people will forever thank you."

Isadora ended her transmission. She then placed her palms at the bottom of the viewscreen and looked out. Other than the small speck of the *Caretaker*, growing slightly, unnervingly larger every second, the other vessels in orbit were invisible. All she could hope was that someone out there was listening.

And willing to put everything on the line for her people.

·   ·   ·

The inside of the *Sanctitude* was grisly. Carson recalled the ruined villages he'd used to patrol through, back during the early days of his time undercover with the Offspring. Back then, he'd only had to contend with burned infrastructure. The Junta flagship, on the other hand, was a graveyard.

Every hallway he and the ex-Offspring moved through was filled with cut-up Junta corpses. As they made their way through an endless number of claustrophobic hallways, working their way to the aft section of the warship, they noticed plasma bolt-shaped holes in the hull. Rended metal peeled back, giving Carson a view of the deadly vacuum beyond. Suggesting that the crew had, eventually, resorted to desperation.

They passed through a pressure door, weapons drawn, but they hadn't encountered anyone yet. That probably meant the boarding teams were bogged down with seizing the CIC and engineering.

When they finally reached weapons control, passing through another pressure door, Carson and the others took cover on either side of a locked door. The fact that it hadn't been breached yet suggested the Offspring boarding parties hadn't seized the gunnery station yet. Which meant there could be Junta soldiers on the other side.

Two ex-Offspring set a charge. Seconds later, sparks flew out of the device. The door snapped open. Carson followed the others into the weapons control room quickly, fanning out on a platform just inside to avoid getting pinned down. But no fire came their way.

The room was a massive cylinder, missile silos running along the entire drum. A series of control stations ran along the length of the room, catwalks providing access points. Carson walked to the edge of the entry platform, but he couldn't make out any Junta soldiers in sight, much less Offspring.

"Perfect!" Emil said. "The Junta and the Offspring are too busy killing each other to notice we snuck in here."

"I don't like this," Harry said. Then pointed to the various control rooms adjacent to the catwalks. "Too many small alcoves that'd make for easy ambush spots."

Carson held up his hand. "I don't like this any more than you do," he said, his eyes constantly darting to every nook and cranny in the room. "But we need to act fast. My guess is, the Offspring have probably already taken the CIC. That means they'll be steering this ship right into the *Exemplar*'s path. We need to make sure this ship's missiles don't fire. Or, better yet, that they fire at the other warships."

Emil and Harry nodded. The rest of the ex-Offspring split up into two fireteams, each one heading to a different section of the room. While Harry's group headed to the right, Carson and Emil went to one of the lower-left catwalks.

When they reached one of the control stations, Carson pulled up his wrister and checked the latest holographic readout data. Sure enough, the *Sanctitude* was closing in on the *Exemplar*. Two other Junta warships were already in position. Carson could only assume the Offspring had commandeered both.

"If either of those warships gets a salvo off, they could overwhelm Nadia's missile scrambler," he said, showing Emil the projection. "We need to target their missile batteries."

Emil nodded. "Sounds like a plan." They walked over to separate control stations and began inputting new targeting parameters.

A voice startled them: "Who the hell are you?"

Carson spun around, sidearm drawn. From a dark corner of the control station, a man in a Junta officer's uniform stepped out. He raised his hands when he saw the gun pointed at him.

Carson recognized the face almost immediately. It was Michael Azkon, the head chairman of the entire Junta. The man who'd backstabbed Nadia, nearly gotten Isadora killed, and sent troops to the

Offspring hideout that killed Russ' spec ops team during his insertion operation. For once, Carson didn't feel bad about waving a weapon in someone's face.

"Well, well, well," Emil said, pacing around the general. "I'm guessing this rat came down here to hide."

Michael gritted his teeth. "I'm a military man. I knew the CIC was lost. The damn Offspring took us completely by surprise." He paused, regarding Carson and Emil's brown enviro-suits. "And I'm guessing you people aren't with the rest of them."

Carson lowered his handgun, confident the general was unarmed. "No, we're not." Telling Michael his real identity would just complicate things. There'd be time to sort it out later.

Emil flashed a taunting grin. "How does it feel, watching your whole empire collapse before your eyes, because you actually *trusted* Tanner Keltin?"

Carson shot him a reproachful look. His haughtiness made sense, though—his own deradicalization process had probably made him all the more judgmental of anyone still blinded by Tanner's wiles. It was the kind of thing he'd have to sort out over the coming years.

"I get it," Michael growled. "I made a bad call."

"Look, none of this matters," Carson said. "We need to target those other warships' weapons systems *now*."

"Right. I'm on it," Emil said, heading back to one of the control stations, where he resumed setting new targets.

"If you fire off a salvo, they'll lock you out from the CIC," Michael said. "And then they'll send their people to storm the gunnery station."

Carson and Emil exchanged glances. The other man gave him a reassuring nod. "Well then," he said, "I guess we'd better bunker down and get ready for company."

He turned to face Emil. "Fire."

·   ·   ·

The *Exemplar* was racing so fast that the cluster of ships they needed to pass through to catch the *Caretaker* seemed to bloom to life. Which included a flotilla of Junta warships heading right for them. Nadia could only assume they were controlled by Offspring.

They could go around the warships, but that would cost them precious time. The *Caretaker* was forty-nine minutes away from colliding with the *Preserver*, and they might not even reach Tanner's ship at all if they recalculated their flight path. That meant the only way forward was through the jaws of enemy guns.

Into certain death, it seemed.

Nadia had faced near-annihilation before, but not like this. Flying straight into a lethal crossfire from multiple warships would overwhelm their missile scrambling systems. And, still, they pressed forward. Because they had no choice. 30 million refugees were about to die, and if they had even a fraction of a chance of succeeding, they had to try.

Already, her body felt like it was sagging under the *g* forces. A headache was only growing in intensity. She was worried about the condition she'd be in if they actually got to the *Caretaker*, but—as always—they had no other choice. And it sounded like making it to Tanner's vessel alive was already a long shot.

A beep from their scanner made Derek jump. "I'm...picking up something," he said, looking over. "It looks like a Union fighter wing has left one of their capital ships and is heading toward the Offspring ship cluster."

"*Exemplar*?" the crackling voice of a Union fighter pilot came over the radio. "This is Cronus Wing Leader. Isadora just gave us the sitrep. Y'know, my brother was on Calimor when the war broke out. He got out thanks to your people accepting war refugees on Sarsi. So this one's personal. We're gonna help you push through."

Nadia didn't even get to thank the pilot when the scanner showed another detachment of Union fighters converging on the Offspring ships. "*Exemplar*, this is Tiberius Wing Leader," another voice came over the radio. "We also got your leader's message. A lot of us were deployed to New Arcena during the Calimor crisis. If it weren't for you and Isadora calling for a ceasefire, we'd have been killed. We owe you our lives, and we're gonna see this through to the end."

Her mouth was agape. She looked at Derek and Boyd, silently asking them what to say. Derek shrugged, Boyd grinned.

The scanner reported a third squadron of fighters deploying. "*Exemplar*? Atlas Wing Leader here. One of my squadmates was vacationing on Haphis a few years back during a Syndicate raid. Turns out, the only reason he's still alive was because your man Russ Kama saved him. Today, we're gonna make sure those actions were just paying it forward. We're with you."

Nadia felt the familiar, dull ache in her heart every time someone mentioned Russ. Her lip wavered.

"Are those gunships?" Boyd said.

Sure enough, per the scanner, five Horde gunships had joined the three fighter squadrons. "Tori Hyrak dispatched us to ensure that the peace negotiations went favorably for your people. We suppose ravaging a handful of Junta warships is in line with that mandate. Happy hunting, *Exemplar*."

A lone Junta frigate fell into formation behind them. "We are part of the Ashkagi delegation from Enther," a voice emerged from the radio. "You have given us our planet back, our way of life. We won't let the Offspring take that from you."

Nadia at last placed a shaky finger on the radio transmitter. "I don't know what to say," she said. "Just *thank you*. I'll make sure we earn it."

"You bet," one of the Union fighter pilots said. "All wings, accelerate to attack speed. We're going in hard and fast. Take out whatever could hit the *Exemplar*. Laser batteries, flak cannons, missile launchers. Anything and everything."

"All gunships, provide covering fire for the fighters," one of the Horde pilots said. "Target the warships' point-defense turrets."

"We'll take out their hangar bays so they can't scramble fighters," the Ashkagi pilot from the captured Junta frigate said.

Nadia drew in a sharp exhale. "Let's activate the missile scrambler. Time to do this."

They were in visual range now. Close enough that she could watch as the motley assemblage of fighters, gunships, and the frigate converged on the Offspring line. Like a surging tidal wave of justice, crashing across space. Six Offspring-controlled warships were in her path.

When they were in range, the white trails of missiles and the blue flashes of plasma fire painted the blackness of space. The hijacked warships lit up in orange plumes as the ferocity of the Union fighters' attacks neutered their defense cannons.

But the warships responded with a ferocity of their own. Dozens of Union fighters disappeared almost instantly, torn apart by point-defense turrets.

"I'm gonna bring us in close to one of the warships. I'm guessing the Offspring won't fire at their own people," Derek said. He swerved the *Exemplar* to pull them right alongside the closest vessel.

"Smart," Nadia said.

"That's giving them too much credi—woah!" Boyd said. Derek had brought them so close that he had to pull up just in time. As they raced around the top of the warship's hull, the rest of the battlefield stretched out in front of them.

The remaining five warships were arrayed in wildly different orientations. Physical columns of Union fighter jets swirled over and around the area like a swarm of angry hornets. Many disappeared in brilliant, tragic flashes of light. All the while, cannons from the gunships and the frigate peppered the battlefield, keeping the enemy's guns distracted.

Derek swerved the *Exemplar* in a zigzagging path that ran between the blockade. A barrage of plasma fire streaked at them, evaded easily. The guns that shot at them went up in fire seconds later, after a Union strafing run.

"The *Exemplar*'s almost through!" one of the pilots said. "Don't let up!"

Derek cursed, causing Nadia to refocus her attention on the viewscreen. Two of the remaining hijacked warships were moving in a pincer formation toward them.

"The *Exemplar*'s in trouble!" another pilot said. "Someone get there!"

It was no use. The other warships had moved into position behind them, cutting them off from their support ships. "It's the *Sanctitude*," Derek said, gritting his teeth. "I'm gonna try to—"

Before Derek could initiate any evasive maneuvers, the missile silos on the aft section of the *Sanctitude* slid open. Warheads jetted out from the hold, swerved about, and streaked straight for...

...straight for the other warship?

Nadia cocked her head in confusion as the strike crippled the other vessel's weapons batteries. That either meant that the Junta hadn't actually succumbed to the Offspring boarders on the flagship, and had suddenly decided to help Nadia—unlikely—or that Carson had managed to sneak aboard. A thin smile spread across her face.

"It's Carson," she said, a rising feeling of warmth in her gut providing a certainty that no hard evidence could. "He's paving the final path for us."

"And we're taking it," Derek said. They broke through the back of the Offspring line. Then approached Bitanu, plunging around its gravity well. Toward the *Caretaker*.

"Looks like you're clear, *Exemplar*," one of the surviving Union pilots radioed. "Good luck."

Good luck, indeed. Now, there was nothing left between them and the *Caretaker*—except time.

CHAPTER 40

Tanner was surprised the *Exemplar* had made it through the ships he'd thrown in its path. The *Sanctitude* had apparently fired on another warship, preventing what would've been a killing blow on Nadia at the last moment.

A pity. Tanner radioed orders to all Offspring on the *Sanctitude* to find and kill whoever had saved her.

But he had bigger issues to turn his attention to. According to the *Caretaker*'s computer, the *Exemplar* would reach them in five minutes, a full sixteen minutes before they'd collide with the *Preserver*. Firing missiles at them would throw off their trajectory.

That meant he'd need to plan a defense of the ship. Which would be a lot easier without the splitting headache, brought on by the intense *g* forces of their slingshot maneuver. The colors of the ship had started to deaden, even. He had to blink to make sure he wasn't imagining it.

Focus, Tanner told himself. It wasn't hard to figure out what Nadia's plan would be. She wouldn't try to destroy the ship, not while the laws of inertia would just end up sending the debris crashing into the *Preserver*. Her only option was to steer the ship in a new direction, which meant she'd be gunning straight for the CIC.

The problem was, he only had six Offspring with him to defend the ship. They outnumbered Nadia and her team, sure, but the narrow corridors of shipboard gunfights—he assumed the newar and her lackeys would bring their own oxygen supply and shoot without hesitation—could easily negate a numerical advantage.

And he had to admit that Nadia's team had seen plenty of fighting. He might even respect her as a worthy opponent if she weren't a newar. As it stood, there was only so much glory he could find in thwarting her.

Tanner reviewed the deployments of his followers from the CIC holo-projector. He hoped he'd sent them to the positions most likely to either catch Nadia and her team off guard, or pin them down. And even if they managed to get to the CIC, he had another card to play.

He walked over to a small elevator shaft at the far end of the CIC, taking it to the very tip of the vessel. The elevator shot past almost a dozen decks until it deposited him at the *Caretaker*'s nose.

Tanner exited into an observation room, capped by a transparent, protective membrane impervious to plasma fire. The kind of thing that used to be standard on old warships like the *Caretaker*.

He had to strain his neck to look directly up, but his delight at the growing size of the *Preserver* more than outweighed the discomfort. They were so close, so *tantalizingly* close. The sacrifice he was about to make would go down as one of the most monumental moments in Natonese history. An act countless generations would thank him for.

When so many other institutions of society had only half-heartedly resisted the newars' encroachment, or even rolled over for the invaders, the Offspring had stood firm. Had held the line. Had been willing to stand up for the entire Natonus System when no one else would.

Tanner walked forward. The center of the observation deck was a raised platform, which dropped off along the far edges. A catwalk ran around the perimeter. It'd be a glorious arena for him to meet his end.

Approaching the edge of the raised platform, Tanner reached a terminal station and used his administrative privileges to lock out the CIC from its control functions. That way, even if the *Exemplar* crew made it there, it'd be a hollow victory.

Once he was done, he looked back upward. With every second that the *Preserver* grew larger, the closer he was to his demise. He closed his eyes and took a deep breath. He wanted his last moments to be free from thinking too much about the future. He was already sure of the righteousness of his cause. He wanted his last thoughts to be about Rebecca.

He'd protected her for so long. Was protecting her even now. He thought about her face, wondering what she would look like, now that she was almost eighteen. Wherever she was, Tanner was sure she'd grown into an accomplished young woman. The kind of person the Natonese people would look to for guidance, for leadership in the uncertain days to come.

"This is for you, Rebecca," he whispered, fixing his eyes on the *Preserver*. "*All* of this is for you. I love you."

.   .   .

Carson was relieved to hear the missiles they'd fired from the *Sancti-tude* had allowed Nadia to break through the Offspring line. He was less relieved when he realized that, any minute now, Offspring hijack-ers would burst into the weapons control bay, guns blazing.

The problem was, he and the other ex-Offspring had already blown the door to get inside. So fortifying the bay was a no-go. And leaving was probably an even worse option. They'd get picked off by the numerically superior Offspring in the flagship's narrow corridors, while at least the bay entrance offered a natural chokepoint.

The others had organized into four teams, each one taking posi-tion on either the upper or lower catwalks of each side of the gunnery bay. He, Emil, and the Junta leader Michael Azkon were holding po-sition in one of the control rooms. As far as he could tell, the latter was little more than an inconvenience at the moment. Hopefully, the general's military training meant he wouldn't get in the way once the fighting started.

"There have to be some Junta survivors crawling around in here," Emil said, glaring at Michael. "Why don't you contact them, tell them to come help us?"

"Okay," Michael snapped, "first thing: I barely even know who you fucking people are. You seem to care about helping the refugees, and you clearly used to be Offspring. Other than wanting to get off this ship alive and having a mutual enemy, we don't seem to share any interests.

"Second: don't you think I'd have *tried* that before? The first thing the damn Offspring did when they took the CIC was cut off our intercom system. And with the comms disruption—which I'm guessing the rest of the Offspring were responsible for—and a lack of a radio, that means I can't contact anyone. Even if I wanted to."

Emil walked forward so the general couldn't see his expression, then rolled his eyes. "Helpful son of a bitch," he muttered.

Carson stifled a grin. "I'm guessing he's still trying to process the fact that Tanner was manipulating him the whole time. Before we judge him too quickly, it's worth remembering just *how* effective of a manipulator Tanner was. He's probably just being an ass as a coping mechanism."

"Oh, from what I know about him, being an ass is just his brand."

Before Carson could respond, he heard shouts. The frantic thudping of plasma fire followed. His head shot up toward the entrance. Two Offspring had stormed through the blown door, but they'd been shot as soon as they entered. It was a four-way crossfire: sure to be deadly to the first few waves, but not impenetrable. They'd lose a war of attrition for sure.

A smoke grenade followed the Offspring advance team. A billowing cloud of charcoal-colored smoke filled the entry platform. Plasma bolts flew out from the hidden depths of the cloud. Two ex-Offspring went down immediately. The others backed up further away from the entrance, retreating down their respective catwalks. They went racing for whatever control station they could find for cover.

Carson, Emil, and Michael all stayed as close to the wall as possible. "Is it too much to ask for a weapon?" the general asked.

"Yes!" Carson and Emil shouted simultaneously.

"Is there any way out of here, other than the main entrance?" Carson continued. "Otherwise, we're all dead."

He darted out from cover, fired off a couple of indiscriminate rounds. To his dismay, a half-dozen Offspring had already established a beachhead inside the gunnery bay. He hurried back into cover.

"I suppose...there *is* an old maintenance corridor running along the underbelly of the ship," Michael said. "This used to be a Theocracy vessel. They used human maintenance workers. Now, we just use drones."

"We're in the middle of a firefight, and this guy's giving us a damn history lecture!" Emil scoffed, firing a couple of blind rounds around the edge.

"Where is it?" Carson pressed.

"At the very bottom of the bay," Michael said, pointing to a patch of metal that didn't look particularly noteworthy to Carson. But he'd take anything that gave them a way out.

Carson got the attention of the other fireteams and communicated the plan via hand signals. While two of the teams laid down a heavy screen of covering fire, he tossed a smoke grenade out at the entry platform. Then fired off a salvo, while the others began rappelling to the bottom of the cylindrical bay.

The sudden maneuver seemed to catch the Offspring off guard. They were slow to respond, but they still picked off one of the ex-Offspring. Once the others had regrouped, they covered Carson, Emil, and Michael as they rappelled to the bottom.

With Carson, Emil, and the five surviving ex-Offspring covering him, Michael quickly got to work on the maintenance tube hatch. Carson urged the others in, while he and Emil continued to trade shots with the Offspring on the entry platform. Once the rest of the team was inside, they jumped in.

The tube itself was narrow, claustrophobically so. They'd have to walk in a single file. Outcroppings of metal, pipes, and cables were everywhere. "If they didn't know about the maintenance tube earlier, they do now," Carson said. "Let's move!"

Considering the confines, however, hurrying was impossible. After only a few seconds, an awful metal screeching sound echoed through the tube. "What the hell was that?" Emil asked, turning to face Michael.

"Could be the elevator," the general said. "As I said, the tube was built for maintenance workers."

Carson stopped in his tracks. If the Offspring controlling the vessel had activated the elevator, they'd be crushed for sure. If they went back, they'd get picked off in the weapons bay. If moving forward and retreating were both deadly, there was only one course of action left that made sense.

Michael had told them that the maintenance tube ran along the *outside* of the ship. Carson pulled a fusion cutter out of his utility belt.

"All right everyone," he said. "I've got an idea. But you're gonna need to make sure you've got your oxygen masks on tight."

.   .   .

Derek had done it. The *Exemplar* had latched onto the *Caretaker*. It would've been too tricky for them to land in the hangar, and it was miraculous that they'd been able to latch onto the hull at all. Plus, Nadia figured that keeping their position unpredictable would give them a better chance of success.

"Okay," she said, as she, Boyd, and Derek headed for the airlock. They peeled open the door and began cutting through the *Caretaker* hull with fusion torches. "We've got about sixteen minutes to get to the CIC and redirect the ship away from the *Preserver*."

"And avoid getting killed by Offspring along the way," Derek said with a grimace.

"We know from Carson's intel that Tanner boarded the ship with a team of twelve," Boyd said. "We know two of them went with him to Bitanu, where we took them out. And I'd bet some others went down during the takeover of the ship in the first place. I think we can do it."

"I agree," Nadia said. "But we should be careful. They know we're coming." They finished slicing through the hull and jumped down into a narrow corridor.

Even being on a warship, where most of the walls were metallic grey, Nadia could tell that her vision was starting to change. Under the sustained high-*g* slingshot around Bitanu, she'd developed a headache. Her vision had darkened at the edges, her sense of color diminishing. The teal mesh of her suit looked duller than ever before.

The idea of facing down an unknown number of Offspring—and Tanner himself—while affected by *g* forces wasn't helping her nerves. But the headache was at least distracting. Her temples flaring made it easy to forget that 30 million lives were resting on her team's success. And at least the Offspring would be similarly impaired.

Nadia and her two crewmates worked their way through the hallways carefully. They kept their helmets on, their weapons drawn. According to the intelligence Carson had dug up, the Offspring managed to seize the *Caretaker* because the Junta crew was unwilling to shoot back and depressurize the vessel.

Nadia and her crew, however, had no such qualms. Not while they were equipped with their own oxygen supply.

Still, they were taking it carefully: checking their corners, covering each other, moving slowly but deliberately. The stakes were higher than ever before, and she'd learned a few things during her time with Russ.

They followed signs for a turbolift bay. And then when they reached an airlock door, it swished open. Three knife-wielding Offspring lunged out at them.

Boyd cursed loudly over their radio channel. Then tripped as he tried to run backward. One of the Offspring closed in on him, swinging his knife madly. Nadia shot him in the chest, then jetted backward.

Another Offspring cornered Derek, who dodged beneath the swipe of his blade, grabbed the Offspring's legs, and tackled him. The two grappled on the floor while the knife skidded away.

The third Offspring ran at Nadia, who turned her gun and started firing. Her first two shots went wide, striking the hull, ripping through the metal. Oxygen rushed out. Everything outside her helmet went silent.

Without the benefit of sound, the only indication that a shot had been fired was the flash of blue from the other end of the hallway. Nadia looked over her pursuer's shoulder to see Boyd shoot the Offspring Derek was grappling with.

Nadia feigned jumping to the right before rolling to the left. Another silent shot streaked overhead, this one from Derek's gun, and struck her attacker. The dead Offspring went flying, collided with the door, then slumped to the ground. She pushed herself to her feet and joined her team.

"One way to get the heart rate up," Boyd panted over their channel.

Derek shot him an incredulous look. "Your heart rate isn't up already?"

"Come on," Nadia urged, "we need to hurry." They moved through the airlock at the other end of the hallway, leading into the turbolift station. No Offspring were waiting for them. They took the central lift, with a sign that read COMMAND DECK.

Soon, they were moving through the uppermost levels of the *Caretaker*. Nadia caught sight of dried blood on the walls, probably the remains of the Offspring's violent takeover of the vessel. She wished she could feel more sympathy for the dead crew, but they'd chosen to ally with the Offspring, knowing full well the kind of man Tanner Keltin was.

They reached the CIC unopposed. When the door opened, Nadia sprinted from the right side of the door to the left side of the room. Derek did the reverse, and Boyd crouched low and covered both of them. But it was a moot point. The CIC was as deserted as the rest of the ship.

It felt like a trap, but she had a hard time caring about that with her headache. And the promise of finally ending the Offspring threat in reaching distance. She crossed over to the central terminal, her footsteps feeling heavy the whole time, and pulled up the ship's piloting functions.

It was only a second after she realized she'd been locked out when the smoke grenade came in.

In another instant, dark grey, billowing smoke suffocated the room. She ducked just before two plasma bolts struck the wall behind her. The CIC was at least insulated in the ship's interior, meaning that stray shots wouldn't depressurize the room. She fired blindly, but the sounds of battle and the lingering hiss of the grenade made it difficult to hear anything.

Boyd and Derek crawled over to her. "We're locked out!" she shouted. "The piloting controls have been routed elsewhere!"

"I can figure out where. Cover me!" Boyd shouted.

Nadia and Derek both darted out of cover, then fired into the impenetrable smoke cloud, unsure if they'd hit anything.

"Got it!" Boyd said. "Looks like executive control's been turned over to a terminal station in the forward observation room. A turbolift at the back of the CIC will take us there."

Boyd crouched again, and Nadia and Derek fell back into cover. "Boyd and I will hold the line," Derek said. "Nadia, go. End the lockout, then I'll use the CIC station to reroute the ship. Until then, we'll cover your back."

Nadia wanted to protest. Especially since they had no idea how many Offspring were pinning them down. But she knew her crewmates could handle themselves, and splitting up would allow her the best chance of success.

"Okay," she said. "Stay safe."

They covered her as she ran to the back of the CIC and took a small turbolift to the very apex of the vessel. Given that the observation deck would make for a theatrical location to watch the Offspring's plan unfold, Nadia thought she knew precisely who would be waiting for her.

As the lift continued to rise, her body felt even heavier. She'd been under high-g stress for almost an hour, and everything hurt. She was pretty sure the concept of color had now turned into an abstraction.

It didn't matter. She looked upward as the turbolift climbed. Toward Tanner, she was almost certain.

· · ·

The first part of Isadora's plan had succeeded. She'd rallied the rest of the increasingly misnamed peace summit attendees to come to her people's aid, and they'd shepherded the *Exemplar* through an Offspring defensive line at a high cost. According to the scanners, the *Exemplar* had now reached the *Caretaker*.

But also according to the scanners, the *Caretaker* would rip through the *Preserver* in four minutes.

Everything now depended on Nadia somehow managing to divert the *Caretaker* in time. If it hadn't been for the adrenaline, Isadora was certain she'd be a nervous wreck. Or that she might've taken the easy way out, boarding an evacuation shuttle off the *Preserver*.

She'd stayed on the cryo vessel because she wanted to do everything she could to save her people, even up to the last moment. But now, pacing in the observation lounge and watching the *Caretaker* grow alarmingly large, she couldn't think of anything to do.

Political appeals for help wouldn't do anything, not when the *Exemplar* was the only ship fast enough to reach the *Caretaker*. She'd moved the *Preserver* as far from the oncoming Offspring ship as she could, but the cryo vessel was ponderous. Destroying the *Caretaker* wouldn't do anything at this point, and there were no militia forces on the *Preserver* to deploy to assist Nadia's team.

Really, all she could possibly do at this point would be to somehow convince Tanner Keltin to stand down. The impossibility of that idea elicited a hollow laugh.

But then a different thought surged to the top of her head. She could radio a transmission to the *Caretaker*. Not to persuade Tanner, but to *distract* him. Anything to give Nadia's team a crucial edge.

Isadora felt a cold realization stir inside her. She knew the exact message to send.

She crossed the observation lounge. A shaky, adrenaline-addled hand pressed the dispatch button. She set the controls to blare her message through every open transmitter on the *Caretaker*. Then reached a hand into her left blazer pocket.

Isadora cleared her throat and began to speak.

CHAPTER 41

Space looked a lot bigger to Carson, now that he was standing on the hull of a warship. He'd activated the magnetic function of his boots, meaning he was now walking along the underbelly of the *Sanctitude*. The surviving ex-Offspring, including Emil and Harry, were behind him. They had Michael Azkon in tow.

The assembled ships that had helped the *Exemplar* break through the Offspring line—the survivors, at least—were still in the vicinity, still engaged in pitched shootouts with the hijacked Junta warships. Every few seconds, a Union fighter jet would race by, chased by a plasma salvo from the *Sanctitude*.

One of the fighters caught a bolt, then careened sharply, before pummeling into the *Sanctitude*'s hull. The fighter disappeared in a plume of fire, but the hull plating beneath buckled.

Carson looked around. The costs of the battle were grimly apparent, with fighter debris everywhere he looked. Along with dozens of vacuum-frozen bodies: the pilots who had sacrificed their lives to give the refugees a fighting chance.

But they'd clearly turned the tide. Three hijacked warships had been destroyed, their husks drifting toward Bitanu's gravity well. He turned toward the white orb below. Watched as fiery debris rained down on the planet.

Emil walked up to him and spoke over a private radio frequency. "You know we can't trust Michael Azkon, right? We should put him in prison for everything he's done."

He was absolutely right. The man was an opportunist—one who'd hurt or tried to hurt a lot of refugees. But he was an opportunist on record aiding and abetting a known terrorist organization. And with the rest of the Junta collapsing in the face of the Offspring betrayal, watching his empire disintegrate and then rotting in jail felt like a suitable fate for him.

But that was a question for when they were out of harm's way. Right now, Carson wanted nothing more than to get the surviving ex-Offspring to safety. They'd risked so much for his people that they deserved to get out of this alive.

Carson looked out over the curve of Bitanu, where both the *Caretaker* and the *Exemplar* had receded from visible range. There was nothing more he could do to help Nadia or Isadora. There was only getting his team to safety.

"We'll figure out what to do with the general later," he responded finally. "For now, I just want to get everyone out of this ali—"

A wing of Union bombers swooped in from the left, cutting him off. They unleashed their payloads on the hijacked vessel, destroying the remaining point-defense cannons in a single maneuver.

But one missile lodged in the impact crater left by the crashed fighter just a minute earlier.

A wall of fire shot out of the *Sancitude*'s hull.

Only when the flames receded did Carson realize that the back half of the warship was floating away. The half they were on began to tumble toward Bitanu's gravity well.

The bombers must've hit a weak spot, splitting the warship in two and effectively trapping him and his team on the other half of the ship from the hangar. And judging from their proximity to the planet, he guessed they were only a few minutes from entering its atmosphere. And being incinerated.

Carson switched his transmitter to dispatch to the rest of the group. "Okay," he said, walking over to Michael. "Know any other way off this ship?"

The general shook his head. "It's an older vessel. Only one main hangar bay."

"Useless," Emil scowled.

"There are still all kinds of ships flying around," Harry Klim said, not even trying to conceal the panic in his voice.

That was a fair point. Carson widened the reach of his transmitter so that it would hopefully reach one of the Union fighters. "This is Carson Erlinza," he said, briefly trying to figure out how to concisely summarize his identity, "I'm one of the refugees, and I'm part of an infiltration team aboard the *Sanctitude*. Specifically, the section that's crashing. We need immediate evac."

There was a long pause before anyone responded. Long enough that he feared no one was going to answer.

"Carson Erlinza?" a voice finally repeated. "This is Cronus Leader.

We just checked the Union's databases. The only record of a 'Carson Erlinza' in the system is someone who lost their Obrigan job to a refugee guest worker. You're marked as probable Offspring."

The fake identity the leadership put in place. Carson closed his eyes in frustration. Everyone in the Natonus System—or *almost* everyone—thought of him as nothing but a terrorist. Not someone who'd put everything on the line to give his people a shot at stopping Tanner's murderous plot.

But more problematically, he had no idea how to explain his story, much less if the Union pilot would find it convincing. Especially with the amount of time they had left.

Emil turned a knob on his wrister as well. "Look," he said, "we're a bunch of Offspring defectors. And we have a captured General Michael Azkon with us. We're happy to go quietly if you'd like to take us all into custody."

Another pause.

"General Michael Azkon?" the pilot repeated in disbelief. "All right. We're sending a shuttle to extract you. Stay put, and stow any firearms you have. Cronus Leader out."

"Well," Emil said, flashing the Junta leader a grin from behind his helmet, "I guess you weren't useless after all."

.   .   .

The turbolift door slid open. Nadia stepped out and saw a single man across a large observation room, with a central, circular raised platform and a catwalk running around the far side.

She'd lost her ability to perceive color, but she didn't need it to know he was Tanner Keltin. The all-important terminal was behind him. She'd have to get through him to access it.

"Nadia Jibor!" Tanner shouted over a general radio frequency, nearly splitting her eardrums. "There's no one I'd rather share these final moments with. And no one I'd rather watch the destruction of your people alongside."

She raised her gun. Fired off almost a dozen rounds. Tanner used his suit to jet from the center of the platform up to one of the catwalks. Nadia continued to fire, her plasma bolts shearing the metal catwalk railing into pieces. Pieces that tumbled down the large drop-off between the catwalk and the raised platform.

Tanner sprinted along the catwalk, firing as he went. Nadia sidestepped, her legs feeling heavier with each footfall. Bright sparks flashed where his shots landed, ripping metal out of the floor.

The two danced around each other, firing desperate shots that continued to miss, until Nadia reached a stack of crates to the right of the terminal station. She ducked into cover.

Nadia looked up through the transparent membrane covering the observation deck. The last time she'd seen the *Preserver* that large was the first time she'd departed the vessel, aboard the *Exemplar*.

They probably only had a few minutes before collision. This shootout with Tanner was superfluous, really. A delaying tactic. All he needed was to stall. She had to act, had to reach the terminal at the far end of the deck.

Nadia spun out of cover, searching for her adversary. But he must've relocated. Searching around for the man, she finally found him. He was standing on a beam running along the dome, his magnetic boots activated. Then he pushed himself off, barreling straight for her.

Plasma fire rained on her. With Tanner coming for her from

above, cover was practically useless. She jetted forward, firing upward as she went. Her shots were poorly placed, slamming harmlessly into the dome. She recovered badly, and went flailing to the ground.

Tanner slammed into the floor and raised his weapon at Nadia. She kicked her feet back, crawling away from him. Plasma bolts streaked toward her. She rolled away, but not before a single shot grazed the top of her right hand. She howled in pain.

And let go of her weapon.

Her instinct was to clutch her hand and keel over, but she knew Tanner could end her if she hesitated. She activated her suit's thrusters once more. Sped back into cover behind the crates, her arms and legs flying wildly. Floating droplets of blood seeped out from the tear in her right glove.

The ominous, triumphant clang of Tanner's boots echoed through the observation deck as he advanced on her. With every one of his footfalls, Nadia's heart rate quickened. She was cornered and unarmed.

She looked back upward. They were *so* close to the *Preserver*. She had to act now, had to do something. Even if she failed. She wouldn't cower in fear while 30 million lives hung in the balance.

Steadying her breath, she resolved to use her suit to propel herself right at Tanner. Maybe he'd shoot her, maybe she'd get there before he had the chance. Considering how close it sounded like he'd gotten to her, a surprise maneuver might just work. She could catch him off guard, then race for the terminal. Maybe she'd be able to return controls to the CIC before he shot her in the back.

That was when she heard Isadora's voice.

"Tanner Keltin," Isadora's voice boomed from the terminal station's transmitter. "I am Isadora Satoro. We've never met—that confrontation on Bitanu doesn't count, I'd say—but I wanted to let you know that we could've been friends in another life. You see, *my daughter Meredith and your sister Rebecca are dating.*"

The speed of Tanner's footfalls slowed.

"All it would've taken," Isadora continued, "was a few different decisions. A few different forks in the road. We could've watched them fall in love together. Could've watched them grow up and grow old together, maybe. To hear Rebecca tell it, I know you would've liked that."

Tanner's footfalls ceased.

"The thing is, Meredith and Rebecca are the future. Nothing that happens here today will change that. Nothing you've done, nothing you'll *ever* do, will stop that. Because Meredith and Rebecca are *both* Natonese, and someday, the whole galaxy will belong to them." Then, a click sounded. Like the start of an audio file playing.

"We all know the future is about togetherness..." a girl's voice said over the radio. Nadia was nearly sure the voice belonged to Meredith.

This was Nadia's moment.

"...about Natonese and Earthborn joining forces, becoming one..." a second girl's voice sounded. *Is that Rebecca Keltin?*

Nadia burst out from cover and launched herself straight for her handgun, still resting on the floor. The audio file was still playing, alternating between Meredith and Rebecca's voices, but it was hard to concentrate on the words. When she turned to face Tanner, she saw an expression beneath his visor she'd never seen before.

"...in unity, there are no challenges too insurmountable, no odysseys too dangerous..."

There was no wrath in Tanner's expression, just confusion. His face contorted, as though he wanted to reject Isadora's revelation, but part of him couldn't help but wonder if it was true.

It gave her all the time she needed.

"...this is why we do what we do..."

Nadia raised her arm, pointed the barrel at Tanner. There was no rage in her movement, no thirst for vengeance, no *this is for Russ and Vincent, you son of a bitch*. Just grim, solemn necessity. Just dispassionate justice.

"...eliminating the threat of miscommunication..."

With a gentle squeeze, Nadia's finger tugged at the trigger.

Tanner's neck exploded.

He crumpled to his knees. His mouth was moving, though Nadia couldn't tell whether he was cursing at her or begging for forgiveness. She supposed it didn't really matter.

Tanner's eyes clouded. His body slammed into the ground. He lay still.

"...creating a safe environment for everyone..."

Nadia didn't have time to linger. She had to get to the terminal station *now*, had to end the lockout back in the CIC so Derek could reroute the ship. Assuming he and Boyd were still alive.

She limped past Tanner's corpse, toward the center of the main platform. Her body felt like it was seeping to the floor with every step. The edges of her vision kept narrowing, closer and closer, till there was almost nothing left.

"...bringing hope for countless generations ahead..."

"Please," she said, though she couldn't tell whether she was saying anything aloud, or whether it was just in her head. Just reaching the terminal station felt like a marathon. A weary hand slammed into the console, searching desperately for the root menu.

Every time she blinked, she worried she was going to pass out.

"Don't give out on me," Nadia urged her body. Her words sounded slurred, unintelligible. "Just a little bit longer."

"...and winning humanity's future." The audio file ended, and the deck fell silent.

She found it. The series of commands that would restore functionality to the CIC. Her finger inched over till it was directly over the final button. Relief surged through her as she pressed down. The console lit up, signalling that full navigational functionality had been restored to the CIC.

That was when Nadia's vision finally failed her. And when she lost all consciousness.

.   .   .

Inches saved the *Preserver*.

Isadora had been busy trying to come to peace with everlasting nothingness, with never seeing Meredith again, while trying to ignore the horrifying crime that Tanner had committed, when the announcement came through.

The *Caretaker* had swerved at the last second, missing the edge of the *Preserver*'s hull by inches.

Isadora had leapt into action immediately. She'd contacted the Union fleets, which dispatched a swarm of thruster-equipped drones to latch onto the *Caretaker*'s hull, slowing it down until they brought it to a stable orbit. Then, a dozen transports filled with Union marines boarded the ship.

They found seven dead Offspring aboard—including Tanner—and the unconscious bodies of Nadia, Boyd Makrum, and Derek Hozan. They'd all passed out from sustained high-g maneuvers, but were very much alive.

Nadia looked like she'd passed out directly after inputting a command that had returned navigational controls to the CIC, which had allowed her crewmates to chart a new path before they passed out, too.

The marines had retrieved Nadia, her crew, and their ship from the *Caretaker*. All three were recovering in one of the *Preserver*'s med bays, while the *Exemplar* sat in the hangar.

Doctors had been monitoring Nadia's condition, assuring Isadora that she was stable. And they'd messaged her right away when Nadia regained consciousness. Isadora left her shipboard office and rushed toward the medical wing.

In the waiting room outside, there was a single man sitting in one of the chairs. He was well-built, with dirty blond hair.

And wore a brown Offspring enviro-suit.

Isadora panicked for an instant, before realizing that he was Carson Erlinza. The therapist-turned-spy who'd discovered a critical piece of intelligence that had bought them just enough time to save the *Preserver*. She'd never even *met* him.

He looked up, an exhausted expression in his eyes, and came to his feet. "Ma'am," he said, raising a weary arm in a salute.

Isadora gently motioned for him to lower his hand. "I believe it is myself—and everyone else aboard this ship—who should be saluting *you*. Especially after everything I put you through."

She thought back to the conversation she'd had with Riley over a year ago, back when the Offspring had just attacked New Arcena. She'd signed off on a proposal to establish an espionage program, but she'd never personally had much involvement with the project. But it had paid off in ways so monumental it was difficult to appreciate.

"Really, it was some of the other ex-Offspring who played the most important role," Carson said. "And Nadia was the one who stopped Tanner. And you were the one who rallied the other fleets to help."

Isadora walked up and placed a hand on the man's shoulder. He flinched under her touch. She wondered for a moment just how much he'd been through. What had it been like, being undercover with the Offspring for so long? She'd probably never know, and she was happy to leave it that way.

"You've endured more than almost any of us," she said gently. "And you're being modest. All of us had a part to play, yes, but you were a critical piece in that. Your intelligence, relayed by Nadia, allowed me to move the *Preserver* ever so slightly away from the *Caretaker*. And considering that mere seconds saved us, you buying us a ten-minute head start made all the difference. You can rest easy tonight, knowing that 30 million people are alive because of you."

She retracted her hand. Carson's lip quivered, and Isadora thought it would be best to leave him be for the moment. "Also, I get to see Nadia first," she said, cocking a wry grin and nodding toward the med bay. "Executive privilege and all that."

He chuckled. "Naturally." He sat back down and lowered his head once more.

Isadora walked toward the med bay, pausing at the door. "And Carson," she said. "If there's anything you need—*anything*—let me know, and I'll make it happen. Executive privilege covers that, too."

Carson just nodded.

She walked into the med bay. Hooked up to a diagnostic station was Nadia Jibor. Tubes were pumping fluids into her, while a wrist cuff monitored her blood pressure. The medical team had stripped her of her enviro-suit, exposing deep red blotches across her arms, neck, and face. There were bruises everywhere along her neck and cheeks. A number of blood vessels in her eyes had burst.

"Isadora?" Nadia said weakly.

She just grinned. "Thank you," she mouthed. She wanted to run forward and embrace her, just like she had on Calimor, on Enther, on Bitanu. After every crisis they'd been through together.

This time, she held herself back. She had a feeling Nadia wouldn't particularly appreciate a hug in her present condition.

"...I look horrible, don't I," Nadia said, letting out a laugh that quickly turned into a cough.

Isadora nodded, her smile widening. "Yes. Yes you do."

"The thing is, I hardly remember any of it," Nadia said. "I remember stepping off the elevator bay. Flashes of a shootout with Tanner. And that's about it. Everything gets really fuzzy. The next thing I remember is waking up here, and a bunch of doctors telling me that I'm going to be fine, that Boyd and Derek are okay, and that we saved everyone."

"Well then. I guess I don't really have anything to add."

"Y'know, if you keep trying to make me laugh, I'm pretty sure one of the doctors is gonna come back in and yell at you."

"Oh, I'll just glare at him icily and tell him to leave us alone. That usually does the trick."

Nadia coughed once more. Isadora walked closer and sat down on a bedside stool. "If I can't make you laugh, then I guess I ought to give you the bad news," she said. "Now that you've saved the 30 million still on the *Preserver*, and since we're about to turn this thing into a giant wormhole, that means someone's going to have to survey a bunch of settlements."

"Pass," Nadia said, managing a weak grin. "I quit. I think I earned it."

"That's funny," Isadora said. "I quit too."

Nadia let out a deep, contented sigh. "So this is really it, huh? After all this time, we're right back where we started. And we're both nobodies once again."

Isadora thought back to her first meeting, with Nadia, Russ, and Vincent. None of them were even supposed to have their jobs—it was only an accident of their sister ship having been destroyed. Her heart ached, wishing Russ and Vincent were still here. Back then, she'd been so naive that she couldn't even be properly overwhelmed by the task before her. And now here she was, on the other side. Just like Nadia.

"Nobodies," she repeated. "I have to say, I kind of like that."

CHAPTER 42

Carson had seen New Arcena once, right after he'd come out of cryo. He'd only been in the colony for a few hours, but he remembered being surprised at how small it was, given its important place in his people's story in the Natonus System.

It was small no longer.

Carson's shuttle landed in the middle of what could only be described as a thriving metropolis, located in the heart of Calimor's red deserts. The leadership had already pulled 10 million people off the *Preserver*, most of them going to newly constructed settlements. Still, the mass thawing had clearly swelled the size of New Arcena.

"Sorry about the dust storms," the pilot said from the front of the shuttle. "The descent really is a hell of a view. You'll have to come back sometime."

"That's okay," Carson said. "I think I could use a little less adventure in my life." He thanked the pilot and departed. Once inside, he lined up behind a couple dozen others before entering a security checkpoint, which was far more crowded than anything he'd ever experienced before in the Natonus System. The shuttle he'd commissioned took off almost immediately afterward.

Isadora Satoro had resigned as chief coordinator by now. But she'd held onto office long enough to recommend one final measure, paying Carson a massive sum of natons for his service to their people. It'd passed the Consultative Committee—marred by bitter political feuds, now—unanimously. He was pretty sure he'd never have to work a day in his life again if he didn't want to.

An innately frugal person, it was almost hard for him to comprehend coming into that kind of money. He'd invested a significant amount of it into the charity organization that Meredith Satoro and Rebecca Keltin had founded. He'd also given a decent chunk to Emil, who'd started a deradicalization program for the hundreds of surviving Offspring to reintegrate into Natonese society and pay back their communities for what they'd done.

Apparently, the two organizations were even working together. With Carson's injection of cash, Emil had hired Harry Klim as a liaison officer to Meredith and Rebecca's charity. One way for ex-Offspring to fulfill the community service portion of their sentences was through aiding in new settlement construction projects.

Emil had asked Carson if he wanted to participate, given his background. But he'd declined. He'd tried being a therapist again, right after the battle of Caphila on Enther. The ethical complications of his spy work had marred the experience. Even now that he'd finished his mission, he couldn't go back to the person he used to be. He wasn't a therapist anymore.

It was his turn to approach the security booth. A guard asked him to press his thumb into a scanning device. It flashed green, and seconds later, her eyes went wide. "Carson Erlinza?" she asked. "You're—"

"—please," he said with a forced smile, "I'd just like to go see my brother. I don't need a big fuss."

It was too late. The people around him started whispering, started staring, started pointing at him. His heart began to race, while sweat oozed down his back.

But the commotion had already attracted others' attention, rippling outward. Soon, everyone in the entire security checkpoint had their attention fixed on him. The applause started with only a single person out of sight, but soon, everyone was clapping and cheering.

Carson faked a smile and waved uncomfortably. He'd never asked for this kind of attention. If anything, he wanted to get away from it.

He'd spent almost a year undercover with the Offspring, constantly worrying about being caught, being discovered. It'd been plenty of time for an unhealthy sense of paranoia to settle in. All he wanted was the freedom to be able to disappear in a crowd again.

Keep breathing, he told himself. *Inhale. Hold it. Exhale. Take your time.* The same drill he'd used with his patients back on Earth countless times.

He should've known something like this was bound to happen. His undercover work had already been the subject of many a media documentary or televised drama. He'd always declined the interview requests, but that hadn't stopped anyone from producing them anyway.

The security guard gave him a sympathetic look. Then pressed a button on her terminal and cleared him through quickly. He nearly sprinted into the settlement proper.

Once inside, he checked his new wrister. *Early*, he thought with a frown, fearing a repeat incident from the checkpoint station. Luckily, the shopping concourse just inside was packed with small tourist shops. New Arcena was home to a massive volume of shipping between the core worlds and the outer rim by now, so it didn't surprise Carson to see these kinds of amenities.

He stepped inside the first shop he could find and immediately found a set of optical-enhancing goggles, the kind the spice farmers used. They were unbelievably gaudy, with the rims designed to look like the sandstone bluffs overlooking the settlement. And they hardly worked. But he still bought them, along with a bandana covered with an artist's rendering of New Arcena.

Carson put the goggles on, wrapped the bandana over his hair, and headed back outside. He still had almost twenty minutes before Stacy was supposed to finish his shift in the editing studios, where his team was wrapping up work on their latest documentary.

He strolled through the corridors aimlessly, passing through throngs of tourists, maintenance workers, off-duty spice farmers, off-world merchants. The settlement's hallways used to feel almost as narrow as starship hallways, and nearly as tubular.

Now, the colony felt like a proper city. Instead of claustrophobic plastic and metal everywhere, the walls had been replaced with large glass windows, which would normally give a great view, but were now blanketed by red dust.

Carson walked past the hydroponics bays where they grew spices. They were massive now, having been rebuilt into multilayer structures, with dozens of plots on each level. He passed by a dozen trade offices and meeting rooms that didn't exist the last time he was here. Each of them seemed packed with merchants haggling over goods or exchanging cash.

And then, when his wrister finally told him it was time, he headed to the nearest cafeteria. He found Stacy immediately, drinking a coffee at a long table. He was wearing a black jumpsuit and a beret cap. He had a smattering of hairs along his upper lip—*big mistake*, Carson thought, *you never could grow facial hair, Stacy*—but other than that, he looked the same as he had when the two of them boarded the *Preserver*.

Stacy looked up and locked eyes with him.

He walked forward, sticking his hands in his pocket and suppressing a grin. "*Hao jiu bu jian*," he said: the only Mandarin he knew. Stacy let out an exaggerated sigh and put his forehead in his palm. "How was my pronunciation?"

Stacy looked up and grinned. "Even more atrocious than usual."

Then he leapt up, and the two brothers locked arms in the tightest embrace Carson had ever experienced.

"Fucking hell, brother," Stacy said, "when the leadership told me you were on a secret assignment, I didn't think that meant you'd *infiltrated the fucking Offspring*."

Carson winced when Stacy called him "brother." Had even a normal, fraternal word of acknowledgment become tarred through his experiences?

And then he winced again at his brother's liberal usage of foul language. Carson had done his due diligence as an older brother, back when Stacy was still learning English, by teaching him all the curse words. He hadn't looked back since.

"If it's all the same," Carson said, "I'd rather hear about what you've been up to."

"Right. Yeah. That makes sense."

Stacy launched into a long explanation about the documentary projects he'd been working on. Which included a bunch of campaign videos for Isadora back when she'd been up for reelection, but ever since, he'd been producing the kind of heart-wrenching, sappy shit— Stacy's words—that got big, rich donors in Union space to get all misty eyed, open up their pocketbooks, and throw cash at their development projects. Again, Stacy's words.

It was incredible, really, how *connected* his brother seemed. All this time, Carson had been thinking he was protecting his brother— and he *was*, to be sure—but it seemed like Stacy was doing well for himself. Rubbing shoulders with the rich, the powerful, the famous. And contributing to the public relations front of their people's colonial enterprise.

But he could only think about that for so long, with the haunting memories of the checkpoint incident still racing through his mind.

"You seem really interested in what I have to say," Stacy said with a grin.

"Sorry. I just had a moment in the checkpoint earlier," Carson said, before launching into an explanation of what had transpired after landing. "I guess I'm just paranoid about the same thing happening in here."

"Must be tough, being around people who are happy to see you and thankful for everything you've done for them."

Carson shot him a look.

"But yeah...I get it," Stacy said, his voice growing quieter and more serious. "I tell you what, let's head back to my room to wait out this dust storm. I'll kick your ass in StarRacerIV—"

"—wait," Carson interjected, "you're telling me, out of all the things you could've packed from Earth, you brought *video games*?"

"Yes. For the purpose of the aforementioned asskicking," Stacy said. "Anyway, after the dust storm is over, I know the perfect place to go."

. . .

Stacy wasn't lying about the asskicking. He also wasn't lying about knowing the perfect place to go.

Now decked out in enviro-suits, they were lying down on the red sand of the plateaus overlooking New Arcena. A sheer sandstone drop-off was only a few feet away. The settlement's growth had even led to embedded pods and wings in the cliff face. But the two brothers had at last found quiet and isolation.

Carson looked up at the red atmosphere, out to the left as the dust storm slithered away, then back up at the Natonus sun, hazy from the clouds' interference. For the first time since he'd come out of cryo, it felt like time was slowing down. It was just him and Stacy on the ridge. No one else to worry about.

Stacy seemed to appreciate that he needed quiet time. Neither of them talked for almost a half-hour. The whole time, Carson's mind went through everything he'd seen: the bombsite at New Arcena after an Offspring suicide attack, the collapse of the Rhavego mining tunnels and Juliet's death, the mission to insert Carson and Russ' death, the battle for the capital city on Enther, and finally, the blood-soaked corridors of the *Sanctitude.*

His mind seemed to have been protecting him the entire time he was in the field. He'd always slept well in spite of the unending violence and hatred he'd witnessed. But he was paying it back now. For the past few months since Tanner's death in the skies of Bitanu, Carson's sleep had been wracked with nightmares.

He let out a loud sigh. "You know, I can't really say I'm doing great."

Stacy looked over at him and nodded, giving him a sympathetic look from behind his visor. "The fight against the Offspring's been over for months, and you're only now coming to visit. I think that's a pretty good sign that something was off."

Carson explained everything he'd been feeling: the nightmares, the restlessness, the inability to stay focused. Stacy listened patiently. "I'm not the therapist here," he said after Carson was done, "but it sounds to me like this is pretty normal stuff. I mean, you've basically been in danger for the past few years. You've probably lost sight of what 'normal' even means."

Carson paused before responding. He supposed Stacy had a good point—after all, their final few months on Earth had been spent fretting over the Hegemony onslaught, especially so after the battle of Mars, and trying to decide whether to flee on the *Preserver*.

He'd had to say goodbye to their parents, knowing they'd be long deceased by the time either of them came out of cryo. He hadn't even had time to mourn, time to reflect on the loss of his homeworld and all his friends and family. He'd just been racing from danger to danger, focused on stopping the Offspring.

What *did* "normal" even mean, now? The closest thing he could come up with was his brief time aboard the *Exemplar* before his insertion into the Offspring, back after Nadia and Russ had finally stopped bickering, and they all got along. It'd been a peaceful week.

Maybe he'd been so desperate to find a sense of normalcy that he hadn't allowed himself to appreciate the depths of his trauma. In all the patients he'd ever worked with, a single truth had emerged: trauma didn't define who you were as a person, but you'd drive yourself mad by trying to go back to a past that was no longer possible.

Change was the only constant in life. You could either embrace that, or wallow in bitterness. Maybe trying to go back to his old, unadventurous life was an impossibility.

"When I finally heard you were coming to visit, I was ecstatic," Stacy continued. "I was actually going to ask if you wanted to live with me, at least until you got your feet under you. And don't get me wrong, I'm overjoyed to see you. The offer stands, if you want it. But I don't think it's what you *need*. You need adventure, you need the road. You need to find out who you are."

Carson's eyes started to water. He'd been so focused on all the things he wasn't—*not* a therapist, *not* happy, *not* at peace—that he'd barely been thinking about who he *was*.

And, damn it, Stacy was right. He'd been on an aimless journey of self-discovery for months, and all it took for his brother to diagnose his situation was a few hours.

"You know, I got this job offer from the ISB," Carson said. He figured that was a good sign—whenever a patient suddenly blurted out something, that was usually the first step to a real breakthrough.

Stacy gave him a confused look.

"The Union's Intelligence and Security Bureau. They said I did really good work undercover. I mean," he allowed himself a cocky grin, "hard to argue with the results."

"Fuck yeah! *That's* my brother talking."

"They said they're going to need all kinds of intel after the wormhole back home opens. They'll need reports on what's been happening in the Sol System during the last century, probable threat assessments, whether any further wormholes lead elsewhere, all that kind of stuff. They actually offered me a job in their new fact-finding program. It'd be the first time one of our people got invited to join the Union bureaucracy. Obviously, I wouldn't start until *after* the wormhole opened, so I could stay for a few more months."

Stacy had a sad smile. "I'd beg you to stay longer if I thought that was the right thing to do. But I think the ISB job is where you belong. Up there." A gloved hand pointed to the sky.

Carson's eyes watered once more. For so long, seeing Stacy again was what had kept him going while he was undercover. But now that he was here, he was already making plans to leave. Then again, Stacy seemed to be doing well for himself. Somewhere along the way, his little brother had grown up.

"And no matter how far you get, you're always welcome back here," Stacy continued. "The only thing I'd say is: aren't you gonna need a ship to get there? Or will the ISB give you one?"

A grin crept across Carson's face. "Actually, I know just who to ask."

CHAPTER 43

When they'd left Earth, Isadora had promised Meredith to take her to a beach on some alien world as soon as they came out of cryo. She'd gotten the timing off, but she'd finally fulfilled her promise.

Tricia had invited her to her private island villa on the planet Haphis for a few days. She'd instantly leapt at the opportunity to make good on her promise, bringing both her daughter and Rebecca along.

Which was how Isadora had ended up lounging on a recliner at the edge of the villa, wearing a comfortable beach robe, watching the waves gently roll in. For the first time since arriving in the system, she wasn't wearing her wrister. Hadn't woken up to an alarm. Sleep was a commodity she'd have to relearn how to appreciate.

Especially now that, as of two days ago, the *Preserver* was officially empty. And she'd officially resigned as chief coordinator. Her long crusade was over. She'd done it.

She'd gone further than resigning. In fact, she'd dissolved the position entirely. Now that their society had quadrupled in size in a matter of months, having a single individual with the kind of unchecked authority she wielded as chief coordinator was unhealthy. It made more sense to empower the Consultative Committee instead.

As for her, she would move into a symbolic leadership role. One who would perform ceremonial duties, but who would stay above the fray of partisan politics. The social dynamics of their multiplanetary refugee community desperately needed a unifying figure of her stature. She could do that more effectively by dispersing her day-to-day decision-making authority among others.

Well. She would move into her new role *after* her month-long vacation.

She was halfway tempted to go check her messages. Constantly checking her inbox was a learned habit, a scar from her years as chief coordinator. She'd also have to relearn how to say *no, this is my time right now*, and leave the rest of the universe waiting for her.

Besides, she knew what most of the messages would be: frantic pleas for an endorsement from Katrina and Alexander.

Politics had become even more unbearable, with ties fraying further between the Integrationist faction headed by Alexander and the Isolationist faction headed by Katrina. Riley, Gabby, and Valencia were desperately trying to hold a caretaker government together before another election could be held.

They'd eventually settled on a new position of quorum speaker: a nominee from the majority party in the Consultative Committee, who

would serve as the head of government. Everyone knew the speaker-
ship would go to either Alexander or Katrina, depending on which
faction prevailed in the upcoming elections.

Despite the outward vitriol, Isadora secretly suspected that they
would end up governing similarly. Sure, their respective emphases
might be channeled differently, but she knew them personally. Had
watched them work well together, side by side, for years. Their ani-
mosity was more political theater than anything substantial.

At least, that's what she hoped. Both seemed desperate for her official endorsement, but she'd told them countless times that she
wouldn't. She was fond of both of them, and she felt that both made
solid arguments.

And besides, now that she'd left office after defeating the Offspring and helping save everyone on the *Preserver*, she was at the
peak of her popularity. She wanted to bask in the warm glow of approval, not wade into the newest controversy. And it would be im-
proper for her to offer endorsements in her new ceremonial role.

She heard the soft crunch of sand coming from behind her. Tricia
was walking out of the villa, two fruity drinks in her hand. "I figure
you might want one of these," Tricia said, placing the cocktail down
on a glass table next to Isadora's recliner. Then she unfolded a recliner and joined her.

"We just woke up," Isadora said.

Tricia shrugged. "I think you get to drink whenever the fuck you
want when you retire. Otherwise, why would anyone do it?"

Isadora thought that was a damn good point. She picked up the
glass, clinked it with Tricia's, took a sip. Then winced almost immediately after. Tricia's proportions seemed to be heavily in favor of
more alcohol.

"And what the *hell* is that on your head, Isadora?" Tricia asked, an aghast look on her face.

After landing at the main Haphis spaceport, Isadora had indulged herself in the gaudiest wide-brimmed hat she could find at one of the tourist shops. It was smothered with flowers, wisps of silk, and gilded ornaments. Her purchase had elicited an eye roll out of Rebecca and a horrified look from Meredith.

Isadora shrugged. "It's a hat, and I love it." She took a long drink of her cocktail.

"That's the spirit," Tricia said, taking an even longer drink.

They sat and watched the waves for a comfortable few minutes, until Isadora spoke up. "So, what are you going to do now? What does a retired Tricia Favan even *look* like?"

"A lot fucking happier. Can't you tell how much more easygoing I am now?" she asked dourly. She stirred her drink with the miniature umbrella. "But seriously. For years, I was working as a civil rights attorney. Then I was a fighter pilot. And finally, a prime minister for a decade and a half. I'm not used to this life."

"Having free time, in other words. Should I express...sympathy?"

"No, smartass, you shouldn't." Tricia glared at her. "I'm just saying it's going to be an adjustment. I'm sure you're feeling it too. I know I was prime minister a lot longer than you were in power, but I never pulled the sheer number of all-nighters that you did. And I never had a kid to take care of on top of that."

"It isn't a competition, but I agree. There have been days where I get so restless I don't even know what to do."

In so many ways, Isadora felt lucky. Until the very end, she'd never been on the front lines of the fight against the Offspring. Had never seen combat like Nadia, never had to survive among their enemies like Carson. But the stresses of political life had worn on her in other ways.

She'd only just turned forty, but there were days when it looked like she was pushing fifty. Her eyes seemed deep and sunken, her heart rate permanently elevated no matter how many deep breathing exercises and meditative stretching programs she did.

Her doctors had told her that the stress alone had probably taken years off her life. It wasn't a sacrifice she could compare to what Nadia or Carson had been through—and it especially couldn't compare to the ultimate one Russ or Vincent had made—but it was a sacrifice nonetheless.

"So," Tricia said, "you're probably gonna hate me for asking this, but: what *are* you going to do? I probably only have a few decades left in me, but you have half a lifetime. I have a hard time seeing you as the kind of person who can just kick back and relax."

"No," Isadora said sadly. She wasn't sure she'd ever been that kind of person, but she *definitely* wasn't that kind of person now. There would always be a part of her that yearned for the high-pressure environment of her years as chief coordinator. There was no going back to a time beforehand. She explained her new ceremonial position to Tricia.

"Smart," she said. "Now that your people's politics are getting heated, you bug out just in time to keep your approval numbers high. And then you kick the can down the road for whoever becomes quorum speaker."

Isadora opened her mouth to protest, but she supposed there was some truth to what Tricia was saying. She'd justified her job transition by focusing on what her people *needed*, but, being honest with herself, there was certainly an allure to avoiding the partisan mudslinging that would surely diminish her reputation.

"To be honest," she said, "I keep getting this feeling that nothing's going to calm down. The wormhole will open, and who knows what the expeditionary fleet will find on the other side. My people will continue to argue and bicker over our place in the system. Millions will be moving back and forth between the Sol System and Natonus. So no matter how much I keep worrying there's nothing to do, other days it feels like there's *too much* to do."

Tricia nodded. "It sounds like you still want to be in charge."

She chuckled. "That's all I know, at this point. But I genuinely want someone else to be making the next round of hard decisions."

"You know, a smart person once told me that over the mountains are mountains."

"Now *you're* the one being a smartass."

The two sat in comfortable silence and continued to drink their cocktails. Isadora had only consumed a light breakfast and a cup of coffee this morning, so the buzz hit her faster than normal. Before long, her head was feeling light and tingly.

"So," Tricia said eventually, "Now that you're really out of the game—the chief coordinator game, I should say—you ever think about what kind of legacy you're leaving?"

It was the question every politician thought about, so it surprised Isadora that it'd rarely crossed her mind. Her entire tenure, she'd been so busy moving from crisis to crisis that she'd never really thought about building something sustainable, the thing long-lasting legacies were made of.

"I don't know," she said. "I got everyone out of cryo, and in less than four years. We're on our way to becoming a democratic society, with elections taking place at both the local level and at the main administrative one. No matter what we decide— further integration or maintaining our own cultural cohesion—we'll have friends and allies wherever we turn. I've made sure the Natonese people and their representatives like us well enough. And the Offspring have been thoroughly dismantled."

"Now *that's* a hell of a legacy," Tricia said. "Somehow, I'm getting the feeling that you're gonna be someone who goes down in the history books."

Isadora detected only the faintest morsel of jealousy in Tricia's tone. But she could understand. During career transitions, politicians had a tendency to become preoccupied—obsessed, even—with the idea of leaving a legacy. And she couldn't deny the feeling of joy, of pride, that'd swelled in her chest when Tricia mentioned the history books dwelling on her.

That's just who she was now. Who she'd *had* to become. A creature of politics.

The emergence of two figures from the right side of the shoreline reminded her that her political side, although ever-present, would never have to fully dominate her life again. It was Meredith and Rebecca, returning from a morning stroll around the perimeter of the island.

Meredith was wearing a beach robe similar to Isadora's, while Rebecca was sporting an all-black jumpsuit. Isadora was pretty sure she owned exactly zero beachwear, and that she was also the kind of person who'd never even considered buying some for the trip.

The two of them joined Isadora and Tricia. "Starting early, I see," Rebecca snorted, indicating the cocktails in their hands.

"When you successfully run a solar system for a decade and a half, you get to start early whenever the fuck you want," Tricia said.

"I'll keep that in mind," Rebecca said.

"So," Isadora said, "what do you two think?"

"It's all beautiful," Meredith said, a glowing smile on her face.

"It's okay," Rebecca murmured, her shoulders slouched.

Meredith looked at Isadora. "But I still can't *believe* you're wearing that hat."

Isadora looked over and exchanged glances with Tricia. "I suppose I'll add that to the list of things you can get away with after managing a solar society for years."

Rebecca, meanwhile, was trying her hardest not to laugh at the hat. Which was, of course, the *real* reason Isadora had bought it.

Ever since she'd returned from Bitanu, she hadn't seen Rebecca smile. She'd had to find out about her brother's death from the public media, had to watch it being portrayed as a cause for celebration.

For months, Rebecca had been bombarded with the media narrative that Tanner was evil, genocidally so, and that his death and the destruction of his organization would signal the dawn of a new era of peace, cooperation, and exploration.

The worst part was that all of that was true. And somewhere deep inside, Isadora suspected she knew that. But it didn't make the situation any easier to deal with. So if Isadora had to buy a stupid-looking hat to get a genuine laugh—even a mocking one—out of Rebecca, you damn well bet she would.

"I think we're gonna go wade in a little," Meredith said, nodding toward the shoreline. "Wanna come?"

"Oh, maybe I'll join you in a bit," Isadora said. "Why don't you two go ahead?"

Meredith and Rebecca headed down the beach while Tricia excused herself to go to the bathroom, claiming that the alcohol had gone right through her. Isadora nursed the last remnants of her own cocktail and watched the two young women work their way into the water.

They paused when their ankles were submerged. When a wave came in, the water surged to the top of their kneecaps. Rebecca's movements seemed stilted, although Isadora couldn't tell if that was because of the emotional state she was in—or because she was wearing a soaking jumpsuit.

Still, the two locked hands, faced each other, pressed their foreheads together, and kissed. It was such a touching and unexpected sight to Isadora, who'd never observed them so publicly affectionate before.

In the thin space between their bodies, she looked out at the Haphis oceans, which seemed to stretch on and on into eternity, into an infinite number of future possibilities. That was her real legacy: both their relationship and everything it symbolized. Two different peoples from across the galaxy, coming together. Becoming one.

Maybe her legacy would be defined less by her own personal accomplishments and triumphs, and more about everything she'd enabled others to become, both Natonese and Earthborn.

Isadora smiled and finished her drink, satisfied with that realization. It was someone else's story now.

CHAPTER 44

The Bitanu peace summit had been the largest gathering of starships Nadia had ever seen in her life. And even that was dwarfed by the mass of vessels that had assembled for the *Preserver*'s transformation.

The *Exemplar* hung at the edge, giving her and her crew a magnificent view of thousands of ships from all over the Natonese system. There were military vessels, naturally, but also huge numbers of media, trade, even Ashkagi missionary ships. Nadia knew for a fact that plenty of Earthborn were serving on some of their crews.

It was a visual representation of everything she'd been working toward for all these years. Everything that Boyd and Derek had been helping her with. Nadia looked up at the bulkhead, where they'd installed four holo-portraits: Morris Oxatur, Juliet Lessitor, Vincent

Gureh, and, of course, Russ. It was a dream that all of them had died for, one way or another. Nadia would honor that sacrifice for as long as she lived.

"Looks like the transformation will begin any minute now," Derek said, interrupting her thoughts.

"Oh boy," Boyd said, rubbing his hands in anticipation. "I've never watched a ship the size of your *Preserver* implode before. Hell, all this tech is so advanced, it practically seems like magic to me."

"I know how these things go," Nadia said. When they'd started pulling cryo pods off the *Preserver* in bulk, the leadership had estimated they could do it in a month with the settlement charter ban finally lifted.

Then, it'd taken almost half a year. It was well into 2407 by now. If the transformation process was about to begin "any minute now," they'd be lucky if it started in the next few hours. Especially because the *Preserver* had to be controlled remotely, with all the old crew having been evacuated.

Looking at the gargantuan cryo vessel and knowing that it was completely, utterly empty was somehow upsetting to Nadia. "I'm gonna go check on our new crew member," she said. "Holler at me if anything actually happens."

"Of course," Derek said.

She retreated into the interior of the *Exemplar*, passing through the canteen on her way to the starboard dormitories, where a newly fashioned, personalized bowl sat next to the ones for her, Boyd, and Derek.

This one had the letters CE engraved on the front.

The *Exemplar* had always had four cabins installed, even though they'd rarely used the fourth one. So when Carson had asked if he could come aboard for their preliminary trip to the Sol System, she was more than happy to give him back the room he'd once temporarily occupied.

Nadia knocked on the door. Carson called for her to enter. "Getting settled in okay?" she asked, crossing her arms over her chest.

"Definitely!" he said, using a voice that made Nadia wonder whether she'd known him long enough to assume he was lying. It looked like he was in the middle of moving his belongings back-and-forth between his desk and his cabinet. "I can't decide where to put anything. This is actually the first time I'm settling down somewhere."

It broke her heart when she realized how true that was. Carson had been traveling light when she'd picked him up back on Rhavego, and he'd gone into his undercover work without so much as a single memento. From what he'd told her, he'd been constantly staying on the move since the peace summit.

Nadia had never gotten to know Carson particularly well, but she knew Russ had always admired the man. Had respected his inner strength. If he'd impressed Russ, then that was more than good enough for her.

"Boyd, Derek and I, we've all been uprooted," she said quietly. "Sometimes more than once. So we make sure this ship feels like home. It can be yours, too—for as long as you want it to be."

Carson paused, then took a deep breath and stashed a bag of supplies into his cabinet. This time, he didn't deliberate further.

"C'mon," she said. "I want to show you something."

She led him outside the dormitories, where she'd put up her map of the Sol System. "Remember this?" she asked.

Carson let out a hollow laugh. "I've been in tourist boutique shops from one end of this system to the other. You know that they're selling these maps everywhere now? It's all the rage."

Nadia grinned. "You're avoiding the question."

Carson paused and looked at his feet. "It's weird," he mumbled at last. "This used to look so recognizable to me. But now it looks...strange, somehow."

"I feel the same way. I'm starting to think that maybe *home* is just always going to be a murky concept. Hence, the importance of the ship. It's always been a place where I can come back to when things get rough. And I've been through some dark places these past few years, Carson Erlinza."

He looked away.

"Not like you," she added quickly. "I'm not sure any of us can compare to what you went through. But we'll always be here, and you can always come along. Whether that's here," she said, indicating the map of the Sol System, "or wherever else in the galaxy we end up going."

The two strolled down the corridors of the *Exemplar*, heading back to the cockpit. "You think there will be more wormholes on the other side?" Carson asked. "The old Hegemony network, just waiting to be reactivated?"

Nadia shrugged. "I have to be honest, I like the idea. But," she added, dropping her voice and speaking in an artificially gruff tone meant to mirror Russ, "I know optimistic assumptions are a rookie mistake." They shared a laugh tinged with an edge of sadness.

"The truth is," she continued, "none of us knows what we're going to find when the *Preserver* transforms. I'm just happy to be going in with a capable team, ready for anything."

The two arrived back in the cockpit. Boyd stood up, walked over, and clapped Carson on the back. Nadia had worried whether they would get along, seeing as they'd never met before, but the two had instantly liked each other. "Finally, someone around here who can make a half-decent fucking waffle" was Boyd's initial assessment of their new crewmate.

Derek waved at Carson. Nadia had never witnessed the two of them spend much time together back during the latter's stay aboard the *Exemplar*. So it'd surprised her when she'd caught them up late one night, reading one of Derek's poetry books together. It was hard to get Derek to open up about much, but he'd told Nadia that Carson was interested in trying to write his own poems.

"It makes sense," he'd told her, "after all, storytelling can be therapeutic."

They all strapped in. The three men began joking around about some competitive video game Carson had apparently borrowed from his brother and brought aboard the *Exemplar*. Nadia, meanwhile, was focused on the viewscreen.

After almost four years in the Natonus System, she was returning to her home. To Earth, maybe. She knew it'd look utterly different from when she left. She couldn't help but wonder what else the galaxy had in store for her.

There will always be more Tanner Keltins, a part of her mind said. There would always be dangerous people, people who she couldn't convince.

But that wasn't the full story of their final confrontation. Her memory of the actual shootout was so addled by amnesia that she'd had difficulty piecing everything together. She had no idea how she'd come to shoot Tanner, but she liked thinking that, in the moment, she'd done it to save the millions of lives on the *Preserver*, not to take vengeance. It had been an act of necessity, not wrath.

So it would be elsewhere.

There would be Tanners, but there would also be all the thousands of Natonese who'd helped her in her journey. Like when she and her crew had stopped the near-war with the Union, or when the entire system had come together to help her ship push through to the *Caretaker*.

There would be many of those moments to come. She'd need to make sure she was ready to handle the Tanners of the galaxy so she could appreciate all the little miracles along the way. She looked up at the portrait of Russ on the bulkhead. *Prepare for the worst, so you can cherish the best*, she thought. Come to think of that, actually—

—the *Preserver* began to transform before she could finish the thought.

The cockpit went silent. Thousands of miles away, the giant metal arms along the outside of the vessel rotated, then folded in on themselves, lurching toward the nexus hub at the center of the craft. Boyd let out a low whistle as the second metal arm began retracting.

It was strange to think about the vessel being empty. It had always been an eternal source of life for Nadia's people, and now, it was turning into something else.

Pale, beautiful, shimmering blue light emerged from the central nexus hub. The first metal arm had retracted far enough that the tip disappeared in the light sphere.

"You know," Nadia said softly, "I was thinking. I know we talked about my plan on the way over..."

Boyd put his face in his palm, Derek frowned, and Carson furrowed his brow in confusion.

"We've gone over this a bunch of times," Boyd said. "I love the idea, especially the spirit behind it, but the fleet commanders are just gonna call us nuts if we pitch it to them."

"I wish I could say I disagreed, but I don't," Derek said.

"Someone help me out here," Carson said. "What's going on, exactly?"

Boyd sighed. "Look...before we picked you up from Calimor, we were talking about an alternative to the Union navy's plan. One where *we* went into the wormhole first, once the *Preserver*'s transformation process is complete."

"It's a symbolic thing," Nadia interjected. "This is going to be the first time a Natonese vessel arrives in the Sol System, so sending in a flotilla of warships would send the wrong signal to posterity."

"Boyd and I concurred," Derek said. "But there's no way the navy will."

"Why not?" Carson said. "Hear me out: the wormhole is a natural bottleneck. Sending in waves of ships doesn't really make sense if there *were* a hostile fleet on the other side. We'd just get our ships picked off one by one. But the *Exemplar* has a missile scrambler system. If we get in first and activate the defenses, we'd be a more effective scouting party than the warships."

Nadia was speechless. She'd been so focused on the significance of the *Exemplar* going in first to realize that it was *also* a sound security measure. And besides, the Union military might appreciate risking just four lives instead of an entire warship going in first. Maybe it could both be an important symbolic point *and* a prudent defensive move.

She looked up at the portrait of Russ again. Imagined him giving her one of his winks.

Outside the viewscreen, the second arm of the *Preserver* had disappeared into the growing orb of blue light. The nexus hub had now completely disappeared, consumed by the ever-expanding ball of energy.

"He's right," Boyd blurted out. "That's our pitch right there."

"I agree," Derek said. He'd already turned around to work on a dispatch.

Boyd turned to Nadia in excitement. "Let me guess, you want me to—"

" —fire up the missile scrambler? Yes, exactly. For old time's sake," Nadia said. He pushed himself to his feet and headed for the engine room.

"Derek, can you send a message to the Union flagship letting them know that we're going in first? You can explain our plan nicely if they're skeptical," Nadia said.

"I'm way ahead of you," Derek said, typing away at his terminal.

While Derek finished up, Nadia turned to Carson. "And Carson, you can—I don't know, buckle in? I guess I'll have to figure out something to ask you to do in the future."

He grinned, making sure his seat's chest straps were tight. "I'd like that."

The gentle hum of the missile scrambler announced Boyd's return. "The Union military is asking us what the hell we're thinking," Derek said, scanning over a list of written transmissions on his terminal. "After I explained our rationale, it looks like an argument broke out. Some of the ships' captains are saying that we should stick to the plan already in place. But others are saying that, actually, we're making a good fucking point. Their words."

Nadia grinned. "I think that's our cue. Let's plot a course."

The *Exemplar*'s engines fired, and they slowly accelerated. Outside, the third metal arm of the *Preserver* had disappeared into the blue light sphere. The fourth and final arm was retracting. Nadia felt the acceleration push her back into the chair. The assembly of ships seemed to fly by the cockpit's viewscreen as they sped forward.

As they approached the transforming *Preserver*, the final arm retracted. The light sphere had grown as large as the vessel itself. Any vestiges of the actual ship were no longer visible. They'd received a confirmation from one of the Union admirals saying that, actually yes, their plan was better than the previous one, and would they mind taking point?

They were coming in so fast that Nadia wasn't sure they could slow down if they wanted to. They passed the last line of ships. All that was before them was space—and a massive, moon-sized ball of blue energy.

"Any last words before we head through?" she said, letting out a nervous laugh and turning to face her crew.

"To new frontiers," Derek said.

"To new opportunities," Boyd said.

"To finding ourselves," Carson said.

Nadia turned back around to stare at the growing ball of energy. "To us," she whispered. It was an expansive *us*, encompassing not just their crew, but all Natonese and Earthborn. Anyone and everyone who'd been part of her foray through the Natonus System.

They were so close now that the sphere of light was filling up the entire viewscreen. Until suddenly, it shrank. The edges of pure energy receded, ebbing away. A series of metal emitters emerged from deep within, then circled the shrinking perimeter of the sphere. The wormhole had opened.

Nadia held out her hands and clasped Boyd and Derek's hands. Carson joined in, making a square of human contact. Outside, the sphere of energy stabilized. The *Exemplar* came in fast, until the nose of their vessel slipped through the wormhole. Blue light bathed the entire cockpit.

And the universe opened up before them.

ACKNOWLEDGEMENTS

Finishing this trilogy was a surreal experience. There's a part of me that is blown away by how little time has gone by—this trilogy was conceived on a plane to Massachusetts in late May 2019—while another part of me is blown away by the sheer weight of everything that's happened since then. Let's see: there's been a global pandemic, reckonings over racial injustice, political upheaval and violence, career changes, friendships strengthened and broken. To name a few. Although optimism and hope about humanity's future carry through from beginning to end of these three books, I suppose there's a dark undercurrent there, as well; a feeling that I had to write these books to remind myself that truth and justice can prevail in the end. That believing in redemption, in recognizing our common humanity, flaws included, is How We Win. I'm not going to pretend—will *never* pretend—like these are perfect books, but I hope that you, the reader, will appreciate the honesty that I poured into them. Where there was anguish, it was genuine anguish; where there was idealism, it was genuine idealism.

As with the first and second books, nothing about this project could've ever happened without a group of dedicated friends and family. Angela, Brian, Joe, and Tiffany—thank you for everything. There are days where it feels like this trilogy is more yours than mine...which is certainly for the better! Sarah—thank you for being my life partner, and, slightly more relevant to the actual book in your hands, my alpha reader. Natasha Snow (www.natashasnow-designs.com)–thank you for bringing these books to life with your incredible, jaw-dropping covers. To my parents, my brother, and my sister-in-law—thank you for reading and supporting me (and for blurb advice from the latter!). To you, the reader—thanks for trusting me to take you on this journey. I'm excited to see where we go next.

ABOUT THE AUTHOR

Matt Levin lives in Texas with his wife and two dogs, and is the author of the Natonus Refuge trilogy. He enjoys running, swimming, and backpacking while not writing. Join him on Facebook at @mattlevin-writer, or follow his work at mattlevinwriter.wordpress.com.

34356290R00272